D0586840

A NOTE ON THE AUTHOR

KERRY YOUNG was born in Kingston, Jamaica, to a
Chinese father and a mother of mixed Chinese-African herit-
age. She came to England in 1965 and lives in Leicestershire.
Kerry is a reader and mentor for The Literary Consultancy,
and a tutor for the Arvon Foundation. She is also Honorary
Assistant Professor in the School of English at the University
of Nottingham and Honorary Creative Writing Fellow at the
University of Leicester. She was writer-in-residence at the
University of Sheffield (2014–16) as part of the Royal
Literary Fund Fellowship Programme.

kerryyoung.co.uk

SHOW ME A MOUNTAIN

KERRY YOUNG

BLOOMSBURY

LONDON · OXFORD · NEW YORK · NEW DELHI · SYDNEY

Bloomsbury Paperbacks
An imprint of Bloomsbury Publishing Plc

50 Bedford Square   1385 Broadway
London   New York
WC1B 3DP   NY 10018
UK   USA

www.bloomsbury.com

First published in Great Britain 2016
This paperback edition first published in 2017

British Library Cataloguing-in-Publication Data
A catalogue record for this book is available from the British Library.

Library of Congress Cataloguing-in-Publication data has been applied for.

ISBN: HB: 978-1-4088-6955-0
TPB: 978-1-4088-4314-7
PB: 978-1-4088-4433-5
ePub: 978-1-4088-4434-2

2 4 6 8 10 9 7 5 3 1

Typeset by Integra Software Services Pvt. Ltd.
Printed and bound in Great Britain by CPI Group (UK) Ltd, Croydon CR0 4YY

For more about our authors and books visit www.bloomsbury.com.
Here you will find extracts, author interviews, details of forthcoming
events and the option to sign up for our newsletters.

For my mother
Joyce Monica Young
1930–2015

The highest manifestation of life consists in this:
that a being governs its own actions. A thing which is always
subject to the direction of another is somewhat of a dead
thing.

St Thomas Aquinas

CHAPTER 1

Kingston, Jamaica
1966

I TOOK HOLD of the padded paper bag. In both hands.

'Yu alright?' she asked.

I nodded.

She crouched down in the aisle at the side of me. Knees held firmly together by her navy-blue pencil skirt. Steadying herself with one hand on the seat arm.

'First time?'

I nodded again.

'Nothing to it,' she said. 'I fly up and down, up and down, week in week out. Not nobody ever lose the contents of their stomach yet. Even if sometimes they feel like they want to.'

I smiled.

'Don't you worry about a thing. Captain Byfield know what he doing. Got his wings in the Royal Air Force no less, so that should be good comfort.' She patted my forearm lightly. 'And I am here to tek extra special care a yu.'

Then she stood up and walked away with her BOAC pill-box hat perched on her head.

I replaced the bag in the seat pocket and sat back, wanting to be reassured by what she'd said to me. Forcing myself to believe that everything was going to be OK.

Gazing out of the window I could see the traffic moving on the ground below. The grey metal staircase being retracted. The dusty flatbed of the retreating luggage truck. The re-frigerated wagon now empty of its preprepared food.

But even as I watched all of this, the vision in my mind was of him. Doing the thing I knew he would do. In the haven he knew best. The cathedral. Lying face down, pros-trate on the cold marble tiles in front of the altar. In the darkened gloom. His arms outstretched like the figure hang-ing on the cross high above him. That was the picture I couldn't shift.

And then there was a sudden lurch and we started to move as the stewardess walked back through the cabin checking that all our seatbelts were securely fastened. She smiled at me briefly, encouragingly. A moment later, a crackling on the Tannoy followed by the captain's instruction: 'Please prepare for take-off.'

Palisadoes airport flashed at me as we taxied along the runway. I breathed in deep and slow, because something in my heart knew that this was not farewell. It was goodbye. That is how final it felt. No more lush green hills and gush-ing waterfalls. No more coconut palms or Bamboo Grove or Fern Gully. No more bougainvillaea or hibiscus or wild orchids. No more lignum vitae. No more squeezing between my toes the warm, white sands of Dunn's River, or listening to the clicking legs of crickets as evening sets in. No more feeling the salty sea breeze on my face, or tasting it on my lips. Or smelling the sweet, tangy scent of the eucalyptus. No more Negril sunsets witnessed from a cottage high on the West End cliffs. That was all going. Creeping past me frame by frame through the aeroplane window. Low-rise concrete buildings, shrubbery, scrubland, dry and brown and brittle under the Caribbean sun. Fading. Evaporating, like the musty dampness of rain lifting off a hot afternoon lawn.

I remembered the card I had posted to Gloria Campbell. The one I'd written days ago and dropped into the mailbox just before the departure gate. In the middle of all the commotion. A regular tourist postcard. With a picture of the Jamaican flag, yellow, black and green, and Dunn's River Falls and a sunset on Negril beach. *Look after him. You were always more of a wife to him than I ever was.*

The engines roared as the plane lifted its nose into the air. The wheels losing contact with the ground. First the front one, followed by the others. Taking me away from Jamaica. So beautiful. So vigorous. So ripe with promise and possibilities. This land of mine that I so loved but did not know how to help. Trained as I was for nothing. Apart from being on the wrong side.

Then there was a sudden surge as we rose above the Blue Mountains and headed north. Away into the clear blue sky. I thought of the half-written letter in my bag. Not a blue prepaid aerogramme but actual white airmail paper and an envelope that I would have to stamp and post when I landed. That was the least he deserved.

3

The 'Fasten Seatbelt' sign flashed off. I reached down to unbuckle my belt and saw the paleness of my hands. Too light to be black. Too Chinese to be white. I shrugged off a shiver. Too late now. I was on my way, having done the only thing I could do. I had made the decision to live.

CHAPTER 2

1935

I HELD MY breath. Like I was swimming underwater. And then I closed my eyes. And let everything wash over me. The muffled sound of their angry voices and the sight of Samson standing there in his white shirt and black bow tie trying to explain to Papa why Mama wanted me removed from the premises. Right now. This instant.

The premises. Where the smell of the opium I can still remember. Sweet and heavy like burning maple syrup. Hanging there in the air. Soaked into the walls. Even though, according to Papa, they stopped smoking it a long time back. Not that he ever smoked it himself. So he said.

And as well as the opium, there was the mah-jongg. All day, every day. From early morning until late night. With players taking their tiles from the wall and tossing others gently away into the centre. Not slapping them hard and loud on the table like a game of dominoes. But picking and choosing and reject-ing them just as deliberately. Players sometimes pinching my face or rapping me on the head with their knuckles to be friendly and funny. Other times giving me *sore foot* money to celebrate their luck, when they had won. All with an endless supply of jasmine tea and food, cooked in the lean-to out back. Steaming rice and sausage, boiled chicken, roast duck and sugared pork, pak choi, choi sum, chicken soup. To keep everyone nourished while they set up for the next game.

'This instant? That is how she order me?'

'I cyan say nothing 'bout it, Mr Henry. That is what she say to me.'

And then he reached out and grabbed me, Samson, by my nine-year-old arm and yanked so hard I fell off the chair on to the floor and Papa leapt to his feet overturning his stool. And Mr Lowe came running from the kitchen to see what all the commotion was about, adding to the shout-ing himself and waving the *dow mah* in his hand like he just left off chopping up a duck to come and run off an intruder in his cookhouse. Wearing his long white cotton apron hanging halfway down his calf, and his little wispy beard, all grey and stringy like it was a big effort for him to make it grow.

'Tell Miss Cicely if she want the child she will have to come fetch her. Herself.' Pausing after 'her' like he was preparing to say 'herself' with the weighty emphasis he wanted to make his point. And then he took hold of my other arm so then I was being split in two. Samson on one side. Papa on the other.

'She say di place not suitable fah a child.'

True. But it was my father's substitute home from home. His not-so-secret hideaway from the life he was trying to avoid.

6

'Leave the child alone.' That was Mr Lowe trying to break Samson's hold of my arm. Twisting his hand so that Samson's grip made a burning sensation on my skin.

'No need, Lowe. Not your problem.' That was Papa while he reached for Mr Lowe across the table and snagged the cloth so that everything went crashing to the floor. Blue and white porcelain bowls, rice, soup, boiled chicken and soy sauce everywhere. Smashing and splashing dark, wet stains on to my white cotton socks. Turned down like frilly collars around my ankles because that is how Mama wanted them worn.

Then Samson suddenly let go of me. 'I never mean to be pulling and tugging at di child like dis, Mr Henry. It just dat Miss Cicely waiting in di buggy outside and I cyan step on to dat veranda without Miss Fay at my side. My life not worth it.'

Papa nodded. I waited.

'Go on,' he said, dropping my hand and motioning his head towards the door. 'Yu mother expecting you.'

As I walked away I turned and looked back at him. Papa. Standing there so tall and broad. Taller and broader than most other Chinese men. And I wondered, as I had wondered so often over the years, how such a strong, healthy, successful businessman like him got to be beaten down by a woman like her.

'Get yourself in here.' Her voice was firm and hard.

Samson held my hand as I climbed up into the *mah cha* and then he got in up front with the driver who cracked the leather reins to set the horse moving.

'How many times have I told you to stay away from that place?' She slapped my knee. Hard enough to sting. 'How

7

many times? As if enough prayers not being said over your head. You have to tempt the devil at every turn.'

'I was with Papa.'

'Don't you sass me, young lady.' She slapped my knee again. Harder this time. Leaving behind the red mark of her ample palm. She shifted around and rearranged herself, trying to get comfortable in a seat designed for slender Chinamen, not African women of my mother's proportions.

The driver moved his buggy steadily in the late-morning heat. Through North Parade, along Slipe Road, past Cross Roads market, and headed uptown along Old Hope Road to Lady Musgrave Road. Mama and me comfortably shaded in the back under the black canvas canopy. The driver and Samson with the sun beating down on their heads.

When we got home she ordered me into the house. Up the six whitewashed concrete steps to the veranda, furnished with its wicker armchairs and occasional tables and edged with a flower bed of jungle geraniums and red ginger, and at the far end, a giant angel's trumpet. I walked across the squeaky-clean tile floor, towards the front door. Breathing as I went the uptown air that was a hundred times more refined than the odour of Chinatown, with its crammed streets of cookhouses, grocery stores, bakeries, laundries, betting shops, barbers, hardware stores, dry goods, and gambling dens. And where I imagined they were still holding the pipe over the lamp. Not just locals, but English soldiers wearing the King's uniform and rich white men, and sometimes women, who walked the streets of downtown Kingston searching out every opportunity to indulge themselves.

Miss Allen was sitting on the veranda eating a mango from our tree. Slicing off the flesh and taking it into her mouth from the sharp edge of the knife. Leaning forward and letting the sugary juice drop on to the floor like it didn't matter because some maid would soon clean it up.

'So yu find her then?'

'It not that hard. Her father only have but one bolt hole.'

I stopped and watched as Miss Allen reached a bony black hand deep into her mouth. Then she pulled out a stringy piece of fruit lodged between her teeth and wiped it on the cloth napkin resting in her lap.

'Di mango dem sweet dis year.'

'Yes, my dear.' And then Mama pushed me in the back and steered me towards the piano room.

She kept the bamboo cane in the bag with her embroidery. At the side of the armchair. It was short. Maybe a foot and a half. But when she brought it down on your palm or leg it had the rip of a cat-o'-nine. When properly administered, with the appropriate force and whipping wrist action that takes advantage of the natural spring in the wood. No need for swinging space. So she said.

'Yu think yu too big to cry? Is that what yu think?' And down came her cat-o'-nine once again. This time against my shoulder as I dropped my hand and turned my body away from her.

'Nine years old and yu think yu a big woman. Come here.' She grabbed my arm and spun me around. 'Hold out your hand. Higher.' Thwack. Two more times. Thwack, thwack. The tears rolled down my cheeks as my palm reddened with the rising welts. But my mouth, I kept shut. As tight as I could. Biting my teeth together. Locking my jaw.

She dragged me by the arm to the piano stool and forced me to sit down. 'Stay there till I come tell yu to move.' And then wheeling around as she walked away. 'Yu hear me?'

She paused by the armchair and wiped her brow with the back of her stick-hand. And then she called out, 'Sissy.' Who moments later appeared in the doorway.

'Take her clothes.'

'Miss?'

'You hear me. Every last stitch.'

'You want me to strip the child, Miss Cicely?'

'Sissy, I pay you to do what I tell you to do. So don't act like you gone deaf on me.'

Mama bent down and replaced the cane, tucking it carefully into the bag so that neither embroidery nor threads would become pulled or tangled. She raised herself again to full height.

'Sissy, I mean today.'

But I didn't make Sissy have to undress me. I just removed everything and handed them to her. The little pink shorts and white cotton blouse with the short sleeves, a little too tight on the arm. And the still slightly damp ankle socks.

'Tek her panties as well.'

'Miss Cicely, I don't think …'

'I don't pay you to think, Sissy. I pay you to do.'

But Sissy just stood there so in the end Mama walked over to me and with one hand reached for the elastic waistband and dragged my panties down to my ankles. Then she shoved me lightly in the chest, forcing me to step back. She bent down and picked up my underwear and handed it to Sissy and said, 'How difficult was that?'

I stood glued to the floor as Mama directed Sissy out of the door. Then she stepped out herself, taking the key with her, which she turned in the lock on the other side.

That is when I cried. Actually let out a full-lunged howl. Biting on my forefinger to keep my anguish as quiet as I could. And then I waited. With her half-embroidered table runner wrapped around my waist. Listening to the rain pounding on the roof as it did so often early afternoon. Fiddling with the cane. Turning it over in my hand the way I turned over in my mind what it was that she so hated about me.

A little later when the rain stopped Sissy was outside tapping against the glass with her fingernail. I twisted the catch and pulled up the window.

'Here.' She passed me a shawl and then a tray with a hot patty and a glass of milk. 'Yu mama gone wid Miss Allen and di key. God knows where, or what time she planning on coming back.' Then she started down the ladder only to stop and return a few seconds later.

'You alright?'

'Yes.'

'Yu want pee pee?'

'If I do I will knock on the door.'

'And she come back an hear yu!' Sissy disappeared down the ladder. Next thing, she was back, with a galvanised-zinc pail that she handed to me through the window.

'Use this and afterwards let it down outside. Yu see dis?' She showed me the long piece of rope she had tied to the handle. 'Let it down gentle and I will come pick it up later.' She looked down to watch her step before reaching into the front pocket of her apron for a puzzle book and pencil, which she passed to me.

'In case yu need something to tek yu mind off things.' She smiled weakly. 'It will pass, Miss Fay. It will pass.'

I sat still on the stool. Didn't tinker with the keys on the piano. Didn't smell the pink English roses in the vase or re-position the china ballerina on the shelf. Didn't stack the sheet music that Mama couldn't play even though she kept buying more and more of it. Didn't open and close the chiffon curtains to see them swish along the rail. Didn't plump up the cushions in the armchair or flatten out the flowers in the creases of the material. Didn't run my hands over the silk rug on the floor. Didn't do the puzzles Sissy gave me. Didn't do anything. I didn't even use Sissy's pail.

When Mama came home she unlocked the door and walked away. I got up. Tried the handle. When I stepped out I found my clothes folded in a neat pile resting on a chair by the door. All except the socks, which Sissy had replaced with a dry pair. Just like the clean panties slipped between the shorts and blouse.

At dinner Stanley, home for the school holidays, was silent as always, and Daphne cried. That is all she did. Ever since she was born and they brought her back from the hospital. Two years of crying. Except when Sissy hushed her. Or when she was asleep.

Later, out on the veranda, I told Stanley what happened.

'So what is new?'

I shrugged my shoulders. 'She never drag me outta di cook-house before, Stanley. Not like dat. Actually come downtown.

Bring herself in a buggy from mighty Lady Musgrave Road to di
likes a Barry Street to fetch me.'

'She nuh like yu being down there. Yu know dat.'

'Being down there or being with him?'

'Papa?'

I nodded. Stanley was squatting on the floor cutting out a
piece of wood to make his model aeroplane. A box kit he got
from America. Because Stanley loves aeroplanes. All he wants
to do is go to England and join the Royal Air Force. But he is
only seventeen years old.

He stopped the knife moving. 'Yu should learn to leave
well alone. Just do what she want.'

'She strip me, Stanley. Stark naked.'

He looked up at me. Narrowed his eyes. 'She do that?'
Then he said, 'Yu should shut yu mouth.'

'About what?'

''Bout why she carry on so bad wid yu. How many
years yu been asking dat same question? And nuh get no
answer.'

'Long, long time.'

'So what yu keep asking fah?'

Sissy stepped aside to let me stand squarely at the board as I
took up the iron.

'Yu pester me but I shouldn't be letting yu iron no kerchief
or pillowslip like this. Yu know that?'

'Is OK. Mama not going find out.' I pushed the hot heavy
metal back and forth as carefully, smoothly and precisely as I
could. Standing out back where Sissy had the flatirons heating
on the fire. Two of them so that as one cooled she could

switch to the other. Holding the handle with a thick, padded white cloth.

'Why yu think Mama beat me so?'

'Pay attention to what yu doing. I don't want no burning here today. Not you or these clothes.'

'Sissy.'

'Miss Fay, yu keep asking me this and I tell yu I don't know.'

'But it not true, Sissy, is it.'

'No?'

'Because yu always know everything.' She came over and took the iron from me. 'Yu think maybe it because I light and Stanley dark like her? Why she nuh pick on him?'

Sissy thumped the iron down on its heel. 'What would mek yu say a thing like dat?'

'Just asking, that is all. Because Stanley got a different daddy. Is that it?'

She lifted the iron again, finished off the pillowcase I'd been pressing and turned her attention to the right sleeve of one of Papa's shirts. Then she said, 'It got nothing to do wid you. Dat is all I am going to say.'

'So who it to do wid?'

Sissy puckered up her lips and gave me no answer, just carried on moving her arm back and forth. And then she put the shirt on a hanger. And hung the hanger on the rail to air. And reached for another shirt that had been sprinkled and rolled and packed tight in the basket of clothes. In readiness for the ironing board.

I sat down on the nearby wooden stool. 'I remember the first time, yu know. She lock me in the piano room.

Like it was yesterday. The day she bring Stanley inside to talk to him.'

'Hush yuself now. Dis got nothing to do wid you excepting being a burden yu have to bear. A heavy one fah sure. But like I keep telling yu. It will pass. Believe me.'

How many times I'd replayed that day in my mind. School vacation time, two years ago. Porridge, boiled egg, bread and butter for breakfast. Sitting in the yard watching Stanley fix the bicycle and then pushing it all the way up to the top of the road. Settling myself in place. Feet resting on the pedals. Stanley holding on to the back of the saddle and running behind. Down and down the hill we went, until he let go and moments later I was in a heap again. Right knee bleeding.

'Yu supposed to balance the thing.'

'Alright. Next time tell me when yu going let go. Just shout "now" and I will be ready.' So we'd do it again, over and over until the blood ran down my leg and Stanley pushed the bi-cycle, with me sitting on it, back home for Sissy to have a look.

'What the two a yu been doing?' I was sitting on the hard, straight-back chair in the kitchen while she bathed my wound and smothered it with iodine.

'Learning to ride the bicycle, Sissy.'

'So yu learn yet?' She measured the bandage before cutting it to size.

Stanley laughed. 'She never going learn.' He walked off. When he came back he was carrying a grape soda from the icebox, for me. Sissy wrapped up my knee, firming everything with a tight squeeze of her hand.

'Well next time tek off yu clothes. Skin mend itself. This thing ...' she held up my torn skirt, 'somebody going have to put needle and thread to.' Then she said, 'It nearly lunchtime anyway, so go wash up now.'

Afterwards, the Barretts came over. Dudley and Elizabeth. And Peter Malcolm too. We were playing musical chairs on the veranda when Mama arrived home.

'Stanley, come inside, I want to talk to you.' He got up and followed her into the living room. The others smelt trouble and left. I waited. But after all her hushed tones behind a closed door, there was silence. A long, long silence. And I wanted Stanley back. So I knocked and entered the room in one single, flowing motion. And what I saw was Stanley standing there with his hands loose at his side and Mama sitting in the chair with her elbows on the arms and hands together, fingertips meeting in an arc. What was she saying? I didn't know because as soon as I opened the door she jumped to her feet and grabbed me. I never knew she could move so fast, covering the width of the room in no seconds flat. And then she marched me into the piano room where she was reaching for her cane and I was putting out my hand. And the bamboo was landing with a sting.

But no matter how many times I replayed it there was nothing I could understand. What sense does a child make of these things? Stanley stopped talking to her, though. So I knew it was serious. Oh, he would say a good morning or good evening. Pass the rice or the chicken. Please and thank you. But that was it. And if she came into a room he would get up and walk out. He couldn't even bear to look at her.

It made me remember the other time. Two years before that. The morning I went into her bedroom running an errand for Sissy to collect the empty glass from Mama's bedside. The water she kept by her each night. And there she was, sitting on the edge of the bed with Stanley standing between her legs. Soothing him she was. Rubbing his back like he was upset about something and she was saying, 'There, there.' Except she wasn't actually saying anything at all. It was more like she was singing, or humming softly to him. The minute she turned and saw me, there was a horror on her face. Deep shock, like she'd seen a duppy. And I ran because there was some dread that she had put into me. I locked myself in my bedroom and didn't come out until dinnertime. And afterwards, I didn't say anything to anybody about it. Not a single word to not a single soul. Not even to Stanley or Sissy. Because he was thirteen years old and I knew I had seen something I shouldn't have. I just didn't know what it was. And it was after that, that she started to find fault with me at every turn. That is what I knew. Knew it in my heart. Never mind what everybody said about it, making out that her spite started when the blonde hair I was born with turned to brown. I knew that wasn't the truth. Not the whole truth.

After the day Mama told Stanley the secret he was out of the house most of the time. And even though we would still sometimes play cards or chequers or dominoes, in secret because Mama thought it was sinful, mostly it was just him and Dudley and sometimes Peter, going off to do whatever it was that fifteen-year-old boys do, saying to me anytime I asked about going along, 'You stay at home. Get Elizabeth to come over.'

But Elizabeth didn't come over any more. Mama put a stop to it. 'The child is rude.' That is what she said. 'I don't want her in this house.'

'I could go over to her house.'

'I don't want you mixing with her. Find a decent girl to spend your time with.'

But there was never anyone decent enough for Mama. Every girl I brought home from school was too noisy, or insolent, or stupid. Or too black.

'What is too black?'

'I am not here to argue with you, child. I don't want the girl in the house. That is all there is to it.'

'But why, Mama?'

'If you think I owe you any explanation, young lady, then you had better think again.'

I looked at Mama's African head that she had the hairdresser straighten every week with the hot iron and Vaseline. And each morning fight and argue with the maid because nothing she did could satisfy Mama's idea of what perfectly relaxed hair should look like.

'Are you too black, Mama? Because of your hair? Is Stanley too black because he had a black papa? What about Daphne? Dark like she is. Even though Papa her daddy. Is she too black?'

'Who do you think you are? A little bit of light Chinese skin and some yellow hair and you think you can talk to me any which way you choose?'

No dinner. That was my punishment on that day, and every other day when she lacked the strength or inclination to raise her cane. So I would sit outside on the back steps listening to the clatter of plates and knives and forks, and wait. Wait. Because I knew she would change her mind. That sooner or later I would hear her voice and it would say, 'Fay, come and get your dinner.' And when that happened I didn't want to be out of earshot. I wanted to be there. Ready to spring to my feet and take my place at the table.

But she never did change her mind. Not even once. Not ever. Stanley would save me scraps from his plate, smuggled in his napkin. Sissy would rescue leftovers from the table or sometimes even give me her own meal. Mama? She never showed one ounce of concern. But still I waited. Never straying further than I thought her voice could carry.

'What are you talking about? Boarding school.'

'I'm going to board, Fay.'

How could he leave me like this? 'Why, Stanley?'

'It's better.'

I was sitting on the swing under the mango tree. He was lying on the lawn. On his back. Propped on his elbows. The sun was setting. Evening coming in. Crickets and croaking frogs.

'How will it be better?'

He looked down, plucked at a few blades of grass by his side. Scattered them on the breeze. 'She'll be better with you when I'm gone.'

'So is it to do with you? Why she hates me?'

'She doesn't hate you, Fay. She's your mother.'

After that, the rain didn't bother me, even though it went on day after day for weeks like the whole Caribbean Sea was pouring down from the sky. To me, it was a welcomed excuse for sitting inside with my puzzles and colouring pens. Stanley stayed at home too. Sometimes. And sometimes Dudley and

Peter came over. But the only outside activity was riding the bicycles, which I could do now, through the flooded streets, legs outstretched hip-high. Or making paper boats from old newspapers and sailing them into the unknown.

The night the gullies burst their banks the water washed away homes and drowned the people sleeping in them. So Sissy said. Twelve inches of rain in just twenty-four hours that damaged the mains, which is why we could only get water out of the pipe certain times of the day. A shortage, Sissy said. They had to ration it. The people? Sissy said that's how it goes. That's what happens if your house is too feeble to withstand the weather.

The day Stanley left I threw my arms around him and wouldn't let go. 'I'll be back for Christmas. Promise. It's only a few weeks away.' But I couldn't say anything. Couldn't form words with a mouth so full of wailing as he tore himself away from me and headed for the waiting taxi cab.

Stanley did come home for the holidays, but he wasn't the same. He was lost to me. I could see it in his eyes.

CHAPTER 3

I'D PUT UP my hand before the end. Long before Sister Angelica rose from her chair, straightening her white habit and the long ebony rosary that hung from her waist. I needed the toilet. But she wasn't interested. What she wanted to do was write on the blackboard. So I called out, 'Sister, please.' Which made her swivel her head, covered in skullcap and veil, to see who was causing the disturbance because Sister Angelica demanded absolute silence. Except if she asked you a question. When, if that happened, you had to speak up loud and clear and give her the exact answer that was in her mind. Word for word.

'The lesson is almost over. You will have to wait.'

I thought I could hang on and did, minute after creeping minute. But then I was desperate and knew I wouldn't make it through the final prayer of the day.

'Sister, please.'

'Five more minutes. You will have to wait. Now be still and pay attention.'

But I was bursting. So much so that I could feel the cold, clammy panic rising in my body and the reddening in my face like I was about to explode.

'I can't wait, Sister.'

Then we were all standing. Shuffling around and positioning ourselves behind our wooden chairs with their extended writing arms. I was hopping from one leg to the other. Did she not hear me above the clatter of thirty girls preparing themselves for the Lord?

So I said it again. 'I can't wait, Sister.' But she was already crossing herself. In the name of the Father, the Son and the Holy Spirit. And we were bringing our palms together and reciting in unison: 'Our Father who art in heaven ...'

The second we finished, I made a dash for the door. Didn't even bother to cross myself. So swiftly did I move that all the other girls were still standing silent and upright behind their chairs, while right there in the middle of the room, in that open, empty, deadly space surrounded by the horrified faces of my classmates, I started to pee. Felt the hot liquid running down my legs with no way of stopping it. I couldn't even move. I just came to a halt and stood there watching the puddle between my feet grow larger and darker. Flowing like a river across the wooden floor. A torrent that would not end. And then I heard the laughter and felt Sister Angelica's hand on my arm, shaking me like one might a water jug to make sure it had surrendered all of its contents. But she wasn't trying to empty me out. She was trying to wake me from the trance I had slipped into. Mesmerised by the slow, gradual seepage into the floorboards and the echoing hiss of the girls' voices.

I was still standing there when Sister told everyone to walk around the mess and go home. Just like the day I myself had avoided stepping on the boards where Claudeth had fallen, her whole body wriggling like a cut-off lizard's tail, and frothing at the mouth. Remembered how I had stared at her thinking she was going to die. And afterwards, making sure not to tread on the spot in case I too caught whatever it was she had. But most of all feeling relieved that she had tumbled two girls ahead of me as we stood in the circle, so that Sister never got a chance to ask me to spell the word that was next but one on her list. Whatever that was.

Sissy said Claudeth had a fit and I couldn't catch it. She said I should feel sorry for Claudeth, which made me wonder if I had a fit would anyone feel sorry for me. And if I died, would anyone miss me. That was the first time I thought about killing myself and making everyone feel sorry. Especially Mama. But I knew I couldn't do it because it was a sin. And in my child's mind, I knew God wouldn't like it.

Sister Angelica sent me home wet. Not before putting the cane across the back of my legs three times. The first stroke for letting Satan take hold of my body. The second one for weakness. The third for lacking discipline and control.

When Sissy met me at the school gate she held my hot, sweaty face in her hands and kissed me on the forehead. And then we walked home because I was too ashamed to get on the tram and let everyone see and smell what I had done. All she said was, 'Come, let's get you cleaned up.'

We never told Mama about what happened that day. Nor about the damp sheets at night. What I told Papa was that I never wanted to go back to that school again.

'Trouble at school, Fay? More trouble with your mama?' I was silent. 'Yu have to go to school, Fay. Ten-year-old girl can't just stay at home.'

'Almost eleven, Papa, and I can. Just tell Sister Angelica that I'm not coming back. Stanley finished school himself now. He can teach me until it time for me to go to high school.'

'What all this about, Fay?'

'I beg you, Papa. Please.'

'What I going say to yu mama?'

But as it turned out, Mama didn't care. All she said was: 'Let the child do whatever she wants.' Because she was more interested in what was going on in England with their kings. Why that should matter to her I didn't know, but Papa said it was because the missionaries who educated her as a girl were English and she had a mighty liking for them.

'So that is why she has the tin salmon and cucumber sandwiches, and tea and Victoria sponge cake every day?'

'Every day, Fay. Four o'clock like clockwork.'

So I was at home with Sissy. And Stanley sometimes when he wasn't downtown helping Papa in the shop. I didn't feel like doing anything, though. So I just wandered about aimlessly. From room to room and around the yard with all its trees and colourful flower beds and lawns, which Mama thought made it look like an English country garden. In her mind anyway.

I'd have a swim and then sit under the almond tree wondering why they bought a house with a swimming pool when Mama couldn't swim and Papa never went in it. Maybe he couldn't swim either. That is what I thought. Or maybe he just didn't want to strip down to his trunks, because my whole life all I ever saw him wear was black trousers and a white shirt. And actually, if you looked at the washing line or in the closet or drawers in his bedroom you would discover that he didn't have any other clothes, just hanging black trousers and jackets and neatly pressed and folded crisp, white, cotton shirts. And underwear of course. White shorts and vests. And socks. Black. All black. That was it. That was all he had in the stripped-down room he slept in, on an old Chinese canvas cot with one sheet and no pillow whatsoever. Two brushes and a comb on his dresser and his *chop*, carved in ivory with the head of an ox on the top, because that was the year he was born, with the pad of red ink for when he wanted to seal something with his real name. Not Henry Wong, the name the British immigration officer gave him when he landed in Jamaica. But Hong Zilong. Which is why he called everything by that same name. Hong Zi Grocery Store. Hong Zi Wine & Spirits. I would sit by the pool for a while, pondering all of this, and then I'd go look for Sissy.

Next, knock off a few balls and wonder why they had bought a house with a tennis court when neither of them had ever set foot on it. Not just because it was hidden behind a huge red hibiscus hedge so maybe they forgot about it, but because Mama thought game playing, any kind of game playing, was verging on the sinful. So I'd pick up the balls, put them back in the bin and go look for Sissy.

Wait for the ice-cream man with the wooden box strapped to the back of his bicycle, filled with dry-ice. That was another activity. Or watch Daphne crawl around the floor, fiddle with her wooden blocks, listen to her cry. Then go and look for Sissy. I didn't even want to ride the bicycle any more. What fun was that on your own? What was the point of anything on your own?

Sissy said I had to find something to occupy myself because she had her work to do but no matter how many puzzle books and jigsaws she piled up in the corner none of them could interest me. There are only so many words a person can be bothered to find, only so many mazes to trace, or crosswords to complete, or Spot the Differences you want to run your pencil over. Only so many pictures of English castles and gardens you want to spend your time slotting together.

Some days, when Mama wasn't there to stop me, I went to Papa's shop and stood behind the counter on an empty orange crate passing a packet of flour or sugar. Or I'd sit in the corner reading the comic strips from the newspaper. Sometimes I would even be let into the drawer to give some change, watched carefully by Papa or Stanley. And when nothing was doing, I played kick-can or shove-ha'penny out back with Alvin, the little boy who ran errands for my father. The wine and liquor store? Papa said no. I was too young, even though we still used to pass through the old opium den from time to time. Mostly to get something to eat.

When Stanley was home we would make out like we were doing lessons, but mostly we fooled around. Play-fighting. Rough and excited. Bouncing on the sofa or rolling on the floor. And we would laugh. But Mama didn't like it. She said we made too much noise and it was unladylike. So in the end, Stanley stopped. He was nearly a grown man anyway, too old to be tumbling around with me. I reckon he had more interesting things to do, especially at night when he was always out some place. Doing the devil's work, according to Mama, but I think he was just getting away from her.

And then Nancy Lee moved in next door with all the furniture they must have imported direct from China. Not like the English oak that filled our house. And out back, they had a big room packed to the ceiling with all the goods her father must have been busy selling in his shop downtown. It was like the story I'd heard about Aladdin's Cave. Dim and shadowy with untold treasure.

'Yu not going to school?' That is what Nancy asked me.

'I waiting till high school.'

We were squatting at a small square table of dark wood carved at the edges with cranes and flowers, drinking water that should have been tea from little china cups the likes of which I'd never seen at home, only in the tea shops I'd visited with Papa.

'What you do all day?'

'Nothing.'

We paused and sipped some more water. I looked around at the cramped space we were sitting in. At the Chinese cabinets and screens, the hanging woks and pans, tablewear and glasswear, rugs on a rack, ornaments in china and stone and metal.

And then I said to her, 'How come yu mama never leave di house?'

'How yu mean?'

'She always in there, Nancy. All I ever see a her is she come to di door once in a while. In her nightie mostly, never mind di time a day.'

She stared down into the cup, turning it around in her hand.

'She sick.'

'What she sick with?'

She didn't want to tell me. I could see it in the way she tightened her lips. But she did.

'In her head.'

'Her head?'

'She talk to herself. That is what I mean.'

I laughed. 'Everybody talk to themselves. The man walking down the street talk to himself. The woman at the bus stop. Even Sissy talk to herself sometimes.'

'I don't mean like that.'

'So what yu mean?' But she wouldn't say. She just put her head down and shut up. I looked over and saw the sadness in her. Even as a child I could see it, a deep well of despair as she sat there staring into the empty cup.

Soon after, we started riding bicycles together. Every afternoon when she came back from school. And we made lemonade from the limes we picked off her tree, sweetened with brown sugar. And drank it from the little cups in her father's backyard storeroom where we'd created a home with all the wonderful things he had in there. Pretending we were the doctors who were going to cure her mother. And when Nancy was at school, I watched the house to see what Mrs Lee was doing, which was nothing except walking up and down, and around and around. That was when I asked Papa for a doll.

'You not too old for that, Fay?'

'I need the doll, Papa.'

'Need?'

Yes, need. Because my doll and Nancy's doll could sit opposite each other or lie down on the grass and talk about how Mrs Lee was doing that day. And it didn't matter what I said because it wasn't me saying it. It was Mary. And Nancy could say what she wanted because it wasn't her. It was Betty. So Mary and Betty could look at each other and talk. And we could look anywhere we wanted to, even into the clear blue sky.

And that way Nancy didn't have to look me in the face when she said, 'Half the time she thinks she is God.'

'God? For truth? What she do when she God?'

'She worry 'bout the world that coming to an end and she not done fixing it yet. So she rush 'round the house moving everything. Like maybe she put some shoes in the stove or some sheets in the icebox. And then she walking 'round and 'round only every time she pass the table she have to touch it, on that same exact corner. And all the time she talking because she can hear the voices telling her she is wicked and arguing with her.'

So I started to practise talking to myself. To see if it would help my loneliness. Counting out loud how many steps it took me to get from home to Nancy's. How many times the pedals turned when I cycled around the house or to the corner of the road; how many mouthfuls it took to eat my breakfast. Telling myself you are cycling. Now you are walking. Now you are brushing your teeth, putting on your blouse, fastening your shoes. But I never heard anyone answer me back.

The next thing was sloppy dress and not washing yourself. But Sissy wasn't in favour so that had to stop. Talking in a way that didn't make sense. Better still, not talking at all. But nobody noticed or if they did they didn't mention anything to me about it. Withdrawal, that is what Nancy said they called it. Social isolation. And I would sit under the big mango tree for hour after hour with nobody paying me any mind. Until finally I would give up and go inside and Sissy would say to me, 'Yu feeling better now? Something upset yu?' But why didn't she come outside to ask? 'I reckon yu go out deh to find some peace and quiet. That is what I figure anyway.'

Mama? Nothing. Not even after I started imitating Mrs Lee by touching the dining table every time I passed it. And telling everyone that a mad man was coming to kill me in my bed at night. Papa just said, 'Too many stories, Fay. Time you go back to school.'

Except Mrs Lee wasn't a story. She was in that house day after day not wanting to go anywhere, or do anything, or see anybody. Not even Nancy or Mr Lee. And especially not the daily help who came in to see to her meals and such but who she couldn't be bothered to even exchange a few words with. Like the woman was a ghost who was cleaning the house and doing the laundry and preparing the food by magic.

When Nancy and I were in the house she would ask us to brush her down. And we'd do it because Mrs Lee was always afraid that she was going to set herself on fire even though she never smoked a cigarette in her life.

Sometimes we would hear her in the next room crying or talking her gibberish, or shouting out, 'No, no. Stop it,' like somebody was attacking her. Or, 'You can't come in here.' Even though there was no one there. On a good day, she was happy and cheerful for no reason whatsoever. Offering us whisky from Mr Lee's drinks cabinet, taking off her clothes like she was stripping for a shower, and telling us all sorts of personal things she should have kept private between her and her husband.

Nancy said the doctors gave her mother tablets for her moods and the voices, and the people she saw from time to time. And every so often they took her to the asylum for hot and cold baths and electric shock.

'Electric shock!'

'Yes, Fay. They stick a thing on her head and switch it on. Just like that. And my father says they doing experiments in America cutting out people's brains.'

'Cutting out their brains?'

'Just a little part off the front.'

'And that going cure her?'

'So they say.'

It was the electric shock and them cutting out your brain that really frightened me. Especially since nobody seemed to know what made Nancy's mother that way. Including the doctors who were planning to cut open her head. So if they didn't know with all their learning and certificates how was I supposed to know? How was I supposed to know whether or not the thing plaguing Mrs Lee was the same thing that was wrong with me? The thing that Mama could see and was trying to beat out of me. For my own good. While I was still young. Before it set in. Before it was too late. Before I got as old as Nancy's mother and they had to cut out my brain.

Maybe that was Mama's way of saving me from a life of misery and confusion like Mrs Lee. That is what I thought. Because in truth it wasn't a game any more. Some days I really didn't feel like showering or taking off my pyjamas, or talking to people, or going out of the house. Sometimes I couldn't think straight, or remember things, or react the way people expected me to. The worst part was sometimes, for no apparent reason, I felt unhappy. But if I was turning like Mrs Lee then I never wanted anybody to find out because one day they came in an ambulance and took her. And Nancy and her father moved and I never saw any of them again.

So from that point on I kept everything to myself, working things out in my own head so as not to alert people to my strange ways or disorganised thinking. That is what they called it. Like the day I left Nancy's bicycle in the middle of the driveway and her father reversed his car over it. I stopped wetting the bed as well. But most important of all, I found things to busy myself with. Just in case anyone should think that I was doing nothing all day.

CHAPTER 4

WHEN THE TIME came to go back to school it was a relief. Just to leave the house and catch the bus to Old Hope Road because that was where Immaculate moved to after the fire burnt down the school in Duke Street. But that was it. The journey. Because when I got there it was all the same faces. All the same girls who had stared and laughed at me on that last afternoon ages back, come up from the prep school because we were all twelve years old now. Hazel Brown, Henrietta Thompson, even Marjorie Williams who'd been standing at the desk right next to mine when it happened, and seated next to me again in our alphabetical order. Sister Angelica wasn't there, though. Thank heaven. I don't think I could have spent another year with her.

The lessons. English language, literature and grammar. Algebra, geometry and arithmetic. Geography. Biology. Spanish and Latin. Elocution and penmanship. And I didn't have the faintest idea what was going on. It seemed like in my absence these girls had taken a giant leap the likes of which I could only dream about. They talked about Virgil and Shakespeare, particles and participles, acute and obtuse angles, temperate climates and enzymes like they were discussing what they'd had for breakfast. And of course, everything was *como estas* and *muy bien*. It sent me rushing home straight away at two o'clock every day to see what I could do to save myself from further embarrassment. Stanley helped as best he could but my shame stopped me from asking him the things I felt convinced I should have known but didn't.

'It cyan be so bad, Miss Fay. Yu only been gone little over fifteen months. How much learning can deh do in dat time? And still in di prep school.'

'I'm telling you, Sissy. They all know everything.'

She finished clearing away the plate on which I'd just eaten my corned-beef sandwich. 'No. Cyan be so. Yu too bright for dem to all know everything and you nuh know nothing. Yu must know more than yu think yu do.'

It seemed to make sense but it didn't make me feel any better. Especially since half the time I was studying in the locked piano room, with hands sore from the sting of Mama's cane and a troubled mind turning over and over the events of the day wondering if I could have prevented her wrath by doing or saying something different. Different words. Maybe a different tone. Or just been different. Somehow. If only I knew how. If only I could read her mind. If only I could understand why a mother who loved her child would treat her this way.

But I couldn't. So I decided to avoid her. If Mama was going to be out, rush home as quickly as possible, go straight to my room and do my homework. Do not emerge until dinnertime. If Mama was going to be in, dawdle. Stay in the school yard under the big guinep tree. Slip my legs over the board seat and rest my books on the bench, after wiping away the crumbs from the lunchtime sandwiches. But, and this was crucial, do not stay too long. Not so long that I would risk hearing her voice on entering the house: 'Where have you been until this hour, madam?'

And I would say, 'At school, Mama.'

And she would say, 'The school day finishes at two o'clock. Two pm precisely. You think I don't know that?'

'After-school activities, Mama.'

'I didn't pay for any activities. If you want activities join the Girl Guides. Until then, you will make your way home after school and be here where you are supposed to be.' And after a short pause: 'Yu hear me?'

On other days, she would be waiting for me in the piano room, cane in hand.

'Get yourself in here, madam.' And with every swing of her arm she would shriek, 'You-stay-out-all-hours, this-is-what-you-get.' A stroke of bamboo for each and every syllable.

Sometimes Miss Allen would even sit in the corner and watch. Satisfying herself that her investment was being put to good use. Because it was Miss Allen who always bought Mama the next cane every time one split or broke. And if I was let go as opposed to locked in, I would hear them talk. Loud and carefree like it didn't matter to them who might be listening.

'Lord, give me strength.' That would be Mama.

'The devil's work,' Miss Allen would say. 'Yu know di kinda trouble young girls get up to dese days?'

'Yu telling me? Think I don't know a daughter is an affliction. The wage of sin.'

'Whose sin, Cicely? Not yours, I know dat fah sure.'

'Di sin a di father. Di sin dat pass down from generation to generation. Since Adam and Eve. Di original sin dat child is determined to carry on. You mark my words. She have it in her.'

'I can see that, Cicely. I can see that.'

The sin of the father? My father? Is that what she meant? So I searched my mind for anything and everything that Papa had ever said to me. Every place we had been. His grocery store, the cookhouse, the bakery, the betting shop to pay a debt or to collect his winnings. The constant walking from store to Chinatown store. The fresh coconut water and jelly, pineapple tarts, shaved ice with cane syrup. Rice or noodles. *Shao bow. Wah moy.* Dried shrimps. Instructions on how to parcel the rice and flour and sugar. How to fold the strong brown paper to wrap the perfect bag. How to cut a perfect two or four or six ounces of butter. How to weigh a perfect four or eight ounces of saltfish.

I thought about the day he took me to Immaculate to be interviewed by Sister Ignatius so she could assure herself that I was suitable material for the challenges and rewards the school had to offer. That is how she put it. Never mind that Papa was paying the fees. All that happened there was talk and more talk because I had already taken the entrance exam and, by some miracle, had passed it.

I replayed these times with Papa over and over in my mind. Like a movie on a loop. But there was nothing. Nothing to constitute the sin of the father. What was I searching for anyway?

* * *

The first time I went to see Madam Chin-Loy, Papa took me there himself. In a buggy. Under the canopy to shelter us from the worst of the rain. 'I don't want your mama getting herself into a fluster. Especially if Peggy decide not to take you on. No point in that.'

'Is she a good teacher, Papa?'

'The best private tutor in Chinatown.' He smiled at me. A broad grin from ear to ear. 'Teacher to the best of them. For years and years.' He patted my knee. 'Don't you worry about a thing. What Peggy Chin-Loy don't know about school lessons not worth knowing.'

She tested me. Reading, writing and arithmetic. With each passage and sum more difficult than the previous one. Books taken from the pile on her desk. The specific pages already marked with small pieces of blue card sticking out of the top. 'Read from the paragraph beginning …' Or, 'What do you understand the writer to be saying?' Or, 'Now write something for me. Perhaps a poem you can remember or a chronicle of what you did yesterday.' We were sitting in her little office overlooking the dainty but colourful backyard. Orderly. Like her. With her grey hair in a neat bun and her tidy bookshelves, and precise handwriting. With a black-ink pen noting down my every utterance. Finally, she took the paper from me. Addition, subtraction, division and multiplication. Rubbing her forehead as she passed her eyes over it.

Then she stood and said, 'Let us step outside.'

Papa got to his feet as soon as she opened the door. 'Not yet, Henry.' She didn't even stop walking. Just waved her arm in the air to tell him to sit down again.

In the dining room, lunch had been set for one.

'Eat.'

'Me, miss?'

'Do you see anyone else here?'

So I sat down in front of the plate and knife and fork. And slowly worked my way through the warm macaroni cheese and salad. Remembering to chew with my mouth closed, and to wipe my lips on the napkin so as not to leave a greasy smudge on the glass as I sipped the lemonade. And Madam Chin-Loy watched. Without saying a single word to me.

Afterwards, she told Papa to bring me to her twice a week. Mondays and Wednesdays. From three to five pm. And then she handed him an envelope with a note of her charges.

On the way home I asked him about the Girl Guides.

'Girl Guides, Fay? You have time for that?'

The day Marjorie Williams almost drowned at Sigarney beach was the day I became the class heroine. Because of all the little Girl Guides I was the only one who actually knew how to swim. Everybody else just tricked people by walking along the seafloor swishing their arms in the water. The ridiculous part was she was only a few inches out of her depth. Waving her arms about she was. So at first it wasn't even clear she was in trouble, more like she was showing off to us how far out she could go. The Guide mistress was still unloading the picnic from the bus. And in truth, Marjorie should not have been in the water. She, like the rest of us, had been told to wait.

As soon as I realised she wasn't fooling, I ran into the sea and swam like I had done so many times before in the pool at home. When I reached her I put my arm across her chest and gripped her in her armpit. And then I towed her back to shore. How I knew what to do? Playing with Stanley.

After that, any help I needed with $a^2+b^2=c^2$, the war in Latium, or the difference between fate and divine intervention, was mine only for the asking. And Marjorie Williams became my first schoolfriend. So much so that six months later she invited me to her birthday party. Never before had I been so honoured. But Mama said no. I wasn't going to any party.

'Next thing you know boys swarming all over the place. And if I know anything, then I know that one thing will always lead to another.'

'I am thirteen years old, Mama. It is a little girl's birthday party.' The word 'please' was on the tip of my tongue but I didn't say it. I'd promised myself never to plead with her for anything. So I didn't go. The Saturday afternoon came and went with me sitting on the veranda looking out at the lawn wondering what Marjorie, Hazel, Henrietta and all the others were doing. When we went back to school on Monday they were all full of the fun and games they'd enjoyed. I felt left out. Excluded.

'Shame you missed it, Fay. It was really good.'

'Thank you, Marjorie. Maybe next time.'

But there was never to be a next time because after that a slow and gradual distance grew between us until we were reduced to nodding terms. My regret? That I hadn't made the effort to offer any excuse or explanation. I'd simply said, 'I can't come.' Why? Because I was too ashamed to admit that after Papa had talked her into letting me go, Mama refused to buy a present and forbade him from doing so. Why didn't I make up a lie? I don't know. What I did instead on that

Saturday afternoon was sit silently on my own feeling sorry for myself. Thinking about how I hurt Sissy by turning up my nose at her suggestion that she find a gift for me because I knew that whatever she came up with would look pitiful next to the lavish offerings of my classmates.

It didn't matter anyway because the worry in the house wasn't about me. It was about the strikes and riots that were bringing Kingston to a standstill. It was about the police and soldiers who didn't seem able to do anything to stop or control the marauding crowds that wandered the streets causing mayhem including looting Chinese shops and burning some of them to the ground. It was about the governor declaring a state of emergency and Mama's fear that my father would lose his fortune.

That was when Sissy decided to leave me. I knew it was going to happen the moment I saw the red-skin man standing on the doorstep, dressed in a brown suit with his hat in hand.

'I am looking for Miss Florette Cecilia Wint.'

'Sorry, mister. Nobody called that living here.'

Mama brushed me aside. 'And what business would you have with her?'

'It is of a personal nature, madam. Does Miss Wint reside here?'

The man was a lawyer under instruction from solicitors, so they said, in England. And what he wanted was to tell Sissy that her father had died and left her money. Quite a tidy sum, it turned out, because her father was an Englishman who went back to his home leaving Sissy with her mama in West Kingston, where he found her. But even after her mother passed and Sissy went into service, her father still made it his business to have somebody track her down and give her the chance of a new life. That is how much money it was.

'A boarding house, Miss Fay. What I always dreamed of. Wid young ladies staying there and being fed and looked after. Meking a home for dem dat maybe deh wouldn't otherwise have.'

I was sitting on the chair in the kitchen.

'Yu leaving me, Sissy?'

She stooped before me and took my hands in hers. 'Yu want me to be a maid my whole life? Fetching and carrying after people morning till night, six and a half days a week. Never having my own roof over my head.' She pointed upwards. 'Never being able to decide for myself what it is I want to do. Is that what you want for me, Miss Fay?'

I couldn't argue with her. Even I could see that she would have a better life in her boarding house than the one she had with me.

'Deh will find someone else to look after yu. And she will be fine, Miss Fay. Just fine. And then one day yu will grow up and you will leave her. And until then yu can come visit me at di boarding house anytime yu want.' She smiled and stood up.

'I going miss yu, though, Sissy,' I said, looking up at her with tears in my eyes.

'Yu never have to miss me.' She bent down and kissed me on the forehead. 'All yu have to do is close yu eyes and hold on to dis and I will be there.' She pressed into my hand a doll made from a lollipop stick dressed in a traditional Jamaican costume of red and white, with a black face and a bandanna wrapped around her head.

'Does she have a name?' I asked.

'What yu want call her?'

I thought and then I said, 'Athena.'

'Athena?'

'She is the goddess of wisdom and courage.'

'Good name.'

After that, I couldn't breathe. My lungs wouldn't fill. All I had was a shallow in and out breath. In and out. In and out, while I was gasping for air. I came over tired as well. Couldn't keep my eyes open. All I wanted to do was sleep even though I pinched myself to stay awake so that I could share with Sissy every last minute she had left in this house. Willing the days to stop passing; imagining that if I could hold my breath for long enough I could make time stand still and she would not have to go. Or maybe make myself sick to keep her here. But it didn't work.

The day she left I sat in her room and watched her pack the small brown cardboard grip, wondering how it could be that she had so few things. Two cotton dresses, and a third which she called her Sunday frock. Some underwear that she turned her back to me when she folded. A rattan hat with a bright yellow ribbon tied around it. Her church bonnet, so she said, even though I couldn't remember ever seeing Sissy go to church. An ancient but well-polished pair of brown and white shoes. The black and white uniforms Mama had given her were washed and ironed, and hanging on the rail. And the sensible black shoes were on her feet. Mama said she could keep them. Thirteen years of service and that is all she had to show for it.

When the taxi arrived I stood on the veranda steps while the driver loaded Sissy's case. And even though my chest felt like someone had tied a belt around it and pulled it tight, and my eyes prickled from being forced wide open, I didn't cry.

Sissy said goodbye to Mama and nodded her head at me before walking slowly to the Checker Cab. And then at the last minute she turned around and came back. Climbing the steps until she reached the one just below me where she stopped and enclosed me in her arms. Not close like she would usually, but loose. And then she leant into my ear and whispered, 'You are perfect. Don't let anybody mek yu forget it.' And then she let me go and walked to the waiting car. Got in and shut the door. And it drove away.

Mama looked at me with that 'What did she say to you?' question on her face but I didn't tell her, I just turned around and went inside to my room where I threw myself on to my bed and sobbed. Away from Mama's prying and disapproving eyes.

The next week I caught the bus after school and went to Franklyn Town to visit Sissy in her boarding house. It was a huge ramshackle place with bedrooms galore and bathrooms and a kitchen that had seen better days. 'Yu right,' she said. 'It not much. But it can fix up. Some hammer and nail. A lick a paint. You wait and see.'

I smiled. Mostly because, despite the condition of the house, Sissy's happiness was written all over her. Her joy was absolute and complete.

'Come.' She led me out into the small backyard. 'Even dis going turn beautiful. Nice and cool and shady for all di young ladies dat going sit out here and read their book or do their embroidery.'

Afterwards, resting in the creaking veranda chairs while we sipped some cold sorrel, Sissy reached into her pocket and pulled out a clay pipe. Stuck it in her mouth and lit it.

'Smoking, Sissy?' I said in shock.

She laughed. 'A secret yu mama would never have approved of.' She took a puff and released the smoke slowly. 'But now, I am my own woman. Do any damn thing I like.' Looking at me out of the corner of her eye to check how I felt about her saying 'damn'.

I had never seen Sissy like that before. With her greying hair tied in a bun that was still loose with stray strands. A casual, floral, cotton frock with a break-neck and patch pockets. And slippers. Flat, open-toed slippers. The pipe in her mouth was nothing. It was the expression on her face that said it all. Sissy was free.

I was clutching Athena in my hand the morning I woke up to discover I was bleeding to death. All over the white sheets. Lying there overcome with grief while Pearl was knocking on the door telling me it was time to get ready for school.

'Yu going to be late, Miss Fay. And yu know the Sisters nuh like that.'

I didn't answer. Instead, I ran my fingers over the red wetness in the bed. And at the edges of the circles now turning brown and hard in their dryness.

'Miss Fay. Miss Fay.' The knocking grew louder. More insistent.

'I can't come out, Pearl. I'm dying.' That is when she opened the door, marched over to the bed and pulled back the bedspread and top sheet.

'Yu not dying, Miss.'

Pearl helped me to clean up and sent me to Mother Murphy who showed me what to do with the elastic and how to fold the napkin and fit it between my legs. And when they are soiled, she told me, put them to soak in the covered bucket under your bed and I will see to them. And that was when I finally understood what Mother Murphy did, because all my life I'd never seen her do anything other than sit on a stool in the yard and argue with the other maids. Sit and argue, and rub coconut oil on her skin because it was so dry it was practically dropping off her. Why Papa kept her on? Because 'Mother Murphy too old to go anywhere else'. That's what he said.

So for five days once a month Mother Murphy collected the bucket from under my bed and replaced it empty and disinfected. And the napkins washed and bleached white, neatly folded in the bottom of my drawer.

When I told Sissy about it she wasn't surprised. She said I was a woman now.

'Mother Murphy explain to yu 'bout babies?'

'Babies?'

'Yu mama then?'

I just opened my eyes wide and looked at her. She took the pipe from her mouth and spat brown saliva over the veranda railing into the yard. And then she told me how it would come to be that one day I would make a baby. But I didn't believe her. It didn't seem likely that I would ever want to do a thing like that with a man, or that something as big as a baby could possibly get pushed out of a person. Especially not out of me.

★　　★　　★

As soon as the war started, Stanley went straight away to find out if he could join the Royal Air Force. They said he had to take some tests and have a medical examination, which he did and passed.

'So yu going to England, Stanley? To fly an aeroplane?'

'It a war.'

'There not no war here in Jamaica.'

'Everybody got to make their contribution, Fay.'

I stared across at him sitting next to me by the pool. Fiddling with his toes he was, like he couldn't bring himself to look me in the face.

'Yu think yu ever going come back?'

'Not if they kill me.'

'Yu want to die, Stanley? Is that what yu want? Yu only twenty-one years old and yu want to die.'

'I never said that.' He paused. Then he lifted his head towards me. 'But it a war. That is what happen.'

I breathed in and out three times. To steady myself. 'Tell me something.'

'What?'

'Tell me what happen that day I come in the living room when Mama was talking to yu.'

'That such a long time ago, Fay.'

'Maybe, but everything changed after that. How you were with her. How she was with me. I know it was something bad, Stanley.'

'What difference it mek now?'

'I need to know because yu going to war and maybe never coming back and I cyan spend the rest of my life wondering if it was something to do with me. Like if I am such an evil person that whatever went on could affect everybody so bad.'

'Don't talk rubbish. Yu not evil. I already tell yu it had nothing to do with you. Didn't I already tell yu that? Long time back.'

'Don't just say that. Tell me something that make sense. Explain it to me.'

So he told me that Mama's own papa had forced himself on her and that was how come she get pregnant and give birth to him. That Mr Johnson, whose name was also Stanley, was his father and his grandfather at the same time.

'That is what she tell yu that day?'

'I just told you.'

And then the true horror of it took hold of me. 'He do that to her? His own daughter?'

'More than once, Fay. Over and over.'

'And she was just little more than a child?'

'A child that was old enough to know better.'

'Yu nuh feel sorry for her?'

'Sorry? For her?' He stood up to walk away.

'No, Stanley. Wait.' I grabbed his leg and forced him to sit down again.

Then he said, 'She should have run away. That is what any self-respecting woman would have done.'

'Run away to where?'

'I dunno. Somewhere. Anywhere. That is what she should have done. Or otherwise stick a knife in his ribs.'

'Really? Yu think so?'

He stood up again. 'Enough.'

'One more thing, Stanley.' He looked down at me. 'That time. Just before she started beating me. When I

47

came into the bedroom and she was stroking your back and humming to yu.'

His brows furrowed. 'I don't know what yu mean.'

'And I ran off but never said anything to anybody. And then a few days later she started beating me.'

'Because of your hair?'

'No. Not that.'

He thought about it and then he said, 'Nothing happened.'

'Nothing?'

'Like what? What you think happen?'

'I don't know, Stanley. That is why I am asking you.'

He leant over and picked up his towel. And then, walking away, he said again, 'Nothing happened.'

Stanley packed his bags and got on the boat. And he sailed out of Kingston harbour at six-thirty in the morning just as the sun was rising to light up the day. And while Mama lay in her bed, Papa and I stood on the dock and waved to his back because he never looked around. He just strode up the gangplank and disappeared. After all, he had told us not to come. But Papa insisted and I pleaded with him to let me along.

The night before he left, Stanley promised to write. The night after, the house was empty and silent. Dark and dismal like a hollow cavern.

His first letter came a few weeks later. It was short and cheerful. He said England was fine. Different. He was stationed just outside London where he had everything he needed and life was good. But he wasn't flying any aeroplane. He was working in the stores.

CHAPTER 5

I REMEMBER I was waiting at the bus stop. That was all. Just standing there in Old Hope Road because I had stayed too long at school and missed the tram. So now I had to catch the bus with labourers and domestics not the office workers and shop assistants who looked so neat and tidy and kept their belongings together in an orderly fashion. On the tram. No. I had to cram myself on to the bus with people who had no idea about giving a person a little space. People who would squeeze up tight next to you and raise their arm to hold the rail never thinking about the smell of the armpit I would catch. A child standing there under them. People who didn't bother to wipe the sweat from their brow or stop it from dripping off the end of their nose. People who carried their possessions in brown paper bags instead of the pretty handbags or faux-leather cases of the tram travellers. And worst of all, people whose shoes needed a damn good clean and polish.

And so I endured the journey. Getting off opposite King's House to walk the length of Lady Musgrave Road home. And maybe it was that, my preoccupation with the people on the bus, that distracted me. Left me lacking in attention and disarmed. Because the first thing I noticed about him was his shoes. Shiny, black leather. In good condition. And then the rest of him: a presentable light-blue shirt and steamed navy trousers. He looked ironed.

'Excuse me, miss.' I stopped. 'I wonder if I could bother yu for any change yu might have?' I hesitated. He continued: 'I have just been robbed, yu see. My wallet lifted from my pocket right here.' He patted his left leg to show me exactly where his wallet had been. 'As I was trying to help a man who had fallen down drunk in the road.' He paused. 'So now I am in need of bus fare to Constant Spring Garden.' Well, I thought, in my child's innocence, he can't be that bad if he's trying to get to Constant Spring. That's a good area.

'Sorry, mister. All I have is little over a shilling.' He watched as I rummaged in my bag for the change. And then held out his hand for me to drop the coins into it.

'This is all yu have?' I nodded. 'Chinese from Immaculate and dis is all yu have?' So he'd recognised the school uniform.

'Sorry,' I said. 'But I think it might still be enough to get to Constant Spring.'

That is when he slapped me and I fell to the ground. He grabbed me by the hair and hauled me up again, with tears streaming from my eyes and snot running from my nose. And then he started to drag me. Not caring that my schoolbag was left on the sidewalk or that my shoes were being scuffed against the hard surface of the road. I didn't even cry out. That surprised I was. That stunned into silence. The pain in my head was like my scalp being pulled off while my feet fumbled to regain their balance and I flailed my arms about trying to catch hold of him. Any part of his body or clothes that, as it turned out, I could not reach.

He steered us off the road and into the bush, where another slap and a shove left me lying in the dirt. In my white school dress.

'What yu doing, mister?'

He looked at me, confused. So no plan then. That is what I reckoned anyway: just the sight of a light-skinned Chinese who he felt sure would have money.

'Who yu father?'

'My father?'

He knelt down and put his hands around my throat. Squeezed it. Tight but not too tight.

'Yu father got money if yu going to Immaculate.'

So that was it. I was right. I brushed his hands away and sat up. It was easy, that undetermined was his grip. Then I pulled up my knees and wrapped my arms around them.

'Are yu going to kidnap me?'

He didn't answer. He just leant back on his heels with a slight heaving in his chest and tiny beads of sweat rolling down his shiny, black face. Resting himself after his exertion.

So I asked him, 'What yu want to do now?' He didn't answer. 'My papa got a shop downtown. We can go there and get some money if yu want.' Except we had no way of getting there. Not with the coppers I gave him now scattered on the road beyond. Not both of us anyway. 'Or do yu want to just forget about this?'

He adjusted his feet and shifted his body to squat down on his haunches. That was when I realised he was only young himself. Maybe just a couple of years older than me.

'I never mean yu no harm, miss. I just see di uniform and reckon yu would have something in yu pocket.'

Someone walked past on the other side of the bush. Should I have cried out? I didn't. It didn't seem necessary somehow.

'What's yu name?'

He licked his dry, cracked lips and then bit into the thick flesh of the lower one.

'Delton.'

'Well, Delton, my pocket was empty.' I stood up. Dusted off the dirt from my dress as best I could. But white marks so easily. I examined the black and red streaks. Twisting my head around. And then turning my back to him. 'How bad is it?'

'Not too bad,' he said, brushing me down with his hand.

'Come on, let's go pick up the change and my bag and go get ourselves a cream soda.'

But when we returned to the spot my bag was gone. And the money too. All except the thruppence that had rolled into the gutter. He picked it up and handed it to me.

'So yu don't want to kidnap me for the ransom or go to Papa's shop then?'

'No.'

Delton and I walked down the road together while he told me his story. A good-for-nothing drunk of a father who beat his mother and all the children. And everyone in the house around the corner as well where the woman was another one of his baby mothers. And how many more women and children his father had Delton didn't know. His mama throwing him out when he was ten years old because she had too many mouths to feed. Living by his wits and now a trainee carpenter on a government youth scheme. Was it all true? Maybe. It would have explained why he was dressed so nicely.

'So what yu doing accosting children in the street? In broad daylight?'

'Broad daylight?' He laughed. 'And it wasn't no children neither. It was just you. Because yu look so fit and full a yuself strolling down di road like yu own it. Wid yu head hold high as a kite. And I say to myself dis girl got money.' Which made us both laugh.

'And then yu slap me and go drag me in a bush?'

'Dat was just a reaction. I sorry 'bout dat. Yu hurt bad?' He turned and examined my face. 'It still little red, yu know.'

'It will pass.'

And then he rubbed his hand on his trousers before offering it to me. So I took it and we shook just as we reached the gate and stopped walking. His hand was dry and rough so maybe he was a carpenter after all.

'Delton, yu right. I do have money, just not in my schoolbag. Yu want to come inside for some ice-water or lemonade or something?'

He held up his hands in protest. 'No. It not dat sorta thing. I should be on my way. Honest to God I don't know what come over me back there. It just dat sometimes, yu know, when yu got nothing and yu see somebody wid something, a urge come over yu. I just glad yu not hurt bad, dat is all.' And he bowed and carried on walking, turning around a few yards away to wave goodbye.

I sauntered up the driveway to see Mama sitting on the veranda with Miss Allen.

'Who is that yu walking up the road with?'

'Nobody.'

'Nobody? Well it look like somebody to me.'

I stood on the veranda, looking down at her with the crochet square in her lap. A tiny section of what I knew would grow into a magnificent centrepiece to be washed and starched in epic fashion to grace someone else's dining table. Most likely Miss Allen's or some other member of Mama's church group, because she always preferred to give away her efforts so as to bask in the gratitude of those less fortunate or less adept with the hook than herself.

'Where is your schoolbag?'

'It fell on the road.'

'Fell on the road? And yu leave it there? With all the books and whatnot your father paid good money for?'

'Good money dat yu so careless wid.' That was Miss Allen. Muttering under her breath but never missing the chance to add her tuppence to the brawl.

Mama stood up and walked over to me. 'Turn yourself around.'

'It's just a bit of dirt where I tripped.'

Miss Allen sniggered. 'Oh yes, so it's tripping now, is it?'

'Turn around,' Mama shouted. So loud it brought Pearl running outside to see what the commotion was.

'It nothing, Miss Cicely. Little bit a soaking and rubbing and it soon come out.' Pearl was fingering the back of my dress.

'Stand aside, Pearl. You did not witness the odious behaviour to which I have just been subjected.'

And Miss Allen added, 'With her own two eyes. Yes sir. Tell no lie.'

'This child,' Mama said, pointing her finger at me, 'has been walking the street like a hussy, with a man on her arm.'

'He wasn't on my arm. We shook hands, that was all.'

'A man, Pearl. A big, black man no less. Under God's good heaven. Throwing away her schoolbag and rolling about in the dirt with him like a common ...'

But Pearl cut in before Mama could finish. 'Miss Cicely, please.'

'Marching in here with a red face and a filthy dress to show off to all and sundry what she has been doing.'

Pearl took me by the hand and started to lead me away.

'Not one more step. You hear me? Not one more. Pearl. Inside with you.' Which sent Pearl scurrying back into the house. 'You. In the piano room.'

'Mama, nothing like that happened.'

She took me by the hand and dragged me away, while Miss Allen chewed her cud and nodded her head and muttered to herself, 'Yes, yes. Wicked girl.'

Mama shut the piano-room door behind her.

'Mama, Delton tried to rob me on the street.'

'I close my ears, O Lord, to the lies of this child's twisted tongue. Have mercy on me for what I am about to do. Because without the sting of the lash, evil will prevail, sealing her fate in the fires of hell. Give me the strength, Lord Jesus, to save her soul from eternal damnation.' And then down came her cane against my back and legs and arms as I tried to protect my head. Strike after frenzied strike as I ran to escape the worst. Throwing the piano stool between us. And the standard lamp.

Overturning the table with its vase of roses. And finally, crouching down behind the armchair. Pursued by her in a rage that I thought would see the end of me.

That is when Mother Murphy stepped through the door.

'Enough now before yu kill dis child.'

And Mama stopped. Sweating and panting. And exhausted.

Pearl bathed the cuts on my arms and legs, and asked Mother Murphy if she should call the doctor. But she said no, they were just surface wounds. They would heal. A few days off school and some rest till the swelling went down. That was all I needed.

Papa looked horrified when he saw the state I was in.

'Your mama do this to yu?'

So I told him what happened. With Delton and the shilling and the schoolbag and the red face I got when he slapped me and how my uniform got dirt on it and what Mama said about what she thought I'd been doing.

'What she say when yu explain all that to her?'

'I never told her, Papa. She never gave me a chance.'

He glanced back at the open door before sitting down on the edge of my bed.

'She most likely not believe yu anyway.' And then he gently stroked my forehead and said, 'I think maybe she gone too far this time.'

Did he say anything to her? I never knew. Never heard a thing. No angry confrontation. No comforting little chat. No hushed conversation in the dead of night, which it would have been because Papa was out of the house from sun up to sun down. Gone to the shop and then to Barry Street to do his business. No whispering from the maids. Telling the tale and retelling it amongst themselves, which is what they did about everything. Nothing. Except sorry looks and a sympathy for me that led to a fussing over my welfare. My clothes and hair and food. And the tidiness of my room. And a letter from Madam Chin-Loy expressing regret that my parents had cancelled our sessions, and wishing me well for the future.

When I asked him about it he said, 'Peggy? Well maybe it time yu finish with her anyway. Only so much catching up a person can do.'

'And Mama?'

'Your mother doing her best. She don't intend to be mean to yu. Is just her own sorrow inside. Coming out. In the wrong way.'

'But did you say anything to her?'

'Oh, Fay. What I going say? I ask her not to do it again. That maybe next time yu end up in the hospital and what good that would do.'

'What she say?'

'She? Nothing. But I don't think she will tek the cane to yu like that again. I think she even frighten herself with how much her own vengeance tek a hold of her.'

It was three whole weeks before I went back to school. Mama told Sister Ignatius I had a fever and vomiting and needed bed rest. During that time I lay in my room or wandered around the house in a daze. Doing nothing in particular except think about how much simpler everything would be if I could kill myself. Or just go to sleep and never wake up again.

* * *

57

'Yu papa not a bad man. He just lost, dat is all.' That is what Sissy had to say.

'But if he loved me, Sissy.'

'Oh he love yu, Miss Fay. He love yu. Don't yu ever have one doubt in yu mind 'bout dat. He love yu more than Stanley. More than little Daphne. Even though maybe I shouldn't be telling yu dat.'

'How yu know?'

'It stand to reason. Stanley not his own so you his firstborn and a man always feel special 'bout his firstborn.' She paused before adding, 'And a daughter at dat.'

'Yu think it mek a difference?'

She knotted her brows at me while she considered my question. 'I reckon. Always seem dat way to me anyway.' And then she let her gaze drift to the street as we sat in the shade of her veranda. On the new chairs. Steam-bent rocking chairs with cane backs that she said had been a gift from my father.

I sipped the cool lemonade. 'What Mama got against black men anyway?'

'Black men?'

'That's what she called Delton. A big, black man no less.'

Sissy sighed. Slow and heavy. 'Oh that. She just think deh lazy and troublesome. Good for nothing. Dat is all. Just sitting around waiting for the next easy thing to come their way. Not wanting to put their back into anything.'

'I think it is more than that.'

She took another puff of her pipe. It was out, so she leaned over and tapped it on the railing. And then she reached for a match and poked the dead tobacco loose.

'Well, maybe with good reason.'

'Not all black men like her father. Doing what he did to her.'

'Yu know about dat?'

'Stanley told me.'

'U-hum.' She finished repacking her pipe. 'Not all fathers what she think either.'

And just then, before I got a chance to ask her what she meant, a young woman opened the gate and walked towards us.

'Good afternoon, Miss Sissy,' she said as she came up the steps in her blue school uniform, nodding her head at me before going into the house.

'Marcia,' Sissy said. 'One of my young ladies.'

I thought on it and then I said, 'Yu never wanted to have children yourself, Sissy?'

She laughed. 'Me? When would I have time to do dat? Anyway,' she patted my arm, 'I already have my baby right here. From di day I come to di hospital to fetch yu home and deh put yu in my arms. And I kiss yu little head for di first time.'

And then she lit her pipe and sucked on it. While looking across the street at the two women prancing and dancing on their veranda. To the music from radio station ZQI.

CHAPTER 6

WHEN THE THREE-STOREY stone-built hotel opened in 1931 it was palatial, with beautifully landscaped grounds, tennis courts, a rattan gazebo and stables. It was the first building in the West Indies to be constructed for earthquake resistance, with furniture and fittings the most lavish of the time. And next door, a superb golf course was laid out. But by 1936, the operation was in financial difficulty and in 1940 the government decided to put the Constant Spring Hotel up for sale. The governor at the time, Sir Arthur Richards, offered it to Mother Xavier, the Franciscan superior, and Sister Davidica, the principal of Immaculate, and in January 1941 the school was established at Constant Spring.

Immaculate Conception High School for girls was magnificent. All in pink and white with the arched windows and doors downstairs and the little balconies upstairs where the boarders slept. And on the top floor, the rooms for the Sisters. Gardens with flowers and steps and four columns at the front door. Tiled areas with armchairs for people to sit in, with vases of flowers on tables and reading lamps pointing down to the exact spot that a person would want if they were sitting there with their book. With the ferns and palms and banana trees and two tennis courts, and a swimming pool with waterfall. And in the chapel, behind the statue of Our Lord, a message on the wall that said 'Peace I Give To You'. Peace. That is what the place was full of. Inside and out. A school of peace and splendour. It didn't surprise me none that it had originally been built as a hotel.

Looking at it, I thought, yes. I understand. Because when I'd asked Papa about the swimming pool and tennis court at home he'd said, 'This house built years back by white man more used to building hotel. Who sell it to his friend who, when he go back to America, sell to me because your mama, she wanted it. It what white people have.' It made perfect sense.

And even though it was all the same girls and all the same nuns who had moved here together from the old school site, it still felt new. Like I was starting over again from the beginning. As a regular. Not like the first time I went to Old Hope Road. A stranger returning to the class after a self-imposed exile.

But the best thing about Immaculate. What made Immaculate so immaculate. Beverley Chung.

She was standing in the garden by the statue of Our Lady surrounded by a small group of girls all listening eagerly to her American drawl. I decided to walk on by. I didn't think she needed any more attention. Certainly not mine. But she called out, 'Hey, gal.' And when I turned around I saw she was talking to me. She raised her left hand and with her index finger beckoned me over. I sauntered towards her.

'You have a name?'

I thought her presumptuous, bordering on the brazen, but I answered her anyway. 'Fay Wong.'

She scrutinised me. The other girls followed suit. Suddenly, the white school uniform made me feel like a pale ghost. Not that they looked any different, all light-skinned as they were.

'You have anything to say for yourself, Fay Wong?'

Mama would have called her insolent. I called it arrogant, so I said, 'You are the one who called me over here. What do you have to say for yourself?'

She laughed. Good-humoured with a tinge of embarrassment. I turned and walked away.

The next time I saw her she was strolling across the lawn. When I got abreast of her she said, 'Come with me.' I followed her to the swimming pool and then behind the changing block where she produced a packet from her pocket. 'Want one?' I shook my head. She tapped out a cigarette, put it in her mouth and stuck a lighted match to it. I watched the smoke furl up into the air.

'Your father owns Hong Zi grocery stores?'

'Have you been checking up on me?'

Beverley Chung was tall for a fifteen-year-old. She was slim. Elegant. Self-assured as she puffed on the Chesterfield. 'You notice anything about us?'

'Who?'

'Us. You and me.'

I thought about it while looking her up and down. I too was tall for a fifteen-year-old. An attribute I'd inherited from Papa. Slim. Yes. But elegant? Probably not. And certainly not in possession of Beverley's confidence. 'No. What should I have noticed?'

She sighed. 'We are the only ones.'

'The only what?'

'Fay Wong, are you really as stupid as you are making out?' I started to walk away. 'Half-Chinese,' she shouted after me.

I turned to face her. 'Everybody else,' she said, 'is black, Venezuelan or full Chinese.' She paused. 'Yu nuh notice dat?'

'What happened to your American accent?'

It turned out that Beverley was Jamaican-born, taken to America by her parents when she was two years old because her father was an accountant and got a job with a company in New York. The year before the crash. So she said. But even though everybody was broke, her family was OK because people still needed somebody to count the money they didn't have and help them invest what was left to make a better future. But she never liked it. She couldn't settle with the crowds and the horns honking up Fifth Avenue, and people looking down their nose at her because they reckoned she was Chinese and poor, which couldn't have been further from the truth.

'And as for my mother, being a black woman, if she went into a store they all started locking up their cabinets. No, really.' She laughed. 'And hiding their goods like they thought she was about to burgle the place. A woman with two children in tow. If she tried on a pair of shoes they wiped them out with a damp cloth before putting them back into the box. If she wanted a sweater they never had her size. I don't know how she put up with it. Especially because everybody took her for the maid. The nanny with her two little Chinese charges. I felt angry all the time. Even in Mott Street where, if you didn't talk to them in Chinese, you couldn't get so much as a cup of tea.'

So when the money situation improved she talked her father into letting her come home. And his one condition was this: she had to be a boarder at Immaculate. The other thing – going to her grandmother's every free weekend and holiday – was Beverley's own idea. Not that her father objected to it. 'He thinks Grandmother is keeping an eye on me, which just goes to show how little he knows his own mother.' And then after a snort she said, 'Despite the things he himself told me about her and her years in China.'

Grandmother Chung had a huge monster of a house off Hagley Park Road. Even after all the time I spent there I never figured out how many rooms that place actually had. It put me in mind of some princess's forgotten palace, minus the decay and cobwebs, because that place was pristine and sparkling from top to bottom. That many maids she had running from here to there. And some dusting and polishing it would have taken too with everything made out of Chinese pottery and porcelain, filling every inch of every table and shelf in every room. Ornaments and jars in all colours, shapes and sizes adorned with flowers, fish, dragons and phoenixes. Chinese rugs on the floors, paintings and silkscreens, wall-mounted fans, lacquered cabinets, crystal chandeliers dangling from the ceiling, delicate little glass shades over every table lamp. But the thing that really caught my eye was the vase in the entry hall. Like a gigantic brass tree with tubes of pink glass at the end of each branch holding the varying arrangements of white lilies she had nestling there. Filled so it was busting. And no matter what time of day or day of the week you went there it was always radiant and fresh like those flowers had been put there just the second before you stepped foot through the door.

The other thing that you couldn't ignore was the shelf in the living room. A highly polished Huanghuali rosewood mantelpiece with a lattice back and arms, and a pale-honey golden sheen, that hung high on the wall. Not like in the picture books where a log fire would be burning beneath it to keep out the winter cold. No, not like that. There was no fire, just the wooden shelf, which had standing on it three magnificent and bedazzling Ming urns, a dragon on one, a fish on another, birds on blossom branches on the third, containing, so Beverley said, the ashes of Grandmother Chung's three late husbands.

'So which one of them is your grandfather?'

'Far right. The last one. She gave up with husbands after that.'

Where Grandmother Chung got her money and decorating sense from I didn't know. When I asked Beverley all she did was wink at me which meant she didn't know either.

'Parties. We had such wonderful parties.' That was Grandmother Chung, dressed in peach satin and twirling around the room like a young woman with her beau dancing a quickstep. 'Dancing and laughing until sunrise. Every weekend. With the whole of Kingston flowing in and out of that door because no one dare let a Saturday evening pass without calling in here.' She smiled at us. 'Can you imagine that?' She sipped her champagne. We were enthralled. And she knew it.

Beverley said that her grandmother was related to Chiang Kai-shek but she never said how and I wasn't sure I believed her anyway. Yet, true or false, Grandmother Chung ('Call me GC') had something. A devil-may-care attitude and instinctive decadence that even now, at a grand old age of I didn't know what, was completely irresistible. Looking at Beverley I could see she had it too. That was what drew me to her in the garden and later behind the swimming pool. Her absolute refusal to conform. And the delight she took in it.

'He died of food poisoning. Vomiting and the other thing from some bad meat or fish or something. That is why she started eating this.' Beverley jutted out her chin.

We were standing on the back veranda looking out at the vegetable garden.

'Your grandmother only eats vegetables?'

'Vegetables and more vegetables, darling. Not from anywhere, though. Only the ones she cultivates herself.' She glanced over at me. 'Not herself personally, you understand.'

'Of course.' I surveyed the expanse of land stretching out in front of us. 'But why so much? She could feed a small army on what she's growing here.'

She laughed. 'Haven't you noticed, dear heart? There is a small army living in this house.'

'What, all the maids have to eat the vegetables as well?'

Beverley turned to me wide-eyed. 'My dear,' a smile crept across her lips, 'GC says she couldn't bear it if one of them should fall prey to the malady that took my grandfather.'

And then she linked my arm and we strolled through the callaloo together.

But as much as life with Beverley was heaven, so was life with Mama hell, with her finding fault with me at each and every turn. Because even though she had stopped swishing her cane her tongue was still in motion.

'You think you too old now for me to take a cane to you? Think you can come in here and treat the place like the Constant Spring Hotel the way you carry on at school? Well this is not and never was a hotel, let me tell you that.'

When the school report came with news that I was in the top ten per cent she waved it around at dinner.

'You think you smart now? Too clever for your own good. That is what you are. But no matter what the Sisters have to say it not going make you white. You still have my thick black blood running through those veins and always will have. So don't let none of this go to your head.'

And then she took the report and tore it in half. And again and again. Until it was shredded into ribbons, which she tossed on to the table in front of me.

'You just remember your place.' That is how she left the room. With Daphne watching on.

And after I had my hair cut. 'Who tell you to go do a thing like that? You have my permission? No. I don't recall that. The Sisters tell you to do it?'

'No, Mama.'

She glared at me. One hand on her hip. 'So this is your idea of a joke?'

'My hair look like a joke to you?'

'Don't you sass me, young lady. You think that is what you can do now? With your papa paying all that money so you can get an education and all you do is backchat? You are fifteen years old, Fay Wong, and you would do well to remember it.'

Actually, the makeover was Beverley's brainwave. We'd been sitting watching the hairdresser preen and beautify her grandmother when she suddenly said, 'Let's cut our hair.' To which GC clapped her hands and immediately leapt from the chair for Beverley to sit down. But Beverley's idea was more than that. What she wanted was for the two of us to have the exact identical style. Shoulder-length. Cut straight across the front in a square fringe. Ironed out and dyed the same shade of black. It took hours. And afterwards, Cleopatra had met Kingston Chinese. It was magnificent.

That is how it started. The twin-look. Same hair, same dresses, same shoes. But there wasn't any 'Reach me down' for us, waiting while some woman with a long pole fetched a frock off a nail hammered in a wall. We didn't even have to visit the dressmaker like I did with Mama. No. The dressmaker came to us armed with fabric samples and numerous catalogues of patterns from America, which we flicked through sitting in GC's living room, sipping root beer. So one day it might be a shirt dress or a fitted blouse and flared skirt. Maybe even a peplum skirt if it took our fancy or one cut on the bias to look more elegant. Mostly in cotton, plain, floral or stripes. In colours tame and wild. Shoes? He came to us. With his boxes piled high. Kneeling down to ease the footwear gently on and off. Heels, flats or brogues. The bill? On GC's account.

The gesticulating hands, throwing our heads back when we laughed, sitting cross-legged on the sofa, that was all there too. I even started to say 'Darling' and 'Dear heart' from time to time.

Mama hated it. And the more she hated it, the more I loved it.

'Who tell you to dress like this? The white girls up your school? That what you doing now so you can run 'round town with them? Maybe you should wear your school uniform on Saturdays and Sundays as well.'

I stood up from the table. 'Yu got no idea what yu talking about.'

She slammed down her knife and fork. 'In this house we speak the King's English. You understand me? Not this Back-O-Wall yu coming with now. Is that what they teaching you at Immaculate? I very much doubt it.'

And then, standing herself and walking away, she said, 'There not nuh shortage of money. If yu want to spend, spend. Yu father have it. Just try to get yourself something decent. God forbid that people think this family so broke yu have to go 'round the place in rags.'

Rags! Is that what she thinks? But then I had to smile because Mama can never hear the Jamaican in her own voice.

When Papa came to my room it was to ask me to simmer down with my mother.

'She have her ways, Fay. You know that. You can't just abide it while you in the house?'

I thought about it and then I said, 'Let me be a boarder.'

'Boarder? The school only a tram ride away up Constant Spring Road.'

I raised myself up from the edge of the bed and started to rearrange clothes in my drawer.

'Fay, it don't do to be arguing like this with your mother every day. Believe me, I know.'

'I am not arguing with her, she is arguing with me.'

'Same thing.'

'It is not the same thing, Papa. What she is doing is criticising and judging me. What I am doing is defending myself and trying to reason with her.'

'No, Fay. I don't think that is how it is. Maybe it used to be that way long time back. But now, since you grown, it more like the two of you just thinking every day how to be a thorn in each other's side.'

'Then let me board and I will only come back in the holidays and you can have some peace.'

But I didn't come back. Not really. Once in a while maybe. Because boarding school was all-consuming. Not just with the lessons from eight am to two pm and the mountain of homework; and the after-school activities of the Sodality; and the games we played at night swapping pyjamas from a jumbled pile and, at the end of term, throwing our unwanted belongings down the corridor for anyone who wanted to grab them in the scramble; but every minute of every day practising our reverence for God, self and others; learning discipline and goodness so that we would become honest, competent, responsible and compassionate citizens. Because, according to Sister Ignatius, the purpose of a good school was to create an environment in which young people learn to be virtuous. Pure in thought, word and deed. And, she said, that was also the definition of a good family. It made me laugh inside.

And when we weren't doing that, we were at GC's twirling and dancing and eating vegetables.

Papa I visited downtown. Either at his grocery store or at the opium den turned mah-jongg hall cum cookhouse, where we shared rice and sausage or dried pork, and greens. And gallons of jasmine tea.

'You know your sister growing and you don't hardly see her.'

'How old is she now?'

'I don't know. How old you?'

'Seventeen.'

'So that mek Daphne ten.' I didn't say anything. I just continued to drink the tea. 'Why yu nuh go see her sometime?'

'I see her, Papa. Only maybe last month I go over there.'

'Fay, even I know that not true.'

So I went. The place looked exactly the same. Just like it did at Christmas three months earlier. Mama was sitting on the veranda with her crochet as I climbed the steps.

'Decided to grace us with your presence, did you?'

'I sent a message.'

'Yes, you did,' she said, nodding her head but not looking up. Concentrating her attention instead on her hands as they moved smoothly and deftly. 'And I got your message. And now you are here.'

I sat down in the wicker armchair across from her and admired the shawl that was coming to life in her lap. 'How are you, Mama?'

She raised her eyes to me. 'You are asking me? Since when you take any interest in how I am?'

71

I crossed my legs. 'I am asking you how you are, that is all.'

She turned back to her thread and hook. 'I am tired. Exhausted by the time and effort it takes to run this house. Every day another thing. If it is not this, it is that.'

'The maids not doing their work? Samson not fixing and mending and gardening like he should?'

'I had to let him go, if you must know.' I didn't say anything. 'We have a young boy doing for us now. Edmond.'

We sat there quietly while I took in the bright array of colours in the flower bed below.

'Smells like rain in the air,' I said, finally.

'So they say. Later on.'

We fell silent again.

'I've been meaning to come over for a while.'

'Is that so?'

'I miss being home.'

'Home? Is that what you call it? Seem to me that wherever you spending your time must be more agreeable.'

I breathed in deep and slow. 'You mean with all my white friends?'

She put in a slip stitch. 'Swimming and playing tennis up at your fancy school so much so you can't even spare five minutes to come see how your little sister doing.'

I looked away at the distant mango tree with the swing hanging below it and thought of Stanley, and his latest letter in which he wrote: *The English need our help right now but their friendliness is only skin deep. Beneath every smile is resentment, and a fear of us and our alien ways. Thinking we have come to steal their women. And when this war is done, steal their jobs and homes as well.*

And then I turned to Mama and said, 'Yes, being with the white girls is all I want to do. Going to the beach, playing tennis, partying. They know how to have fun and enjoy themselves. Not like sitting around here being miserable with you.'

'So you finally admit it. About time. Passing yourself off like you think you special, like maybe they too blind to see that whatever your airs and graces you still a half-caste. Not one thing nor the other. And no amount of money and expensive frocks is ever going to change that. Especially since neither half of you is white.'

In truth, Beverley and I had next to nothing to do with the white girls. We didn't even think of them like that, because with the girls it wasn't about colour. It was about money. Who had it and who didn't. Although it was fair to say that the lighter your skin the more likely it was that you had a rich daddy. That is how it was. But were they white? They came from Cuba and Latin America. Venezuela we said. I don't know why. The Canadians, they were white and we did sometimes force ourselves into their company just for the hell of it. But it wasn't genuine. Our time with them. We all knew that.

The real division was between boarders and day-girls. The boarders were wealthier and lighter. Like me. But not like me because, as Mama so often and so eloquently pointed out, I was not white, but neither was I full Chinese. I was half and half. Not fully anything.

I got up and walked inside. Daphne was out back reading a book. When she saw me she threw it on the ground and ran into my arms. I grabbed her and swung her around letting her legs fly in the air.

'Pearl told me you were coming.'

'So what you want to do? There is a Tarzan movie with Johnny Weissmuller.' She shrugged her shoulders but we went anyway.

Daphne was growing up hushed and terrified. She had no opinion about anything. If you asked her 'How is school?' she said 'Fine'. The lessons? Fine. Homework? Fine. Friends? Fine. Things at home? Fine. If you asked her what she wanted to do, she shrugged her shoulders. Movie? Shrug. Beach? Shrug. Play a game? Shrug. Ice cream? Shrug. For Daphne, opinions were dangerous.

What Daphne did? She read. Constantly. Book after book, sometimes the same one over and again. Engrossed in another world. Withdrawn from this one. It was her protection. Camouflage for her disengagement.

Beverley and I graduated high school in traditional Immaculate style. Parading along with our classmates in the march of the zombies. White dresses, white shoes, white gown and white mortarboards, which at the end of the passing-out ceremony were flung into the air despite Sister Ignatius's insistence that no such thing should occur.

Afterwards, I went over to Papa and hugged him. Mama had decided not to come and had kept Daphne away. Grandmother Chung was there, though, as were Beverley's parents. That was the first time I met them because, according to Beverley, there was no need for me to suffer them when they made one of their infrequent visits back to the island.

'You would be bored out of your mind.' So she said.

And sure enough, they were quiet, Mr and Mrs Chung. Restrained. Uninspired. But certainly not the tiresome duo I had been led to expect. Tyrone, Beverley's older brother, was a different matter entirely. He was handsome with short, slick-back hair, dark mysterious eyes and a smile that exuded confidence and mischief. When Beverley told me that he was not returning to America with his parents I knew that life was about to change.

CHAPTER 7

'DON'T YOU THINK you should be finding something useful to do with yourself? School is done with. So that makes you a grown woman. A responsible adult. Not a child sitting around waiting for her papa to provide.'

This was how Mama carried on every day, so I didn't bother to answer. She was shouting at me through a closed door as she wandered about the house looking for extra chores for the maids and I sat in my bedroom reading another sad letter from Stanley about his loneliness and not fitting into life in England.

I didn't understand anyway how she had the nerve to criticise me. Big and fat and pregnant as she was with a child that any woman her age would be ashamed to be carrying. Hanging on to her back and steadying herself on the arm of every chair or table she passed. Sweating and puffing and dragging her feet. It was disgusting.

Beverley's parents thought she should go to college in America, but she didn't want to do it. She said she was happy in Kingston living with her grandmother. She would find work. Actually what we did was dance, mostly at the Bournemouth Club because it had a proper ballroom. Not like the tile dance floor at Club Havana under the hole in the roof that closed the place any time it rained. As rare as that was. But whereas we had taught ourselves to swing and jive in the gazebo with the other girls and practised our steps late at night along the boarders' corridor, Tyrone could really dance. Showing us all the jitterbug moves he learned in Harlem when his mother thought he was in Midtown learning the dry-cleaning business.

GC was in her element, sitting on the sofa clapping and cheering Tyrone as he whirled and swirled Beverley and me or sat at the piano pounding out a Fats Waller tune. I never realised a piano could sound so good. Not being played by an amateur in the privacy of his own living room. Mama certainly couldn't produce anything like this. Listening to her you would think that music was something to be endured. A Sunday-morning service in a dark Methodist hall in St Ann where some rickety old man is hunched over the keys using three fingers to provoke the faithful to turn their backs on sin. Because that is how Mama heard music. Like a threat from God. Tyrone's playing was nothing like that. It was bright and uplifting with all his ten fingers moving so fast you would think he had fifteen or twenty. Sitting there upright and solid, only bending over when he wanted to get in the groove. It was pure joy. Mama would have called it pure sin. Because, for her, sin was the word for every pleasure imaginable, from laughing at a joke or reading a detective book to the demon drink and the absolute unmentionable.

Bournemouth was a club full of white people who had nothing better to do than swim and sun themselves and sip gin and tonics all day, even after they opened it to the public. That was where we met Freddie, one night when Tyrone was worn to a frazzle dancing with Beverley and then me and Beverley again. I was sitting alone at the table when he came over and asked if he could join us. I'd never seen anybody with such blond hair before. Blonder than mine when I was a child. Hair that he flicked back with his right hand every time it flopped across his forehead. He offered me a cigarette and I took it hoping I wouldn't cough and splutter too much. When he leant over with his lighter I held his hand to steady it just as I'd seen in the movies. The band was playing Duke Ellington's 'Satin Doll'. I could barely hear a word Freddie was saying. So he moved closer until he was practically sitting in my lap.

'You and your friends are members here?' English. Even though I couldn't smell that musty odour we call wet fish. Like when you put on a piece of clothing that hasn't been properly dried.

'It's not a members' club any more. Not since 1937. Any riff-raff can come here now.'

He laughed. Embarrassed. Then he cast his eyes around the room. The polished dance floor, tables nestled at its edge, the long mahogany bar with the mirrors behind it reflecting the chandeliered ceiling.

'You and your friends come here a lot?'

He puffed. I held my cigarette at a distance, tapping it over the ashtray every now and again.

'Sometimes.'

'It's just the three of you?'

'Excuse me?'

'You are not with anyone? I mean not with him or anyone?'

He smiled, showing off perfect, white teeth like an American.

When Tyrone returned to the table he ordered more whisky. I drowned mine with ginger ale, which was my custom. Beverley and Tyrone poured water into theirs. Freddie swallowed his neat, not even cooled with a cube of ice.

After that we became a foursome, with Freddie driving us in his jeep from Grandmother Chung's to the Bournemouth Club especially when Eric Deans was playing, or Club Havana or the Silver Slipper in Cross Roads, which was stylish and where the sound system played calypso and the rhythm 'n' blues that Freddie liked so much, even though he always seemed more relaxed at Bournemouth.

Freddie was in agriculture. So he said. Part of some commission planning and co-ordinating farming projects across the Caribbean. But we didn't believe him. He looked too young to be that important. More like he was talking about his father. It didn't matter, though. Freddie was good fun and we were happy enough to share his company even if he was nowhere near as good a dancer as Tyrone.

'Staying out all hours of the night. Coming in here smelling of liquor and cigarettes after you have been running around the town with God knows who doing God knows what with money in your pocket from God knows where. You think I don't know what you are doing? The Good Book

79

says "Flee fornication. Every sin that a man doeth is with-out the body; but he that committeth fornication sinneth against his own body" and that applies to every woman as well.'

I just looked down at her ridiculous belly, kissed my teeth and walked off.

When I asked Beverley about us spending so much time with Freddie she said, 'Are you enjoying yourself?'

'Yes.'

'So am I.'

What Papa wanted to know was how come I was getting through so much money every month.

'It goes, Papa. You know how it is.'

'As long as it not bad trouble, Fay. Things that out of your control.'

'You mean like losing money every night playing mah-jongg in Barry Street?'

He laughed. 'Now you chastising your papa?' He reached into his pocket. 'At least I have chance win back. All your money only go in one direction.'

Sissy thought maybe it was good for me.

'A woman got to have some down time. I grant yu dat. Serious life going come pon yu soon enough. Husband, chillen, house to run.' She squinted at me cheekily out of the corner of her eye. 'Maids to order.' She rocked gently back and forth in the chair. 'But a bakra?'

'Not every white man is a slave-driver.'

'No?'

'Sissy, it is 1946. We just finished fighting a war together. On the same side. Even Stanley went to serve his king and country.'

'Which king and what country would dat be?' I didn't answer. 'You are twenty years old. Dis man, how old?'

'I don't know.'

A disapproving pout came across her lips. 'So what he do?'

'Agriculture. So he say, but we don't believe him.'

'Yu see, dat is what I mean! Yu cyan trust a 1946 bakra any more than yu could trust di ol' slave-master way back when.'

I stood up. 'Yu want something to drink?'

She stuck the pipe into her mouth and sucked. I walked inside. When I returned I handed her the lemonade I'd poured from the fridge. She took it and sipped and then rested the glass on the table next to her.

'What all the tablets yu have there in the kitchen cupboard?'

'Oh dat not nothing.' I stared at her enquiringly and waited for more. 'Di big ones fah pressure and the likkle ones fah sugar. Or maybe it di other way 'round.'

'High blood pressure and diabetes, Sissy?'

'Yu father send di doctor. And he bring dem here. All his boxes. So I put dem in di cupboard.'

'Yu should be taking them.'

'Oh stop yu fussing. I tek dem when I remember. In fact I tek a whole heapa dem yesterday so dat should keep me going.' She paused and turned to me. 'Di important thing is you remember to be careful.'

'What yu mean?'

And then she reminded me about the talk we had when my bloods came. So I told her that we went dancing. Nothing like that was going to happen.

She raised her eyebrows. 'Careful, dat is all I am saying. And double so because a bakra is a bakra. Deh different from us. And you a island girl, Chinese. Yu will smell like mango and sweet sop and June plum all rolled into one to him.' She thought for a while and then she said, 'Anyway, I don't want yu coming over here no more.'

'Yu don't want to see me?'

'I never say dat.' She paused. 'See yu but not here, dat is all.' She finished off her lemonade. 'Yu getting too old now to be coming 'cross town on yu own. People dem leave a chile alone. But a well-turned-out young lady? We asking fi trouble wid yu coming over dis side on di bus.'

'I don't take the bus, Sissy. I catch a cab. You know that.'

'Same thing. Never know who yu might bump into.'

'Bump into?'

She was irritated. 'This too long and draw out. Just meet me at Cross Roads next time. Outside di market.'

'Sissy getting old. These things happen.' That is what Papa said when I asked him about sending the doctor to her.

'And the rocking chairs you bought?'

'That? Long time now, Fay.'

I thought about what Sissy said about who I might bump into. 'Is there something going on with you and Sissy?'

'Sissy!' He laughed. A great big belly laugh. 'Me and Sissy? Like that?' And he laughed some more.

'You haven't answered my question.'

'You really need answer to that?' I didn't say anything. 'Serious?'

He finished his tea. 'No. Nothing like that.' And after another chuckle: 'She old, Fay, and she not got nobody but us.'

The thing about Freddie was his electric-blue eyes. I'd never seen anything like it before. They sparkled, beckoning you towards them. Pleading and promising all at the same time. And no matter what kind of dance you were doing with him, somehow it was his eyes you were following not his hands or feet.

And then we started eating. Not just the club supper plates late at night when we were famished from dancing, but going out to dinner, to a restaurant, early evening, in places uptown I didn't even know existed because the only eateries I had been to before were the cookhouses in Chinatown Papa had taken me to. With chefs doing things with food I never could have imagined. It was an entire world away from rice and peas and chicken, curry goat, saltfish, pumpkin soup, sweet-potato pudding. Nothing like the downtown Chinese food or the polite dishes they served at school. I didn't even know what I was eating half the time. All I did was sit and watch Freddie read the menu and then get my mouth and stomach ready for the most delicious things I was going to put into them from a plate so beautiful you didn't want to disturb it. Except you did because it was there to be savoured not just stared at.

Freddie enjoyed himself. You could see the pleasure he took introducing us to beef Wellington and chateaubriand. And wine, the likes of which I'd never ever heard of because Jamaica isn't a wine-drinking place. It got so that we couldn't wait for Freddie's next excursion because no matter how much we ate it was never enough. We always wanted more.

More of the last. More of the next. With the liquor making your head spin with glee.

But the thing that really made us laugh was Freddie's ganja cigarettes. Boy, did that split your sides. And make you hungry. In that place of his in the hills above Kingston, which was more like a tree house on stilts, sitting in the most beautiful gardens high up where the air was fresh and cool. Small but gracious with mahogany floors and wood-slatted windows with no glass, that we would push up shut at night while we sat on his railed veranda sipping his Appleton. Silk embroideries hanging on the wall. Silk rugs on the floor. And where you expected something solid like a bathroom door, there was only a frame panelled with bamboo, which I reckoned if you got close enough and put your eye to the gap you would probably see through; bamboo ceiling fan; bamboo furniture in the living room and on a low shelf in an alcove a statue of the Buddha with a vase of flowers and burning incense next to it. It was sumptuous.

So I was wide awake all night, dancing and drinking and laughing, and tired all day, sleeping in my bed until all hours of the afternoon with Mama banging on the door shouting, 'You intending to get up today, madam?' And me turning over and putting my head under the pillow.

Later on I would say to her, 'You can't leave me to sleep? What am I doing to you? How is my life injuring you?'

'Injuring me? I already tell you that you injuring yourself and the price you will pay will be in hell. As God is my witness.'

'I already have hell right here on earth listening to you every day.'

'Lord, God Almighty. Strike me down dead this instant for the ungrateful wretch of a child I have brought into this world.'

That was how it was with her in the mornings and sometimes late at night when she would even get up out of her bed to come and argue with me about the hours I was keeping.

Then Tyrone got a job at D&G selling Red Stripe and soft drinks. He was the quintessential salesman with his good looks and charm, driving all over the island convincing shopkeepers to take his latest special offer. So four became three because Tyrone needed his sleep. And after we started playing tennis at Liguanea where Freddie was a member, three became two.

'What is happening with you, Beverley? You don't want to come any more? Freddie do something to upset you? Or was it me?'

'Fay, yu nuh notice what is going on?'

'What?'

'Freddie only interested in you.'

'Me?'

'Don't get me wrong. I not got no complaint 'bout it. Is just that it awkward. Yu know, the three of us together all the time.'

'Tell me what yu want me to do.'

She took my arm and linked it through hers as we strolled through Issa's department store. And then she patted it with her spare hand.

'Yu don't need to do anything. Enjoy yourself. Just be careful.'

'Yu think Freddie bad?'

'No. Nothing like that. He is a man, that is all.'

*   *   *

85

When Beverley turned up with Audley I was jealous. I sat all night watching them dancing on Bournemouth's polished floor and even though Freddie kept trying to coax me out there I didn't want to go. All I wanted to do was study precisely the fun that Beverley was having in the arms of this slightly tubby, red-skin man. It looked different. Different from how she had danced with Tyrone, where you could see she was there for the music and the pleasure of feeling her own body move. Or with Freddie, which was more controlled. Friendly but courteous. With Audley it was something completely alien to me. Like she was dancing with her body not her arms and legs. A body that had tension in it even though it was in fluid, constant motion, turning and twisting, and gliding through all the exact same routines. And each time they came back to the table she sat so close to him that her hand could rest on his knee or his shoulder or stroke the back of his neck. How I felt? Like I was the awkward third person Beverley was talking about. As if Freddie wasn't there at all.

'Where yu find him anyway?' I said to her as I was sitting crossed-legged on GC's sofa.

'Audley?' I didn't answer. 'Tyrone met him at Sabina Park.'

'Didn't know Tyrone was such a cricket fan.'

'Yes, you do.' Then she looked at me. 'Oh Fay. Envy?'

It made me angry. Because it was true. She threw herself on to the sofa and wrapped her arms around me. 'What is there for you to be jealous of? You have Freddie.'

I eased away from her slightly. 'Have you and Audley?'

'Would a respectable woman tell?'

'Would a respectable woman do it?'

'Are you serious?'

I didn't know if I was. What I did know was something was different about Beverley. A new dimension. A quality of being that was at the same time both more carefree and more mature. And what I realised in that instant was that Beverley and I had become separated. She had become a woman while I was still a child. That is what I envied. That is what I was jealous of.

So when Freddie suggested that we go up to his house on our own I agreed. It was the first time me being there without Beverley and Tyrone. We had dinner on the veranda prepared by his daily who promptly saw to the dishes and then left. He poured the coffee and Appleton and rolled one of his cigarettes. Watching him, I felt strangely calm. Not nervous like I had imagined. I was completely composed. More relaxed than I remembered ever being with anyone, apart from Beverley. But it was different. It was grown up, not like two schoolgirls playing.

And after hours of talking about Jamaica and watching the sun disappear over the horizon, he asked if I wanted him to drive me back to town. And I didn't say anything. I just reflected in my mind the journey I had already set in motion by telling Mama that I was staying at Beverley's. He got up and took me by the hand and led me into the bedroom with the mosquito net hanging over the bed like a giant white tent. I'd never actually seen one before, growing up as I did with the burning green coil.

What I discovered was my love of two things. Being held in someone's arms, and talking in the dark in the dead of night. Because that is when truths come out. Open-hearted and undefended truths. That was when I found out that Freddie's name wasn't Freddie and he wasn't involved in agriculture.

His name was Thomas, after his father. Frederick was his middle name, and going by it saved confusion for his family and created, for him, the distance he cherished between himself and a man he had grown to despise.

'You hate him that much?'

He didn't reply. He just lay there on his back with his arm around my shoulder. Firm so I knew I was held. Loose so I knew I was free.

'It's not like you and your mother. Verbal and violent. It's cold. Controlled. Impersonal. He is in charge. Daring anyone to question or disagree with him. So anything you say is either ridiculed or pounced on from a great height, like an almighty fist landing on your head from twenty feet above. That is how he is with everyone. What I hate most is watching him patronise and belittle my mother, reducing her to tears over something as trivial as the temperature of his soup or the state of her hair. Year after year. Turning a strong, energetic woman into a quivering wreck.'

What was Freddie doing in Jamaica? Getting away from disgrace in England because he refused to fight in the war, his father being an army colonel.

'Conscientious objectors had to register and say that they objected to warfare as a means of settling international disputes. That was the precise phrase you had to use.'

I rolled over on to my elbows so that I could look at him, even though it was just his outline in the semi-light.

'They wanted to put me into the Non-Combatant Corps but it was still military-related work so I said no, and went to prison instead.'

'Prison, Freddie? Why?'

'Because I loathe him and everything he stands for.'

'Was it the Buddhism?'

He laughed. 'I can't lay claim to being a very good Buddhist, I'm afraid.'

He reached out a hand to smooth my hair. 'Prison was my choice but, believe me, a military detention barrack isn't something you ever want to experience. Honestly.' He was silent for a while as if lost in his memories. 'Anyway, when they let me out they sent me to do farming work, hence my lie about being in agriculture.'

I smiled even though he couldn't see me. 'Why Jamaica?'

'Exiled to the colonies in disgrace.' He let out an embarrassed snort. 'Too many people coming home after '45 asking my father where I served in the war. It was too much for him.' And then: 'He has connections here.'

'So?'

'So when he's ready I'll be sent for and I'll go home.'

'And you'll go?'

'I guess. I'm not trained for anything, Fay. Got no way of earning a living here.'

The other thing wasn't what I expected. Not the way Sissy described it to me. It was affectionate and reassuring. Full of tender caresses and sweet little kisses. Even though I had stiffened and withdrawn when he first started to unzip my dress. And he'd stopped and asked, 'Are you OK?' And I'd said, 'Yes.' And proceeded to unbutton his shirt. Remembering all the times that Mama had made me strip. Wondering why my nakedness felt so natural with him. Not shameful. The rubber tube? Sissy hadn't mentioned that at all.

*　　*　　*

From that point onwards all I could think of doing was tell Freddie I wanted him to stay. But I didn't. I kept my mouth shut. With my heart breaking every minute of every day that our time together was coming to an end.

When the letter from his father finally arrived he left it on his coffee table for me to see the postmark and official seal of Colonel Sir Thomas Anthony Smithers. I looked at it but I didn't say anything. I just let it sit there for days and weeks while we went to the beach and played tennis and ate dinner and danced at the Silver Slipper and Bournemouth Club and he read poetry to me in bed at night. Yeats and Wordsworth and Shakespearean sonnets that I didn't understand any more than I had my schoolgirl Virgil but which sounded beautiful and exquisite on his lips.

Until finally he told me that we had two more weeks before he had to leave. And that time we spent almost entirely in bed. Raising ourselves only for food and the bathroom.

I watched him pack, sitting quietly on the chair in the corner of his bedroom. And then he drove me home. Dropping me at the gate as I had asked so I could avoid a barrage of questions from my mother. Just before I got out of the jeep he took my hand and put it to his mouth. And kissed my palm.

'I know,' I said to him, 'that whatever is waiting for you in England will be better than any life you could have here in Jamaica with me.'

'Don't you believe it.'

CHAPTER 8

AMAZINGLY, MAMA DIDN'T say anything about the absent two weeks or my coming and going before that. I wondered if perhaps she had been struck mute except I knew that wasn't so. Not from the amount of piano playing and hymn singing that was going on. Actually, it was me who had become almost silent. Because despite the absolute devastation I felt inside not one single tear did I shed over Freddie leaving. I'd spent so many years forcing myself not to do it. Not to give Mama the satisfaction of knowing she could hurt me. So much so that I'd forgotten how to cry. Forgotten how to let out my grief.

A few weeks later, Beverley threw a party for my twenty-first birthday. A splendid affair at GC's house, lit and decorated in grandiose fashion with a live band and a temporary dance floor put down on the back lawn. Tyrone brought his latest, Cynthia, and Audley played host graciously.

When I spotted Marjorie Williams and Hazel Brown across the room I went over to them. I had no idea Beverley was still in touch. They were reserved. Perhaps I'd been too gushy in reminiscing about our time together at Immaculate.

'Well, the boarders had a different life, didn't they,' Hazel said. I nodded. We all knew what she meant. Different experience from the darker-skinned day-girls.

I changed the subject. 'So what are you both doing these days?'

'Working at Woo-Tong Travel Service,' Marjorie said.

Hazel had just returned from America where she had been studying English and American Literature. She said she wanted to be a writer.

'Not that anyone can seriously expect to make a living out of that. So I'll probably end up teaching but who knows eh? Maybe one day.'

'Maybe,' I said and smiled. Politely. 'The future has yet to come.' And I held up my glass in a toast.

Where Beverley got the rest of the guests from was a mystery to me, but the place was packed and jumping. Tyrone and Audley danced with me all night until the sweat was running down my back. When I finally slumped into a garden chair GC came over to sit with me.

'Twenty-one years old, Fay. A woman now. Not the child I met so many years ago.' She patted my hand.

'Thank you. It's kind of you to have this party for me.'

'Nothing kind about it. This is your home. Has been for a very long time. And a very long time to come, I hope. So enjoy, even if Freddie isn't here to wish you well.' She took my hand in hers and squeezed it tight.

Mama ignored my birthday. She was too busy fussing over Kenneth. Two years of cooing and wooing this over-indulged boy-child like she'd never seen one before. Still, she was the only one doing it. Nobody else was interested.

The maids did what they had to, following their instructions. But real attention? No. Not one ounce since the day he was brought into the house, because in some way everybody felt disgraced by his arrival.

Papa gave me an envelope with money, which was welcomed. Daphne made a beautiful card with a dried pink rose pasted on the front and inside she had written 'To the best sister anyone could wish for'. It made me feel guilty. But I hugged and kissed her anyway, while she wriggled and finally tugged herself out of my arms and ran away.

Freddie sent a card telling me of his safe arrival back in Wiltshire and of the rolling green hills and frosty air he now realised he had missed. And how he was looking forward to the snow and had started a small publishing house in Oxford, specialising in Caribbean literature, which he had called Bamboo Tree House Press. And at the end he wrote: *It is better that I am back in England. We were too good to last and I never want to see you dancing with anyone else but me.* I didn't know what he meant. Not like when he told me England wouldn't suit me. Or when he said the two of us together would not be accepted there. I already knew that from Stanley's letters. But how can anything be too good to last?

Isaac was standing outside the Carib theatre when Beverley and I came out. Just standing there smiling at all the young women passing him by. He was big and black. So black he was almost blue, with enormous hands you couldn't help noticing every time he gave a wave or lifted his hat to another unsuspecting stranger. And just to spite my mother I turned to Beverley and said, 'I'm going to take him home with me.'

'Yu joking?' She looked excited and terrified all at the same time.

'Can you imagine it? Mama's reaction.' And so saying I walked straight up to him and asked his name. When he smiled, his even, white teeth surprised me.

'Isaac.'

'Well, Isaac, what are you doing for the rest of the evening?'

He placed an open palm flat on his chest. 'Me, miss?'

I looked him up and down, standing there tall and broad in his dark-brown trousers and yellow shirt. A man who obviously didn't know that men should not wear brown after six pm.

'Yes, you.'

'Nothing, miss.'

'Then come with me.'

I hailed a cab, expecting all three of us to get in, but Beverley said no. She was going back to GC's to listen for the explosion.

So it was just me and Isaac sitting on the veranda at Lady Musgrave Road when I asked a bewildered Pearl to bring us a couple of beers.

'Now, Pearl. Go.'

When she returned she poured the cold beers into the glasses and retreated into the house. Seconds later Mama appeared. Prompted no doubt by the loud whispers in the kitchen.

'And who might this be?'

Isaac stood and extended his hand, not before giving it a quick wipe on his trouser leg. 'Isaac Dunkley. Pleased to make your acquaintance.'

She glanced down at his hand disdainfully, making no attempt to shake it. 'And what is Isaac Dunkley doing on my veranda this evening?'

'Ma'am?' He gave a fleeting, anxious glance to the now empty chair in which he had been sitting.

'He's having a beer with me.'

Mama's eyes darted in my direction. 'So I see.' And with tightly drawn lips she walked inside.

As soon as she had gone, Isaac made to leave. 'No need to bother yourself, miss. I can find my own way back to town.'

'Sit yourself down, Isaac, and finish your beer. You and I aren't through yet.'

After that, I invited Isaac to the house regularly. Just to watch him sit there with his knees together sipping the beer as carefully and delicately as he could manage. He was nervous, maybe even a little frightened, but he kept coming. Never refused an invitation.

Mama continued to fume but didn't say a single word to me about it, which in a funny way added to my pleasure because she couldn't even have the release of letting off some steam. Not in a house full of black maids. That would have been in very bad taste.

To Isaac she said nothing, avoiding him with fierce determination. So we both knew what the game was. And we both knew that I was winning.

Beverley thought it was delicious. So I told her to come over to the house one day and witness the spectacle for herself. 'I'll come early to get a ringside seat,' she said. And even though I didn't pay it any attention, there was something between them. Beverley and Isaac. A fascination that I couldn't quite believe.

After he left, I said to her, 'What's with you and Isaac?'

'He is nice, Fay. Easy to talk to. You don't think so?'

I was horrified. 'Beverley, we don't hardly know the man.'

'So how yu going to get to know him? Certainly not sitting down here every other week drinking a Red Stripe.'

I half-smiled in amazement at her daring. And then I put a hand to my forehead and said, 'I don't believe this.' And she laughed heartily before raising the beer glass to her mouth. After she gulped and swallowed she said, 'Yu need to enjoy yourself, Fay. Yu only live once.'

'Beverley, the man is a butcher's assistant who lives in one room above the shop.'

She feigned astonishment. 'Fay Wong. I am shocked. You of all people to display such petty snobbery after everything you have said about your mother. Or are you telling me you actually agree with her opinions about the ills of poor people, and worse, the evils of the work-shy, immoral black man?' She raised her eyebrows at me.

So that was it. We had to do more with Isaac. Audley suggested the Bournemouth Club. I said no. And not Club Havana or the Silver Slipper either. Absolutely no dancing. Dinner? No. Going to the beach? No. Whatever we did, we had to be fully clothed. Drinking in any bar Audley cared to name? No. An outing to the races? No. A movie? Yes, OK. As long as it was something tame. A comedy perhaps. Nothing romantic. Maybe a musical. In the end we settled on *Road to Utopia* with Bing Crosby and Bob Hope, and

Dorothy Lamour, which was fine. And afterwards we went to Monty's restaurant for coffee.

Then one day Isaac did something that took me completely by surprise. He invited me to join him on a walk through Hope Gardens. I didn't know he had such boldness in him. The Royal Constabulary Band was playing, so he said, and he thought I might enjoy the music. Imagine that. Isaac Dunkley taking the initiative. So I said yes. When we got there he dusted off the seat for me, bought cream sodas, which we drank from the bottle, with straws, and, in the interval, ice creams.

And while the band, dressed in full uniform, including their peak caps with the red band around them, played all sorts of calypso, Isaac talked about his life as a boy in Trench Town. It was horrifying to think of people living with such hardship day after day; sharing one toilet and a standpipe in a dirt yard with dozens of other families; eating boiled dumplings and roast breadfruit for dinner or a small piece of bony fish on a special occasion; running around barefoot and never attending a single day of school beyond the age of ten. On this same island. It was shameful.

He sat back in the chair and crossed his legs. Right ankle resting on left knee.

'What does it make you think, Isaac, when you come up to the house and see everything up there? The way we live.'

'It Jamaica. How things are. Di rich live soft and comfortable. Di poor scratch di rock-hard earth. Always been dat way.'

'And always will be?'

He looked at me squarely but didn't say anything. And then he turned his attention back to the bandstand. He had a different kind of confidence talking about the life he knew. Less reserved than he'd been these past months. Less subservient than that first night outside the Carib.

'What brought you to town?'

He gave me a sideways glance. 'Truth?'

'If you want to. Not much point answering if you don't.'

He hesitated and then he said, 'I did a lot a bad things. I mean real bad. To mek ends meet. I mean wid a mama and eight chillen to feed. Being di eldest boy. Yu have to do something. Not that I meking excuses. I did what I had to do but it wasn't nothing any man would be proud of.' He paused. 'The worst part? I didn't think nothing 'bout it at the time. Truth was it made me feel like somebody.' He looked at me. 'Can yu understand dat?'

'So what happened?'

'One day, deh run me out.'

And then the music started again.

Sissy said she thought I was playing with him and it wasn't fair.

'He just a poor bwoy. He would do anything yu want him to, just so he can look pon your skirt tail.'

'Poor but bad, Sissy.'

'What he do?'

'I don't know. But even by his own admission it was shocking. Enough to get him run outta Trench Town.'

'Bad enough to get run outta Trench Town? Dat is bad.' She tapped her spoon on the side of the sundae glass to loosen off the ice cream, and then she rested it in the saucer. 'No guessing what a man like dat got in his head. But whatever it is, I tell yu now, won't do yu no good.'

The first time I went to the butcher's shop was a rainy Sunday afternoon when we couldn't think of anything else to do. Actually, I think Isaac was brave taking me there, even though he resisted when I suggested it.

'What yu want to go there for?'

'To see it, Isaac. So I can imagine you in your room. Yu don't think that is important? To see how someone lives and what their life is like when they are not with you.' He wasn't convinced. 'You've seen where I live. Don't you think it's fair that I should see your place as well?'

The shop was closed with the calico window blind pulled halfway down. It was bare. All the marble and glass wiped clean and sparkling, and the counter stripped. We passed around it and found the staircase behind. Narrow and rickety with a handrail so barely fixed to the wall it moved when you took hold of it. When we reached the top there was a long dark corridor with three doors. A storeroom to the right, so he said; a bathroom to the left which I could smell well before we reached it; and Isaac's room at the end.

'Wait here a minute.' He opened the door and slid through, closing it promptly behind him. I could hear muffled sounds of hurried tidying as I paced up and down peering into the dingy bathroom, which, surprisingly, was relatively clean even though old age had made the sanitary ware and fittings scaly and scruffy. But the smell, that was something else, the pungent consequence of two, he and the butcher, less than careful men sharing a toilet. I tried the knob on the storeroom door but it was locked.

'Alright.'

I turned. He was standing in the doorway. Isaac's room was too small to be housing so much furniture. A big iron bed, a wardrobe, a tall bureau with drawers, a table in the corner with a straight-back chair, an armchair next to the bed, two free-standing cupboards, stuffed, I was sure, with the debris he'd gathered together to conceal from my eyes. The air was heavy and stale even though the dirty window had been pushed wide open.

'Where do you prepare food?'

'Downstairs. A little kitchen back a di shop where we chop up and grind and such. Got a sink and a burner for boiling the water for di coffee in di day.'

I cleared a space on the table and rested down my purse.

'So yu see it. What yu want to do now because there not much point staying here?'

I sat on the straight-back chair and eased off my shoes. 'Talk to me.'

'Talk to yu? What yu want me talk to yu 'bout?'

I thought a while and then I said, 'Tell me why they ran you out of Trench Town. And how come you ended up here.'

'Yu don't want to hear none a dat.' He shoved one hand in his pocket and with the other pointed to the door. 'Come on, let's go.'

'I do, Isaac, want to hear.'

So he sat on the edge of the armchair and told me about how he used to supply people with the things they needed.

'Yu know, a cook pot, a pair a shoes for di pickney fah school, maybe a frock fah a special occasion. A hat. Hell, I was even putting food on di table. And fah my favours deh pay me back little-little.'

He was growing increasingly nervous. Twitching and fiddling with his collar.

'So?' I asked.

'So?'

'What happened?'

'Yu really want to know?'

I nodded. He slumped further into the chair.

'One night when I come home a whole bunch a dem was waiting fah me wid machete and burning torches like di Ku Klux Klan. And deh tell me to get out.'

'Why?'

He sighed deep and heavy. 'It was over a woman. And di men dem was mostly her brothers and their friends. About eight a dem if I count right.' He paused. 'So anyway, I come to town and see di job in di window and here I am.'

'And your family? Your mother, brothers and sisters?'

'Oh, I wasn't living wid dem at di time. Deh show me di door long before dat. As soon as the little ones get big enough to provide. Didn't want to know me no more.' He raised his eyes to me. 'Enough a dis.' He stood up.

I slipped on my shoes and picked up my purse and we left. I knew there was more to it but the stench of raw meat coming up from below was beginning to get to me.

Next time I saw Beverley she handed me a small package. When I unwrapped the brown paper and looked inside the box I saw it was a soft little rubber thing shaped like a brassière cup. I held it up dangling between my thumb and forefinger.

'Put it back in the paper! What is the matter with you?'

I rewrapped it and slipped it into my bag. After she told me what it was I said, 'Yu use this with Audley?'

'Every man, Fay. You need to keep yourself protected. Not all of them prepared like Freddie.'

'Where yu get a thing like that from anyway?'

'GC. Next time yu coming over the house she going get her doctor to come fit it right and show you what to do. So mek sure yu don't get up to nothing before then.'

Isaac had more to him than you would think because most of the time what he wanted to do was talk about communism.

'Yu nuh pay any attention to di election?'

My mind was a blank so he said, 'Kingston and St Andrew.' He pulled a packet of Four Aces from his pocket. 'And what Mr Bustamante say 'bout how the wealthy class a di country not paying a penny to fight communism.' He tapped out a cigarette. 'And is him got to find di money to protect their business from nationalisation.' He rummaged for some matches. 'Because the communists are coming. Yu nuh know nothing 'bout dat?' He put the cigarette in his mouth and lit it.

I had no idea what Isaac was talking about. So one day he took me to the public library on East Street to show me year-old copies of the *Gleaner* reporting on strikes by the railway workers, public works, post office, printing office, prisons and hospitals, and told me about how this year there was a printer strike at the *Gleaner* company itself.

'Yu nuh read di newspaper?' Which he said too loud for the prissy librarian who put her finger to her lips to shush us.

He leant towards me and whispered, 'High unemployment, Fay. Starvation wages and misery that Mr Bustamante cyan do nothing 'bout since he get elected.' I sat there feeling the heat of his passion, incensed as he was at my lack of awareness.

'People been fighting out on di street getting themself killed and facing police and tear-gas and yu nuh know nothing?'

The shame that overcame me left me silent. Then I said, 'What does all this have to do with communism?'

'Di masses losing patience, Fay. Deh want a better life. Decent wages fah honest labour. Di revolution is coming.'

'Revolution, Isaac?' There was an involuntary sneer in my voice.

'When the hard-working black man, and woman, who was born wid nothing, not even deh own name, and made to suffer first on di plantation and now in a rundown dirt yard crawling on deh knees, finally stand up and claim di living dat is theirs by right of being a human being. And when di owners a everything put up deh hands and say: "Tek it, bredda. It is yours."'

Out on the street I tried to hail a cab, but Isaac's hand on my arm prevented me from doing so. Instead, he led me up the road to the stop. Not since Delton had I waited at a bus stop. And if I thought the bus had been crowded that day then woe betide me because when the green corporation number 32 finally arrived it was packed solid. People jowl to jowl. Elbow to elbow. So tight you couldn't even scratch yourself if you wanted to. Isaac forced his way up the three steps pushing me ahead of him. He paid for two tickets to Cross Roads and shoved me further into the assembled mass. The smell of sweat hung in every inch of air. The exhaustion on every inch of body. The misery on every inch of face. I couldn't breathe. Wanted to reach for a handkerchief to cover my nose, maybe even my eyes. But didn't dare do it. Not just because I couldn't and wouldn't open my purse but because I realised I was already a spectacle. Completely out of place. Despised for who I was and what I had. I didn't want to add insult to the injury. So I just tried to steady myself against the constant jolting of the bus, with Isaac's arm around my waist and every eye in the coach burning through us with disdain. Angry that I was standing there. Riding a Kingston bus. With him.

Isaac's room was, by comparison, familiar and comforting. It felt safe. As did I in the generosity he'd shown at not condemning me. And his perseverance in trying to help me understand. So when he wanted to hold and kiss me and fondle me into his bed I let him do it. In payment for the guilt I felt about Lady Musgrave Road, Immaculate, my father's money, Grandmother Chung's house, the tennis club, every night I had danced at the Bournemouth Club, every mouthful of chateaubriand I had eaten or candlelit beach-fronted bar in which I'd drunk champagne. Every drive in Freddie's jeep with my hair blowing in the evening breeze. Every night I lay in his bamboo tree-house Sea Island cotton sheets. In payment for every day, minute, second of my light-skinned privileged life. I let him do it. Slipping into the bathroom just before with Grandmother Chung's rubber cap.

CHAPTER 9

THE BABY SURPRISED me. Beverley just said: 'These things happen.'

'What do you mean these things happen? What about the rubber cap?'

'Accidents happen, Fay.'

'Accidents happen?'

She sighed and stirred her coffee. 'It's done. The question is what are we going to do now?'

Beverley said going to one of the old maids down some back alley was out of the question. I didn't need her to tell me that. We were Catholics after all. Besides, that sort of thing was illegal, to say nothing of dangerous. Adoption? Too many official forms to complete. It would leave a paper trail, so we decided no. Just keep it? Beverley wasn't in favour.

'Raising a child at our age? In our circumstances? Life is just beginning, Fay. Would you let a thing like this ruin your whole future?'

How I felt about it? Betrayed. Not by him. Isaac didn't really mean anything to me. Not like that. Not even after all the weeks and months I had spent with him going to rallies and listening to speeches and reading everything he put in my lap. And talking together all hours of the day and night about what needed to happen to make Jamaica a better country for everyone. Rich and poor. Black, white, Chinese, Indian, Jew. Lying in that stinky room of his above the butcher shop.

No, it wasn't him who hurt me to the core with all his chat of equality and revolution. It was her. Because I had trusted her. More than anyone else in my entire life, because more than anyone else, I believed she was on my side. Wanting the best for me. Like Aristotle said, wanting for someone what you believe is good for their sake and not your own. That was friendship. Doing things out of concern for the other person not yourself. So if she was my friend whose interest was Beverley serving?

'It just happened, Fay. What can I say to you?'

'Things don't just happen like that, Beverley. At some point you made a decision. People organise themselves and their time so they end up in a situation and then they decide. Sometimes they even plan it beforehand. Is that what you did?'

'Plan it?' She threw down the dresses she was gathering together to give to the maid to press. In her bedroom at GC's. Then she stomped across the expanse of floor and opened the door.

'If that is what you think you may as well leave right now.'

I stayed put on the semicircular window seat overlooking the back lawn. One knee raised with my arms tucked around it. 'I was asking. That is all.'

She slammed the door and returned to the bed. 'I don't know how you could even think a thing like that.' And then she picked up the clothes from the floor. 'Isaac is a low life. Why would I deliberately do something like that?'

'But you did, Beverley. That's the point. And I'm guessing it was more than once.'

'Fay, for God's sake. I'm in a predicament here. Are you going to help me or not?'

The idea that I might have had any feelings about it seemed beyond Beverley's comprehension. As far as she was concerned we were friends. She was in a jam and I should help her. No big deal. About Isaac she just said, 'You're only playing with him yourself. For reasons I can't even begin to fathom. Not like he's any Freddie Smithers. In a year's time this will all be history and you and I will still be here.' And then she laughed, tossing her head back the way we liked to. And it was over.

What it made me realise? No one can be trusted. Not completely. Not absolutely. Sometime, somehow, somewhere everyone will either let you down or desert you. Or both. A mother who beat you. A father who was too afraid to stand up for you. A brother who ran away to boarding school and later to England. Freddie who took flight at his father's call. Even Sissy. And now Beverley too. All for the same reason. Every single one. They wanted to make their own life. The way they saw it. The way they could conceive it. Whether or not it included me. Not that Beverley was casting me aside. Rather, she was reminding me of my place. Just like every other person in her life. Like GC who was there to provide. And Tyrone who was there to entertain. Like the maids who were there to serve. We serviced and supported Beverley Chung. And in exchange she gave us her charm.

So there was nothing to talk about. Even after I asked her point-blank: 'Didn't you think that maybe I would be hurt? About you and Isaac.'

The way she looked at me so wide-eyed and innocent it was clear the thought had never even entered her head.

'Really?' And then her eyes narrowed as a question mark formed on her brow. Which made me wonder if maybe everyone in my life felt the same. If all of them were simply oblivious to my feelings or baffled by the idea that what they did had any impact on me whatsoever.

Grandmother Chung's reaction was different.

'Beverley Chung, how could you do a thing like that? To your own dear friend. Friends since you were fifteen years old. How could you do that?'

We were in GC's living room. The two of us sprawled on separate sofas. GC was dressed in turquoise linen, standing by the mantelpiece with a margarita in her hand.

'Answer me, girl. I am talking to you.'

'It happened, Grandma. It happened. How many times do I have to keep repeating that to everyone?'

'As many times as it takes for me to understand.'

GC lit one of her little cigars. Shorter than a cigarette. Slightly fatter. Cuban. With a full-bodied aroma that put you in mind of fried beans and sombreros, and the sound of guitars and 'Guantanamera' filling the air.

'I have been married three times and had more men than I care to remember and I know, with absolute certainty, that these things never, and I say never, just happen. And definitely not more than once.'

GC walked, as she spoke, over to the sofa on which Beverley was lying and removed from her granddaughter's hands the magazine she was flicking through in search of enticing new designs.

'Your next dress can wait.'

Beverley looked up at her, frustrated. 'GC, there is nothing to say.'

'Absolutely not. There is plenty to say. Plenty to explain. Plenty to apologise for.'

I got up to leave. 'Fay, you stay right there. I want you to hear every word this granddaughter of mine has to say for herself. Sit down, which is what I am going to do. So we can all listen with full attention.'

And then she raised her brows at Beverley as if to say, 'Now you should begin.'

Beverley sat up. Crossed her legs on the sofa. Fiddled with her bare feet and red-painted toenails. In that moment she looked like twelve years old not twenty-two. GC settled herself in the armchair and rang the little bell on the table next to her. When Theresa appeared she raised her glass and said, 'Could you bring me another one of these?'

We waited in silence while Theresa retreated to the bar and returned with the drink on a small silver tray. Glass chilled and rimmed with salt. Lime slice dangling on the side.

'Do you need anything else, miss?'

'No, that's fine, Theresa. Thank you.'

So then we were alone and it was time for Beverley to speak. But before she could open her mouth GC interrupted.

'What about Audley? You think about him any more than you thought about your friend here?'

'What Audley doesn't know won't hurt him.'

'That is your plan? To keep it from him?'

'The only reason I told you is because I need your help.'

GC rubbed her face, pressing hard on her nose and pinching her top lip between thumb and forefinger. I'd seen her do it before. When something had angered her. A careless maid, a task left undone, something out of place, someone's unkind behaviour or thoughtless comment. It was her way of holding her tongue while she decided what to say. A bad, old habit, she once told me, because it smudged her make-up, especially at the sides of her nose that were prone to being greasy.

Then the door opened and Tyrone was standing there.

'Family conference.' He went over to the bar and poured himself a drink. Appleton Special.

'Anyone else?' he said, holding up the bottle.

We all shook our heads. He eased on to the sofa next to me. Glass in hand. Then he crossed his legs. And sipped his rum.

'So what we talking about?'

'About your sister being pregnant with Isaac Dunkley's child.'

Tyrone choked and spluttered Appleton down the front of his shirt. He wiped his chin and brushed himself down.

'Yu serious?' And then, after a short pause, 'Who is Isaac Dunkley?'

So Beverley had to explain to an increasingly stunned Tyrone about us meeting Isaac outside the Carib; and me and Isaac. 'Fay and a butcher's bwoy?' And how she bumped into him in town and started seeing him on the odd occasion; and how one thing led to another; and so on and so forth.

'So on and so forth? Is that what yu just say to me? That is your way of telling us yu pregnant?'

Beverley didn't reply. So Tyrone just sat there with his dropped jaw, clutching the glass in his hand like he dare not bring it to his lips in case by doing so he inadvertently added further tragedy to Beverley's story.

'So what going happen now?'

We all looked at Beverley. 'Don't expect me to keep it. That is all I am saying. Fay and I already been over all a this.'

GC turned to me. 'Is that so?'

I nodded. 'Beverley says she can't keep it. But she can't get rid of it either.'

'What about Audley?' Tyrone asked.

Whereupon we all three of us shouted at him, 'Forget about Audley!'

And then GC added, 'That is for another time. Except you, young man, must know to keep your mouth shut. Understand?'

Tyrone held up his arms in surrender. 'I wouldn't even want to get myself in di middle a dis.'

So it was settled. GC had a friend with a house in Montego Bay that most of the time was unoccupied. It was a good spot. A big, bustling city far away from Kingston that had too much going on for anyone to notice us or care about what we were doing. Not like going to Port Antonio or Savanna-la-Mar where everybody knew everybody and where an unknown pregnant woman, Chinese at that, would make for curiosity and careless talk.

'That is it?' Beverley asked GC.

'What more do you want? You are the one who got yourself into this mess. And I am the one who is having to bail you out. I think a simple thank you would be in order. Don't you? To say nothing of the apology you owe to this poor girl who for seven long years has considered you a friend. Don't you think you should have something to say to her?'

Beverley looked over at me. And then, with her eyes downcast, she said, 'I'm sorry.' Speaking the words into her chest so that they were barely audible.

'Speak up, Beverley,' GC told her. 'We all want to hear.'

Beverley raised her head. 'Sorry.'

'What are you sorry for? Tell us.'

Beverley flashed a face of anger at her grandmother, who sat there still and calm as she said, 'Life doesn't demand much of you, Beverley Chung. Everything has been handed to you on a plate. So there is nothing for you to do except one thing. Try to be a decent person. That is all. But it seems even that you cannot quite manage. All we can hope is that you learn from this experience.'

'Like you did? Running around China like Chiang Kai-shek's whore.'

'Who told you that?'

Beverley didn't answer; she just lowered her head with an expression of such shame that I knew she already regretted the words escaping.

'You are a child. You have no idea. It was years ago. A different time. A different place. Whatever your father told you is untrue. Simply because of this. No one point of view can ever be the truth. No one perspective or opinion absolute. The facts of life cannot be disputed. Witness you and what is in your belly. But the whys and wherefores. They are something else. So perhaps you are right. You have nothing to be sorry for.'

And, so saying, GC got to her feet and walked from the room.

Before the baby started to show, GC had her driver take us to Mo Bay. I didn't tell anybody at home what I was doing. All I said to Papa was that I was going to stay with a friend. And I packed a bag and left.

But the place wasn't in Mo Bay. It was actually well outside the city. Up in the hills near Wiltshire, which I thought was funny because of Freddie. But unlike the rolling carpet of green Freddie had described, our Wiltshire had tree-covered mountains, and valleys and gorges. And GC's doctor coming up every week to check on us. And a local midwife staying in the house sharing quarters and domestic duties with the live-in maid. She'd made all of the arrangements, GC, in a cool and detached manner. Giving Beverley instructions about what would happen as if she were a total stranger upon whom she, GC, was bestowing some act of kindness. Towards me, her spirit was more generous. But not like before; because, really, Beverley and I were in it together. So to some extent, I'd been tarnished with the same brush.

Up in the hills, we played cards and chequers and read Agatha Christie because the owner of the house seemed to have every single novel she'd ever written. Near on forty of these books we read in the six months we were there. Occasionally we went down to Mo Bay to visit the beach at Doctor's Cave or stroll around the market. And once or twice we went to the theatre. Sometimes in the afternoons when Beverley was resting I took myself off to Great River. Just to sit. Not on a bamboo raft but in a boat. With a book. So actually, it seemed like we were on a long, extended vacation and the baby was just an excuse for it.

When the time started to draw near I did feel nervous, mostly because I had no idea what to expect. Dr O'Keefe said he would have preferred a hospital birth. Nurse said she'd successfully delivered hundreds of babies in homes across Mo Bay and the hills. Beverley said we should let her grandmother decide.

When GC arrived she said it was best to keep things simple. O'Keefe should sterilise whatever he needed to sterilise. Nurse should boil water and prepare fresh towels. And we should all get ready. There wasn't going to be any trip to the hospital.

And as it turned out everything happened exactly according to GC's plan. Even the baby flopped out like he was under her instruction. I don't even think it hurt that much, it was all over so quickly. One minute Beverley's waters broke and the next I was being handed a shiny black baby boy to hold. Screaming his head off so we knew everything was alright. And Beverley was grinning from ear to ear, not because of the child whom she refused to touch, but out of gladness that the whole tiresome affair was over.

Afterwards, everybody had their own look. Dr O'Keefe's was relief as he packed back into his bag all the little metal things he hadn't needed, muttering to himself about what a small miracle it was for a first-time mother. Nurse rolled her eyes at him as if to say: 'I told you so, you stupid man.' GC had an air of self-congratulation. That superior confidence of knowing you have control over everything. Me? I still couldn't believe that such a huge thing could have come out of such a tiny hole. Even though, as babies go, Nurse said Junior was on the small side. She reckoned maybe he'd come earlier than he should have.

We stayed in Mo Bay a few more weeks just to recover and regain our confidence. And then we went back to Kingston. All forgiven between us. And did what Beverley had always said she would do. We went to Cross Roads and gave the baby to Isaac.

'What yu expect me to do wid a thing like dis? I cyan keep no baby in here. What I going do trying to be father to dis?'

Beverley put the baby in his arms. 'Yu should a thought a dat before yu do what yu do.'

'Come on, Beverley, this not fair and yu know it.'

'Yu know di baby was coming, Isaac. What yu think was going to happen?'

He stood there in his little room holding Junior at arm's length. 'Yu cyan do dis to me.'

'Watch me,' she said as she headed towards the door, turning around briefly to add, 'And if yu ever tell him I'm his mother I will hit yu so fast wid a lawsuit it will mek yu head spin. Or better still, advertise to every man in Trench Town where he can come and find yu.'

And then she took me by the hand and led me down the stairs through the shop and into the street. We didn't even look back. What I remember feeling? Sorry for Isaac. And sorry for baby Junior too.

CHAPTER 10

I DIDN'T SEE anything of Isaac for months after that. Not until after he left a note for me at home and I went to join him downtown at the procession organised by the Trade Union Congress to support the bus workers' strike. I'd actually been paying attention this time, following it in the newspaper. So I knew about the strike and the operation of buses by strike-breakers; and the union's appeal for a public bus boycott; and the armed police and special constables; and guards at bus stops and terminuses. All over a one pound, seven shillings and seven pence per week pay rise for drivers and a pound, two shillings and thruppence for conductors. And paid holiday and sick leave. It seemed like a pittance and a travesty. Especially given all the money and resources that was being put into stopping these people from earning a decent wage.

At first I didn't think I would go. What finally took me there, to Victoria Park that day, was thinking about the families of the strikers; and the relief driver who'd been shot and killed; and the other two stabbed with broken bottles;

and worse, the parcel bombs left on buses to explode. It made me remember that bus trip with Isaac coming back from the public library. The look of despondency on the faces of those poor, dejected people and the fact that they couldn't even travel safely any more.

Isaac was pleased to see me when I arrived to meet him. We started at the park and paraded down King Street and through the busy corporate area. Hundreds of people carrying banners and singing a song that Isaac said was called 'Workers of Jamaica', with bystanders cheering us along to show their support, and many more people joining the parade on the way back to Victoria Park. Isaac told me about a public meeting that was planned for that evening at the corner of Windward Road and Water Street and asked if I wanted to go.

We went. The place was packed with people eager to listen to the stream of speakers who stood on the platform telling us about what had transpired between the union and the company because of the company's refusal to negotiate over the wage increase or agree to the joint labour–management committee the union wanted.

'A joint committee,' one man said, 'so that in future workers cannot be dismissed without knowing the charge against them and having the opportunity to defend themselves through their union.' It seemed a fair enough request to me.

On the way back to Cross Roads I asked Isaac about the baby. He told me he had given him to his sister to take care of.

'You still have contact with her?'

'Why not?'

'Because of what happened. I thought they'd disowned you.'

He quickened his pace. 'Dis not worth talking 'bout. Di baby is fine. Yu can tell Beverley.'

Why I spent the night with Isaac I don't know. Maybe it was because I hadn't actually felt betrayed by him. Because our relationship, such as it was, was founded not on desire or anything like it, but on my longing to understand Jamaica. This island on which I had lived my entire life but about which I seemed to know so very little. Isaac was my way into that, my access door to long conversations deep into the night. Not being comforted in his arms as with Freddie, but locked in the grip of his passion for a fairer Jamaica. Half-wondering as I lay there if he'd laid like this with Beverley. Here in this bed. Somehow I couldn't see it. No more than I could imagine her taking him to GC's.

The union appealed to the public not to cause damage or endanger life but it didn't work. There were more bus bombings and violent action, and letters to the governor threatening destruction of government buildings. So every other day there were headlines in the *Gleaner* from the chief minister, Mr Bustamante, denouncing communism and criticising the governor for not doing enough to suppress the strike.

'So what yu think, Fay? Yu agree wid Mr Bustamante dat di communist are everywhere? In the PNP and such?'

'To tell you the truth, Isaac, I don't really know what a communist is. Wanting a decent wage or fair treatment doesn't seem that unreasonable to me. But the violence, that is something else. And as for all the bickering to and fro between the PNP and Labour Party, that seems sort of pointless to me, because the governor is just sitting there in the background watching us tear ourselves apart. And the British are still in charge. So it seems like a waste of time and energy when what we should be doing is all working together for a better future.'

'I'll drink to that,' he said, raising the Red Stripe bottle to his lips.

What Beverley wanted was for us to go down to the Chinese Athletic Club to watch Tyrone play in some ping-pong competition.

'Ping-pong? Tyrone?'

'His team been playing in the knockout for months. And now the final is at the athletic club and he wants everybody to come support him.'

'That place is for kids, Beverley.'

'Not true. Anyway, it nuh matter. The point is, Tyrone needs you.'

So we went. Sunday afternoon when I would rather have been doing something else. And we sat in the stands and cheered when Tyrone was at the table and when he wasn't we stood around drinking lemonade waiting for the next round to be completed, with man after man coming to that square of green board and smashing that little white ball to kingdom come. It was boredom beyond belief.

Afterwards, we went to Monty's for curry goat with Tyrone basking in the glory of victory and Audley talking about how ping-pong was nothing like cricket. Beverley and I just sat in the booth relieved that it was all over.

An event to forget except that three weeks later Mama told me that someone was coming to visit me.

'Visit me?'

'You know him. A fine young man you met at the Chinese Athletic Club.'

'I didn't meet anyone at the Chinese Athletic Club.'

She threw down her embroidery. 'Well he is coming. So tidy yourself and be on the veranda at four o'clock.'

When he showed up he was a near-scrawny Chinaman a little bit shorter than me. Not bad-looking, as it turned out, and well-presented but with his hat in his hand and head bowed like he was docile and already obedient to Mama's every command. What would I want with a man like that?

'Miss Cicely, always a pleasure to see you.'

The sight of him kowtowing to her made my stomach turn.

She waved her hand at me. 'You already know Fay, of course.'

He nodded and smiled. And then he sat and watched Mama pour the tea, Earl Grey, with tinned salmon and cucumber sandwiches cut into triangles, crusts removed, and Victoria sponge cake. Just the same nonsense she did every afternoon.

'How is business?'

'Very good, Miss Cicely. Cannot complain.'

As she passed him the cup she said, 'What use is there in complaining? We have to face each and every day as the good Lord presents it to us.'

I laughed inside. What a ridiculous scene. The three of us sitting there like flowers in an English country garden. So I drank the tea and drifted off into a lazy half-sleep, wondering what I would wear when I met Beverley that evening.

'Fay would be delighted to accompany you.'

I woke up with a sudden start. 'Accompany him where?'

They both turned and stared at me in surprise.

'To the Chinese Benevolent Society garden party.'

'Garden party? No. I don't think so.' I stood up.

'Fay, the man has come here to ask you out. The least you can do is to show some courtesy.'

'I've never seen this man before in my life.' I looked down at him sitting there in the wicker armchair. 'I'm sorry, whatever your name is, but I'm not going to the garden party or anywhere else with you. My mother has misled you. My apologies.' And I walked inside.

Mama waited until he'd left and then followed me into my bedroom where I was reaching into the wardrobe for the evening's dress.

'You think you are so high and mighty that you can insult the man like that?'

'Who is he anyway? Where did you find him?'

'Me find him? You are the one who met him.'

'I did not.'

'And he had the good manners to bring your father's wallet back after he lost it in Barry Street. With every last shilling still in it. An honest businessman with his own shop in West Street.'

'West Street! Are you serious? That is just two stops short of Trench Town.'

She slapped the edge of my skirt. Years earlier it would have been my legs.

'Don't you start with me now, madam. As if you can afford to be so fussy. Twenty-three years old and how many men have shown any interest in you? And don't mention that Isaac person, you hear me. I mean men. Decent, hard-working men.'

'You mean not black.'

She stamped her feet. Actually stamped them like a two-year-old.

'Think you can talk to me any way you like? Well let me tell you, for all your fancy friends and fancy clothes you are still a woman. And a woman needs a husband and, that being the case, it is better to have one who can provide rather than one with nothing in his pockets but his empty hands. A Chinese shopkeeper is as good a catch as you are going to get. You should be counting your blessings instead of turning up your nose.'

Beverley thought it was a big joke.

'West Street?' Laughing and holding on to her stomach as she rolled around the floor in GC's living room.

'If you are rude enough he will get the message and give up.'

But no matter how indifferent or offhand I was with him, he kept coming. Week after week laden with ice cream and chocolates for Mama. Sitting on the veranda with her talking about nothing and drinking the weak tea she served with milk so it had absolutely no taste whatsoever. Eating her white-bread sandwiches. A Chinaman eating sandwiches. Papa would have bolted at the very thought of it.

Every now and again she insisted that I join them, and I did. It was easier than arguing with her. Five, ten minutes tops. That's all I would give it and then I'd go back inside or leave, sometimes for Beverley's, other times to meet Isaac. Anything rather than sitting there with them listening to their pointless conversation.

Papa told me his name was Yang Pao.

'You know him?'

'Not exactly. He shopkeeper, Fay.'

'Yes, I know about the shop.'

'Why you so hard on him? What he do upset you?'

I looked at him through the steam rising off his soup, sitting in his usual haunt in Barry Street. The bowl of rice in front of him on the red and white chequered tablecloth. The pieces of boiled chicken at his elbow. The soy sauce in the dish. It reminded me of Mama in the buggy sending Samson to fetch me while Papa ate that exact same meal.

'She think you too old still live at home. Need home of own. So two of you not cross swords any more.'

'So that's it? She just wants me gone?'

'She think it time I stop keep you.' I narrowed my eyes. 'No need look like that, Fay. I happy keep you.' He slurped some soup. 'But maybe she right 'bout all the cantankerousness in house. Better gone than fighting with her every day.' He scooped some rice into his mouth, chewed and swallowed. 'Or if you want own place we look together for rent house.' Dipping a piece of chicken into the sauce and holding it with his chopsticks over the dish to drain. 'Unless you want stay with Sissy.'

'No, I don't think she would want that.'

The crunch came when Mama told me she had agreed for me to marry Yang Pao.

'Are you out of your mind? I'm not going to marry him!'

'You will do as you are told or you will get a begging bowl for the sidewalk at Cross Roads market. I am not putting up with your antics in this house any longer.' And, so saying, she slammed the bedroom door and walked away.

Later when I saw Papa I told him there was no way I would marry Yang Pao.

'Is OK. He not rich now but one day he make plenty money and get better business arrangement and move uptown. You see. Everything work out and your mama she keep happy.'

When I told Isaac he just sat there in the bed smoking a cigarette like it had nothing to do with him. Not that I thought Isaac was planning to marry me or that I would ever have considered marrying him. But I did expect some kind of reaction, even if all he wanted to do was ask me how I felt about it. But no. All he said was, 'Do whatever yu want.' His callousness took my breath away. For a moment. And then I thought, well maybe I had that coming.

Sissy told me she'd heard of Yang Pao. It wasn't good. That's all she said. No details. 'But then, who on dis island not up to something? He not as bad as some. Nowhere near as bad. I can say dat much fah him. And he look after his mother.'

How Sissy knew about Mama's plan for me to marry him?

'Yu father tell me.'

'Really? Yu see much a him?'

'The man paid my wages for thirteen long years. And every now and again he drop by. Anything wrong wid dat?'

'No. I just surprised, that is all.'

'Well yu can stop yu surprising and think 'bout what yu going do. Yu going marry dis man or what?'

We had just finished listening to the military band playing in Victoria Park.

'Yu want an ice cream?' And then I remembered. 'Or maybe not.'

'Yu mean di sugar? Yu think I going fret over what going kill me? And then I start worry myself and get the pressure. No, man. Dat is not di way I intend to go.'

'So how yu going go, Sissy?'

'Sitting in my rocking chair smoking my pipe.' And then she smiled and laughed out loud.

In Sissy's opinion, she didn't see how I could get out of it. The marriage.

'Because in truth yu need a roof over yu head. And money to put food on di table. And I cyan see Miss Cicely letting Mr Henry stick him hand in him pocket fah dat. Not after all di trouble she go to fi get yu outta di house. No sir. Dat not going happen dis side a hell. And as fah earning a living. Well, yu know I love yu like me own so yu won't mind me saying. Yu not trained fah anything. So as far as getting a job concerned, that don't seem likely.'

'Maybe I could work fah you.'

She shot me a disapproving glance. 'I tell yu before. I don't want yu coming over deh. I will help yu all I can, yu know that. But not over Franklyn Town.'

We continued to walk away from the bandstand. 'What about Stanley?' she asked. 'Maybe yu could go fi England. Plenty people looking that way. *Windrush* and all.'

'Wid all dat rain and cold and fog?'

'Maybe, but deh say di streets dem paved wid gold. Dat is what deh say. And dat di English got wide-open arms and a warm fish-and-chip welcome.'

What Stanley had written to me?

The English resent us being here. That is the truth. And as far as finding a decent job or room to rent with more than a cold water tap, you can forget about it. The host nation not feeling that hospitable. According to them we are a social parasite. Welfare scroungers who are stressing their services to breaking point. Even though it's us that's keeping everything running in the hospitals and post office and London transport.

And then Sissy said, 'Or the bakra. Freddie what's-his-name. What about him? Yu hear anything a him?'

Freddie's letter?

I think I already told you about my mother dying last year. A brain tumour. She went so fast. Within weeks of her diagnosis. The thing that's been absolutely astounding is how badly my father has taken it. Not just mentally and emotionally but physically. All he does now is sit and read the newspaper. Raising himself occasionally to let the dog in or out. His body has practically collapsed in on itself so now he is but a shell of the man he used to be. He's in a pathetic state and wants me to marry the daughter of an old friend of his. Catherine. And since I'm not doing anything else (with my personal life) then why not? Why not make a tired old man happy? Especially after all the disappointment and disgrace I caused him.

And then, as a postscript, he had written: *But I'll never dance with her the way I danced with you.*

'Because,' Sissy said, 'yu cyan go get on di boat just like dat. Yu have to have somebody sponsor yu. And have a job to go to. Like maybe training as a nurse. Yu ever think a dat?'

Me a nurse? I couldn't see it somehow. I wouldn't have had the bedside manners.

★   ★   ★

'The thing is, Beverley, I need money and I need somewhere to live.'

'Didn't your papa say he would keep you?'

'Yes, but I can't go on like that for ever. I have to do something.'

'But we not trained to do anything, Fay.' She laughed. 'Apart from have a good time.'

Two days later, Beverley had her big solution. Join the army.

'The British army?'

'It's three years, Fay. They will train us to do something and they will pay us. So we can get ourselves a place.'

'You would leave all this?' I surveyed the splendour in GC's living room.

She shrugged her shoulders. 'I'm tired of the vegetables anyway.' And then after a short pause she said, 'Besides, things aren't how they used to be. There's a distinct chill in the air these days.'

So we went and filled out their forms and took their tests and submitted to their medical examinations. And we became privates in the Women's Royal Army Corps. Ancillary Territorial Service.

CHAPTER 11

WE WERE DUES In/Dues Out clerks in the Ordnance Corps, responsible for the supply of weapons, armoured vehicles and other military equipment: ammunition, clothing and general stores; vehicle storage and spares. Requisitioning, warehousing and consignment of every damn thing the British army used, from uniforms and boots and cans of soup to tanks and jeeps and guns. Everything imported directly from England, landing at the dock and taken by truck along South Camp Road to Up Park Camp. Most of the provisions I could understand, but what they needed all this heavy artillery for I didn't know. Playing boy soldiers at the camp, I guess.

I didn't say anything to Mama. I just got dressed and left the house in the mornings and went to GC's to change into my uniform. And then together Beverley and I caught the tram downtown to the depot, which was right on the harbour. We could even see the sea from our desks through the office window. And in the evening, I did the whole thing in reverse.

What mattered to me was that I was learning. Shorthand and typing; invoicing; filing; making inventories of all the incoming supplies; and, as they were issued to the camp, knowing when and how to order replacements and keep the warehouse stocked. I was even learning to drive and fire a gun, which, as it turned out, I was quite good at. Army life was fun. With dances at which you were never short of a partner.

The best part was having my own money. My very own cheque account at the bank. Not having to ask Papa for hand-outs any more. I was my own woman with enough for my half of the deposit so Beverley and I were going here and there looking for a place to rent. My plan, when we got ourselves sorted, was just to leave Lady Musgrave Road, and in the mean-time I didn't reckon there was any point in taking aggravation from Mama about what I was doing. So I let her carry on plan-ning the wedding because that is what she wanted to do.

Daphne suspected something, though. I even caught her searching my room one day, when I came home early and found her all flustered and harassed saying she'd gone in to close the window. Since when did anybody in our house do something like that? I didn't say anything about it, just decided it was better left alone. There wasn't anything for her to find anyway. So I smiled at her knowing that pretty soon it would be over.

And then one morning they sent for me. Just like that. Out of the blue. An army jeep with two military policemen to take me uptown to the camp. When I got there, they marched me into the administrative building, up the stairs and told me to take a seat and wait outside the colonel's office. I sat there sweating and racking my brain for near on forty minutes trying to think what it was I had done. When the door finally opened it was by a corporal with plump, feminine hips, who told me to come in.

Colonel Stephenson was tall and thin with a skinny face and pointed chin. But the weird thing about him was his shoulders, which were hunched up and stiff like someone had nailed a piece of wood across his back.

'Private Wong, please sit down.' He was standing behind his green leather-topped mahogany desk. Hands clasped at his back.

I sat. Organised my skirt to look presentable.

'It has come to my attention that you are betrothed.'

Oh God, I thought. He's going to throw me out. 'I'm not going to do that, sir. It's my mother's plan but I have no intention of marrying anyone.'

'Ah, that is what I wanted to talk with you about.' He sat in his chair and swivelled his back to me so he could look out of his first-floor window at the parade ground. 'This man, Yang Pao. What do you know about him?'

'Nothing, Colonel. Nothing at all.'

He swung around suddenly, plonked his elbows on the desk and stared at me. 'A Chinatown racketeer. That is what he is, Private Wong. Involved in all sorts of protection, illegal gambling and stolen goods.'

'The man is a crook?' I wanted to sound surprised, even though Sissy had intimated as much to me.

'We are not interested in him. That's a matter for the local constabulary.'

My stomach began to churn.

'Tell me, have you heard of the four Hs?'

'Sir?'

'Hill, Ken and Frank. Richard Hart. Arthur Henry.'

And then I remembered the night two years earlier when Isaac and I had listened to Hill and Hart address the crowd supporting the bus workers' strike. I swallowed the sour bile that was gathering in my throat, but said nothing.

'They are communists. And pretty soon they will be exposed and disgraced.'

Oh my God, he thinks I'm a communist. 'Colonel Stephenson, sir. I don't know anything about these men. Are they really communists?'

He tapped his baton on the edge of the desk as his mood softened. 'My dear, I don't expect you to know anything about communists. A girl like you from your background.'

It felt like being in a bad B movie, with two cardboard characters reading from a really awful script.

'Now tell me, what do you know about a West Indies federation?'

I didn't. So he explained about the conference in Montego Bay in 1947 where representatives of all the British Caribbean islands had come together to talk about uniting into one federal government. And how some committee they set up was about to report.

'The creation of a single political state, eventually independent from Britain. Do you understand?'

I nodded my head but, no, I didn't understand. Not really. And especially not what it had to do with me.

'And the last thing anyone wants is a communist Jamaica at the centre of it.' He leant back and rested his feet on his desk, hands behind his head. Full of confidence. 'So that is what I want you to do. Help in the fight against communism.'

'Me, sir?'

'Yes, you, Private Wong. And the first thing to do is marry this Yang Pao.'

'Because he's a communist?'

Colonel Stephenson looked at me as if in disbelief of my naivety.

'Colonel Stephenson, sir. I really don't know anything about communists. And I don't know anything about Yang Pao.'

'Ah, but Zhang Xiuquan?'

I was hot and sweaty, and wanted to vomit. 'I don't know who that is.'

'You don't know? He will be your father-in-law. When you are married, that is. A known communist. Came to Jamaica in 1912 after fighting for the People's Republic on the side of Sun Yat-sen. Wanders around Chinatown, even to this day, extolling the virtues of communism. You really don't know about him?' I sat stunned. 'You will,' he said and put both his feet firmly on the floor. Then he stood and reached across the desk to shake my hand. 'Go back to work now and next week we'll get together for another chat.'

When I told him I wasn't going to do it, he raised his brows and said, 'So you would prefer detention?'

'Sir?'

'Do you have any idea what military detention barracks are like? How it would be to spend the remainder of your three years there? It is three years, isn't it, you signed up for?'

My body went into a rigid, clammy shock. 'Colonel Stephenson, sir. I think there must be some mistake. I have no idea about any of this.'

'That is what makes you so perfect, Private. All you have to do is look and listen. And report what you see and hear to me. Nothing to it. No thinking or analysis required. You are an innocent that no one would ever suspect.' He smiled a self-satisfied grin of slightly yellowing, uneven teeth.

'It's this or detention, Private Wong. I am serious.'

'Don't you think that's rather extreme?' And then I hastily added, 'Sir.'

'These are extreme times, Private.' Spittle was spraying from his mouth. 'Bus bombings, shootings, stabbings, threatened destruction of government property. Illegal public meetings. All of which is telling us something. Do you know what that something is?'

I shook my head.

'That the communists are everywhere and must be stamped out. Whether they are members of the People's National Party or Chinese soldiers from the old country.'

Beverley said we should contact Freddie. We knew his father had connections in the British army in Jamaica. Maybe he could get someone to pull a few strings to keep me out of jail. So I told her about his letter. She frowned and pouted. 'Anyway,' I said, 'how could I do that when he himself chose prison?'

Grandmother Chung was sympathetic but there was nothing she could do. And since we couldn't go blabbing to everybody about it, including Sissy, which was sad because it was my first secret from her, my trip down the aisle with gangsterman Yang Pao seemed more and more inevitable.

The following week Colonel Stephenson sent for me just as he'd said. No more working at the ordnance depot. No more uniform. Just the simple life of a married woman caring for husband and home.

So as Mama's excitement grew so did my sense of doom. And the more she chastised me about my lacklustre attitude towards the dress fittings, bridesmaid gowns, invitation list, menu selection, flowers, beautician, hairdresser, orchestra, the more my silence consumed me.

The atmosphere in the house was full of ambivalence and foreboding. The maids carried out Mama's instructions but without energy. Only the new girl, Ethyl, seemed to show any enthusiasm for what was happening. Edmond persevered with Mama's remodelling of the garden under her tireless harassment and constant criticism. Daphne feigned interest but really I think she suspected the wedding would be called off at the last minute. Kenneth played with his toy trucks and trains as any four-year-old would. Oblivious.

I asked Papa if he knew about Yang Pao's activities and why he would let me marry a man like that.

'Illegal,' he sighed. 'What is illegal? Chinese. We like gamble. Little *pai-ke-p'iao*, that all it is. Everybody chip in. It more like community lottery. No harm in it. Not hurting anyone. The British, they only worry 'bout their taxes.'

'What about the protection racket?'

'Oh, Fay. That not racket. That go way back when old man Zhang first come here. You know the shopkeepers actually ask him to come. Paid passage from China so he come protect them against all the thieving and burning and looting going on. Nobody in Chinatown mind about that.'

'And the stolen goods?'

'That is US navy surplus. Yang Pao not stealing that. As for other things, he will grow out of them when he married and settled.'

I should have asked 'what other things?', but before I gathered my thoughts to do so Papa said, 'You don't have to marry him if you don't want. I will pay for you have own place.'

But I didn't feel I could tell him about the army and Colonel Stephenson's threat. Couldn't explain to him that the marriage was already signed and sealed. So I left it.

'The man has been waiting on that veranda for well over an hour. Do you have any intention of going out there to him?'

I was sitting on the backyard steps with Daphne, making plans for her birthday party. Not that she was involving herself much. She didn't even seem to have anybody she wanted to invite.

'Yu going to be eighteen, Daphne. That not worth celebrating?'

'If you want,' she said and shrugged, which made my own shoulders sag a little.

'We'll make it fun, I promise. Music and food and liquor. Champagne. That's what we'll serve. Want to come to the shop with me?' She shrugged again. I wondered why I was bothering. But still, I wanted to make the occasion special.

I patted her on the knee as I got up. 'And maybe some dancing, eh?' And then I walked inside, brushing past Mama as she hovered in the doorway.

He was sitting. Feet together, hands in his lap. Holding the teacup. He stood as I came towards him. Bowed his head even. Ever so slightly. And waited for me to sit down before retaking his seat.

'Edmond seem to be doing a good job with the garden.'

'Yes,' I said.

He shuffled his feet to break the silence. 'The new girl Ethyl working out OK?'

'She somebody to you?'

'No,' he said hastily. 'I just asking, that is all.' He paused. 'Just making conversation.'

He rearranged himself in the chair.

Then I said, 'I don't mean to insult you, Yang Pao. I don't even know you. I just wasn't planning on marrying anybody right now.'

'I understand.' He looked out over the lawn watching the sprinkler splash its water back and forth. And then he said, 'So ask me something.'

'Ask you something?'

'So you can get to know me.'

He surprised me. I don't know why. Maybe it was just the unexpectedness of it. The humility of him, sitting there like an eager schoolboy exposing a vulnerability I had not anticipated. It wasn't the picture Colonel Stephenson had painted. So for the first time I actually allowed myself to look at him. Really take him in. Not just the crew cut and two-tone shoes, but his strong frame that still somehow had a softness about it. Like he was steel covered in cotton wool. It gave his body a gentleness that matched the kindness in his deep-brown eyes.

'What do you want me to ask you?'

'Anything you want,' he said. 'Or maybe I will just tell you some things.'

136

His hands. That is what I noticed. As he reached across to rest the cup and saucer on the table. They had an energy about them. Open and flowing. I could imagine them holding a baby or writing a poem. Not clenched into fists the way I imagined the hands of a man like him would be.

'When I saw you at the athletic club, I thought you were the most beautiful woman. Perfect, you were. Screwing up your eyes and throwing back your head when you laughed. And so that very day I decided to make it my business to come find you and get you to marry me.'

'But you don't even know me.'

'Not yet, but I will. In time. Plenty marriages start this way in Chinatown.' He sat forward in the chair, resting his elbows on his knees. Hands clasped, almost like he was praying. Or begging maybe.

'All I ask is that you give me a chance.'

When the day finally arrived I felt like I was in a dream. Looking from the outside at my own life as if I was an observer and it wasn't really happening to me. Papa wore a black tuxedo with a starched white shirt and black bow tie. The brides-maids, Beverley and Daphne, were dressed in yellow and white to match Mama's outfit. But whereas their headpieces were based on a simple tiara style, Mama's hat was a colossal, wide-brimmed affair decorated with a vast ensemble of ribbon and feathers like she was presenting herself for a day at Ascot, which I knew about from the photograph of Freddie with his mother that sat on the table next to his bed. Yang Pao chose a white tuxedo and white tie. And actually he looked quite elegant. Clean and sharp.

Mama had decided on the cathedral. Holy Trinity. With its white-domed roof and Byzantine splendour. The service? I didn't hear a word of it, except when we got to the moment when he put the ring on my finger and I came to and realised that was it. With this ring, I thee wed. The deed was done. Even though I couldn't actually remember saying 'I do'. The kissing of the bride? I'd told Mama to instruct the priest to leave that part out. And as for cherish and obey, richer or poorer, sickness and in health until death do us part, we asked him to skip over that too.

The organ played I don't know what as we walked back along the aisle towards the open door. That was when I noticed how completely packed the church was. It was bursting at the seams with people I'd never seen before. All invited by Mama, obviously. Most probably hired for the occasion, dressed in clothes so colourful and outlandish they were probably hired as well. Yang Pao invited a grand total of seven people. Apparently.

When we reached the door, he tried to take my hand but I pulled it away and he got the message. To make sure, I fiddled with the dress, rearranging the skirt that had so much material in it and the long train behind that Beverley and Daphne had to follow and fuss over every step.

The midday sun blinded me, so it was a while before I could focus on the crowd waiting outside. Standing there in the street they were, peering through the fence. Why waste your time coming to see a thing like this? It seemed pathetic. And then there was a hand on my arm directing me towards the statue of Our Lady where they wanted to take the photographs. The bride and groom. The bride with her parents.

The groom with his parents. The family of the bride. The family of the groom. The bride with her bridesmaids. The bride with her bouquet. It was all such a farce. Such a ridiculous display given what every single one of us knew.

And just like we were throughout the preparations, we all had our own look. Yang Pao looked frightened. Maybe even he realised at this point that he'd made a mistake. Papa looked worried. Beverley? Numb. Which is exactly how I felt. The rest of the assembled? They just looked vague, like they were waiting for the proceedings to be over so they could dash off to the next engagement for which they had been booked. Maybe another wedding. Perhaps a funeral. Who knew.

The only person with any sign of life in them was Mama. Cheerful and satisfied, she was, with what she had pulled off. The beautiful, perfect wedding of her firstborn daughter. To a Chinaman, with prospects. A man who, in her mind, would seek out prosperity. But most of all, I was out of Lady Musgrave Road, which is what she wanted more than anything else.

The reception at the house was all canapés and pink champagne. Cocktail-size patties and triangle sandwiches made with coloured bread: yellow, red, blue and green. Standard Jamaican party fare. But where my mother learned about devilled eggs and devils on horseback God knows. The six-piece band? That was fun. Playing all the old standards from Ellington and Basie, with a smattering of Sinatra and calypso to mix it up. The crowd enjoyed it even if Mama frowned at them for not playing something more cultured. Dancing? There was none. Thankfully. I don't think I could have faced doing that with him. So I just walked around grinning and curtsying to various strangers, steering clear of conversation and drinking glass after glass of cool bubbly.

Later in the afternoon they served rice and curry goat. Buffet-style. Beverley and I ate ours sitting out by the tennis court, hidden behind the hibiscus hedge, away from the throng. We stayed there for the rest of the day, laughing about the situation and remembering the school motto 'Through Difficulties to Excellence', wondering how the excellence was going to materialise. Then just as darkness began to fall, Ethyl came to tell me that it was time to leave.

'Really? Where am I going?'

'The honeymoon, miss. Ocho Rios.'

'At this time of night?'

'Yes, miss. Your husband said that maybe yu should stay and travel in di morning but Miss Cicely say no. Yu should go tonight so yu have di wedding night there.'

'I haven't packed anything.'

'I do it fah yu already, miss. That is what Miss Cicely tell me to do.'

I stood up and followed Ethyl back to the house. The guests were gathered. I looked at her.

'Yu case already in di car, miss.'

Beverley hugged me tight just before I got into the blue and white Chevy next to him. He didn't even look at me. He just started the engine, put the gear lever into reverse, rested his arm on the back of my seat, turned his head to check behind, released the handbrake and pushed his foot down on the gas. As soon as we changed to forward motion I snuggled down into the seat, closed my eyes and went to sleep.

By the time we arrived at the hotel it was late into the evening. I slumped into the comfortable chintz sofa and waited while he checked in at the small office window bordering the otherwise open reception area. The old-fashioned furniture and cool, colonial blue and white decor had unassuming sophistication written all over it. Even in the dark I could sense that the garden was luscious and beautiful. The sound of the gentle breeze in the banana trees alone told me that.

We followed the porter to our room along a red-tiled external corridor planted with vines of enormous deep-green leaves, and in the bed below creepers of emerald. Actually, it was quite stunning. Gorgeous. I couldn't imagine how he found the place or what gave him the confidence to come here. It was so far away from downtown Kingston, in elegance and spirit not just in miles.

The bedroom was simply but graciously furnished. Dark wood headboard on the double bed with its fluffy pillows and crisp white cotton sheets. Side tables with lamps. A small dresser with mirror. A ceiling fan. At the far end, white, full-length, folding louvre shutters instead of doors. The bathroom? Marble vanity unit containing the basin. Bath with shower over. Flowers in a vase. Jug with ice-water. Two glasses. That is where I changed into my nightgown. And then I went straight to bed. Lying on the edge with my back to him. Pulling the sheet completely over my head.

When I awoke he was already gone. So I showered and dressed, relieved and grateful that he'd had the good manners to bring us to somewhere civilised with hot water and fragrant soaps. And even though I could already tell that he had dug deep into his pockets, opening the shutters still took my breath away. Not just the veranda with its scattered sofas and occasional tables, but the view. The wide-open bluest sky, and beneath it banana trees, coconut palms, blushing jacaranda, purple bougainvillaea. And beneath that, beds of red and yellow shrimp plant and red ginger. There was even a croquet lawn set with its little hoops. And beyond? The sea with its own white sandy cove. It was paradise. Jamaica at her best.

He was fully dressed in slacks and a sports shirt. Sitting in the armchair flicking through one of the hotel brochures. When I looked closer, it said 'Jamaica Inn'.

The thing about Yang Pao was his silence. He barely said two words to me. And I barely said two words to him because all I wanted to do was sleep. So every morning after breakfast I settled myself on the beach under the shade of a palm and closed my eyes. And a little later I would hear him sorting himself out on a lounger next to mine.

That is how we passed the week, with nothing between us while I exchanged pleasantries and made casual conversation with the hotel owner and American couples from Washington and New York and wherever else. Asking them about their trips to Dunn's River Falls, or rafting down the Rio Grande, or shopping at the craft market in town. In turn, they congratulated me on my wedding and hoped I was enjoying the honeymoon. Actually, I was thankful for the rest. But as the days moved on I realised that I was drawing ever closer to facing the reality I had left behind. The life Colonel Stephenson had fashioned for me, as wife to a hoodlum and informer for the British army.

The strange thing was that Pao, in his withdrawn acceptance, was almost endearing. There was a solidness about him, a resolve that stayed constant despite my complete lack of affection towards him. He was attentive, making sure that I had absolutely everything I needed. A dry beach towel, enough shade, a rum punch, a glass of ice-water. He even negotiated with waiters over what was being served for dinner and whether it would be to my liking. He wanted to please. Wanted me to have a good time even though I didn't care for one second what kind of time he was having. So in the end, I started to think that maybe I could afford to unfreeze a little because what was happening was so unfair. And so unkind, especially the sleeping arrangement with my back to him and the sheet over my head. Him on the far side of the bed so close to the edge he was practically falling on to the floor.

Pao married me for his own reasons, that was clear, but why I married him wasn't his fault. And now we were stuck together for better or worse. A part of me wanted to tell him, felt I owed him an explanation. But what could I say? So I just sat there or slept while he watched me and I watched him out of the corner of my eye.

The last night while he was in the shower and getting ready for dinner I sat on the darkened veranda thinking about returning to Kingston and what was waiting for me. And I started to cry with silent tears running down my cheeks. He came out and sat on the sofa behind me. And then, after a while, he got up and walked over to look me in the face. To check his suspicion. He reached into his pocket and handed me a clean handkerchief, which I took and mopped my eyes while he returned to the sofa and resumed his seat.

Then I said to him, 'My father told me it would be better for me to marry you than spend the rest of my life fighting with my mother.' So there. That was my story.

'You didn't have to marry me. You could have waited for someone more suitable to come along.'

'What, after my mother had set her sights on you?'

'I'm sure Miss Cicely not so stubborn to stick to her own view if maybe you happier with somebody else.'

I laughed. Then I turned around and looked at him. 'You think?'

It wasn't my intention to say any more. There wasn't any need or any point. I'd already made up my partly true reason for marrying him. It would suffice.

I stood up to walk back into the bedroom. But just as I was passing him he reached out and grabbed me and hugged me to him. The closeness of his warm body and deliberate arms, being held like that, in the dark, breached my defences and unlocked the emotion that had been buried inside me since that afternoon in the colonel's office.

I sobbed so much and went so weak in the knees it took all of his strength to stop the weight of me from dragging us both to the ground. Wave after wave of howling and heaving, that is how I was. Not saying anything and him not knowing what to say to me as I reeled in self-pity, grieving about life with Mama, life without Freddie, all the bad decisions I had made, fear about what lay ahead.

After a while he said, 'Do you want to get some dinner?' And the spell was broken. That night when we went to bed I reached out to him, pulling him back from the abyss, and rested my head on his shoulder. And he put his arm around me.

When we returned to Kingston he took me to his home. It was unbelievable. I couldn't imagine how he expected me to live in a place like that. A concrete yard behind a door in a fence in downtown Matthews Lane. A row of five separate bedrooms each with its own door and steps into the yard. A covered area open to the elements with a long wooden table beneath it. A zinc shower cubicle. A toilet at the top of the yard next to the duck pond. He'd been so many times to Lady Musgrave Road, how could he possibly see me living here? I was so stunned I couldn't say a word. Not to his mother, Ma, or to Zhang Xiuquan, the communist, or Hampton, Pao's man who lived there like a constant bodyguard.

So I went to bed. And the next morning I walked to Barry Street, and caught a cab home.

CHAPTER 12

BUT IT WASN'T any good. No point to it. Because all I found at Lady Musgrave Road was Mama.

'The honeymoon not over five minutes and you back here snivelling into your pillow. Time you wake up, gal, and face the fact that you are a married woman now. With responsibilities.'

I called Beverley but all she did was remind me that Colonel Stephenson was waiting in the wings. She was still working at the ordnance depot but had left GC's. Where was she living? With Marjorie Williams. Sharing a two-bedroom house uptown in Osborne Road. Marjorie's roommate had moved out so there was space and she'd asked Beverley if she wanted it.

'Well,' Beverley said, 'I'd been staying there on and off for yonks. Yu know, when I needed some privacy.' And then she laughed that embarrassed laugh of hers so I knew that's where she'd taken Isaac.

'And GC?'

'Oh, she's fine. I'm still over there every other day. Things aren't that bad. I just needed to spread my wings a little. Know what I mean?'

The following day I went back to Matthews Lane. But I couldn't stop crying. I never realised I had so much regret in me. Or maybe that wasn't it. Regret. Maybe it was that crying was the only positive thing I could think to do.

'I know this house not what you used to but it not so bad. We can do something fix it up.'

I listened to him but Pao had no idea. How could he possibly think that place could be fixed to compare with Lady Musgrave Road?

'It better than fighting with Miss Cicely.'

Better? I didn't know. It was different, I'd grant him that. Less injurious because every time Mama opened her mouth it was like a dagger being thrust into my heart. But still, it had energy. Vigour. Not like the lethargy inside me now. Like I was slowly drowning with no desire to save myself. I couldn't even be bothered to wave my arms in the air. Not like Marjorie Williams at Sigarney beach.

'What on earth made you think I could come here to Matthews Lane and live in a place like this?'

'It's my home, Fay. This is my family with Ma and Zhang. What do you want me to do, leave them? Look at them, the two of them old. I can't go leave them just like that. And I don't want to. I am the son, they my responsibility. You forget you Chinese?'

'You think I am Chinese?'

'What you talking 'bout?'

I walked out of the bedroom because I didn't feel like explaining anything to him. Even if Pao could understand what it meant to me, all these years, not to be full Chinese it wouldn't change anything. Wouldn't change the fact that, as

147

Mama so frequently liked to remind me, I am neither one thing nor the other.

Pao did what he could to make things better. Talking each night about his antics downtown, as if I cared, and bringing gifts of silk blouses and stockings, and vases from Chinatown to brighten up the bedroom. But it didn't help. The room was still as dingy and miserable as before, with the rickety narrow double bed and side table with the lamp, and the old wardrobe with the big drawer beneath, and tall dresser standing in the corner. So much dark furniture in such a small space. A tiny window looking out on to the concrete yard and a solid wooden door at the end, which when opened provided welcome air and sunlight but which also let in the uninvited ears and eyes of everyone in the house as they passed about their business. So mostly we kept them shut and confined ourselves to the semi-darkness that enveloped the room, and our life.

There I cried. Not that I thought it would solve anything. But just because I could. Could cry to my heart's content in a way I had never allowed myself to at Lady Musgrave Road. I could feel sorry for myself and weep out twenty-six years of pain and hurt, sorrow and suffering, without Mama's rebuke or worrying that I was adding to her satisfaction.

'No use bury head under sheet. Everybody in this house work. Me, Tilly, Hampton, Pao. Zhang, he old man. He already do everything for everybody. He finish now. Deserve rest. But you still young. What you do?'

I grew tired of listening to Ma's complaining, so I got up. Got up one morning after I heard Tilly, the daily help, come through the gate at five-thirty am to boil the saltfish and pick the flesh from the skin and bone, and drop it into the batter that Ma beat with a wooden spoon in a big bowl she balanced in the crook of her arm, to make fritters that they would fry and drain. Over and over until they had four dozen, which Tilly packed and carried to Barry Street to be sold from some grocer's hot cabinet. Every day of the week except Sunday. Come rain or shine.

And when she came back from Chinatown, Tilly and Ma would sit down together and pluck the duck feathers to stuff the pillows. For sale.

But that wasn't all Tilly did because she also washed and cleaned. And ironed. And when Ma wanted, Tilly would help with fixing the dinner or even cook it herself if the old woman was too busy playing mah-jongg in the yard with her friends. Or felt too tired or irritable to want to bother.

Zhang? He sat. On the wooden rocking chair he took from his room and placed in the shade by the duck pond. Sometimes he'd walk to Chinatown to visit the herbalist or to get his hair cut. And every Wednesday morning he made a trip for the newspaper. Not the world news written in Chinese, but news from China itself. News of home and abroad. As approved by the Chinese government.

Other times he'd play cards or dominoes with the old African, McKenzie, who, as folklore had it, committed some atrocity that Zhang had to punish when he was godfather of Chinatown and a law unto himself. So why was McKenzie now his best friend? Because Zhang showed mercy, nursing the man back to health after practically trying to kill him by hanging him upside down on a scaffold in the hot afternoon sun. Hanging there for hours, he was, in public view so that he could be a lesson to others.

'Tilly not here to play housemaid to you. She here to help me make a living.'

'I know, Ma.'

'Just so you do,' she said as she carried on with the hard yard broom, sweeping up the duck shit and scooping it into the crocus bag for Tilly to take to the garbage at the corner of the road.

That was Matthews Lane. All coming and going. Chopping and stirring. Scooping and shovelling. Listening to Ma's grumbling tone as she chuntered away in Chinese. Watching Zhang hawk and spit. Feeling the wrath of Pao as he instructed and reprimanded his men. The silent and long-suffering Neville Finley, who they called Judge, and Hampton, who was as much at Tilly's beck and call as Pao's. Being her younger brother.

Then one day, for no reason whatsoever, Pao decided we would go out. Together.

'What yu want to do?' he asked me. I was so shocked I didn't know what to say. Didn't even know if I wanted to be seen in public with him. In case someone recognised me. 'Maybe see a picture? Yu want do that? What tek yu fancy?'

He came home and showered after work on the appointed day. And put on a clean shirt and trousers before we walked up to Barry Street and caught a cab to Cross Roads. The film he wanted to see was *The Virginian* with Joel McCrea. I didn't care.

He bought the tickets. Best seats in the house. 'Nothing too good for you this evening,' he said, dropping his Jamaican lilt and grinning as he waited in line for popcorn and soft drinks. He took my hand as well, after we were seated, and rubbed the back of it gently.

The film drifted over me. Half the time I couldn't even hear what was being said, that much of a daze I was in. Bewildered at his sudden attention and lightened spirit. What I did catch made me wonder if Pao had taken us there specific-ally to send a message to me. If he really imagined that I could be Molly Wood, Vermont schoolteacher who goes out west to encounter and resolutely dislike the Virginian only to later fall in love with him. Is that what he thought? That he was a Wyoming cowboy and I would get over my aversion and ride off with him into the sunset.

Afterwards, I asked him, 'Has something happened?'

'Happened? Yu think something happen?'

I looked at him. 'You seem different.'

'I seem different to you?'

I didn't answer but there was definitely a new air about him. A new gait in his stride. A playfulness in his manner. He seemed fresher. Younger. More wholesome somehow. Handsome even.

'Yu know things not as bad as yu think. Home is fine and business is good. All yu need to do is settle into the house. Mek like family. Yu know wid Ma and Zhang. Everything will be irie. Yu will see.' And then he started to sing. Standing right there outside the picture house. The voice that came out of him was the most unexpected tenor you could have im-agined. 'Roses of Picardy': that is what he chose to serenade the street with. In a smooth, melodic tone that was soft and gentle. And soulful. Not sharp and jagged the way he so often was. This was a different Pao. More like the one I observed that night on the veranda. A Pao whose hand I decided to take as we sauntered through the crowd together. With people stopping to cheer and clap him. And him giving a little bow to his appreciative audience.

Yet despite the cheer in the atmosphere I couldn't take the squalor. That was something I couldn't get over. The slime in the zinc cubicle of a shower, slippery underfoot, with green, greying, furry mildew around the edges. Hair in the plughole from Ma's long black strands, which blocked the drain so that no matter how little water you used you still found yourself standing in inches of a soapy morass, grimy from the floor and the red mud that slipped from the pipe time to time.

The duck shit that floated down the concrete channel, the full length of the yard into the gutter outside the gate. That was odious. Like the toilet shed with its high-hung cistern and long metal pull-chain. Funny thing was, it didn't smell. Not like Isaac's place because every day Ma would scrub the whole interior from top to bottom. And pour Jeyes fluid in every corner. To keep out the rats as much as to dampen the stench.

The kitchen? Cockroaches. So bad that if you turned on a light at night the entire place moved. It was exhausting. Just to get up each morning to face it. And to go to bed at night knowing that all of that biology was alive and multiplying as you slept. Lying there as you did, covered in a full-body sweat. In the heat of that room. Locked up like an enclosed tomb.

That is why I decided to go home. For some fresh air, a decent shower and a swim in the pool.

'You back again?'

That is how Mama greeted me when she returned from her church meeting. She and Miss Allen. The two of them locked together in the gossip of the day.

'That a problem for you?'

'Me?' And then she said it again. 'Me?' Standing back this time with an exaggerated look of surprise on her face and a hand resting on her cheek like she was imitating Miss Lou in a pantomime. Which made Miss Allen laugh. Which started Mama prancing around, holding her skirt hem and swivelling it as she twisted and turned. Repeating all of the time 'Me? Me?' as she stopped to strike a different pose for her amused companion.

I picked up my coffee from the side table, kissed my teeth and walked inside. And God what a mistake that was.

'You come here when you should be gone. And use everything like some white boopsie at the Constant Spring Hotel high school and then kiss yu teeth? Just like that?'

So I stepped back on to the veranda, which I should never have done.

'Who you calling boopsie? If I am a kept woman then what are you? You who never worked one single day in your entire miserable life.'

'Work? I work every single hour of every single day. Yu think this house run itself?'

And Miss Allen added, 'With maids to order and chillen to keep on the straight and narrow so deh remember which side a di fence deh come from.'

'Which side a di fence? Which side a di fence do you call this? Maids and swimming pool and tennis court.'

Mama intervened. 'I am a black African woman. Strong and proud, and don't you ever forget that.'

'So that is why every afternoon right here on this veranda they busy serving you salmon sandwiches and Earl Grey tea?'

'Don't yu dear talk to yu mother like dat. Who yu think yu are coming in here like dis?'

'Miss Allen,' I pointed a finger directly at her, 'shut your mouth or I will shut it for you. This is my home before it is yours.'

'Don't you talk to her like that.'

I looked over Mama's shoulder at Ethyl and Pearl standing in the doorway, which made her and Miss Allen turn around to check what I was staring at.

'You two go back inside. This doesn't concern you.' That is what Mama said to them. And they obliged. But their presence, as brief as it was, lowered the fever.

'Mama, this is the truth. You are ashamed of being black. That is why yu never have one good word to say about the black man. And why yu drive Stanley away. And drink tea and eat cake every single day. To mek at least some small part a yu white English. That is why yu convert from Methodist to Catholic. And send me to Immaculate so the whole world could see how much money Henry and Cicely Wong have. As long as I didn't mix with the white girls or be too smart at the lessons. And as for being a boopsie, that is what you fear and have feared my whole life. Even when I was a child and Delton try to rob me on the street that day, and all you could fuss over was how I was rolling 'round in the dirt with him.'

Miss Allen started to open her mouth but Mama rested a hand on her arm to stop her. She, Mama, wanted to be the one to speak. She stood there stony-faced and then she said,

'That is your truth. Now this is mine. You are not welcome in this house. Go back to Matthews Lane where you belong.' And then she took Miss Allen by the elbow and led her inside.

I went back to Matthews Lane. And cried.

Pao couldn't take it so he started to sleep at the shop, after which I barely saw him. Sometimes a mid-afternoon visit for tea with Zhang or to check in with his mother. Dinner most evenings, followed by the collection of clean clothes and his departure, which in some bizarre way seemed to add to my sadness.

'Unhappiness so deep is old. Not new.' That was the first thing Zhang ever said to me. Directly.

I looked up at him standing there with the tea bowl and Chinese newspaper in hand. Something about him reminded me of my father. The tall squareness of him, and the dead-straight, flowing grey hair. But in Zhang there was a stillness. An inner calm that Papa didn't quite have. He pulled up a straight-backed chair and sat down next to me, resting the bowl and paper on the floor.

'When I was boy in China, whole country at mercy of warlords. Men with no shame or conscience. So many, many terrible things they do. But people, if they believe in self, can overcome anything. Even a mountain of suffering.' He held his arms above his head. Fingertips together. To show me a mountain. Then he put them down again. 'You are free. Let go of thoughts that keep you prisoner.' And then he stood, replaced the chair at the table, picked up his tea and paper and clomped his way towards his room. His wooden slippers slapping noisily on the concrete path.

* * *

155

Eventually, when Pao decided that something had to be done, he came to me. I was sitting on the edge of the bed when he knelt down on the wooden floor and took my hands in his. It felt reassuring. I even let him wipe away a few strands of hair that had become stuck to my wet face.

'What we going to do, eh?'

'Why did you marry me, Pao? You married me because my father is Henry Wong. Isn't that the truth? Honestly?'

He hesitated. And then, looking me straight in the eye, he said, 'Yes. Yes it the truth. That is how it start, Fay, but that not how it is now, not since the honeymoon. When we was at the Jamaica Inn I see a different side of you. You must admit yourself we cross a bridge that week you and me. Don't tell me it didn't mean nothing to you.'

I was grateful for his honesty, because I had never believed his speech about how perfect I was. Not for one second. But being the son-in-law of Henry Wong? I could understand that. It was a step up for him.

'I can't live like this, Pao. Can't you see that you and this house are the punishment my mother picked out for me? This is the suffering she wants me to have for the rest of my life.'

'What suffering?'

So I told him about the beatings and starvation, and so many lonely afternoons of being locked in the piano room. He was sympathetic, saying that we could make our own life not just let Mama decide it for us, which was sweet of him. But I knew that Yang Pao was no match for my mother. I'd seen him kowtowing to her on that veranda far too many times.

CHAPTER 13

THE NEXT MORNING I showered in the disgusting gloop of the zinc cubicle and dressed in a breezy lemon linen shift and walked to Barry Street where I caught a cab to Bishop's Lodge.

There was no answer at the front door so I followed the path into the rear garden. What greeted me was a magnificent expanse of lawn with flower beds packed with poinsettia, bird of paradise and wild banana plants with their red lobster claws. I approached the old man sweating as he weeded in the bed. He straightened up. Looked at me. Wiped his forehead with the back of his earth-encrusted hand and rested his weight against the border-fork stuck in the ground.

'I will fetch Miss Crawford fi yu.'

Miss Crawford turned out to be the maidenly housekeeper in a white pinafore apron who told me that there was no one at the lodge for me to speak to.

'No one at all? Not one priest in this entire place?'

'It not customary for people to come here like this, miss. The Fathers are busy with their ministry every hour of every day. So usually you would have to make an appointment.'

That was when I spotted him. Dressed in a long black cassock. Going into the house from the far end of the garden.

'What about him?'

She turned and looked. 'You mean Father Kealey? No.'

'He's a priest, isn't he?'

She drew in her ample chin as she prepared to stand her ground. 'The Father not long out of the seminary. Better yu come back another time.' Then she started us in motion towards the house. 'If yu come inside I will get the appointment book.'

I followed Miss Crawford into the cool back hallway of the lodge with its tiled floor and wooden panelling.

'Wait here.' And so saying she disappeared into the house. But before she returned, he stepped through the door. Standing there with a dimple in his chin and pale grey eyes.

'Can I help you?'

What I noticed about the Father, what hit me straight away, was that he was mixed, with the broad nose of an African but with thinner lips than you would expect. And wavy hair. Not a head that was tight and kinky. And since I didn't reckon the Father to be a man busying himself with a hot iron, I figured the hair was natural. Not straight-straight like pure Indian, but straight enough to betray the fact that he was like me. Even if he wasn't quite as light.

I put out my hand. 'Fay Wong.'

He shook it. 'Michael Kealey.'

His hand was the softest, most welcoming hand I had ever touched. The gentlest handshake I had ever experienced. From anyone. Woman or man. Not that I was used to shaking hands with people. But still, it was something to remember. Remarkable in the confidence that it inspired.

'I was hoping to talk with someone. One of the Fathers.'

He smiled with eyes filled with grace and generosity. Right then, Miss Crawford appeared in the doorway clutching the over-large, red-leather-bound lodge calendar.

'Sorry, Father. I was just going to make an appointment for this young lady.'

He looked at her and then back to me. And back to her again. And then he hesitated slightly before saying, 'I can see her, Miss Crawford.'

'You, Father?' Her eyes widened in surprise and disapproval.

He deliberated on her implied scepticism. 'Yes.' He nodded. 'I think I can see her.' And then he waved his arm in the direction of the door and we passed through a hallway into a small office, leaving Miss Crawford's dropped jaw behind.

He sat at the desk with his elbows resting on it. Palms clasped together in prayer.

'How can I help?'

So I told him about being married to Pao. And the British army. And Colonel Stephenson.

'I can hear your dilemma and your distress, Mrs Wong, but how do you think a priest can be of help?'

'Wong is not my married name.'

He looked at me quizzically but tenderly. And he waited.

'Maybe I just need someone to talk to.'

'I see.'

I gazed out of the floor-length window and let my eyes follow the gardener as he cut the lawn with a machete in one hand and a long, thick stick in the other. Catching the grass between the blade and upright pole. Shorter and neater than any mower would have managed.

'The truth is, Father, I want to enquire about a divorce.'

He was startled, almost sitting back in his chair with alarm. And then, after considering me for some good time, he said, 'That is completely out of the question and you know it.'

'My husband is a crook, Father. Involved in the worst evils of man's weaknesses. Gambling, racketeering. Don't you think that is enough reason?'

'I am not talking about reason. I am talking about the Church's view on such matters.'

'Perhaps an annulment then.'

'Miss Wong. Really.' He scrutinised me a little more. 'And on what grounds would you be proposing this?'

I braced myself and delivered my carefully researched and practised answer. 'That my husband is incapable of discharging the duties and obligations of marriage because of his immoral and illegal activities, which I believe demonstrate a serious personality disorder.'

He smiled. 'No.' And then after a brief pause he said, 'How do you know all of this about him?'

'I know, Father, believe me. The British army is also aware of him. Even my father knows.'

He unfurled his hands and stood. Panicking that he was about to dismiss me I hastily added, 'Is there any chance Rome would consider special dispensation?'

He was exasperated. 'The Church is highly unlikely to grant such a request.'

'I am in a desperate situation, Father.' This I said with as much pleading in my eyes as I could muster.

His compromise was to offer to meet with me. On a regular basis. Really I think with every intention of counselling me out of wanting the divorce. Because Yang Pao, Father Kealey was sure, had many redeeming qualities that we should seek to discover.

'And, who knows, perhaps in the fullness of time your husband will find his way to a more wholesome livelihood. And a better life. Let us put our faith in God, shall we?'

Why I agreed? Because I wanted to feel hope. How he wanted to begin? In the confessional. So he marched us out into the street with the sun forcing tiny beads of sweat on to his forehead, towards the copper dome of the cathedral's Byzantine roof. Past the pink oleander hedges and the statue of Our Lady where I had posed for so many wedding photographs. Through the main doors. Weaving our way along the red, blue, green and gold of the murals and wall art, and inlaid brass leaves now fading and fragile with decades of age and moisture.

And then, looking up, I saw the white faces of the Holy Trinity and the choir of angels surrounding them, and the ceiling with its rays of gold and tiled message, 'This is the Church of the Living God. The Pillar and Ground of Truth.'

Father Kealey pulled open the confessional's heavy velvet curtain and stood back for me to enter. I obliged, kneeling down at the window to wait while he seated himself in the adjoining compartment. Once settled, he slid open the wooden screen covering the wire mesh between us. I crossed myself. In the name of the Father, the Son and the Holy Spirit. Amen.

And then I began. 'Bless me, Father, for I have sinned. It has been ...' But what could I say? I had no real recollection. So I just said: '... five years since my last confession.' And my sins? There were so many. 'I have disobeyed my mother and detested her for dreadful deeds. Deeds I have not forgiven. I have quarrelled with her and criticised her for her failings. I have hurt people.' And then, for good measure, I added, 'I have committed impure acts and taken the name of God in vain. And, through my own fault, missed Mass on Sundays.' I thought that would give him a sense of it. Even if it hadn't covered all of the terrible things I had done. Like thinking about killing myself, which I knew was something no Catholic should ever admit to. Especially not to a priest.

He gave me my penance, and then I repeated the Act of Contrition that had left my lips so many times as a schoolgirl.

'O my God, I am heartily sorry for having offended Thee, and I detest all my sins because of Thy just punishments, but most of all because they offend Thee, my God, Who art all good and deserving of all my love. I firmly resolve, with the help of Thy grace, to sin no more and to avoid the near occasions of sin. Amen.'

Father Kealey waited in a pew while I knelt at the altar praying to God to forgive me, and then we walked back to Bishop's Lodge together. In silence. Where he consulted his diary to arrange our first appointment. When I left, the gardener offered me some cut flowers from the garden, which I took back to Matthews Lane and stood in a vase in the bedroom to show willing. Did absolution bring me peace? Yes.

But it didn't change my circumstances. And no amount of 'Our Fathers' and 'Hail Marys' was going to fix that. I needed some information about communists to report to Stephenson because no matter how much I explained to him that Zhang was no revolutionary, or not any longer, the colonel was having none of it.

'You haven't been asking the right questions.' 'Pay better attention.' 'Take your time.' That is all he said to me from across the desk in his orderly office or strolling along the edge of the parade ground as we watched grown men with rifles over their shoulders marching like toy soldiers.

Another time he snapped at me, 'I am not interested in the PNP and their antics with the 4H's.'

'But Mr Manley is purging the party, Colonel. Most likely Hart and Henry will be ejected with Frank and Ken Hill when the tribunal reports.'

'I told you a long time ago that they are communists. Their moment has come, that is all.'

'It doesn't matter to you?'

'Every communist matters,' he barked. 'Remember that. But what you talk about is common knowledge, Private Wong. Every casual reader of the *Gleaner* knows about the Marxist sympathisers in the PNP.' He twiddled his baton and then stuck it back under his arm. 'What I want you to do is concentrate on the Chinese. Tell me something I don't already know.'

And what a lot there was to concentrate on. Because not only was there a mammoth number of businesses in downtown Kingston, but also a huge range of organisations attending to every aspect of Chinese life and death. Including wholesalers, bakers, retailers, soda-fountain and restaurant associations; the Chinese Freemasons Society, the Chinese Athletic Club and the Chinese Benevolent Association which funded and operated the Chinese Benevolent Society Temple, the Chinese Public School, old folks' home, sanatorium and cemetery. Plus, Chinese and English-language newspapers like the *Chinese Public News*, *Pagoda Magazine*, *Chung San News* and the *Min Chi Weekly*, variously supporting the Kuomintang and Chiang Kai-shek or alternatively Mao Zedong and his communists, which bickered back and forth their opposing political opinions.

But no matter how many garden parties I attended, or how much I went from one organisation to the next volunteering my services, my inability to speak Chinese was an insurmountable barrier. Sometimes even a source of amusement or simple dismissal. Despite my Hakka heritage.

I asked Papa for his help. 'Office work, Fay? You?' He swallowed some more chicken soup. 'What you know about that?' Mr Lowe placed the steamed rice and roast duck down on the table.

'I know, Papa. They teach you everything at Immaculate.' No need to mention the British army.

'Good school.' He thought about it. 'Maybe Cecil Fong can help you. Put in good word in right place.'

'Thank you, Papa.'

The duck was sweet and tender. Succulent. 'Anyway,' I said to him, 'how come you never taught me Chinese or sent me to any lessons?'

'Your mama wasn't in favour.' He scooped some rice into his mouth. 'She say you Jamaican. No need learn Chinese or find out about Hakka traditions. Not like other people send children back to China. Besides, when your time come it was war. You know, with Japanese invasion. Travel not safe.'

Cecil was secretary to the Wholesale Provision Merchants' Association. The position he found for me was helping out at the Tower Street temple, where I typed and filed and dealt with general enquiries. As best I could. Without any Chinese. And even though I felt bad about getting Papa involved I still went there three times a week to listen to what I could listen to. And learn what I could learn.

And it was there, one busy Sunday morning, as he was descending the steps after having chanted his respect and devotion to his ancestors, that I overheard Lue Fah Yee. He was talking to his brother about a letter he had written to the newspaper complaining about its fervent anti-communist stand and his outrage at its unashamed propagandising on behalf of the Chiang Kai-shek government in Taiwan. How furious its response had made him. He felt like burning the place down.

I didn't think too much about it at the time. After all, emotion was running high with the public airing of disagreements and frustration between old-guard Kuomintang supporters and pro-communists, many of them young men recently returned from China.

It wasn't until I heard about the fire at the newspaper office. And Stephenson was pressing me for what I knew and I told him about Lue Fah Yee, because before that I had told him precious little. And in that one moment of carelessness, in which I was more concerned about accounting for myself than weighing the consequences of my actions, I started a sequence of events that really I would have foreseen had I bothered to pay better attention.

The army arrested Lue. Marching him from his grocery store like a common criminal. Telling his assistant to inform

Lue's wife that he was being detained. Indefinitely. If she wanted more information she should go up to the camp. I was in the office when I heard about it. Trying to get as much information as I could out of the boy delivering the boxes of incense sticks while pretending it had nothing to do with me. Like it was idle curiosity. But all he had was gossip. Handcuffs, some people said. Others said no. They just had two soldiers, one either side of him, with a sergeant leading the way.

'Did they say what they arresting him for?'

The boy shrugged his shoulders. 'Deh just ask him name and when he say Lue, deh say he 'ave fi go wid dem.'

'That is all?'

'I don't know nothing else, miss. Dat is all I hear tell.'

The next day when the bakery boy brought the coconut buns and pineapple tarts he told us that it had to do with the fire.

'Are yu sure?'

'Nobody not sure 'bout nothing. His wife been up there, but deh not telling her nothing neither. Only thing she say is that deh musta give him a beating because di man all mash up in di face and moving like he hurt all over.'

'So they let her see him then?' I looked over at Cecil Fong taking an interest as he sorted through the arrangements for the next meeting of the Merchants' Association.

'Through a hole in di door. Like a window wid a little wood shutter dat deh slide 'cross after di two minute deh let her land eyes on him.'

'Bad situation then,' Cecil said. Almost distractedly. Flicking over the papers as he leant against the grey metal filing cabinet.

Then he turned to me. 'Yu hear Maurice Chin want to invite the new policeman to the meeting?'

'New policeman?'

'The one they just bring from Montego Bay and put in North Street station to fight corruption in the downtown area.'

'Really?' I said, thinking of Pao. 'So is that going to happen?'

'Chin say he want the policeman to tell us what he going do to help the Chinese merchants' community.' And then he winked at me, a big overblown closure of the right eye, before he said, 'As if we don't already know how to tek care a things ourselves.' And I at once felt flushed with embarrassment. So much did I colour up even my ears were on fire. That surprised I was by his unprecedented directness.

'Leave di buns right there,' he said and flicked the boy a sixpence. 'We have business to attend to.'

All I heard after that was how Lue seemed to be getting worse. More and more fatigued. Skinny. Withdrawn. And then I heard that they'd let him go. No charges. Turned out the fire had been an accident. Some kind of electrical problem. I breathed a sigh of relief. The other thing, with Cecil. That was his idea of a joke. Just wanted to let me know that he knew who I was. Not that I'd been trying to hide it. More like I preferred to be known as Henry Wong's daughter rather than the wife of Yang Pao. Godfather of Chinatown. Although he always referred to himself as Uncle.

The next time I saw Lue was in the temple, on a Sunday morning a little while later. He looked thin and haggard with his skin practically hanging off his bones. Like he'd aged twenty years in a matter of weeks. He wasn't running his shop any more. So Cecil told me. His brother was doing it, with the help of Lue's assistant.

When I asked Colonel Stephenson about it he just said, 'Some you win. Some you lose.' I knew he was single-minded about communists, but even so, how could he be this cold-hearted and callous about the suffering of an innocent man? Suffering inflicted by him and his men. That took me aback. And in that one moment I knew never to expect any leniency or mercy from him.

How I felt about Lue Fah Yee? Ashamed and disgusted. At myself. And so very sorry that I had involved Papa. Even if I was the only person who knew what had transpired as a result of my selfishness.

Stephenson told me to forget about Lue Fah Yee. 'There are plenty more fish in Chinatown.'

When I told him that most of the Chinese were not communists but enthusiastic Chiang Kai-shek devotees who had come to Jamaica to escape Mao and his policies, he didn't believe me.

All he said was, 'You are not paying attention. Mao Zedong would not be in charge of China right now if it were not for the fact that under the bed of every Chinese there is a communist. Hiding. Lying in wait.' And then he flexed his shoulders in a circular movement as if to relax them and said, 'I suggest you concentrate on what is close at hand.'

'Sir?'

'Zhang Xiuquan.'

I swallowed hard. Not only because I'd promised myself never to tell Stephenson anything else ever again, but because the Zhang I had come to know was genuine and sincere. Why would I betray him like that?

'Zhang?' Papa looked up from his inventory. Checking off boxes of liquor against the list in his hand, standing in the semi-dark of the wine merchants with its stacked shelves and long mahogany counter at the far end.

'The saviour of Chinatown. From the moment he land and put stop to all the looting and burning and murder that negroes visit upon Chinese shopkeepers. In 1912. When the police still prejudice against us.' He ticked off items on the paper. With the pencil he tucked back behind his ear. And then he sat down on the high-backed chair-stool he liked so much. And folded his arms. 'Even 1938 open riots in streets. You too young to remember. And politicians snubbing their nose at us. One time, 1940, shopkeeper get killed when he closing up. Murdered just like that. By some rascal who just step foot inside shop and finish him off. When trial happen, judge declare death accident. That is how it was, Fay. Zhang? All he do is help people defend themself and their livelihood.'

What Zhang told me?

'More than three thousand chests opium every year did British East India Company smuggle into China.' He was sitting in his rocking chair. By the side of the duck pond. Late one afternoon. Under the shade of the small banana tree in the yard. 'For fifty long years. The people? Zombies. Could not lift heads. Never mind do day's work. When Chinese author-ities want them stop, British send warships and soldiers. How end? China beaten into ground and have to pay foreigners war

169

indemnities. Imagine that. Pay them for destruction they bring upon us. And open Chinese cities for foreign trade. Christian missionaries allowed to spread their religion. Let British and French hire Chinese labour in colonies. Force give Hong Kong to British. Worst part? Opium trade legalised. Can you believe that?'

He paused, sipping his tea as he rocked back and forth. 'What we fight for? No more foreigners and warlords ruling over us.' He lowered an arm to shoo away the ducks gathering at his feet. 'And after all that? Japanese. You know where Japanese get war materials they use against us? United States. How about that? The United States of America.'

He turned to me wide-eyed and jutted out his chin. 'You think Mao wrong to want decent life for masses? Honest work. Roof over head. Food in stomach. Liberty, equality, fraternity?'

How could I argue with that? Wasn't that exactly what the workers on the buses, railway, public works, post office, printing office, prisons and hospitals had marched and gone on strike for? And which, at Isaac's side, I had supported.

So as Hurricane Charlie swept over the island, with howling winds that tossed and buffeted and tore roofs from buildings and sent everything that wasn't bolted to the ground flying through the air, leaving fallen trees, telegraph and electric poles, destruction and death in its wake, all I could think of was the dirt yards of West Kingston, and the shacks and standpipes that no longer stood in the shanty towns of the city.

Afterwards, I asked Sissy: 'What was it like growing up in West Kingston?'

She removed the ice-cream spoon from her mouth. Rested it on the saucer and then turned to me as we sat next to each other at the soda fountain.

'Like? It was like hell. Di people not called di sufferers fah nothing.'

I swallowed down the shame of my thoughtlessness. 'No, I guess not.'

Then she said, 'There is something I want to talk to yu 'bout.' And that is when she told me about Pao 'visiting di house deh 'cross di road'.

'The house I think you mean? That house?'

'Same one.'

'The prostitutes?'

Sissy shrugged. 'Men will be men.' And then she said, 'Come on, let's go tek a walk before yu fall down off dat stool.'

We strolled out of the pharmacy and headed towards Half Way Tree, past the coconut cart and the smell of hot, roasted peanuts.

'I wasn't sure if I should tell yu but it seem to me a woman ought to know a thing like that.' She paused. 'About her husband. Even if it only so she can have di chance to protect herself.' She looked at me. 'And who else going tell yu?'

'Protect myself?'

She stopped walking and turned towards me. 'From disease.'

'Disease?' My voice raised high in dismay.

'Yu nuh know what I am talking about?'

And then she told me and my absolute revulsion made me realise that my life could not be worse.

The final twist of the knife? The sea salt in the wound? Was when I found out that Pao, not satisfied with the three visits a week he was making to the whores across the road, had also dug deep into his pocket in Chen's jewellery store for a 24-carat gold and jade necklace the likes of which so enthralled the assistant that he couldn't resist asking me, 'Did you like the necklace, Miss Fay?'

'The necklace?'

'That your husband buy for you.' And then, grinning from ear to ear with delight, 'It one of the most beautiful pieces I think I ever sell. Worth every penny. I'm sure you must agree.'

The embarrassment rose in me so swiftly that I couldn't remember what I had gone into the store for. So when he asked, 'How can I help you today?' there was nothing I had to say in response. I just gathered myself, turned and hurried out of the door.

And then Sissy told me about the argument over the necklace that had taken place across the road and that is when I knew that the whore Pao was seeing was the country bumpkin, Gloria Campbell.

I felt like I was drowning. Being pulled underwater by Stephenson's British army tugging on one leg, and marriage to Pao dragging like a concrete weight on the other. And then Beverley told me that all I had to do to secure an immediate army discharge was to get pregnant. So that was the plan, however disagreeable to implement. Consoling myself with the fact that it was no worse than being with Isaac. But how was I going to get pregnant if I had to protect myself the way Sissy said?

CHAPTER 14

FATHER MICHAEL DIDN'T seem to care when I told him about
Gloria Campbell. Maybe he thought consorting with prostitutes was no worse than all the other things Pao was doing.

'Men fall, Fay.'

'Fall?'

'From grace.'

'I hope you are not going to tell me because they are
tempted by women. Like Adam and Eve and the apple.'

We'd stopped meeting in the office at Bishop's Lodge.
Now we were driving around in the Father's cream and
peppermint-green Chevy. An old battle-axe of a car with
cracked and creaking leather seats but with a shine you could
see your face in and an engine that ran as smooth as silk. We'd
also started to take long walks in the botanical gardens or travel
out to catch the breeze at Port Royal. Sometimes we sat under
the mango tree at Lady Musgrave Road, because even though
Mama had all her feelings about me being there, she couldn't
actually bring herself to keep turning me away. Not repeat-
edly. And especially not after Papa told her to leave me be.

She didn't like it, though. Father Kealey being at the house. So every time we sat on the veranda she made sure she was inside thumping down on the piano, singing about hell and damnation and how sinners will forever die because they are greedy for eternal pain. That was what made the far-off mango tree more comfortable. Me gliding gently back and forth in the cool swing, my hands gripping the rope. Michael, because that is what he told me to call him, sitting on a chair we had Ethyl bring from inside.

'Fay,' because that is what I told him to call me, 'that particular fall had to be. It was the making of humankind in all our fallible glory. For how do we learn anything except by trial and error? Except from experience.'

He rearranged the skirt of his cassock. Tidied himself. 'After all, what was Eve's sin except to believe that she could exercise her power of choice? Albeit enchanted by a trickster. And Adam, what was his sin? Desire for the fruit of knowledge. And those sins, Fay, wanting to know and wanting to choose, plague us all each and every day. Every one of us who is obliged to walk this earth and make sense of our existence.'

I was, and remained, captivated by the sound of his deep, even voice. Steady and deliberate. And the precise way in which he thought about things and expressed himself.

Another time he told me, 'This talk of divorce is because you imagine there is an alternative. But what is the alternative, Fay? A woman on her own with nothing to guide her. Nothing to hold on to but her freedom. Excommunicated from the Church and her salvation. Is that the loneliness you want?'

Was that the price I had to pay? Loneliness? For wanting to know who I was and understand my fall; and decide for myself where ignorance or innocence had been an adequate excuse for the mistakes I had made. Was that the price for understanding what I would do if I could exercise free will? Or was I like Eve? Choosing a forbidden kind of life simply because I assumed I should have the right to do so. Whether or not I understood the consequences.

Those were my questions, and my aspirations, while Michael's desires were becoming increasingly unclear, because what he seemed to want, more and more, was my presence and my attention. My freshness, he once told me, was 'like a spirited shower of rain cooling a hot afternoon'. What I saw was the delight in his eyes every time we met.

I didn't protect myself like Sissy told me. I couldn't figure out how I could do it and get pregnant at the same time. So when the army doctor confirmed to me that the deed was done all I did was count my blessings.

Before I left Up Park Camp I telephoned Beverley but could not reach her. So I went back to Lady Musgrave Road. Daphne was there. And on a wild impulse I just grabbed her hand and said, 'Come on, let's go down to Nathan's and do some shopping.'

'What you so happy about?'

'I'm celebrating.' She raised her brows. 'I'm pregnant.'

Ethyl was standing in the doorway as we walked down the veranda steps. I wondered if I should have been more discreet. But then I thought, What the hell. Everybody is going to find out sooner or later.

We exhausted every department in the store, and then we ate chicken and rice and peas, and took in a movie. When we got back to the house it was late. All I wanted to do was step into the shower and go to bed, but instead what I had to face was Mama, dressed in her nightgown and robe, telling me that Pao had been there earlier in the evening.

'What did he want?'

'Want?' she shouted. 'His wife. What do you think he wanted?'

She did not wait for a response. 'Yu think yu can spend your whole life running between here and Matthews Lane? When are you going to settle down, girl, and realise you have responsibilities?' And then she walked into her bedroom and slammed the door. Hard.

The next morning I got up early and left. I was standing in the driveway fiddling with the car key in the lock when Daphne appeared on the veranda.

'Where you going now?'

'To see Beverley.'

She looked down at the ground, kicking her foot like a two-year-old doing a soft-shoe shuffle. Except Daphne was nineteen years old now. Out of school with nothing to do.

'You want to come?'

She looked up, suddenly bright-eyed as she ran down the steps and got into the car, the beaten-up old green Dodge that I'd bought off a used-car lot the same afternoon, months ago, that the sergeant signed the slip and tore off the voucher for me to collect my licence.

Beverley was eating breakfast on the back veranda. Corned beef fried with onions. With an egg on the side. 'So it's official. No mistake?'

'It was an army doctor, Beverley. So the discharge papers are on their way.' I smiled a big, broad, full-teeth grin.

She held up her coffee cup. 'I told you.' And then a toast. 'To freedom.'

'I still have a baby to contend with.'

'Oh that. We've done all of that before.'

'No, Beverley. I'm going to keep it.'

She turned to me, astonished. 'Yu serious?'

I nodded. Daphne shifted about in the chair next to me. Her mind was turning over so hard I could almost hear the grinding of her questions drifting over the backyard.

I turned to her. 'That was just something that happen a long time ago, Daphne. It don't concern anybody so you just forget about it. You understand me? Not a word of this are you to mention to anyone. And nothing about the army either. Not a single soul.'

And then I glared at her with such intensity that she knew with absolute certainty I was not to be crossed over this. Beverley broke the silence.

'Well, we have cause for celebration. What do you want to do?'

I thought about it and then I said, 'Let's go dancing. You and Audley, Tyrone and Cynthia. Just like we used to.'

Beverley looked at me kind-heartedly. 'Are you sure?'

I knew what she meant. Without Freddie. 'Yes,' I said. And then I became aware of Daphne sitting there.

'Would you like to come?' I asked her, cementing our new-found conspiracy. She nodded enthusiastically. So that would be our first time socialising together.

When we got back to Lady Musgrave Road, Pao was there. Standing in the driveway. Daphne scurried inside the house.

'What you doing here, Pao?'

'What you doing here, Fay?'

'This is my home.'

'No, this is your papa's home. Your home is with me, downtown in Matthews Lane.'

I thought: not for much longer because after the discharge comes divorce. But I didn't say it. I just walked off and he followed me up the steps on to the veranda. God knows why, because all I wanted to do was see the back of him. What he wanted, Pao, was to quarrel and complain about how a wife is supposed to stay with her husband and not make a fool out of him running back to her papa every other day of the week. It was laughable. But just as I made to go inside he grabbed my hand and that turned on my anger like water from a pipe.

'Take your hands off me.' And we started to argue, which I think was actually the first time for us, yelling and screaming at each other like that.

'You are not downtown now with your little whores and hoodlums. You are in a respectable place and you need to act like it.'

'You think this is respectable, you and me bawling at each other right out here on the veranda?'

'You should be the last person on this earth to talk about what is respectable. If you weren't so pathetic you would make me laugh.'

But then two things happened. First, the look he fixed me with. So completely cold. So absolutely terrifying. I'd never seen anything like it before. It ran through me like a shard of ice piercing my entire body. The second thing. He asked me if it was true I was pregnant. And I wondered how he knew, before remembering Ethyl in the doorway. So the news was out. Sooner rather than later. Did it matter? Did I care?

'Remember you are a Catholic.' That made my blood boil. The insolence of him to assume to threaten me with that.

Then he reached into his pocket, pulled out a small box wrapped in the familiar green tissue of Chen's jewellery store and offered it to me.

'Take it.'

'What is it?'

'Take it and see.' I reached out and took it from him even though, really, I didn't want to. I didn't want to unwrap it either but he coaxed me into doing so. When I saw the ring I thought my heart had stopped beating. Because all I could see was the dark green of the jade and the subtle sparkle of the expensive gold band. And all I could think about was what the assistant had said to me in the store.

So I reached into the box, picked up the ring, raised my arm and threw it as far as I could into the yard.

'That would be the companion piece to the jade necklace you bought for your whore in East Kingston.' And then, staring directly at him, 'You think I didn't know?' And I walked inside the house and closed the door, displaying an outer strength of character that was a complete contradiction to the humiliation I felt inside. The shame of having been offered a gift meant for a prostitute. From my own husband. And at the gossip that would abound from the fact that he had spent six times more on her than on me.

And the most insulting yet, the idea that my forgiveness and affection could be bought with a piece of gold. Was I really that much of a spoilt brat?

CHAPTER 15

DAPHNE TURNED OUT to be quite a good companion for our evening at Club Havana. Taking to the floor with Audley and Tyrone like she'd danced with them a hundred times before. Turning and swirling in their arms. I didn't even know where she'd learnt to move like that. Laughing with an abandon I had never ever seen. Swallowing the beer straight from the bottle and licking her lips to savour every last drop of that bitter taste. She was like a butterfly that night, emerging from her chrysalis. Radiant as she spread her wings.

'You not going to tell Mama, are you?'

'You don't want her to know?'

She looked at me with wide, fearful eyes. 'I don't think she would approve.' And then she lowered her gaze to the table.

So what I told Mama was that we were at Grandmother Chung's, which actually wasn't much more palatable than the truth. But at least it didn't immediately conjure for her a vision of men intoxicated with drink and driven uncontrollably to lust by the devil's pulsating rhythms.

The important thing about it was that Daphne and I finally recognised each other. Saw the other as a separate being. Distinct from Mama and who she thought we were. No longer viewing each other as though through her eyes.

And the important thing about that was that when the headaches started I had someone to tell. Not that Beverley lacked sympathy but she took things less seriously so that in the end it was Daphne who put me in the cab and held my hand as she sat next to me on the way to the hospital. Because, as ordinary as it seemed – the vomiting, dizziness, sore breasts; even the itchy, blurry eyes, which everyone told me was normal – I always knew something was wrong. How? Because I could feel my body telling me that lying in a dark room with a cold compress on my head, and drinking plenty liquid, and eating and resting, wasn't going to solve the uneasiness I felt deep inside.

When I told Dr Howard about the numerous trips to the toilet, dramatic mood swings and craving for pickled vegetables and hot red-pepper sauce, he laughed. And the pain in my chest?

'Do you mean your stomach or your chest?'

'In my chest, doctor. But low down. Not high.'

'So in your stomach then.'

'Not exactly.'

He scribbled in my case notes lying open on his desk. Then he said, 'Indigestion. Maybe a little heartburn. Some milk of magnesia should do the trick.'

When I talked to him about the exhaustion he said, 'What do you expect, carrying all that extra weight? In this heat. Bound to feel a little tired, don't you think?'

My anxiety? 'A little hypertension. Nothing to worry about.'

So I just carried on doing everything the same way I always did. Worrying as I went. Especially when the swelling started. Not too noticeable at first, but it was definitely there, in my hands and feet and face. And as it became more pronounced, so too did the headaches increase that everyone said I should have gotten over by now. So it was Daphne, the afternoon she pressed my hand and left an indentation, who made the decision that we should go to the hospital.

And even after we arrived Dr Howard was still unconvinced. It was the skinny nurse in the starched, white cap who said to him, 'She is swelling, doctor,' which forced him to look at me properly. 'How long has this been going on?' When I told him, he said, 'Why didn't you come to me sooner?'

'Because I have been coming and coming only to be told that everything was fine and just as to be expected.'

And Daphne added, 'She thought she was becoming a nuisance.'

That was when the nurse stepped back through the door – I hadn't even noticed she had gone – with two porters and a trolley that they put me on and wheeled me to a private room.

What happened after that I have no idea. There was a drip feeding something into my arm. I could feel that. People were coming and going. I could sense that. But mostly what I did was drift in and out of sleep. So tired I could barely keep my eyes open for more than five minutes at a time.

High blood pressure. Protein in my urine. And a busyness in the room that had a distinct air of concern bordering on panic.

Sometimes when I came to Daphne or Beverley would be there. Michael too. Papa. And Pao. But the moment I knew for sure that I was dying was when I opened my eyes and saw my mother sitting by the bedside. Still and composed and silent. I just lay there gazing at her without saying a word because I had never seen her like that before. With a face absent of criticism or disdain, and a tongue devoid of cruelty. For the first time in my life she actually looked like she didn't hate me. So when I involuntarily closed my eyes again I was convinced it was for the last time.

What shocked me back to life was the sound of his tiny voice. Crying out because he wanted me to wake up and know that he was here. How he managed to get born without me I didn't know. It was almost like I'd slept through the whole thing while he, determined as he was, brought himself into the world. When the nurse placed him in my arms I felt a surge of energy. An electric current pulsing through an invisible umbilical cord. Direct from him to me. A gift of life.

I put my face to his tiny body and breathed in. And what I smelt was vanilla. Not the essence you get from a bottle but an actual open vanilla pod. Fresh and warm and damp. Soft and tingling sweet. I pulled back the shawl to check if the yellowness was all over him, not just in his face. And it was, which surprised me because in some distant dream I thought I heard someone say he was blue. So I guess it had been both. Blue from the breech birth and being so premature. Yellow from the jaundice because my liver had been failing so badly. So much so that they had him in a tiny cabinet with a fluorescent lamp for days trying to get as much light as possible on to his skin. There he lay with minute goggles over his eyes like he was sunning himself on the beach.

When that was over everything went back to normal. I was just another extremely tired mother with a healthy baby boy. And Mama never came back, despite me spending three weeks in the hospital drifting in and out of sleep and recovering from the trauma of what had happened. Vowing that I would never put myself through it again.

That Michael came to the bedside with rosary in hand did not surprise me. The most holy of rosaries. The Seven Sorrows of Mary. The prophesy of Simeon; the flight into Egypt; the loss of the child Jesus in the temple; the meeting of Jesus and Mary on the way to Calvary; Mary stands at the foot of the cross; Mary receives the dead body of Jesus in her arms; Jesus is placed in the tomb.

The suffering of Mary. That is what it was all about. Her suffering in union with her divine son who was made to be born and suffer and die to save mankind. Prayed by Michael with an open and repentant heart so that I could have God's forgiveness for my sins and my soul would be free from guilt and remorse. Because he, like everyone else, was convinced I was about to die.

'Hail Mary, full of grace. The Lord is with thee. Blessed art thou among women, and blessed is the fruit of thy womb, Jesus. Holy Mary, Mother of God, pray for us sinners, now and at the hour of our death. Amen.'

What did surprise me was Pao. Sitting there day after day looking at me in earnest even though he had nothing to say. Wringing his hands most of the time because he didn't know what to do with them, although in his heart I knew he wanted to touch me. So every now and again I reached out and stroked his arm just to let him know that I appreciated him being there, because, despite everything, right then it seemed appropriate that he should be there and fitting that I should be grateful.

And lying there like that, looking at him so quiet and fretful, I understood for the first time that he wasn't any different from Isaac. Doing what he thought he had to do to survive. And then I remembered what Michael had said to me. 'The fall, Fay, does not happen in one sudden transgression. It occurs in incremental stages. In tiny steps almost insignificant in themselves, imperceptible to the naked eye.'

So I thought of Pao, a bewildered youth of fourteen, marooned in a strange land. Disorientated but grateful for being saved from the Japanese and a war-torn China. Fatherless. In search of a new beginning. A new identity. A new home. Being instructed by Zhang into what my own father considered an honourable way of life. For wasn't Zhang the saviour of Chinatown? A hero of the people. Why wouldn't the young Pao follow in his footsteps? First one thing and then the next. Sweep and stack. Run some errands for the shopkeepers. Collect Zhang's gambling money from the *pai-ke-p'iao*. Then the war, and Zhang retires. So he expands, purloined chickens and eggs; surplus goods from the US navy; glut from the wharf; Gloria Campbell and her friends.

Incremental stages just like Michael said. And before you know what, Yang Pao is no longer a boy but has become a man and the Uncle of Chinatown. 'Uncle,' he once told me, 'because Uncle is family. He not yu papa but he watch over yu just the same. He got your interests at heart.'

Sitting there in the hospital he didn't even look threatening. No fiendish hoodlum, just a terrified husband and father hoping against all odds that everything would work out alright.

'Yu want me to go get yu something? To eat. To drink.'

I shook my head slowly from side to side. 'No.' And then after a short while I said, 'Just sit there. It's nice to see you.' Which made him smile and relax the tension that was gripping his body.

And after some more silence: 'The baby looking good. All the yellow gone and he eating and everything just fine.'

I smiled. 'Yes. So the nurse told me.'

'I been thinking 'bout names and I wonder if it alright with you if I call him Xiuquan after Zhang and my brother.'

'Your brother who went to America?'

He nodded. Funny thing was I hadn't thought of the baby as Chinese. Not as Chinese as that name. I'd seen him as Jamaican. And even though I was anxious that the name Xiuquan would set him apart and make him feel an outsider in the way I had done my entire life, I still said, 'Yes, OK.' Because right then I thought I owed it to Pao. To give him something to salvage from this mess of a marriage with me.

When Papa came that evening he said Hong Xiuquan was the peasant schoolteacher who led the Taiping Uprising when the masses took up arms against the foreign capitalists, feudal landlords and Qing ruling class who had, through burdensome taxes, driven them to poverty, bankruptcy and the menace of death from starvation.

'A man who way back in 1845 wanted to confiscate land and give it to poor. And have equality between women and men. How about that, Fay? Long before Sun Yat-sen talk of liberty, equality and fraternity.'

'So you think it's a good name for the child?'

'Me?' He held his palm to his chest. 'I am not saying anything about baby. I am remembering Hong, that is all. Hong like me. Hong Zilong.'

Beverley was indifferent. 'Well, I suppose if that is what he wants.'

Daphne: 'I think it is nice he wants to name him after Zhang. Wants to show that respect to his stepfather and benefactor, if you like.'

Michael said nothing but his face fell.

'You don't like it?'

'It is not for me to like or otherwise.'

But his refusal to speak up didn't fool me. So I just asked point blank, 'What is it?' Because that was the level of intimacy between us. No longer parishioner and priest.

And after a slight hesitation he said, 'The name Karl came to me.'

'Came to you? Where from?'

'It just came to me.'

'Don't be coy, Michael. It came from somewhere.'

He eased back in the chair. 'There was a child I came across when I was at the seminary.'

'In Washington?'

'Yes. He was just a few months old. Sick with meningitis, which they thought he would not survive so his mother sent for a priest and I accompanied him.' He paused. 'Father Perry and I held hands with the baby's mother and prayed all through the day and night non-stop for three days, until his fever broke and the doctor said he might be through the worst. And after that we carried on visiting and praying. And three weeks later he recovered and was sent home. That was the healing power of faith.'

'And the baby was called Karl?'

When I was finally well enough to go back to Matthews Lane it seemed like I had left the old world and was about to re-enter a completely different one. Or maybe I came back as a different person because I no longer resented the squalor quite as much as before, or felt as agitated by Ma's high-pitch whining, barking in Chinese like every utterance was the continuation of some ongoing argument. I didn't even feel that irritated by Pao any more.

Why? Because I had faced death and survived. And Karl too had faced death and survived. So maybe God had not forsaken me after all.

'He just like Pao when he baby.'

Ma had Karl gripped under his armpits, tossing him into the air and catching him again.

'Pao strong baby and smart. Very smart. He learn everything quicker than any baby and he happy. His papa throw him up in air and Pao laugh. Just like throw baby.' And up she hurled him again while I held on to the table to steady myself of my anxiety, which was soon relieved as she quickly tired from her exertion.

Then she talked to me, for the first time, about missing China. The rice fields and open skies. The village. The farm. Missing Pao's father, now dead so many years. Murdered by British and French soldiers, Pao told me, supporting strikers on a peaceful march. Missing Xiuquan, Pao's brother who went to America in 1943, to help with wartime farm work.

'Ah,' she said. 'Too much talk 'bout miss. What good it do you? This happen, that happen. War, death, a new country, a son leave, a baby born. Who tell the world to make these things happen? That is why the Buddha say to be happy is to suffer less, and to suffer less is to be free from wanting.'

I realised then that I had lived in the house for almost two years, on and off, and still had no idea who this woman was. Actually, I couldn't even remember ever having had a conversation with her. And now suddenly here she was with her own past, her own sorrows. Suffering that she let go of with an attitude that said: 'You accept what you have. Now I am here with Pao and Zhang.'

I was there with Pao and Karl even though his birth certificate said Xiuquan and everyone in the house frowned and shuffled every time I used the K word. But, in some way, it didn't matter. Because what I sensed was everyone's relief that I had finally settled. That motherhood had calmed me in some way. I was no longer running away to Lady Musgrave Road at the drop of a hat. I was changing diapers, mixing and warming and delivering feeds, bathing and dressing, making him comfortable. Even softly singing a lullaby as I rested a hand on his cot and gently rocked him into sweet slumber. It didn't even bother me when he awoke at two or three in the morning crying with hunger. Because every wave of his arm or kick of his leg or burst from his lungs was a miracle that might never have been.

The funny thing? It also made me feel more at home, with more attention to the daily grind of Matthews Lane. Of Ma and Tilly boiling and picking the saltfish and beating the batter for the fritters, plucking the duck feathers, cooking and cleaning, washing and ironing. Things I had taken for granted from a young age because a dependable army of women had tended to my every need and desire without a single murmur about the food I had left uneaten, or amount of laundry I produced, or personal items I'd left carelessly strewn, or demands I made or changed or revised. Never a complaint or suggestion of criticism did I ever hear from them, because nothing was ever too tedious or menial for them to do for me. Including Sissy brushing every strand of my hair over and over every night of the week. And Mother Murphy washing and replenishing my sanitary napkins. A ghastly chore that I continued to avoid by returning to Lady Musgrave Road at that time of every month.

But that is not how life is. Not for the majority of Jamaicans the majority of the time. Even the drudgery at Matthews Lane was still less arduous than the gruelling labour of the yards of Back-O-Wall and Trench Town. If Isaac was to be believed anyway. And what reason did I have to doubt him? Didn't Sissy herself tell me that West Kingston was hell?

'The baby,' Zhang said, 'is reminder.' He leant over the crib and gently stroked Karl's head. 'A lesson to learn from.'

'You want to hold him?' I asked.

'No. I just look and see how fresh and new he is. Like young sap. Bend in breeze. Not old man. Dry and brittle like me. He light and supple. Float on water. Not drown in sorrow.' He patted me on the shoulder. 'You not run so much since he come. Maybe you take time now. Look into own suffering. Deep. Into roots. So you understand where it come from and have compassion to make self new again. With original heart you born with. Like baby.'

And then, before turning and clattering back to his room, he said, 'No need remember unworthy deeds you do or do unto you. No need worry for past or future.' He paused and looked down at Karl with a kindly smile in his eyes. 'It time for the Buddha's other shore.'

CHAPTER 16

BEVERLEY WASN'T ENTHUSIASTIC.

'What yu want to go do a thing like that for?'

'To see for myself. To experience it.'

She sighed and turned her head away dismissively. 'Yu not going to experience anything. You are an outsider. At best a tourist. At worst a voyeur.'

I continued to stir my coffee as we sat at the small grey Formica table in the ice-cream parlour in Times Store, a convenient meeting point for Beverley as she made her way home from the ordnance depot. It was late afternoon, so the place was empty apart from us and a young couple sitting at the far end.

I changed the subject. 'You still happy being a Dues In/ Dues Out clerk?'

She brightened. 'I'm learning. I reckon when my time is done I'd like to open a store.'

I laughed, throwing my head back and letting out a great guffaw. 'Beverley Chung, Chinese shopkeeper?'

She smiled meekly. 'Why not?' Trying to sound up-beat even though I could still hear a slight defensiveness in her voice.

'Yu surprise me, that's all. I didn't expect that from you. A New York socialite, London, Paris. Maybe. But a Kingston shopkeeper? No.' And then I added, 'I guess I always thought you'd be like your grandmother. Partying and dining, and dancing the night away.'

She lowered her eyes and pouted her lips. 'Well, I'm not like GC after all. Or maybe not so much as you like to think.' At first I thought I'd offended her but then I wondered if maybe that wasn't it.

'Has something happened?' I asked. And then for no good reason whatsoever I followed it with, 'Was it to do with what you said? About her and Chiang Kai-shek.'

Beverley looked sharply at me but really I knew she was hurt. 'I thought you were supposed to be hunting out communists?'

'I didn't mean it like that.'

But no matter how much I tried to explain that I had just been careless and clumsy, Beverley would have none of it. She'd taken umbrage and could not be appeased.

Sissy said I shouldn't do it. 'Go over there? You?'

'I'm not planning to go alone.'

'I wouldn't tek yu over there. What for?' I stared at her tumbling grey hair with the pipe smoke swirling around it. 'What is it yu so interested in?'

Honestly, I didn't know, except I could feel something pulling me, an invisible force compelling me to go over there. A powerful tugging at my conscience, telling me that if I could see Bumper Hall I would understand what it meant to be poor. So poor that you would scavenge in a mountain of garbage, in the blistering sun, to salvage from it the things you needed to sustain your life. How could that be possible in a country rich in bauxite and home to the white sandy beaches and clear blue sea Americans were flocking to in their droves? How could it be possible in a country in which the likes of Fay Wong and Beverley Chung danced and dined and picked the best from Issa's or Nathan's department stores?

I knew I couldn't go over there alone. That was for sure. So I went to Cross Roads to see if Isaac was still working in the butcher's shop. And there he was standing behind the counter with his white apron covered in blood. He laughed when he saw me, showing off his big, even white teeth.

'What brings you to dis end a town?'

'To check you, Isaac.'

'Really?' He finished wrapping the pork leg and handed the parcel to the inexperienced young housemaid waiting on the other side of the counter. How I knew, despite her day clothes? The sensible black laced-up shoes, and her inattentiveness in judging the meat's suitability. No, that job would belong to some cook or housekeeper who would turn the pork over in the paper, smell it for freshness, poke the skin, prod the flesh, examine for hair, and check for fat. This girl was just on an errand which, given her negligence, she might have to run again later in the day.

She paid Isaac, took the change and squeezed past me as I stood in the open doorway. He wiped his hands on a damp, grey cloth sitting by the large, well-scarred wooden chopping board.

'So what can I do fah you? Pork chops? Minced beef? Oxtail? Chicken, maybe?'

'I've come to ask you a favour.'

When I told him what it was he said, 'No.' And then he asked me, 'What yu want to go over deh fah?'

I explained the pull I felt and then I said, 'I thought you of all people would understand.'

'Understand what?'

'That when you have benefited from privilege you have a duty to recognise it and seek to contribute to the common good.'

The thing that got to me about Bumper Hall was the stench. Pungent. Caustic. All that garbage in all that heat, brewing into a sharp and bitter cocktail that burnt its way through your nostrils. What I saw? Raggedy people climbing on heaps. Digging in and stumbling over a mess of discarded food and cans, boxes and bags, clothing, paper, furniture, shoes, old iron. Things made from cardboard and plastic, metal and wood; solid, jagged or slimy, to stub the toe or slice the sole or squelch underfoot. All amassed and jumbled together. Shifting and swaying beneath them.

And they, searching with a conviction that turned their endeavour into a vocation because what they found would be used or traded or sold. It horrified me to see it. The reality of what poverty had forced upon them.

I turned to Isaac standing next to me at the perimeter. 'Take me to Trench Town.'

'I cyan, Fay. It been years since I set foot over deh. Not since deh run me out.'

'You can, Isaac,' I said as I walked back to the Dodge and eased behind the steering wheel.

'No, Fay. It would be like taking my life into my hands.'

'Back-O-Wall then.'

What we found was alleys between zinc fences and doors, behind which the yards. And as we walked we turned into more and more a spectacle with a following crowd gathering steadily. Until someone shouted, 'Isaac Dunkley.' And they started to run.

Isaac grabbed me by the hand and set off at a pace, moving so fast I could barely keep up. Take a left here. Now a right. Weaving his way through the maze of narrow, dusty lanes with the mob gaining on us yard after yard. And then finally we turned a corner and found ourselves face to face with three of them who had veered off and circled around us. We came to a halt as we heard the rapid footsteps behind us slow and cease.

'Isaac. Yu setting up business over here now?' The voice's owner was wearing loose trousers and a shirt completely buttonless and open down the front, revealing his bare, hair-less chest. In his right hand was a piece of wood, thick and round and smooth, like it had been pared and planed, and polished over and over again. Perhaps an inch in diameter, maybe eighteen inches long. Slapping it against his left palm like a watchman with a cudgel standing his ground while the rest of them crowded in around us. Pressing their point. Their home advantage.

'So who dis yu bring wid yu?' That was coming from behind. A younger voice. Eager. Excited. More playful than menacing. But still it sent a chill through me. And then I felt a hand fingering the back of my blouse. Feeling the material like he was judging the quality of the cloth.

'Nice. Nice.' And then he moved his attention to my skirt. Stroking the fabric and the contours of my buttocks within it. 'Nice. Nice.'

Isaac became agitated. 'She not nothing to do wid you.'

'So what yu bring her here fah? Or maybe she working fah yu. On her back like how yu turn every woman yu meet.'

The fondler was getting rough and insistent. Isaac reached out and brushed his hand away.

'Yu business wid me. Yu nuh need to be bothering dis woman. Just let me walk her back to her car and yu can do what yu want wid me.'

'Serious? Do what I want?' He smiled a crooked, rotten-mouthed, toothless grin and slapped the baton against his palm once more. And then he stepped aside to make way, glaring at us as Isaac took my hand gently and we started to walk. We moved slowly and deliberately, with the whole posse follow-ing behind and the sun beating down on us making me feel faint from the heat as well as the chase and the fear.

After many turns that Isaac seemed to have memorised, we finally came around a corner and I saw the car parked in the distance. I told myself to relax. We were almost there. But as we drew closer I saw something else. The rear end of Michael's Chevy. We kept walking. And then I saw him. Pacing up and down in his black cassock in the middle of the deserted road.

He raised his eyes, saw me and rushed over. 'Fay.' He took me by the arm. 'What on earth are you doing here?'

I said nothing as we continued to walk. Michael fell in next to me. Until a voice said, 'Stop.' But Isaac didn't stop. So we heard the command for a second time. 'Stop or I will shoot.' Someone in the crowd laughed.

Michael spun around. 'Shoot! Have you taken leave of your senses?'

'Michael, no,' I whispered to him as I tried in vain to turn his body to face forward.

Then Toothless pulled out a gun, an old-fashioned Colt with a revolving cylinder straight out of a cowboy movie. He waved it around. Holding it sideways on. For effect not effectiveness.

'You,' he barked, pointing his gun at Michael. 'Get in yu car and go.' The gang became energised. Animated. Shifting from one foot to the next in anticipation.

'I'm not leaving without her.'

Toothless looked at me. 'She? Isaac's whore.' And then, turning to Michael, 'What she to you? Your whore as well?' I heard sniggering.

Isaac intervened. 'We can all just get in di car and go. And it over.'

And then he started to walk and lead me towards the Dodge. But a man in a tight khaki shirt blocked our way. Suddenly, there was a scuffle, and I was being pushed into the car by Isaac while he used his other hand to do battle with Khaki Man. And Michael had launched himself at someone else. And Toothless was shouting and making all sorts of threats, while hands were dragging me from the car and blows were being exchanged with more and more men appearing and piling into the affray. And then what I heard was a shot. A single bullet fired into the air and everything stopped.

'I not fooling wid yu people no more.' Toothless was standing there. Gun in one hand. Truncheon in the other. Then, pointing the Colt at me and waving it towards Michael's car, he said, 'Tek her over deh and lay her on di back seat.' Two men grabbed me. I struggled. Isaac lunged at Toothless, knocking away the gun and the truncheon. Michael attempted to free me. And we were all in turmoil once again.

Then someone shouted, 'Look at how he swinging him fist. Like a battyman in him frock.' And someone else shouted, 'Get him.' And suddenly they were all after Michael. And he ran. And they pursued. And Isaac followed. But I didn't have the energy. I just leant against the car trying to catch my breath. And after a while I realised I was completely alone in the abandoned street.

I gathered myself and set off walking in the direction in which they had disappeared. And although they were out of sight I could hear the harrowing din of their jeering and laughter. What I saw, when I caught up, was their backs. Formed in a tight circle. A shield against what was happening within.

I could see feet. And Isaac kneeling on the ground, his hands held high, like maybe they were clasped behind his head. And the legs of the cart. Strong and sturdy, with the wooden wheels juddering slightly like they were buckling under the strain.

And then there was Michael's voice which came to me resolute but pained. 'Hallowed be thy name. Thy kingdom come … forgive us our trespasses, as we forgive them that trespass against us.' Over and over. 'Our Father which art in heaven. Hallowed be thy name.' As the cart rocked and the crowd mocked and Isaac cowered and I, unable to force my way through the wedged wall of men, sat in the dirt. And cried.

Afterwards, as they were slowly walking away, I saw Isaac with the gun nozzle lodged against the back of his head. Red-eyed. His face streaked with the tracks of his tears. Then Toothless lowered the revolver, stuck it into the waistband of his trousers and strolled over to the cart where Michael lay prostrate. He picked up the wooden baton before wandering off down the road swinging it in his hand as he sauntered.

And even though everything in me wanted to rush towards him, I couldn't move. There was even a part of me that felt like turning away, to save Michael the shame of me seeing him like that. The shame of me knowing what had happened.

So it was Isaac who went over to him. Isaac who raised him up and tidied his cassock. Isaac who comforted him in his arms. Isaac who said to me, 'Go get di car.'

We drove back to town. Me in the Dodge and Isaac driving the Chevy with Michael prone on the back seat. We went to Cross Roads, to the closed butcher's shop where, between us, we carried Michael up the stairs to Isaac's room. We didn't even discuss it. Isaac simply pulled up at the back door and we took Michael inside.

We laid him on the bed and, while Isaac removed his torn and bloody cassock, I fetched warm water and fresh towels. Isaac washed him and settled him to rest with none of us uttering a single word.

Afterwards, Isaac disappeared downstairs and returned a little later with a bowl of hot Campbell's chicken soup. I didn't imagine Michael as a canned-soup man. But, surprisingly, he wanted to eat it. So I sat in the armchair holding the bowl low down while Michael lay on his stomach in the bed and scooped up the contents. One shaky spoonful after another. Isaac sat in the straight-backed chair smoking a cigarette, watching silently until the bowl was empty.

I wanted to ask Michael how he was feeling but it seemed pointless and ridiculous.

'I was returning from running an errand when I saw your car.'

'In Back-O-Wall, Michael?'

'It's complicated.' He looked slightly secretive. 'And I was worried.'

Isaac lit another cigarette, took a couple of drags and then said, 'Yu think we need a doctor?'

'No. I'll be fine. Just get me back to the lodge. If you could do that I would be most grateful.'

'Yu not going nowhere, man. Yu can barely walk.'

'I can't stay here.'

Michael raised himself to get out of the bed, but stopped, not wanting to expose his naked body to me. He pulled the sheet up to his neck and repeated, 'I can't stay here.'

I turned to Isaac. He puffed on the cigarette and scratched his head.

'We can just tek him back and say somebody jump him and he need to rest.'

'What about the doctor?'

'No.' Michael was firm.

So that was it. I went outside while Isaac helped Michael to dress, and under the cover of dark we returned Michael to Bishop's Lodge where Isaac escorted him to his room and I waited in the hallway until Miss Crawford insisted I sit in the office.

'Yu friend putting the Father to bed? Something happen to him?'

'A fright. They jumped him thinking he was carrying collection money.'

'So yu say.'

She didn't believe me. I could tell from the suspicious look on her face the moment she opened the door. Father Kealey coming through the back with two strangers in the dead of night. So after that there was nothing we could say to alleviate her doubt.

'Yu call di police?'

'No. The Father didn't want us to. They didn't get anything from him.'

'But deh beat him?'

'Not really, Miss Crawford. All he needs is a little bed rest.'

'I will call di doctor.'

'No, Miss Crawford. No need for that. We already asked him and he said he doesn't need a doctor.'

She folded her arms and rolled her eyes. Then Isaac appeared in the doorway.

'All done,' he said with an air of finality.

Miss Crawford turned to him. 'All done? Nothing is all done till I tell Bishop Langley what happen. He di one to decide if all is done.'

I stood and made my way to leave. Outside in the Dodge, Isaac produced Michael's torn cassock which he had bundled up in the back of his shirt.

'Yu can go do something wid this. Burn it is what I would recommend.' And then, as he got out of the car at Cross

Roads, 'That man should see a doctor. God knows what could happen to him after a thing like that.'

He closed the door but the window was still wound down.

'I'm sorry,' I said.

'What yu sorry fah?'

'Sorry for forcing you to go over there this afternoon. Sorry for what happened. Sorry for what else might have happened, as if things aren't bad enough as they are.' I paused. 'It was stupid of me.'

He shook his head. 'You rich girls always think yu can do whatever yu want. But most times it not you dat pay di price.' He started to walk away. Then he turned back and, leaning down, stuck his head into the car. 'It go without saying but I wouldn't go breathing a word a dis to anybody. No telling what other tribulation yu go bring down on everybody's head.'

And then he pulled back and headed towards the shop while I shouted after him, 'Thank you, Isaac.' And he, with his back to me, raised his arm in a wave as he disappeared into the darkness.

I thought of going back to Matthews Lane, mostly because I couldn't face Mama. But I didn't. I went to Barry Street instead.

'Fay. What bring you here this time of night?' Papa got up from the mah-jongg table and walked slowly towards me. 'What happen? You alright?' He took me by the elbow and led me to the cookhouse out back. 'Sit down. Tea?' And then he studied me more carefully. 'Rice wine?'

That is when I burst into tears.

'Fay, Fay,' he said, brushing the hair away from my eyes and holding up my chin. 'Something terrible?'

But I couldn't speak. I just wailed like a two-year-old, which brought Mr Lowe rushing over with a fistful of paper napkins that he thrust into my hand. And still I cried.

Papa stared at me in bewilderment. Lowe stood back in shock.

'You want me call Pao? Police maybe?'

'No, no.' That is all I managed to say before being engulfed by more grief.

'It alright, Lowe. You go back kitchen. I see to what go on here with her.'

And while Papa sat patiently stroking my hand as it rested on the table, my crying slowly eased and finally stopped. And I wiped my face and blew my nose on Lowe's napkins.

'Yu mama?'

'No.'

'So what so bad?'

I told him. 'Fay, yu not responsible for everything. It terrible what happen to the Father. But you blaming yourself?'

'It was me, Papa, who wanted to go over there. Me who took Isaac. Me who forced him to go to Back-O-Wall. Me. A stupid, selfish, ignorant rich girl with nothing better to do than ruin people's lives.'

He took both my hands in his. 'No need be so hard. You make mistake, that is all. Everybody make mistake. Some time or another. That is life.'

Lowe reappeared with a jug and two cups into which he poured the rice wine.

'Everybody still alive. The Father will mend. I sure the bishop see to that. And as for Isaac, he grown man. So nothing that happen ruin beyond repair.'

Lowe patted me lightly on the shoulder. 'Drink.' He raised an imaginary cup to his mouth and threw his head back. 'Calm nerves.' Then he took my hand and placed it around the porcelain cup. And, nodding his head, forced the wine to my lips.

'You, Fay,' Papa continued, 'convince self that you the one bring all this badness into world. Ever since you little girl. But it not true. Not true at all. Things the way they was long before you born. Your mama take it out on you. That is all. But it not to do with you. It to do with her.'

He waved his hand for Lowe to go away.

'I know I not been good father. That to do with me. Not you. All I say is sorry. Sorry for my weakness when it come to how your mama treat you.'

'You don't have to apologise, Papa.'

'Yes, I do. You grown woman now but when you little I should have stop her.' He paused. 'So you would know you didn't deserve what happen. Know you wasn't responsible for it.'

The next day I went to Bishop's Lodge but Miss Crawford wouldn't let me see Michael. I pressed her some more.

'He is resting. I already tell you that.'

'But is he OK?'

She scrutinised me, deciding what she was prepared to divulge. 'He talk to Bishop Langley last night and afterwards bishop ask me to call di doctor. So he come over and see to him and now the Father is resting.'

I was grateful. Even bowed my head slightly to her. 'Thank you, Miss Crawford.'

'Yu nuh need to thank me for nothing.' But the look on her face was sour.

I walked away but then turned back. She'd already closed the door so I had to knock. When she saw me she settled her weight on to her right leg and folded her arms in preparation for standing her ground.

'Do you think I could come in and leave him a note?'

She stared at me for a good while. But then she softened and stepped back, opening the door wide but without saying a word.

I went into the office and sat behind the mahogany desk while she watched me scribble on a piece of the lodge letterhead. I signed and folded it into three. I looked up at her. She motioned her chin towards the right-hand side of the desk.

'Top drawer.'

'Thank you.' I reached in, pulled out a crisp, white envelope and wrote 'Michael' on it. And then, as an afterthought, to make it respectable, I wrote 'Father' before his name and 'Kealey' after it.

Miss Crawford stepped forward and took it from me. 'I will mek sure he get it.' And for the first time there was a whiff of gentleness in her. To show me that she knew it mattered.

It was almost three months before I saw Michael again, after a note he had left for me at Lady Musgrave Road. When Daphne put it in my hand she said, 'He must be keen, to be coming all the way up here to deliver this.'

I opened the envelope, unfolded the notelet and read it, all the time conscious of her inquisitive stare. 'It's the details of our next appointment.'

'That is what you call it. Mama is calling it something else.'

CHAPTER 17

MICHAEL HAD LOST weight. And he looked tired and drawn as we strolled around the birds of paradise in Hope Gardens.

'Bishop Langley has been very good to me.'

'You told him everything?'

'Yes.'

'What did he say?'

'He said the Lord moves in mysterious ways. There was a reason for what happened. My task is to fathom what that reason was and understand the lessons to be learned from the experience.' He paused. 'And we prayed together.'

'And the doctor.'

'He helped but mostly my body mended itself. The healing power of faith, Fay.' He laughed. 'We've talked about that before.'

Things were different between us after that. Mainly because, despite what Papa said, I still knew I was responsible for what happened to Michael and I didn't know how to make it up to him. Not that I ever could. How do you appease for something like that? Nonetheless, the more I tried the worse it got because I felt so unworthy of his company and friendship. After all, Isaac was right. I thought I could do anything I wanted.

Michael said that brutality had been bred into the Jamaican psyche from slavery; beaten into every African who had been made to work the fields, gasping for air and water in the blistering heat, tearing their hands to shreds on the sugar cane, surviving on next to nothing and being whipped for every imagined infraction. Men, women and children of all ages, regardless of their state of health.

'Even pregnant women, lying on a concrete floor with their swollen bellies resting in a hole specifically dug in the ground so their bodies remained flat as some massa or overseer brought down a lash on their naked back.'

Lashes, Michael said, made of leather or tipped with wire that would flay a person alive, or leave their torn and bloodied body to be eaten by dogs if the massa thought they were getting out of hand by running away or causing trouble talking about the injustices. Because, of all the islands, Jamaica had the most troublesome slaves, with uprisings every two minutes. Why? Because that was the policy. Disobedient, unmanageable slaves were deliberately sent to Jamaica, especially the rebellious Ashanti from the Ivory Coast. So always, the regime in Jamaica was more cruel, more malicious. Metal collars with protruding spikes; headpieces with metal tongues to insert into a person's mouth; shackles and chains; whipping, hanging, beating, burning, mutilation, branding, confinement. All of it trying to keep down a people who constantly resisted.

What I knew of this? Nothing. Because history in school meant learning about the kings and queens of England. And Christopher Columbus, of course, who discovered Jamaica. Like it didn't exist before 1494.

'What does this have to do with Back-O-Wall?'

'The brutality warped and eroded the slave's sense of his masculinity. He was not a man. He could not do the things a man should be able to do. Reap the benefits of his labour. Make a home. Protect his woman. Hold on to his children. Control his life. There was nothing within his domain. Not even his own agency. So once he escaped from that he had to be more man than man. Independent, dominant, self-regulating, beyond the control of any other human being or social system. He had to be free to spread his seed, and develop the swagger of doing exactly as he pleased, including beating down on anyone who opposed or threatened that sense of self.' He paused. 'Because beating is what he knew.'

So that was how Michael saw it. As I had seen Isaac and Pao, as the result of their history.

'And what threatens is any woman who questions that state of masculine being or any man who fails to live up to the machismo that is the protective shield of the lost and lonely. Because safety lies in numbers. A united front.'

'So you forgive them for what they did to you?'

'Jesus said, "Father, forgive them, for they know not what they do." But we are also responsible. The past is an explanation, Fay, not an excuse. In the end, we are the sum of our actions.' He laughed. 'Free will has its consequences.'

I looked at him enviously as I sat there motionless in the swing. Jealous of his calm, his self-control and his cool, relaxed openness. It made me want to reach out and touch him. Hold him. Feel the warmth of his breath against my cheek. The firmness of his body pressed to mine.

But what I did instead was set the swing moving. 'That is all about the man. What about the woman?'

'The woman, Fay? She has yet to be freed.'

It seemed unbelievable to me that a person could be so dispassionate. Especially after what he had been through. That he could still have kindness and compassion in his heart when all I had in mine was anger and resentment over the way Mama treated me. Feeling sorry for myself when, really, what did I have to complain about? A few strokes of the cane; a locked door; some horrid words. A lot worse was happening to other people.

After Michael left I went back into the house, only to find Mama in the middle of another one of her tirades.

'As the Lord is my witness, may He strike me down dead. Dead, O merciful Father for the heathen daughter I brought into this world. Sinner of sinners. Jezebel that she can be cavorting with a holy man of the cloth.'

She was sitting at the piano with her arms raised to heaven. I came to the door and leant against the frame.

'Yu still not finished with this?'

She turned to face me. 'Nothing will be finished with until I am in the grave.' And then she thought some more and said, 'Unless of course you beat me there, which would be a blessing for everyone in this house. And the Father too. Poor, weak, misguided soul he must be.'

I felt my anger flame. 'You have no idea what you are talking about. So just shut yu mouth before yu say something we both regret.'

Mama shot off the piano stool so fast I couldn't believe a woman of her age and generous proportions could move like that. Like a jack pouncing out of the box. Only the face on her wasn't painted cheerful and happy. It was pure rage as she raced up to me, pulled back her hand and slapped me square across the cheek.

I stared at her coldly as she stepped back. And then I said, 'Do you know brutality has been bred into the Jamaican psyche since slavery? All you are doing now is continuing that tradition. The same way every Jamaican parent does when they beat and beat their children.'

'What do you know about slavery? All you ever worried about your whole life was how to parade yourself as white. Making your father board you at Immaculate even though the school only little way 'cross town. Running all over the place with your rich friends, dancing and partying and playing tennis and God knows what. Like tennis is any kind of pastime for a girl like you.'

I felt the boiling blood throbbing through my veins.

'I blame your father,' she yelled. 'That is the God's truth. Giving in to every little hoity-toity whim yu have. Spoiling yu rotten since the day yu born. So now yu think yu better than everyone else in this house. Better than me because your skin light. Not black like this.' She thrust her arms out towards me, stroking one and then the other to show me just how black she was. And then, waving her hands in the air as she flounced back to the piano stool, she sat down and started to bang out some awful hymn to demonstrate to me the right-eousness of her life.

I felt like a dismissed servant.

'My light skin? Is that what worrying you? More like you doing battle with how you so black. Sitting on that veranda with your embroidery and crochet. Is that what the slave used to do on the plantation? In her spare time after she finish working in the field, or cleaning the great house, or cooking the massa's food or serving at table. Seeing to the laundry. Tending to the mistress and the children. And lying on her back for whoever wanted to defile her. Is that what she did? Embroidery and crocheting? And drink Earl Grey tea in the afternoon? Is that what the slave did that you are following in her footsteps?'

Mama didn't even turn around to face me. All she did was play the piano louder and louder so that I had to scream in order to be heard. 'So who is the one that is ashamed of her colour, Mrs Airs and Graces from Lady Musgrave Road?'

That is when Mama's fingers stopped moving and silence descended on the room. And then, turning to me, she said, 'The slave lived in misery and that is why I pray to the Lord Our God each and every day I breathe to have mercy on my soul.'

'Well maybe you could have shown some of that mercy to me.' And I walked out of the room.

Daphne was sitting on the veranda reading a book.

'When will the two of you stop arguing like that?'

'You asking me?' I went towards the steps.

She shouted after me. 'Something not right between you and the Father. Any idiot can see that.'

I didn't feel like discussing anything with her. So I just kept going. Into the Dodge and reverse gear. And away.

*　　*　　*

Then Papa told me he wanted me to buy a car and teach Daphne to drive.

'Time Daphne learn drive car so she can get away from her mama.'

'Really?'

'She go work, follow man, take photograph, but what kind of life that? She drive car, she can go about own business. Not rely on anybody for what she want to do.'

'You ever think that maybe she is happy doing what she's doing?'

He looked at me through the steam from his soup. Unconvinced. 'You tell me which one better. Drive car or always telephoning taxi cab. What you choose? Which one say freedom to you?'

He'd made his point. 'What kind of car do you want me to buy?'

'Not just buy car, Fay. Teach sister drive.'

He removed the protective white-cotton napkin. Tucked as it was into his shirt collar. Folded it neatly and placed it on the table. Then he took me squarely in his gaze.

So I just said, 'I hear you.'

'Mercedes-Benz,' he said, matter of fact. Because that was the only make of car Papa knew.

'You drive too. Like it your car. Dodge too old to be running round di place.'

When I went to the showroom I didn't know how to choose. Knew nothing about cubic capacity or brake horse-power. So all I could say was automatic because I thought that would make it easier for Daphne to learn. And maroon because in that moment I remembered what Papa said about the freedom the car would give to Daphne, and thought of Nanny rebelling against the Spanish and the English, and the word 'maroon' popped out of my mouth. Besides, I couldn't see myself driving a black Mercedes. Not like every other Chinese man and woman in Kingston. The salesman looked surprised. More than that. Shocked. Especially after I said cream leather upholstery. Thinking of the seats in Michael's Chevy. That was when his eyebrows almost went through the roof.

I was stiff at first. Teaching Daphne to drive. Because I was still stinging from her comment about me and Michael. But sitting in the car with her, hour after hour, I finally discovered how incredibly lonely my younger sister was. Booking appointments; arranging the studio backgrounds for portraits of families, couples, individuals or babies; minding children who were bored or exhausted; carrying the lamps and stands and setting up in people's homes or shops; keeping the records on location in this hotel or that beach, birds, flora and fauna; a wedding; a christening; a child's birthday party. Did she like it? This job.

'I'm not qualified to do anything. Anyway, who cares? If I dropped down dead no one would notice.'

She was turning right into Oxford Road, across the street from the telephone company. The smell of fresh bread wafting over to us from the bakery on Osborne Road.

'You could get training. What do you want to do?'

She didn't say anything. Concentrating on the green light turning to amber as she hesitated waiting for the oncoming traffic to ease. And in truth I heard the thump more than felt it. Quite a gentle little thud. Just enough to roll us into the car in front. A silver Continental stationary on the corner. The driver behind didn't even stop. He just pulled out and passed us with his passenger leaning out of the window to tell us something about women who should get back into the kitchen where they belong. In graphic, unpleasant terms.

I stepped out of the car and let the noonday sun beat on to my bare head. The driver of the Continental was deep in conversation with her friend.

'I'm sorry about that.'

She glanced disinterestedly at me as she tapped her pink fingernails on the steering wheel and chewed her gum. 'Nuh matter.' She continued to scrutinise the line of motionless cars ahead.

'I checked your fender and it seems OK.'

'Honey, this car been bashed and banged and scratched and scraped that many times I surprised there is anything left for you to check.' Her friend laughed. Good-humouredly.

I rested my hand on the window as I bent down to say, 'You don't want to look at it?'

That is when she actually turned to me. 'It doesn't matter. Honestly.' And then she shifted gear and edged her way forward.

But back in the car Daphne was horrified. 'I don't know how it happened.'

'It doesn't matter, Daphne.'

'It does, Fay. I try so hard to be careful. Everything I do. Every little thing. I hate making mistakes. What if something worse had happened? A car wreck. Not just a fender bender but a real accident. People getting hurt. Other drivers. Pedestrians walking on the street. A child crossing the road.' Her voice was shrill.

'Nothing happened, Daphne. Don't let your imagination run away with you. Just concentrate on what you are doing right now.'

At which point I reached out and tugged lightly on the wheel to bring us more centrally back into the left-hand lane.

But Daphne's driving was never the same after that. Even after she passed the test. It was still full of apprehension and trepidation, which made her slow to move, slow to stop, slow to turn, slow to decide what to do. And she would never overtake. Not even a horse-drawn cart or a man on a bicycle if she could not take up the whole of the oncoming lane. So she was dangerous. And I wondered if it would have been better if she'd continued to call a taxi cab.

But, to be fair, Papa was right. It did give Daphne a new-found independence and a new set of skills to bring to her photographer, meeting him here and there, all equipment loaded into the Mercedes, or transported back to the studio. No longer relying on him to drive her home at the end of a long day.

Social life? Nothing that I observed.

'What is it that you want to do, Daphne?'

'Oh I don't know. What is there?'

'Are you serious? The whole world is out there. Parties, dancing, wonderful food, the beach, the mountains, movies, the theatre, tennis, water skiing and every other land and water sport you can think of. None of that appeals to you?' She shrugged. 'You have a driving licence and money in your pocket. You can go anywhere, do anything.'

'Who with, Fay?'

'Who with? You don't know anybody?'

'Where am I going to meet anybody?'

'You meet people all the time.'

'Not anyone who wants to know me.' Tears welled up in her eyes.

I put my arm around her shoulder as we walked from the car to the veranda. Safe in the knowledge that Mama was at her Bible reading group all afternoon.

'Not even from school, Daphne?'

She sniffed and drew a Kleenex from her bag just as Ethyl stepped out of the door to greet us.

Later, when I asked her about men, she remained silent. And when I talked about getting married she said, 'Who would marry me?'

'You don't think you deserve to be loved? Deserve to be happy?'

'What you deserve and what you get in this life are two completely different things. You of all people should know that. Look how happily married you are.'

'That wasn't my choice.'

'It wasn't mine either.'

'I don't know what you mean.'

'It doesn't matter.'

CHAPTER 18

THE THING WAS, Beverley and I had become estranged, ever since I asked about her grandmother and Chiang Kai-shek. Oh, we still had coffee and sometimes we danced. But there was an emptiness between us. A void, that every now and again one of us managed to breach, to exchange a few uncommitted words. Not anything genuine or real, just a pseudo reaching across the divide so that one day, if ever we gathered the courage to talk about what was really troubling us, deep down, a door would still be open. And if we never came to that, never felt brave enough to face ourselves and each other, then there would still be the semblance of a friendship that we could rely on for simple things.

For me, it was the money. Or rather, Beverley's attitude towards it. How she took so much for granted, wallowing in luxury without ever a thought for the other Jamaica and the other Jamaicans who inhabited the townships of West Kingston. Or the country folk who were still carrying water on their heads for miles while she sent her clothes to be laundered, and showered twice a day.

But really, it wasn't Beverley. It was me. It was the disgust I felt every time I saw her kick off her imported shoes and laugh as she settled into yet another tale of extravagance and excess. Including stories of the various men she was dating behind Audley's back.

'Don't you worry he will find out?'

'Oh, he knows,' she said offhandedly as she peeled the orange, not with a knife like most Jamaicans, but with her fingernail, imitating some starlet she'd seen in a movie.

'You don't care?'

'You worry too much. Anyway, what is he going to do? Call it off with me? After all these years? Audley wouldn't know what to do with himself without me.'

And right then I realised I was Beverley Chung, with my casual indulgence and the things I took for granted. Because no matter what, I always had my privilege to fall back on. Always had my backstop. Like she had GC, despite their upset. I had Papa, and Lady Musgrave Road. And I hated it. I hated myself.

So that night when Pao came to bed so late and so drunk and I knew what he wanted I was in two minds. The Fay Wong who would resist, who would fight tooth and nail, scratching and kicking, and twisting and turning my way out of his grip. Who would even have hit him with the bedside lamp if the cord hadn't stopped me short. Why? Because I was not a slave. I had free will and nobody could force me to do anything I didn't want to. But I was also the other Fay Wong. Spoilt and ungrateful. Who deserved every appalling thing that happened or would happen to her. Things that were nowhere near as horrific as had been visited upon Michael, and the burden of every woman from time immemorial. It even made me think about the whore, Gloria Campbell, doing this day in day out with men she didn't know or was barely acquainted with. Including my husband. Just to make a living, because this was Kingston, not some country hamlet where she would be a schoolteacher or a seamstress, growing a few vegetables in her backyard while her man went to his farm or business or dressed for work in his postman or policeman uniform. And where their children would play in the yard knowing that food would be there for the eating come dinner-time, and kerosene for the lighting at night, and church for the going on Sunday. No, this was town, where the sufferers suffer.

So my struggle was half-minded and half-hearted as he pinned my arms to the bed and did what he did. Before I made it to the bathroom with GC's rubber cap.

Afterwards, he said he was sorry.

'I don't know what come over me. It just that sometimes the look on your face so nasty. Like yu screwing up your nose at me and everybody I care about. Thinking yu better than all of us put together.'

The funny thing was? I understood exactly what he meant.

I didn't want the baby, though. That was the truth. Cried nonstop for weeks after I discovered I was pregnant. Said Michael's Rosary of the Seven Sorrows over and over. Working the beads between my thumb and forefinger until they were sore and raw. Actually even considered doing something else about it but couldn't face it. Not some grand-mother in her apron or maybe spinster nurse hidden away in the backstreets of downtown Kingston, on a table that would later provide the surface for somebody's dinner. Or, if done late at night, somebody's breakfast. And who would I take with me? Not Daphne. Not Beverley. Not at the moment how things were between us. Not Grandmother Chung. Obviously. One whiff and she would have had the woman come to her, with a chauffeur escort for good measure. And I didn't want to owe her or anybody else that kind of debt. Sissy? She would have done it, but I couldn't bring myself to ask her. Not a woman who missed having a child of her own. I couldn't make her witness that.

Adoption? Giving it away? Even to Sissy? No. Those things always catch up with you in years to come. I hadn't forgotten about Isaac and Junior.

So, to strengthen my resolve, I told Michael. And I rested. And when the time drew closer I went to the hospital with weeks in hand because I wasn't about to have a repeat perform-ance of what happened with Karl. I slept and ate and wandered in the opulent gardens, read books, eavesdropped on the nurses' conversations and consulted with Dr Morrison, newly here from Scotland. So new, he had not yet learnt how to skate along the tile corridors. Not like the other doctors. Sliding the final few yards and coming to a halt at precisely the desired door. Sometimes I just lay there in the bed and stared out of the windows. Mindlessly. As if I hadn't a care in the world. And I said Michael's rosary.

Papa visited. Beverley. Dutiful but distant. Daphne. Pao, occasionally with Karl. Michael. Tyrone, laden with flowers. Even Sissy made it to the hospital although she was careful to keep early-morning hours because, she said, 'I don't want to be bumping into anybody unexpected.' Mama? She never set one foot near the place.

When the baby came it was a girl. Calm and quiet as you like, with her arms folded across her chest like she'd been waiting in that position for the whole nine months. She didn't make a squeak. Not a murmur. She just rested while they cut and wiped and cleaned her up for my arms. But one look at her and I told them to take her away. Because all I could see in her face was Matthews Lane. And my misery.

Pao picked up the basket with her in it when he came to take me home from the hospital. Me? I looked for Michael's rosary, which was nowhere to be found. Searching high and low, and asking the nurse if perhaps someone had come across it. But no.

He carried the cot gingerly. More gently than a dozen trays of eggs. Resting it on the back seat of the car because I wouldn't hold it as he asked. And even after weeks of him saying we needed to think of a name I wasn't interested.

In the end I told him, 'Call her whatever you want. Just like you did the first time.'

Mui was what I heard him telling Dr Morrison on the telephone. Spelling it out for him. M-U-I. Little sister. While I exchanged pleasantries with Tilly. Standing there with the hard yard broom in her hand. Leaning her weight on it as she paused for a breather.

'Yu seem happier, Miss Fay. Motherhood to your liking?' I didn't reply. 'Little man doing good as well.'

'Yes.' And then, to change the subject, I said, 'How are things going with your bus driver?'

'Oh good, miss. Good. We well settled. Thank yu.'

Pao cooed over the baby when he came off the phone. And then he play-fight with Karl like any ordinary father would a three-year-old. Smiling and laughing. And tussling with the boy in the safety of his enclosed arms. Looking over at me every now and again as if to say, 'This is us. Family.' Like he was having a quiet celebration to match the noisy one that was going on out in the street. The one that went on all year long, 1955, with singing and dancing and athletic events. There was even a touring bandwagon show, to cheer us along in remembering the landing of Penn and Venables three hundred years earlier. As if it was something for us to be proud of. Our association with Britain. As if slavery was forgotten and forgiven.

The other thing that happened that year? The People's National Party won the general election and Norman Manley took office as chief minister.

And a little later Pao and Papa went into business together. I was shocked when Sissy told me.

'Doing what?'

'Running liquor and groceries to di new hotels on di north coast. So I hear.'

'Where yu hear it from?'

'Fay, it all over town. How yu father supplying di goods and yu husband supplying di transport and muscle, humping crates and whatnot.'

'What mek it so big news?'

'It not nuh big news. Is just dat I have a special ear when it come to you. Yu want me stop telling yu di tittle-tattle dat come my way?'

I thought about it. 'Who else going tell me anything?'

224

She nodded. 'Dat is what I reckon.' And then she puffed on her pipe.

What Papa said? 'It is business, Fay. Business, that is all. And who better to do business with than your own son-in-law? That is what family is for.'

So I had to swallow how I felt about it. Betrayed.

'What is it that you want?'

'I want to be free, Michael. I want to own my own life. Not Mama's life for me. Not Pao's. But my own. Where I decide for myself what I will do and where I will go.'

'With two small children?'

'Does that have to stop me?'

'It limits you.'

I looked at him, his head framed by the poinsettia wafting on the breeze behind him. Michael Kealey is a beautiful man, with his wavy hair greying at the temples, and the dimple in his chin. And his sorrowful eyes.

'Have you ever loved anyone, Michael? A woman.'

'Me?' He smiled. Just a half-smile across his lips. 'No.'

'Never? Not even thought about it?'

He hesitated. And then, looking straight at me, he said, 'I have thought about it. But I am a priest. Did you forget?'

And I knew. Just from the way he was looking at me, with an intensity in his eyes that I'd never seen before. I knew he meant me. So I didn't say anything. I just turned and carried on walking through Hope Gardens. And a while later I said, 'Ever since I was a little girl I wondered if there was something wrong with me.'

'Wrong with you?'

So I told him about Mama sending Samson to drag me from the cookhouse, and wetting the schoolroom floor, and about Nancy Lee and her mother. And how I tested my own madness, hoping against hope that someone would notice, but they never did. And having no schoolfriends until the hare-brained times with Beverley. And Freddie. And everything else, including the marches and bus journeys with Isaac. Colonel Stephenson and Lue Fah Yee. All in one continuous stream that went on for days during which Michael listened and listened and barely said a word.

I told him about the hours and days and months and years I had spent in torment trying to understand my life.

'Everything is inside my head, Michael. Thinking and thinking and thinking some more. Replaying incidents from twenty-five years ago, trying to make myself remember every minute detail. Checking over and over in my mind what I might have missed. Around and around in circles examining every look or comment for meaning. Then and now.'

'And how is that?'

'Exhausting.'

He reached out and took my hand as we sat on a bench in the shade of a mahoe tree. The kindness in his touch sent a shiver through me. A surge of energy that propelled me into his arms. Where I rested my head. And wept. Just like that. Without thinking. Without feeling like I was an observer looking at myself from the outside. Not even with Freddie in the darkness of night had I done that. Because, as close as we were, there was always a part of me that remained separate. A part of me that I kept protected. The part of me that knew he would leave.

I lay in Michael's arms forgetting he was a priest. Because, actually, his arms welcomed me and his body melted into mine. How it felt? Like faith and courage were being breathed into me. It felt like I was embracing hope.

When I finally pulled back, I told him about losing the rosary and not being able to find a replacement. Despite searching Kingston high and low.

'I bought that rosary when I was at the seminary in Washington. It won't be easy to replace.' And then he smiled. But it was a different smile. Not formal like in the beginning. Or slightly guarded as it had been more recently. But open and unprotected. A smile that acknowledged we had moved on. Taken another step along some unnamed road.

CHAPTER 19

WHEN THE BLACK Rover pulled up next to me in King Street, I knew I was on my way to Up Park Camp. Sitting in the back of the car for a silent journey with two plainclothes officers up front. They parked, marched me into the building and deposited me in a well furnished but empty office.

'You have heard about the Federation, I assume?' He hadn't even bothered to introduce himself coming through the door. He knew who I was and that was enough for him.

'I heard.'

'It is all Mr Manley cares about since he got elected.'

'Not all he cares about, I'm sure.'

He was irritated at my insolence. 'You don't seem that enthusiastic.'

'Should I be, Colonel?'

He twiddled his moustache. A long, twirled-up thing like a bicycle handlebar. It made him look ancient, like some old German Kaiser or a Confederate general with his short hair slicked back so neat. Or Wyatt Earp. Yes, that was it. All guns blazing at the OK Corral.

'I am not a colonel. I am a major.' He tapped his epaulette to show me the lonesome crown.

We sat. Quietly. Until finally I said, 'I don't know what you want from me.'

'You don't know?' he said mockingly.

I sighed. 'We've been through all of this before, Major ...'

'Hutton.'

'Major Hutton,' I said, repeating his name. 'I can't help you.'

He opened the file on his desk. Flicked over some pages. Fiddled with the edges of the paper. 'I think you can.'

I didn't say anything. And then he said, 'Isaac Dunkley.'

'Isaac Dunkley? Are you serious?'

'I couldn't be more serious, Private.'

'I am not a private any more. I was discharged.' I got to my feet and started towards the door.

'The man is a communist deeply involved with all sorts of undesirables and Cuban revolutionaries.' And then he waited a brief moment before saying, 'And maids in your service.'

I stopped and turned to face him. 'Maids in my service?'

'A Miss Tilly Stokes. Maid at Matthews Lane. Am I correct? And her bus-driving – what shall I call him – man friend?'

Tilly? Really? So meek and mild about her chores. And the bus driver she told me she was happily settled with.

'I still don't understand what this has to do with me.'

There was a tentative knock at the door. A nervous corporal entered with a note in his hand, walked across to Hutton and handed him the envelope. Then he brought his feet together, saluted and left.

Major Hutton reached for his letter opener. A paperknife in the shape of a ceremonial sword.

'A present from my wife.'

As if I should care.

He unfolded the piece of paper, read it and then looked up at me.

'I now have in my hand the telephone number of the police station where your Mr Dunkley is currently being held.'

'He isn't my Mr Dunkley.'

'Arrested by the local constabulary for unlawful assembly and public affray.' He raised his dark, bushy eyebrows. 'That makes you guilty by association.'

'Association with what?'

'Or perhaps you would prefer me to tell the *Gleaner* news-paper about how helpful you were a little while ago spying on Chinese communists.'

'I did no such thing!'

'I will not mention Lue Fah Yee by name, of course, but mud sticks. Private Wong,' he paused, 'can you begin to imagine how that mud would smell on you right now? And on your father's business? To say nothing of the reaction from your husband's – what shall I call them – associates?'

So I sat down and listened while he made a phone call to arrange Isaac's release and in exchange I agreed to find out what Tilly and her bus driver were up to. And what Isaac was doing with his Cubans.

'It was some massive crowd, yu know. Down in Duke Street. At di opening a di new House a Representatives.' He was excited. Isaac. 'People climbing trees and clinging on di fence so deh could strain their neck to see di new ministers parading into di House. In victory. Because it was time for a change and change had come!' I knew what he meant. 'Time for a Change' had been the People's National Party election slogan. 'Wid di party flag flying and a thousand voices singing "Jamaica Arise". It was glorious, Fay. Yu really should 'ave been there.'

We were in the soda fountain at Half Way Tree, where Isaac was drinking a beer he'd brought into the store himself and sipped openly despite the waitress twice telling him, 'I am sorry, sir, but you cannot consume your own beverages on the premises,' which he ignored. With a smile.

'So yu get arrested, Isaac?'

He shrugged. 'Ah, it was nothing. Deh didn't have nothing on me.' He stretched out his arms. Palms up. As if to demonstrate the absence of chains. 'So deh let me go. Simple as dat.'

Then he leant his head slightly to the side and observed me. 'But what dis got to do wid you?'

'I was worried 'bout yu.'

'You? Worried 'bout me?' He laughed. A great belly laugh that was so familiar it warmed my heart. But underneath it, beneath the carefree joviality, he was serious.

'Father Kealey alright?' I nodded. 'So what yu want wid me?'

And that is how it all started again, with Isaac going on and on about how Manley had become obsessed with rooting out so-called reds from the PNP. 'Because he fraid he going lose support if people really believe di Party under communist influence. So now every little thing dat anybody do, like di sugar workers' strike, got dem shouting communist from di rafters.'

The other bee in Isaac's bonnet? Alexander Bustamante.

'Yu know he even try get di governor to mek a law so communism become illegal? And force di person deh accuse to have to prove he not a communist. Whatever happen to innocent until proven guilty?'

Isaac's indignation was relentless.

'He even have di affront to put dat advertisement in di newspaper day before di election. "Bustamante's Final Appeal: Save This Country From Socialism". But it didn't mek no difference, Fay. Manley still win. Never mind Governor Foot's big speech up di Myrtle Bank Hotel 'bout how all sections a di public must reject di communists. He didn't mek no law. We still here.'

And that was the first and only time Isaac ever came close to saying he was a communist. Mostly he just talked about inequality and injustice and oppression. For months and months. And how a man is the consequence of his circumstances.

'He also chooses, Isaac. He decides to do one thing instead of another. This thing instead of that. Like the mob who ran us down in Back-O-Wall.'

He looked at me over the top of the old copy of *Public Opinion* he was busy studying.

'That he does,' he said with resignation. And a sigh of irritation. 'But he does so within the limited options he can perceive.' So this was a different Isaac. An Isaac who was certain and who used words like limited options and perceive. No longer the awkward, tongue-tied bumpkin I met outside the Carib theatre all those years back. No longer Mr Tentative from Trench Town. That was over.

The new Isaac said, 'He does so within the limited actions he can visualise for himself. Based on his skills, his resources, his confidence, his past experience, his expectations. He does so within the limits of his social context.' Which made me physically sit back in wonder. 'And his feelings or fears about being embraced or ostracised. He does so within the limits of his imagination and the consequences he can predict.' And then he removed the spectacles he'd taken to wearing when he read.

The day he asked me if I wanted to go to a gathering I feigned surprise even though I'd been waiting for it. Cautiously edging my way towards it.

'What's it about?' I asked him.

'The people's programme. Housing and education, medical services; employment; equal pay for equal work; right to union membership; guaranteed markets and fair prices for small farmers; lower prices for essential goods; protection of Jamaican industry; nationalisation of foreign-owned companies like the bauxite, electric and telephone.' He recited the list like he was reading from a manifesto etched on his brain. And then he stared at me as he leant against the bus stop, there in Cross Roads.

So I said to him, 'What about the Federation?'

'The Federation?' He licked his lips while he composed his response. 'Well, on the surface of it, it seem OK. Good thing to strengthen our economic development and trading position. Yes sir. But the way they have it right now, it half free and half slave, with the British still ruling over everything. So, no. Our Federation should be completely free of the British government. And each country should have control of its own internal affairs. That is how I would see it. Plus, the money. You have to have control of the bank and taxes. Because without that, you not controlling anything at all.'

'What about the rumours?'

'Well if it true, really true, that they only trying to sever Britain's preferred trade arrangements with its Caribbean colonies so the US can sell goods to Britain, then that is not a good situation for us.'

'Yu believe it?'

'What do you think?'

'Karl.' I was calling for him to come in from the yard. 'What are you doing out there?'

'Nothing. Just with Uncle Kenneth.'

I'd started to take him with me on my returns to Lady Musgrave Road. Old enough now at five. Mui? I left with Pao. Her glorious papa who, as each week passed, she seemed to become more and more attached to. More and more in adoration of. Looking only to him for whatever she wanted or needed. Food, drink, a helping hand, a show of sympathy or soothing comfort. Me? I was always second best. Or, more realistically, last choice, behind Zhang and Ma. And Hampton, who played childish games. A big, beefy man with a mountain of iron that he huffed and puffed with each morning lying on his back on the bench press in the yard. Squatting on his haunches and sitting in the dirt with her.

'What's this?'

'Just stuff.' Karl glared at me, irritated at my interference. He was hopping on one leg, eager to return to whatever was occupying him. Then Kenneth sauntered in, looked me up and down before jutting out his chin at Karl and asking, 'What yu want him fah?'

'You are eleven years old, Kenneth. That is not how you speak to anybody.' He stuck his hands in his pockets and leant against the doorpost.

I turned to Karl. 'Ethyl found these things in your room.' I held up the bag containing the toy cars and comic books. And in my other hand, the roll of money.

'So what?'

'I am not talking to you, Kenneth.'

I turned my attention back to Karl. 'Where did you get all of this?'

He said nothing at first. And then: 'Somebody gave them to me.'

'Somebody gave you this?' I unfurled the bills and counted them. 'Fifty-five pounds. Someone gave you fifty-five pounds? And these other things,' I said, emptying the contents of the bag on to the table. He cast his eyes to the floor.

'It was me, alright.'

'You, Kenneth? And where does a child get this kind of money from? Not saved from the few shillings you get from Papa each week. Of that I'm sure.'

'Yu think yu so high and mighty?' And he turned and walked away.

I knelt down to Karl. 'Do you know where Kenneth got these things from? And the money?'

'He gets them from shops downtown and sells them to other boys.'

'Well, I don't want you taking any more of Kenneth's gifts. Do you understand me?'

There wasn't any point in talking to Mama about it. She and I had never managed a civil conversation about anything in our entire lives. And as for Pao? What kind of role model was he anyway?

When I went to Isaac's gathering I discovered that it was no union meeting or authorised PNP group. It was something entirely different. Not an organised party event at all but a collection of loosely associated people who seemed intent on arguing ferociously with each other and disagreeing about everything under the sun. Not only the wrongs and rights of the PNP and Jamaica Labour Party but also whether or not Castro was sensible to attack the presidential palace in Havana, especially since they failed to kill Batista and caused so much horrendous retaliation from the government.

And sitting there quietly in the back row of these chairs drawn in circles in this comfortable living room was Tilly. Tilly, who'd cooked and cleaned and washed and ironed without a single contentious word or opinion for the seven long years I had known her. And in the seat next to her the bus driver who would later that evening be introduced to me as Vincent, who also remained silent throughout except for near the end when he said, 'Liberty is not begged for but won with the blade of machete.' Which Isaac whispered to me was from Fidel Castro. 'Although, technically speaking,' he said, 'it was Fidel quoting Antonio Maceo.' The crowd appreciated it, though, because they clapped heartily and murmured to themselves, 'Right on, comrade' and 'Yah man.' Someone even raised his voice enough for '*Patria o muerte*' to be heard above the general hum. Homeland or death. My schoolgirl Spanish was good enough to understand that.

Afterwards, when we were standing up with coffee cups in hand, Vincent said to me, 'How long yu know Isaac then?'

I glanced at Isaac. 'A while.'

Vincent laughed. A boyish chuckle. 'Yu cagey wid it.' And then he winked at Isaac, which prompted Tilly to elbow him in the side and say, 'Miss Fay di wife a Yang Pao. Yu know.'

'Oh, I sorry, miss. Yu say yu name Fay. Yu never say Mrs Yang Pao.' He bowed his head. 'I would never 'ave been so presumptuous.'

I surveyed the hot, crowded room now emptying into the street.

'Were you serious about the machete?'

Isaac stiffened next to me. 'Absolutely, miss. Machete and gun and cricket bat and stick. Anything we can lay our hands on to win our freedom.'

Tilly giggled nervously. 'He don't really mean it, Miss Fay. He just like to talk dat way. Vincent wouldn't slap a mosquito on di back a his neck.' She linked his arm and stroked and patted it to reassure herself.

I wasn't so convinced. Not when I looked at the loathing in his eyes. His utter contempt for the system that had spawned us, me and him, and the relative privilege we enjoyed. Actually, it unnerved me. Frightened me, even, as I stepped into the darkened street imagining a strange man lurking behind every corner, with that look on his face and machete in hand. Remembering the toothless gunman in Back-O-Wall with his carved and polished baton.

'Yu think Vincent is right about the machete?' That is what I asked Isaac as we walked to the bus stop.

'Long time ago some old Russian said that so long as society is divided into classes, so long as there is exploitation of man by man, wars are inevitable.'

'Lenin,' I said.

'From his mouth in 1905,' he replied. 'Or was it his pen?'

'He also said that war is a bestial way of settling conflicts in human society.'

Isaac grinned at me. 'Yu been reading.'

'True or false?'

He spied down the road to see if a bus was approaching. No such luck.

'What do you suggest?' he asked. 'Slavery is bestial. Poverty, unemployment, selling your labour at a miserable price, persecution, exploitation, sickness, unsanitary conditions, illiteracy. They are all bestial.' He studied me carefully. 'How are they to be overcome,' he paused, 'if not by war? Or do you think all the rich people will just get up one morning and decide to give away everything they got?' He narrowed his eyes. 'Their supermarkets, wine merchants and wholesalers, and palaces in Lady Musgrave Road?'

'We are just the buffer class, Isaac. The real rich people, they are nowhere to be seen. Not by you, not even by the likes of me. Most of them don't even live here. They far off across the waters in England and America and everywhere else. Just like it always been.'

And then, looking back at me over his shoulder as he walked down the crowded bus, he said, 'Yu damn right about that.'

★   ★   ★

238

I didn't say anything to Tilly the next morning. Nothing about the evening before. But I regarded her differently. She carried herself differently too. That wasn't just in my imagination. She was straighter. More upright. Prouder-looking. With a new disdain on her lips as she picked up the dirty clothes Pao had left on the bedroom floor and rinsed through the dishes from breakfast. And, bizarrely, that was the first time I saw Tilly's black skin. She was African. Not Chinese like Pao and Zhang and Ma. Not light-skinned, mixed, like me. She was black like Hampton and Finley who came and went with Pao and were his to command. Like Tilly was here for Ma to command. And with my eyes now opened to her colour, I saw her resentment.

I continued going to the meetings with Isaac. Never saying a word but escaping scrutiny because I was a woman so nothing was expected from me. Would have been pooh-poohed had I dared to comment. Considered a kind of insubordination. Women were not there to talk, the few of us there were. We were there to listen. And admire.

What I discovered was that a war was already being waged in the townships of West Kingston. One neighbourhood pitted against another. Lines drawn in the dirt at street corners to protect the nothing they had. Nothing apart from opinion about this or that party or leader or policy, and the illusion that one day they would be better off by virtue of having supported one instead of the other.

The truly demoralising and heartbreaking part? People's preparedness to rob, rape, beat and maim over it. Even kill. It was the violence. The physical and mental brutality that I found so very hard to swallow. Almost as if they did not recognise each other as fellow human beings, only as rival targets.

And, even then, when Major Hutton called me to task I refused to say anything.

'It has been months, Private. You must know something.'

'No, Major. Nothing to report.'

I was sweating. Nervous. He was agitated. Irate.

'You are playing the fool with me, Mrs Yang.' He closed the file on his desk. Slamming his palm down on the flimsy, brown cardboard cover as hard as he could. 'But I'm not going to stand for it. Do you understand me? This is not a game we are playing here. An empire is at stake.'

I almost laughed out loud, but stopped myself just in time. It wouldn't have helped matters. I did try to pay better attention, though. What was it that Vincent was actually doing? And, as it turned out, Vincent was a bag man. On his bus route. Collecting donations from the idealistic better-off to support the efforts in Cuba. Funds transported by olive-skinned, Spanish-tongued *compadres* who came and went and who, while on the island, instructed Vincent and his like in the ways of revolution. Lessons he cascaded in living rooms and backyards across Kingston to people eager to fashion a more radical approach to a new society. Not the gradual transition the elected Social Democrats promised but something faster and, unquestionably, more furious.

And then one night in the heat of debate someone said, 'The rich will never give up their riches. The powerful will never surrender their power. Both must be taken by force.'

It was horrifying. Not the thought of my loss, because God knows I didn't deserve what I had. Not even the anticipation of the bloodshed, as wasteful and barbaric as that would be.

But the realisation that these men, sitting so comfortably under the whirling ceiling fan with ice-water at their sides, had no idea that their lofty ideals bore no resemblance to the bedlam unfolding on the streets of West Kingston. Because what was happening over there was not revolution. It was not the roaring of the masses as they brought down the structures that oppressed them. It was something far less grand. Far less noble. It was the whimper of the powerless flexing their muscle against their equally powerless neighbour. With the warlords reaping the benefits on both sides.

And even then I still said nothing. Because who was I to interfere? Who was I to take sides? Who was I to play traitor once again?

'I have a new proposition for you.' Hutton squinted at me. 'Why? Because, Mrs Yang, I know you are keeping something from me.'

Major Hutton's new office was a cupboard with the tiniest of windows over which he had draped a chequered blue and yellow curtain, making the room even darker than it was. In broad daylight. I didn't imagine that was army regulation.

I sat. Crossed my legs. Wiggled my foot up and down. Refused his offer of a cool drink. Neither soda nor water.

'So, this is the thing.'

I waited. He pursed his lips tightly before saying, 'I'm going to arrest your husband.'

My brows raised and eyes widened. 'Yes,' he said. 'I am quite serious. I told you I would not stand for you playing the fool with me.'

'But Pao is not a communist.'

'So you say. And actually I am quite prepared to believe you.' He tugged at his collar. Uncomfortable in the heat. 'Nonetheless, he is a criminal. Illegal gambling, stolen goods, protection, racketeering. There is no end to his talents, it seems.'

I was stunned into silence. He was smug. 'Ah, now I have your attention.' Then he was gloating. 'I have sworn and signed statements, Mrs Yang. This is no joke. A Chinaman on a farm in Red Hills with whom your husband has been falsifying records to procure illicit chickens and eggs. A US navy sergeant, now returned to American soil thank goodness, from whom he has been receiving stolen navy supplies. A practice which it seems has been going on for some good time. So there you have it. Even if the Chinese in Chinatown will say nothing of his antics. Loyal fools.'

He twiddled his moustache. 'What do you have for me? Or would you prefer that I pick up this telephone right now and send the father of your two young and, I understand, quite beautiful children to the penitentiary? Directly to jail. Do not pass Go. Do not collect two hundred pounds.' And then he tucked in his chin and half-smiled with his lips pulled tight across his uneven teeth.

The whole ridiculous scene would have been comical. Except it wasn't. So I coughed up everything I knew about Vincent. And in exchange Major Hutton promised to leave Pao alone. Now and for ever because really he posed no threat to the Great British Empire.

Two days later Isaac told me that the police had waved Vincent down on Old Hope Road and searched his bus. And then taken him and the small canvas holdall of money he had at his side to the station where he was charged with drug trafficking and remanded for trial.

'Drug trafficking?'

'That is what they say.' He carefully scrutinised me before finally raising his head in a kind of acknowledgement, with a look that told me he knew. But he didn't say anything because if he did he would be forced to do something about it and he didn't want to put himself in that position. Not with the wife of Yang Pao.

Tilly didn't say anything to me either. Actually, she never uttered another word to me after Vincent's arrest. She just came to Matthews Lane and did her work and avoided me as best she could. Surveying me out of the corner of her eye when she thought I wasn't looking.

Why I did it? Apart from to save my own skin. And Pao's. Because Vincent and his friends were wounding the country, and the ordinary Jamaicans who honestly all they wanted was a decent life and some prospects for their future. And because the organised violence he was supporting, in word if not deed, wasn't revolution. It was feudalism. With the warlords holding their territories to ransom, and the people of those communities paying them homage and delivering unto Caesar his due. A share of everything they had, including their loyalty and physical support for his posse. Because every warlord saw himself as a cowboy roaming and taming the Wild West. And in return, as these things go, the people received services like healthcare and schools. And protection. From those very same posses who, on another day, would tear them and their homes apart. Not a bad exchange in the absence of anything else. But it was still a confidence trick. A political mirage.

Pao, on the other hand, as much as I despised him, was all above board. Gambling, protection for Chinese shopkeepers, stolen goods. Everybody getting exactly what they bargained for. Including the women in the house across the street from Sissy. Pao wasn't peddling an illusion. He was making a living. Against British law and sensibilities, for sure. But not against the Jamaican people.

So I felt bad about it. Betraying Vincent to the authorities. But not as bad as I felt about the innocent Lue Fah Yee.

CHAPTER 20

'ALL THE CHILD do is read and sulk. You know that?'

That is what Mama continually griped about. Not satisfied with her constant rumbling and grumbling at and about me.

'He is seven years old, Mama. What do you expect from him?'

'He should be running in the yard or riding a bicycle or making something out of a piece of old wood. Not sitting there on the veranda day in day out with his nose in a comic book.'

And even after I reminded her that Daphne did exactly the same thing, all she could say was, 'He is a boy.'

So maybe I should have been relieved the day he told me he'd been out with some other boys. It seemed healthy, until he said, 'Seeing some people Uncle Kenneth knows downtown.'

'Downtown! With Kenneth?'

Karl immediately clammed up and buried his head further in the Green Lantern's latest exploits.

When I asked Kenneth about it he was offhand. 'What yu fussing yuself 'bout? It was only a visit to some people who owe me money.'

'Owe you money? You are a thirteen-year-old schoolboy, Kenneth. Who could possibly owe you money?'

But there was no answer. He just shrugged his shoulders and walked away.

Mama was furious. 'Who give you the right to be chastising Kenneth over anything? The way you gwaan. You so respectable yourself?'

'I am not talking about being respectable. I am asking what Kenneth can be doing downtown for people to owe him money.'

'You should pay better attention to what your own children doing and leave your little brother alone.'

I looked at her in amazement. 'Mama, you don't care what he is doing? You're not interested in or concerned about that?'

'What I am concerned about is my concern. Not yours.'

What I decided? The children needed more organised activities. Evenings of playing cards and chequers and snakes and ladders. Reading. Not Batman and Superman, but real books. *Moby Dick*, *Tom Sawyer* and *Huckleberry Finn*, *The Grapes of Wrath*. Daphne playing the piano. Picking out the odd chord here and there while we sang. Not hymns from the song sheets of Mr John Wesley but popular tunes about carrying our ackee to Linstead Market, and our island in the sun. Songs from movies. *Oklahoma*, *By the Light of the Silvery Moon*, *The King and I*. Saturday-morning picture shows at the Carib. A Flash

Gordon serial. A western. The beach on Sundays with picnics of fried chicken and potato salad.

But I still didn't know how to be with them. Mui even recoiled from my hand the day she got sunburnt and I tried to rub aloe vera on her back.

'Get Ethyl to do it.'

'I can do this, Mui.'

'No, Mama. I don't like the feel.'

My own daughter couldn't bear for me to touch her. And then I thought it must run in the family. Because I couldn't remember, not even once, when my mother had touched me. Maybe to rub white rum on my back to stop me from catching a chill. Or Tiger Balm on my forehead for a headache. Vicks on my chest for a cough. Not even holding the towel over my head while I lowered to the bowl of steaming concoction that would unblock my nose. No. That was all Sissy, who washed and dressed my cuts, and soothed my bruises, and brushed my hair, and tidied my skirt to make it hang just right.

As far as conversation was concerned, that was a complete and utter disaster. 'Are you OK?' 'Good day at school?' 'Much homework?' 'Anything to tell me?' It was all pointless, empty, noise. And nothing the children ever seemed inclined to respond to. Pathetic, really. But that was how we went on. Letting our near-silence cement itself, while I listened to Mui quiz Ethyl about everything, from where the months on the calendar come from to why a lizard's tail continues to wriggle after you cut it off. Questions Ethyl had no answers to.

Sometimes she asked Ethyl about her life in the country, and why her mother had sent her to work in Kingston and what it was like to live in a city instead of roaming free through the open land and banana groves of Portland. Ethyl's answers, despite her trying to dress them up, always sounded sad. There was an emptiness in her heart when she compared then and now, covered over with a cheery tone to make sure that 'Miss Mui' knew how grateful Ethyl was for her job and living in the house, and caring for 'a beautiful young miss like you'. Listening to it reminded me of me and Sissy. Even more so the day I saw Mui standing at the ironing board while Ethyl arranged the pillowcase for her to press. And then I remembered the look of freedom and independence on Sissy's face the first time I visited her at her boarding house in Franklyn Town.

I was leaning over Mui's shoulder as she sat at the table with Hampton.

'Because I want you to come with me.'

'Why?' she asked, looking up from the square of red rice paper she was busy cutting and arranging to be pasted on to the bamboo frame. For the kite she and Hampton were building together.

'Because you want to see Aunt Daphne and Grandma, don't you?'

'No.'

Hampton raised his brows but said nothing.

'Mui, you spend so much time down here, trailing after Zhang with your tai chi lessons and questions about China. And pestering Hampton to make kites and karts and take you to the beach. Don't you think it would be nice to go uptown for a change?'

'I am happy here.' She stood up. Brushed her sticky hands on her dress and shook her head to reposition her plaits down her back. 'Do you know what a revolution is?'

'What?'

'It is when the masses say enough is enough. The people who don't have any power. They say no more. We are tired of having nothing. Tired of being told what to do by other people. Tired of being poor and kept down with no hope. Tired of being oppressed. That is their plight.'

'Their plight?'

'Yes, Mommy. Plight. The plight of the people. In this country. Jamaica. Land we love.'

'Well that's fine but what I'd like you to do right now is gather together whatever you want to take with you and get in the car.'

'You don't care?'

'About the poor people?'

'Or my plight?'

Hampton snorted as he started to clear away and tidy up. Putting the scissors and glue in the box with the paper remnants.

'Yes, I do,' I said. And I did. Underneath my worries of motherhood, and regret about what happened in Back-O-Wall, and shame over Vincent and Tilly. And Isaac. 'And it is important. But you are not a part of the plight, Mui. You are a child who should be more interested in puzzles and games.'

Karl walked over to us. Slowly but deliberately.

'Don't yu want to see Ethyl?'

And that is how we managed to set off to Lady Musgrave Road. With Mui sitting in the front gazing out of the side window and Karl sitting in the back. Reading a comic book. In the silent car. By the time we reached Cross Roads I'd had enough and turned on the radio.

'Do you know where Karl and Kenneth went?'

'No, Mommy.'

'I think you do know, Mui. And you need to tell me right now. This instant.'

Her lips were sealed. Determined not to be a turncoat like me. Mama was standing behind me.

'You speak up now, young lady, before I take a strap to you.'

I turned my head. 'Nobody is taking a strap to her. Especially not you.'

'If you say so, but you still need her to open her mouth.' She kissed her teeth and walked away.

I tried once again. 'It has been dark for hours, Mui. I am worried about them, that is all. Please tell me where they went and at what time.'

'I told you. I don't know.'

The last thing I wanted was to have to telephone Pao. I even thought about getting in the car and driving around but what would be the point? I had no idea where to begin.

'Mama, you don't know where Kenneth hangs out?' I was shouting to her from the dining room where I was still wrangling with the poker-faced Mui.

'Hangs out? What kind of language is that?'

I took a deep breath. An innocent nine-year-old child was being dragged around town by a fifteen-year-old tearaway and she was worried about my language.

'His friends?'

She shouted back from the piano room. 'You should concentrate on getting your stubborn daughter to tell you what she knows. That would be more useful than her sermons about the plight of the poor. And how Jamaica will rise up in revolution.'

At eleven pm, after they had been gone since early afternoon, I decided to call the police.

'I will send a constable to gather the particulars.' That is what the voice at the other end of the line told me. But at three am there was still no officer at the door even though I'd called them again at one o'clock to impress upon them the age of the children, at which point the desk officer said, 'We dealing with something else right now. I will send someone over as soon as I can, but honestly it may be morning before that happen.'

So I sat on the veranda in the dark, wrapped in a shawl, listening to the chirping of the crickets and slapping away every mosquito that tried to settle on my arm or neck. And as daylight broke I suddenly awakened and looked up to see Kenneth and Karl sauntering up the driveway together. Actually I heard their voices first. Cheerfully chatting away as if they didn't have a care in the world.

I stood up as they reached the top of the steps. 'Hello, Mommy.'

'Hello? That is what you have to say to me at six-thirty in the morning?'

He looked surprised, as if my anxiety was completely uncalled for. Irrational hysteria. Kenneth piped up, 'Is my fault, Fay. Sorry. Just a little thing that tek an unexpected turn.

Married to Pao yu must be used to dat.' And then as he swaggered past me, removing his hand from his pocket to open the door, 'Respect to di man.'

Karl followed him into the house, looking back at me as I stood there in the growing light of dawn. I was relieved I hadn't called Pao and alerted him to the way Kenneth was following in his footsteps.

When I finally got to the bottom of it?

'An illegal card game, Karl?'

'Uncle Kenneth wasn't doing anything, Mommy. Just serving a few drinks. That was all.'

'And you didn't think there was anything wrong with that?'

'I don't know what you mean.'

'The police coming and arresting everyone. That is what you said, isn't it? Why you had to spend the night under the house and wait for the buses to start running again.'

He looked at me and sighed. I couldn't even say it was with any sense of remorse. It was more like impatience at my not being able to understand the harmless events that led to him and Kenneth hiding out with the dealer. A rogue who knew to slide out of the back door at precisely the right moment, while the police turned the place upside down searching for money and contraband and then stationed themselves inside and out in order to apprehend the men who continued to arrive throughout the night for, according to Karl, just a game of cards.

'People play cards all the time. And give each other money. The police don't care. Sometimes they do it themselves. What you are making such a fuss about?'

'You are nine years old, Karl, and you were out all night with criminals. What was I supposed to do?'

'If you were that worried you should have called my father. It would have been better than calling the police.' I glared at him.

After a while of standing there in silence he said, in a low repentant tone, 'I love you, Mommy.'

I wanted to say 'I love you too' but I didn't. It seemed so shallow to say it to him right after he'd said it to me.

Mui was sitting on the back steps playing with her paper dolls.

'I don't like you shouting at him like that.'

'I wasn't shouting.'

'You were.'

I sat down on the step next to her. 'He is getting into bad ways, Mui.'

She fiddled with a doll. Lifting the tabs to remove the dress and replacing it with another. 'He didn't do anything. He was just following behind. He is not a criminal.' She paused. And then, turning her head ever so slightly towards me, she added, 'And neither is my papa.'

Karl stepped out of the back door. Walked over and rested his hand on her shoulder.

'Want to tek a swim?'

Mui shot to her feet immediately, putting the paper dolls back in the shoebox and tucking it under her arm as she raced inside to collect her swimwear. Shouting to him, 'Last one in the pool is a ninny.'

The next time I saw Michael I told him about it. 'He is coming up for his first communion, Michael. Don't the discussions with the other children include talking about things like this?'

'In all honesty? No. Not many children share Karl's experiences. Not ones that come to Mass and Bible study classes anyway. His situation is unusual, Fay. Let's face it.'

'You have no idea what is usual or unusual.' I felt crotchety at his offhandedness. 'So what does he talk to you about?'

Michael smiled. A cheeky sort of grin. Most unpriestlike. 'Come. You know that is between him and me.'

My irritation welled up. 'Not every conversation is a confession.'

He smiled again. Tight-lipped this time. 'Don't frown like that. If there was anything to be concerned about I would tell you. Honestly.'

So I decided to leave it alone. Decided to believe that Michael knew best. Decided to trust his priestly judgement. Like a good Catholic.

And because I was at Bishop's Lodge. Downtown, feeling shaky, I decided to go to Franklyn Town and see Sissy even though she had told me so many years back not to visit her at the boarding house. And I had obeyed. But that day, for no good reason, I hopped on to the cross-town bus and paid my fare.

'What I tell yu about coming here? Didn't I tell yu?'

'You did, Sissy. You did.'

'So wat dis?'

She was angry. Seriously put out at seeing me standing there at her front door.

'So yu not going to invite me in?'

She huffed and puffed, looking past me to across the street for inspiration. And then she said, 'Well, time come to everything.'

She made coffee. We sat in the yard out back. Oddly.

'Something wrong with the chairs on your veranda?'

'Yu come here to see me or sit on my veranda chair?'

So I shut up and enjoyed the cool breeze in the yard and talked about Karl and Mui, and how I had distanced myself from them because I didn't want to harm them.

She choked slightly on the smoke from her pipe. Suppressing a laugh that was more a snort. 'Which mother never do that?' She took another puff. 'Since di beginning a time, Fay. The beginning a time.'

Sissy's point was that every mother damages her children. That is life. That is where our wounds come from. Unintentionally. Unavoidably. In small ways and sometimes in colossal ones but always there is impact. Because we are young and their children, and expecting so much from them. Perhaps too much.

'So yu see, it cyan be helped. You being absent in body or spirit not saving dem from nothing. It just meking some other something for dem to have feelings about.' She looked over at me. 'When deh growed. Not that yu can ever guess what yu coming and going mean to dem. Dat is a mystery. All yu can do is be true to yuself. Be who yu are in all yu glory and Him upstairs will tek care a everything else.' She laughed. A genuine chuckle this time. And slapped herself on the thigh. 'Not that I want to start sounding like yu mother.'

We finished our coffee. 'What gwaan is what gwaan. Deh will have to mek sense a it themselves. Just di same way yu doing dat very same thing right now.'

It wasn't until I was leaving that I discovered the reason Sissy told me to stop coming to the boarding house. Because across the street, in broad daylight, stood my father. On the veranda. Talking to some woman. Standing so close to her, so relaxed and comfortable, I knew it wasn't a chance encounter.

I looked at Sissy. 'Gloria Campbell,' she said.

'Gloria Campbell? Pao's whore?'

'Yu always know he know her. Dat is how come she end up here. After he find her wandering di street when she lose her live-in domestic job. And he bring her to me to board.'

I didn't say anything. Actually, I didn't know. How would I? Who was going to tell me?

'Yu even meet di sister long time back. On dis veranda right here when she come back from school one day.'

I stepped back inside the house in case Papa should look over and see me. 'Is he a regular customer?'

'Maybe. Maybe not. But deh have a lot a communication, dat is fi sure.'

CHAPTER 21

THE FIRST THING I heard about Grandmother Chung taking sick was from Tyrone, who came by the house late one evening to tell me.

'I been asking Beverley for weeks if she been in touch with you.'

'Weeks, Tyrone? GC been sick that long?'

'She tek bad two maybe three months back. Took to her bed and not raised herself since.'

'And the doctors?'

'Say there is nothing they can do. She just slowly going downhill.'

What was wrong with her? Kidney trouble. 'Just come see the old woman when yu can.'

The next morning I went over to Hagley Park Road where the maid greeted me with a sober face and the place was sad and silent like maybe GC had already passed. Beverley was sitting in an armchair by the side of the bed. Her grandmother was asleep. A fraction of the woman I used to know. Like she had physically shrunk and was fading away into nothingness.

It was such a long time since Beverley and I had seen each other. I didn't know how she would feel about me turning up unannounced. But she surprised me, standing straight up like she did and opening her arms to take me in.

'I didn't know if you would come.'

'Of course I've come. Tyrone only told me last night.'

How we sat? Next to each other holding hands. That is how we spent the days and nights, sometimes sleeping sometimes not, as we listened to GC's wheezing chest and failing breath. And watched her complexion get more and more grey as the hours and days ticked by. The Chiang Kai-shek incident we never mentioned. No apologies or post-mortem needed. It was gone. Dissolved by time.

The funeral was simple. A glass-fronted coffin. White lilies. Her parish priest. And family, including Beverley's parents who came in from New York, an aunt from Washington and an uncle from England. None of whom Beverley or Tyrone seemed to care about very much. Or know particularly well for that matter.

So we sat. Beverley between Tyrone and me, in the front pew, as we bid farewell to the woman who had shaped so much of our lives.

A week later, when the will was read, we discovered that Grandmother Chung had left everything to Beverley and Tyrone. Every last penny of what was quite a sizeable sum.

'Captain Charles Meacham,' he said, extending his hand to be shaken.

I shook it. 'A captain now?'

'I beg your pardon?'

'I seem to be going down in the world. First a colonel, then a major and now a captain.'

He laughed. A pleasant, easy-going kind of laugh. 'This is just a courtesy introduction. I am not going to hound you about communists like Hutton. The good major has done his duty and is now safely back in England.' He smiled. 'There are other things I find more interesting.'

The things Captain Meacham found more interesting? Having himself a damn good time, which is all he seemed to do twenty-four hours a day seven days a week. Drinking liquor, gambling and carrying on with as many women as he could lay his hands on. The younger the better.

Still, I suppose there wasn't much else for him to do because in September 1961 Norman Manley had to hold a referendum for the people of Jamaica to decide if we wanted to stay in the West Indies Federation. That much controversy there was about whether or not the smaller islands were dragging us down, which was Bustamante's opinion.

So the nation voted and we left the Federation and Manley and Busta went to England to see the Queen who granted us independence. To take effect from 6th August 1962. So really Meacham was just kicking his heels. The British army was leaving and I would finally be free.

But not quite, because actually I was just like Jamaica. Colonised by the British, used for their own ends and now abandoned to my own fate. So I asked Meacham to take me to England.

'I can't do that! On what basis could I possibly do a thing like that?'

'Captain Meacham, I am in danger here. Once you leave. Can't you see?'

'Let's not get melodramatic. People are excited about independence. All those other things will blow over. Trust me. No one knows anything about your involvement with the Lue Fah Yee incident or the bus driver and his friends.'

'They do, Captain.'

He looked at me understandingly. Scratched his ample forehead. 'They will forget.'

Beverley thought maybe Meacham was right. Nothing bad had happened to me so far. Besides, it wasn't the British army that was keeping me safe. It was Pao, or rather the name of Yang Pao, and the Mrs that came before it.

'As long as I am married to him.'

'Oh Fay. Divorce?'

Not in Beverley Chung's book of Catholic etiquette. Affairs, yes. Divorce, out of the question. 'That is why Audley and I never married. To avoid these kinds of complications.'

She fiddled in her bag. Extracted a lipstick and small turquoise mirror in the shape of a fan. And in between tending to her lips and using her little finger to tidy up the corner of her mouth she said, 'Anyway, isn't Father Kealey supposed to be talking you out of that? How long can it take? Doesn't he have other sinners to attend to?'

I ignored it. Poured myself a drink instead from GC's cabinet. Then I asked her what she knew about hiring a private detective.

Her eyes widened in excitement. 'Serious? What for?'

'I need to find out about someone, that's all.'

'Which someone?'

'Gloria Campbell.'

'The whore?' I nodded. 'After all these years? You think it's going to make any difference to anything?' I didn't answer.

She studied me carefully. And then she said, 'I'll ask our attorney. He has to know somebody.'

'Somebody reliable and trustworthy, Beverley. Discreet.'

'Discretion is my middle name. Didn't you know?' And then she smiled as she raised the champagne glass to her lips.

The strange thing? The thought of my father with Gloria Campbell was more upsetting to me than my knowledge of her and Pao. About Pao there was a sort of impersonal acceptance. About Papa there was a deep sense of betrayal.

So when the detective told me that what they were doing together was running an illegal money-lending business I was relieved. It seemed more wholesome than him having an affair with a seasoned prostitute. Because it was the sort of thing my father would do. Make money. Even if it was under as opposed to over the counter. I felt I could look him in the eye again. Touch his hand. Share my woes. Despite reports of a house in Ocho Rios. I just decided to ignore that. Imagined they were counting their money.

The photograph? Taken while she was crossing King Street and looking sideways at the traffic, was a picture of a woman in charge of herself. A woman in control of what she was doing. Serious but relaxed. Her solid black build, with curves in all the right places, I'd already seen from Sissy's veranda. But her satin-smooth skin and the confidence in her eyes I only saw in the close-up snapshot.

The child was harder to swallow: A girl exactly the same age as Karl. Expelled from her prep school for giving backchat to the nuns and fighting with her classmates in the schoolyard.

I got her address in Barbican and drove over there. Late afternoons, sometimes early evening. Occasionally, I took a trip in the morning. Parking the car around the corner and walking past the house like I was just strolling the street going about my own business. Once or twice I even took a cab and let it cruise by.

All I saw was the old woman. So ancient it was a wonder she could manage the household chores. Why employ somebody like that? With a child in the house to be attended to. It was beyond me.

The child I spotted a few times. Coming and going in her school uniform, sitting on the veranda, skipping in the yard with her rope, talking to the old woman. She was black, maybe even a shade darker than her mother. Not like Karl and Mui, light-skinned with Karl's wavy curls or Mui's dead-straight Chinese hair. No. Her hair was African. Tight like her mother's. The sort of hair that needed relaxing and ironing and constant tending with coconut oil; conditioning and moisturising the ends; tying a scarf around it at night to prevent breaking and tearing; a wide-toothed comb for careful disentanglement; hair pomade and grapeseed oil to withstand the high temperature of the Marcel iron. When she is older. But now, the child had short plaits that stuck out at the side, and danced back and forth as she hula-hooped.

Gloria? Yes. I glimpsed her once or twice because it seemed she still spent most of her time in the house across the street from Sissy even though she'd stopped living there years ago, just before the child was born. How she looked? Beautiful. Inside and out.

Pao? Never. Not once in the many weeks I was traipsing over there. But it didn't matter. I could feel his presence. His aura like a giant cloak hanging over the place.

Papa? No. Thank God. I don't think I could have faced that. So I stopped driving to Barbican before that particular calamity occurred.

I didn't say anything to Papa about Gloria. That was his business. His secret. I didn't say anything to Pao either. But I knew.

Beverley's plan using GC's money was to open a shop. Just like she'd talked about all those years back.

'In Constant Spring. The premises are perfect. Come and look.'

I did. She was right. It was perfect. One vast open floor to be fitted with display cabinets and counters, and stocked with Chinese rugs and vases, garments and tea, tableware and kitchenware. Everything from silver-tipped ivory chopsticks to oversized lacquered screens. Chung's Emporium. Like Nancy Lee's father's backyard storeroom. Only a hundred times bigger and brighter and better.

The beam on her face could have lit the city for a week. 'Tyrone is going to come in as well. As a partner.'

I smiled. 'That's fantastic.' And then I said, 'Are you sure this is what you want?'

'Never been more sure about anything.' She spun around in the empty space, sending her skirt fluttering in the air. 'Want to be a partner as well?'

'Me? I don't have any money, Beverley.'

'But don't you think we were made for this? Dues In/Dues Out. Procurement, import orders, inventories, storage, distribution. It was all the same thing, wasn't it? The Royal Army Ordnance Corps.'

'That was you, Beverley. I was doing something entirely different.'

She sat down on her haunches, gathering her skirt about her. Such an unlikely pose for a woman like Beverley Chung.

'Ever since I left the army I've been trying to think what it is I want to do. Nothing ever came to mind. Apart from this. Remember?'

I nodded. 'I didn't think you were serious.'

'Maybe I wasn't then. I don't know. But with GC gone it seems like I should make an effort to do something. Not just flit away my days sleeping and eating and dancing. And spending her money.' She looked at me. 'Know what I mean? And the Chinese theme. Because of her. GC. Who she was. How she lived. Seems like the only thing we should sell. In honour of her.' She paused. 'So we going to do this then?'

'You do it.'

She stood up. Came over and linked my arm as we walked towards the door and the smell of roasting peanuts from the sidewalk vendor.

'We will do it.'

'I don't want my name on anything, Beverley. Seriously. Absolutely nothing. I don't want anybody coming to track me down. I've had enough of that.'

'The British are leaving, Fay. Haven't you heard?'

And so they did because on 22nd June 1962 the Royal Hampshire Regiment left Jamaica, bringing to a close three hundred years of British troops stationed on the island. It was the end of an era. The slave masters had gone. We were in charge of ourselves now.

To celebrate independence, we had eight days of singing and dancing and street parades. Her Royal Highness Princess Margaret even came to wish us well in a spectacular ceremony at the National Stadium attended by a multitude of local and foreign dignitaries. Lowering the British flag at midnight and raising the black, green and yellow of Jamaica just before they set off the fireworks. A splendid affair which I did not attend. Why? Because I was cross they had left me behind after changing the entire course of my life. They were gone. And I was still here. Without a handler, which is what Captain Meacham liked to call himself.

So I took Karl and went to the movies. The drive-in at Harbour View. Five films back-to-back. All through the night. Most of which he spent asleep in the rear seat of the car. Me? I was dead to the world as well. With my eyes wide open.

Afterwards, I was relieved it was over. The jubilation. Glad that things could get back to normal with our new prime minister, the first prime minister of an independent Jamaica, Mr Alexander Bustamante, going to work to show us what he could do to make a better life for all. But honestly, I didn't feel that optimistic. And all Pao's prodding and poking did was to make me angry.

'What is it? Yu worried what Busta going do when he make his stand for the working man? Or maybe yu think we was better off under British rule? I know that is how some people feel.' Another time he told me: 'Slavery is over. We in charge of our own destiny now.'

And I said, 'God help us.' Which he didn't like.

'Yu would rather we mek some links with America then?'

I was tired of listening to him. Tired of talking about it. Tired of the sloganising. 'Out of Many, One People', even though we were quite some mixture.

Slaves from Africa; Chinese and Indian indentured workers; poor Scots, Irish and Welsh imported to increase the white population; wage-labourers from northern Europe; Jews given permission by Cromwell to settle in British colonies; Chinese men escaping the civil war encouraged to become the shop-keeping middle class, like the Lebanese dry-goods pedlars fleeing the Muslim Turks; the Maroons, living high in the mountains; and, of course, the descendants of the white planters including their mulatto offspring.

And then thinking of Mama with her afternoon tea and cake, so allegedly proud of her slave heritage but who, still inside, harboured the attitude she had about black men. Maybe about all black people, including herself. Thinking of that and remembering everything I learned from Isaac, I said to Pao, 'My whole life has been spent being white for Cicely to stop her feeling ashamed, and being black for Cicely to stop her feeling alone. I had to be Catholic for Cicely because Methodist was too black, and I had to hold back at school for Cicely because being smart was too white. I had to spend with style for Cicely so she could show off her new wealth and class, and I had to be prim and chaste for Cicely so she could protect the reputation of black womanhood. And where me being Chinese came into all of this for her I don't know. But whatever I did she picked and poked and prodded, and found fault with me because in Jamaica the colour of your skin still counts for everything. You think independence is going to change that?'

But really the whole long speech was unfair. I had pinned it all on Mama when it was me. My snobbery and my acceptance of my privilege. It was my guilt.

So Pao and I left it at that. And Beverley bought her store. Opening it in grand style in the spirit of a new Jamaica. We were in business, with the Chung name above the door and me moving silently in the shadows as I had learnt to become accustomed.

I waited quite a while before mentioning Gloria's child to Michael. The daughter who went to St Andrew High School at the same time Karl started at St George's College.

'You mean Esther?'

A wave of shock rolled over me. 'You know? How do you know? What do you know?'

He patted the bench next to him, urging me to sit down. I didn't feel like it. I wanted to see his face when he gave me his explanation. He crossed his legs. Crossed his wrists over his knee.

'The child was in trouble, Fay. With school.' I knew but still I wanted to hear it from him. 'Her mother brought her to me seeking help. Guidance.' He paused. Studied me a little. 'The only reason I saw her is because of who her father is. When Gloria told me I felt I had to help.'

'Who is the father?' I wanted him to say it.

'You don't know?'

'I want you to tell me.'

He looked down at the ground. Took one hand and brushed his trouser leg like he was removing some unwanted speck from his thigh except nothing was there.

'Yang Pao.'

The jolt I felt was swift and brief. Not the heart-stopping, chest-wrenching quake I'd imagined it would be. Maybe because, in truth, I already knew.

'Are you sure?' I asked him. He nodded. 'How can you be so sure?'

The guilty look on his face and the accompanying silence told me that he'd had it from the horse's mouth. Not just taken Gloria's word for it.

'How long have you been seeing Pao?'

Michael stood up and tried to take hold of my arm. 'It isn't what you think,' he said but I shrugged away just as a gardener passed us with his barrow in what suddenly felt like the most exposed public garden ever created.

'Nothing you have said to me have I ever repeated to Pao. Or anyone else, for that matter.'

I believed him. But my heart was still pounding. Not for the reason I would have imagined, but because I was jealous. Jealous of sharing him. With Pao and Gloria. And now the child, Esther. Because what I wanted was for Michael to be mine and mine alone.

CHAPTER 22

CHUNG'S EMPORIUM SOLD everything Chinese. Imported and delivered to Constant Spring on trucks directly from the wharf. One gigantic floor of traditional *changshan* and *cheongsam*, blouses, jackets and trousers for men, women and children; porcelain tableware; ivory chopstick sets; antique teapots; appliqué table-cloths; fabrics in plain silks and brocades; jade jewellery; rugs, paintings and silkscreens; lacquerware of decorative boxes, jars, screens and cabinets; fans hand-held and wall-mounted; Qing, Ming, Tan and Han vases, ornaments and jars; Buddha statues; temple bells; ceramic and metal miniature pagodas; incense and burners; paper lanterns and parasols; embroidered purses; tai chi suits and swords; books on Buddhism, feng shui, zodiacs and mah-jongg; ancient texts and poetry; traditional Chinese medi-cines. There was even an entire corner devoted to tea.

'Too many fingers in our crates at the wharf. Dat is di prob-lem.' Tyrone was irate. 'Half the stuff going missing before it even leave the dock.'

Beverley was smoking a cigarette. Something I hadn't seen her do for ages. Not since school, behind the swimming pool, and over the years the odd one here and there. But not constantly as she'd been doing these past few months.

'If it carries on like this we'll be bankrupt before the year is out.'

So even though I was in two minds about stepping out of the shadows, I decided to help when Captain Meacham fell into my lap. Listed in the *Gleaner* among those honoured guests attending the anniversary celebrations of independence, which included a military parade from George VI Memorial Park to Cross Roads with the prime minister taking a salute.

The idea came to me one afternoon as I was on my way to see Michael. Parking the car just around the corner and checking the doors were secure before slipping the keys into my purse and straightening my linen dress. And then, walking towards Bishop's Lodge in an absent-minded sort of way, who should I bump into? Of all people. Right there in the street. The words were out of my mouth before I could think.

'My, my. Gloria Campbell.'

After she recovered from the shock of my recognising her, and what seemed like an endless silence with me looking as condescending as I could, I finally said, 'I have often wondered what it would be like to meet you face to face. Have you ever wondered that?'

'We met already. One time long ago, in your father's wine store when you were organising your sister's birthday party.'

'Really?' I didn't remember. No surprise there. But then out of pure spite, motivated by nothing other than plain downright nastiness, I said, 'Are you still enjoying the jade necklace?' Which didn't make me feel as superior as I thought it would. Actually it made me feel rather small and miserly. Impoverished by my own unkindness.

'You and me been sharing a life for a very long time whether or not we like it. So maybe it is providence that we should meet like this because now we don't have to wonder.'

She stunned me with her eloquence and outspokenness. But really I should have expected it. From seeing her photograph and watching her at Barbican. And knowing the business she was in.

I stood there for a while looking at her dressed in that ghastly floral cotton frock. And then I tucked my purse under my arm and walked away. Knowing for sure that she had just come from visiting Michael.

I'd sent a note to Meacham via the independence anniversary organisers. He'd told me to come to the house he'd rented in New Kingston. The place he was staying with his daughter. A pasty, skinny eighteen-year-old with short brown hair, who he told me was on her way to Oxford University to study law.

'Good for you,' I said to her as she passed through the living room picking up the keys to his borrowed Rover car.

'Club Havana,' she said.

'Really?'

After she left, I asked Meacham the favour I had come for.

'I can't help you, Fay. No longer in my jurisdiction. We gave you up. Remember? You are on your own now. All I am here to do is celebrate.' He raised his Appleton-filled glass. Jingling with ice.

'After everything I risked for you?'

'You risked nothing for me.'

'The British.'

'That was a very small contribution you made for the greater good.' He poured himself another drink. Motioned towards me with the bottle. I shook my head.

Meacham sipped his rum while giving my request a second thought. 'OK. You need safe passage for your goods. I can understand that. Customs keep their nose out. Dock workers keep their busy little hands to themselves.'

He picked up the telephone. While he dialled the number he said to me, 'For old times' sake.'

I heard the voice answer at the other end. 'Superintendent Donaldson.'

'Reggie? Charles Meacham.'

And after exchanging a few pleasantries he told Reggie what he wanted, for old times' sake. And Reggie agreed. Seemed they were pals. You could almost hear them slapping each other on the back.

He put down the receiver and turned to me. 'After the holiday weekend. Monday morning, bright and early, we'll go up to Harman Barracks and sort this out.' And then he raised his glass in a conciliatory manner. 'OK?'

But when Monday morning came Meacham had gone. Back to England, so the caretaker at the rented house told me.

'When?'

'Saturday morning. Hurry-hurry.'

So I went to see Donaldson anyway. At Harman Barracks. Home of the Jamaican Constabulary. And he agreed safe passage for our goods. As a favour for Meacham. For old times' sake.

It wasn't until the Wednesday that I saw the notice in the *Gleaner*. Two youths stabbed to death in the car park of Club Havana. On Friday 2nd August. And I wondered if it had anything to do with Captain Meacham's daughter and their sudden return to England.

'Guns now, Pao?'

'It a little plastic thing. Dat is all.'

I snatched the toy from Karl's hand and smashed it under my foot. Grinding it into the Matthews Lane concrete with my heel.

'What di hell yu doing?' Pao shouted as he grabbed my arm to unsteady me and Karl tried to pull him away.

'It doesn't matter, Daddy.'

But Pao wasn't listening. He was on his bended knees gathering together the broken pieces of the Buccaneer pistol. He looked up at me. 'What yu do that for?'

What I should have said? Because I was worried about Karl. Afraid of where Kenneth was leading him. Horrified at the example Pao was setting. What I did say?

'Because I am sick and tired, Pao.' He stood up to face me. 'Sick and tired of you and your little kingdom. Lording over Chinatown like an emperor. Rolling around in your filthy business like a pig in swill every day. Coming back here to play the perfect father. With toy guns no less.'

That was when Mui rushed up to me and punched me in the stomach. Firm but half-hearted like she wasn't completely sure she meant it.

'Don't you talk to my papa like that.' And then she leant back into Pao's open arms. Staring up at me. Just like Pao was staring, with Karl standing by his side.

Pao turned to the children and hugged them both. Together in one embrace.

'You two go about your business now. No need for this to turn into a brawl.' And then he kissed them. A peck on the cheek for each. And patted Mui lightly on the bottom as she and Karl ran off up the yard. Hand in hand. Towards Zhang.

'Yu little brother pestering me to get a piece of my action. Yu know that?' Nodding his head the way he liked to in that upward motion. 'Cornering me every chance he get up Lady Musgrave Road.' He picked up the fragments of the gun. Strolled over to the garbage bin and dropped them in. Then he brushed off his hands. One against the other. And walked towards the gate. And I knew he was going straight to Gloria.

How it started with Louis? Late one night on the wharf when he came up to me and said, 'Miss Beverley Chung?' Because the arrangement with Donaldson meant that we had to be on the dock to collect our shipments. Whatever time of the day or night they came in. Checking off each crate to make sure it was still sealed, and counting every single one on to the truck that Beverley's men would drive up to Constant Spring to the Emporium storeroom. With me signing Beverley's name on the importation docket because I didn't want to be directly implicated and looked enough like her, especially in a dim light, to get away with it. Not that anybody down there was paying any attention. Or cared, for that matter. So it took me by surprise. Being addressed like that. It stunned me into silence. And it was in that brief moment's hesitation that a lie became reality.

'Louis DeFreitas.' He put his palm flat on his chest by way of introduction. As soon as I saw the long fingernail on his left little finger I knew he was trouble. The thin moustache that looked as if he'd drawn it on with an eyebrow pencil. The paleness of his skin. The cunning in his eyes like an animal on the prowl. It all spelt danger, but what could I do? So I just stood there.

'What I find interesting is how yu manage to get yu crates off di ship and on to yu truck without even disturbing di customs officers from their domino game. Zip, bang. Yu gone. Just like that. With all the nails and tape still in place. Not one lid lifted or paperwork stamped. How yu manage to do that? Yu have a secret, Miss Chung?'

I could feel the heat rising in my face. Even my neck was burning.

'I can't help you, I'm afraid.'

'No?' He smiled at me with narrowing eyes that looked almost yellow in the dim light. 'Well that is a shame. I was hoping you and me could scratch each other's back, if yu tek my meaning.' He looked around. 'These bwoys down here do nothing but sit. Five minutes heaving, sit for a hour. That is how deh do things. But not for you. I been noticing that. Chung Emporium get it business done quick-quick. So I reckon a few palms getting greased. But the customs thing, that is a real mystery. Yu nuh think so?'

I didn't reply. And then, quickly looking around, I said, 'The truck is loaded. I have to go.'

'So yu say.'

The next time, after many 'how you dos' and waving from a distance, I made a mistake. It was late, very late, and I'd been waiting on the wharf for ever. It was raining. I was thirsty. Hungry. And he offered me food. Shouting across the dock: 'I have a feast here di bwoys bring down from Barry Street. Nice hot Chinese food, Miss Chung. I bet yu wouldn't say no to a taste a dis?' Which is exactly what I should have said.

He was swinging the beer bottle in the air when I went over to him. Held between his thumb and forefinger. 'I thought di smell a dis would get your attention.' He handed me a pair of wooden chopsticks still in their paper wrap from the restaurant. Then he turned to the men sitting on chairs and benches in their makeshift shelter. 'Mek way nuh. Yu cyan see we got a lady joining us?' And with a flamboyant bow he produced a cloth from nowhere and flicked it over one of the canvas chairs. So I sat down, took the cardboard container from him and started to eat. He passed me a cold beer. I drank.

His men talked excitedly to each other, grumbling and complaining about the government, the violence in West Kingston, how much money they had lost at the races, deficient women, ungrateful children. Except DeFreitas. He spoke to no one. He just sat and watched. A walking stick by his side with a silver fox-head for a handle.

Then he turned to me. 'Yu think any more on what I say to yu 'bout di customs?'

Fear was rising inside me. I looked round but Beverley's men were way off, still loading up. 'I don't know how I can help you.'

'No?' He gazed lazily at me. 'I'm sure we can help each other. It just a question of if yu want to.' He paused. 'What yu want from me in exchange for a piece a yu magic?'

'I'm not in that business, Mr DeFreitas.'

'Louis. Call me Louis.' And he smiled but it wasn't so much friendliness as menace. More like the smile the wolf might have given to Little Red Riding Hood.

I got to my feet, handed him the empty carton and chopsticks. 'Thank you. It was kind of you to include me.'

'No problem.'

Three days later a black Rover pulled up next to me as I was crossing Princess Street. When the two plainclothes men got out and ushered me into the back seat I knew where we were going.

The brass plaque on the office door said 'Superintendent Reginald Donaldson'.

'I hear yu been keeping company with Louis DeFreitas.' Donaldson was tall and hefty with his African hair cut close to his head. A slight tugging on the buttons of his khaki jacket.

'I'm not keeping company with him. I bump into him at the wharf from time to time and we exchange a few words, that is all.'

'What words he exchange with you?'

I swallowed. A sudden rush of saliva. 'He wants to know how it is that Chung's Emporium manages to take delivery of its shipments without clearing customs.'

'How he know about that?'

'He's always down there, Reggie. He can see what is happening.'

Donaldson sat back. Slightly startled at me calling him by his first name.

He decided to let it go. 'So what yu say to him 'bout it?'

'Nothing.' I paused. 'He thinks I'm Beverley Chung.'

He smiled. A big, broad grin. 'Does he now.' And then he mulled it over. Weaving his tubby fingers together across his chest. 'Yu sure he nuh know who you are?'

'I told you. He thinks I'm Beverley.'

'Good. Because if he realise who yu married to he would see you as more leverage than a few customs-free crates. Yu get me? Him and Yang Pao turf too close together without one a dem wanting to tek over the other one. It just a matter a time. And trouble fah me.'

I got it, even though I knew Pao wasn't interested in any turf other than Chinatown. And DeFreitas's interest in the crates and customs was only the thief in him hungry for the plunder.

A week later there was a note from Donaldson inside the post-office box I'd rented in Beverley's name. To keep the inquisitive eyes of Lady Musgrave Road out of my business. It simply read: 'Be nice to our friend.'

I decided to ignore it. But the next thing was, Louis was asking me to dinner.

'I will have dinner with you, Louis. But I'm not coming to Tivoli Gardens.'

'Yu think I so rude as to invite a woman like you to a place like that? What yu tek me for? No, Beverley. You name it and I will go anywhere you want.'

'Yu mad?' That was what Beverley said to me when I told her.

'What yu expect me to do? Yu know what would happen to me if Donaldson decide to go tell everybody he know 'bout what I did for the British those years running up to independence.' The horror on her face mirrored the panic in my voice. 'All I need is a big *Gleaner* headline to finish me off completely.'

'You think the newspaper would be interested in a thing like that? So long ago.'

She thought on it and then she added, 'Well, maybe it not such a long time in the life of a country. Two years. And with all the trouble right now and the politicking that going on; and the feelings that been running so high against the Chinese.'

I met DeFreitas in a quiet, out-of-the-way, not-too-upmarket restaurant. A discreet location, Beverley had called it, and she was right. The chances of anyone recognising me there were minimal. She said non-existent. But still, to err on the side of caution, I chose a table in the darkest corner and positioned myself in the shadows. Facing the room so I could see who was coming my way.

'How yu find a place like this? I thought I was going drop off di end a di earth driving over here.' He smiled and sat down, gulping down the entire tumbler of ice-water and wiping his wet hands from the glass on the napkin before refolding it and placing it back on the table.

'So, Beverley Chung, I finally get yu to myself.'

What we talked about while eating the escovitch fish and rice and peas who knows. All I remember was trying to make sure I didn't trip up over the details of Beverley's life. Not to get caught in a lie.

'What about you, Louis?'

'Nothing to tell. Mother from Back-O-Wall. Father, God knows, except he got to be white judging from di shade a my skin. Run 'round barefoot wid my backside hanging out my pants and not a farthing to my name. Got shoes now, though. And plenty more besides.' He smiled. 'Don't get me wrong. I not complaining. I skinny but I crafty enough to get di chicken when I want it. Yu know, like the fox.' And he lifted up the walking stick to show me the handle.

'What happened to your leg?'

'This?' He tapped his right leg lightly with the stick. 'Polio. When I was young. Tell yu di truth, it a small miracle I walking at all. So every day I feel grateful. As long as I don't overstress myself it don't bother me none.'

I expected him to mention the customs situation but he didn't. He just ate and drank and talked. And actually it was a pleasant enough evening even though a terrified part of me was holding my breath the whole time.

Afterwards, we walked to the car park and I realised I had come in Papa's Mercedes. But then what would Louis know about Beverley Chung's car? He saw me settled inside, smoothing my skirt to make sure it wouldn't get caught in the car door as he shut it. And I drove away, catching sight of him in the rear-view mirror as he stood there watching the tail-lights disappear. The fingernail I never asked him about. I knew it was the mark of a gambler. A card-sharp. A cheat.

Everything I learnt about Louis during the following months I reported to Donaldson. Who his friends and associates were; his men at the wharf doing nothing at all, not even showing up for work half the time, which the authorities couldn't do anything about because complaining could cause union trouble and even strike action; the pilfering of shipments; handling stolen goods; drug trafficking; raids on rival gangs.

But the thing that made Donaldson's eyes light up was the week Louis hijacked an unmarked police vehicle full of pistols, revolvers, shotguns and assault rifles. It turned out there were even some automatic machineguns and a grenade launcher on the truck. Donaldson said they were all confiscated weapons on their way to be destroyed.

'Incinerated. Melted down. But how did DeFreitas know about it?'

'He said somebody told him but I don't know who.'

And I never found out because in no time at all one of Pao's men, Samuels, was selling guns in Chinatown. So Papa told me.

'Big trouble, Fay. Big-big.'

'Like the riots?'

'Oh this nothing to do with burning and looting Chinese business.' He laughed. 'No need for three days' lockdown like before.'

'How you know 'bout all this anyway?'

'It all over the place, Fay. How Pao go buy back all the guns Samuels sell to Chin and Chen, Chung, Lee, Leung, Fung, Huang, Cecil Fong, Alfred Ho. Everyone. Even Lowe buy one because he think Pao order it.'

'So what going happen now?'

'It already happen. Pao go Tivoli Gardens and give back guns. And hand over Samuels as well. Hand him over to boss man. Just like that.'

'In Tivoli Gardens?'

'Tivoli Gardens, Fay. Tivoli Gardens.'

That was when I told Donaldson I had to get out. The situation was getting too close to home. And he agreed. What good all of this was doing anyway I didn't know. A police raid here. A police raid there. But really, nothing much seemed to have changed. Besides, the bedroom thing with Louis was building pressure. Sooner or later he was going to stop taking no for an answer. And I hadn't signed up to that.

Actually Louis took it well when I told him I didn't want to see him any more. I was waiting for the men to load up when he came over to me.

'Something vex yu? Mek yu keep yu distance from me these last weeks?'

I turned and looked at him in the faint shadow of the lamplight. Funny thing was, Louis was quite a gentleman. Old-fashioned. Holding open doors, pulling out the chair for me to sit, being so careful of my skirt every time he closed the car door. He was respectful even though he had to shuffle on his one good leg to do it.

'I heard what happened to that man Samuels. Shot in the back of the head and his body burned and left in an alley.'

'Yu hear all a dat?'

'Your men,' I said. 'Boasting about it.'

He didn't say anything. 'I know yu up to things, Louis. Who isn't? But Samuels, I cyan tek that.'

'No?'

'No.'

'Dat is a shame.'

'And the thing is, I don't really want to be keeping your company any more. I don't even want yu coming up and talking to me like this.'

'No?'

I gazed out to sea so I wouldn't have to look at him when I said: 'It was fun having dinner wid yu and passing the time down here while we waiting hour after hour. But I cyan do it no more. Not knowing what I know about Samuels and God knows how many more. You are different person to me now.'

I heard him tapping his stick on the ground. And saw him, out of the corner of my eye, stroking his moustache. Just with the index finger of his left hand, rubbing along the thin line above his lip. I'd seen that so many times before when he found himself lost for words. So that is how we were. Silent in the moonlight. Me not wanting to say any more. Him not knowing where to take the conversation. Until one of his men shouted out for him and he walked quietly away, limping slightly as he went, and it was all done.

Except for what Sissy told me a few weeks later. That Kenneth was working for Pao now. Picking up the slack left by Samuels. And running errands for Louis as well.

'How did that happen?'

'Di bwoy been chasing 'round town at high speed telling everybody he come 'cross how he a big man now in his brother-in-law employ. Meking quite a show a it according to what I hear. So sooner or later yu would have to say "Yes". Town too small fah him not to bump into Mr Louis DeFreitas.'

'How yu know all this?'

'How I know?' She paused and then she said, 'It come to me on di breeze.'

CHAPTER 23

IT SHOOK ME. The Samuels episode. Not because of Louis. I always knew he was dangerous. But because of Pao. Delivering Samuels into Louis's arms knowing, I was sure, what would happen to him. That was more than gambling and consensual protection. More than stolen goods. It was as close to murder as you could get without actually pulling the trigger yourself.

So I went to Matthews Lane to collect Mui. Karl was already with me from a few days earlier when I'd taken him to Lady Musgrave Road and Mui had refused to come. Telling me she had other plans with Hampton and I didn't have the energy to argue with her.

I told Karl to wait in the car, I would only be a few minutes. All I wanted to do was pack the remainder of my things and collect clothes for the children. And take Mui. Pao spent so little daytime there it never occurred to me that he would be home. But there he was. Sitting at the table drinking a bowl of tea. That was when I realised I hadn't thought it through, hadn't reckoned on an encounter with him. So I decided to brazen it out, walking through the gate with an air of self-assurance, straight past him to climb the two concrete steps into the bedroom.

I reached down the suitcase from off the top of the wardrobe and started to empty the contents of my drawers into it. Then he was standing in the doorway.

'What you think you doing?'

I wasn't planning to say anything. Nothing about DeFreitas or Samuels, but I did. Blurted it out right after I threw the vase of flowers at him that smashed on the doorpost, and he brushed the shattered glass and water off himself and walked back down the steps into the yard. And I followed, venting my anger and bitterness and jealousy, because what was on my mind wasn't just about his racketeering and turf war with Louis. Or his involvement of Kenneth, about which I was still fuming. It was about Gloria Campbell. And Michael. So I ended up saying far too much with the heat of vengeance pulsing in my veins. Too much about Samuels being murdered execution-style, and my disgust at the repulsive excuse of a house he called a home. Screaming at him for being a sleazy, small-time, petty hoodlum, dealing in drugs and guns and murder.

'I am not a drug dealer, and I don't run guns, and I didn't murder nobody.'

And then I said it, the thing that had, for so long, been burning like a hot poker in my heart. 'Well with your little whores then. I think you are still running her, aren't you? Your whore in East Kingston.'

That is when he launched himself at me and we started to fight. Rolling around on the dusty concrete exchanging blow for blow, kick for kick, scuffle for scuffle. Like a pair of schoolboys in the dirt yard. I surprised myself with the vigour with which I punched and shoved, even at times when it felt like he was actually pulling me towards him rather than pushing me away. Never once resorting to the all-too-female scratching and biting and yanking of hair. Just a manly raising of the arm and smashing of the fist. Army-style.

Next thing the whole household was running down the yard. Ma shouting and waving her arms in the air. Hampton with his head down for a faster pace. Even Zhang was sauntering up to see what was happening. All of them finally standing there and looking at us in horror. But the thing that really made me stop was the sight of Mui on the step in her pyjamas, and Karl coming inside the gate. And then, being held by Pao at arm's length, I spat in his face. It was my last line of defence. An instinctive reaction. And he let me go.

Karl came over and took my hand. And then I walked across to Mui and took her hand also. And looking at me with both children, one on each side, he said, 'What you think you doing?'

'You don't think I'm going to leave them here with you, do you?'

'You not going anywhere with the children.'

And in that moment what I saw, maybe for the first time, was the reality of Pao. Not the explanations and excuses that Isaac had put into my head about limitations and alternatives, and the possibilities a man can perceive, but the true revulsion of Pao's life that I had closed my eyes to and trained myself to discount. What I saw was the dishonesty and corruption that he paraded as business. And what I wanted to do was lash back at him for it. I wanted to hurt him.

'What, so I can leave them here to grow up with pimps and whores, and thieves and thugs and murderers? So that one day maybe they become just like you? Is that what they should aspire to? To become just like Papa? Papa's little boy and girl?'

And he slapped me. With an open palm. Firm and hard. It stung. I could feel the blood rushing to my cheek in the imprint of his hand. Tears wet my face. That was the last thing I wanted to do. The last thing any woman should do in a situation like that. Cry. But as he reached into his pocket and handed me a handkerchief a softness came over me, remembering the first time he'd done it, given me something to mop my face on that last night of our honeymoon in Ocho Rios, when, just as now, there was nothing more to be said.

So I took the handkerchief and dried my tears as I watched Mui step across from me to take his hand.

'You are a grown woman, Fay. You can do what you want, but the children staying here with me.'

I looked at Zhang, Hampton and Ma standing there. And then at the children, Mui next to Pao, Karl beside me with his arms dangling loose at his side.

I felt weak and ridiculous when I said, 'This isn't over.' As if that was any kind of threat. And I left. Empty-handed. Thinking that perhaps Karl would run after me but he didn't.

A week later when I saw Michael he was horrified at the state of my face because by then it had turned a greenish shade of yellow and was blackening at the edges. I just said, 'Fighting with Pao.' Said it straight like that, like it wasn't an issue. And he raised his eyebrows. Not like a priest, but like a man. A priest's expression would have had less anger. More compassion.

'Did you see a doctor?'

'It wasn't that kind of fight. He slapped me, that was all. Harder than he meant to.'

'Harder than he meant to?' He looked at me with a disbelief that was completely justified.

So I said, 'It was a brawl. As much my doing as his.' But I could see Michael was waiting for more. 'I went to clear my things from the house and to collect Mui but it got out of hand.'

'And there was a particular reason for that? Clearing your things from the house.'

'It's complicated.'

I didn't know how to gauge the look on his face. Was it surprise about Pao? Disappointment in me? Distress at the situation? Frustration that there was nothing he could do? Who knows what he was feeling. There was a deep, heavy sigh accompanying it, though, whatever it was.

We were in Hope Gardens. A favourite of Michael's for the wide, open space. He said he could breathe there, and be reminded of his own insignificance every time he looked up at the towering mountains and the royal palms stretching into the sky. He could be anonymous, surrounded by the dancing of the coral hibiscus as it fluttered on the breeze, and the remnants of so many post-wedding photo calls. On the ground, a sprinkling of confetti, rice, a rosebud lost from a buttonhole.

'I fear I may be losing my way.' That is what he said as he walked and I followed, matching step for step, breath for breath.

'My whole life, all I ever wanted was to be a priest. The first time it came to me I was seven years old. A neighbour had died. After a lengthy illness, so it was neither sudden nor entirely unexpected. But it was a catastrophe because she was the heart of the yard's community. Even as she lay there with death's door opening ever wider, people would still flock to her bedside for words of comfort and guidance. Not for her, but from her, because she was an obeah woman. She could see the future and cast spells and tell people what to do to keep their demons at bay.'

We passed the empty bandstand. 'When she died, the whole yard was inconsolable. You could hear the wailing all hours of the day and night. Like lost souls wandering in the wilderness. Even my own mother would burst into tears for no apparent reason, and fight with neighbours as she had never done before. Not out of anger, but out of dread.' He stopped and stared at me awhile before starting to walk again, while making the longest speech I'd ever heard from him.

'Then one day, out of the blue, Bishop Langley came into the yard. He was just a young priest then, fresh from the seminary. I don't know who invited him but he came and right out there in the sun and dirt he set up a rickety old wooden table and celebrated Mass, with everyone going about their business ignoring him. Week after week he came until people started to pull up a chair or crate and sit down to listen. And gradually the weeping stopped and a quiet peace crept over the place, which, over time, turned into a gentle kind of relief. And I thought to myself: What is such a gift that people's grief and fear can be transformed by one man's prayer? Not that it was a swap, the obeah woman for God, but because they had gained something inside themselves. Not outside direction but an inner strength with which to meet the challenges of their wretched lives. And what I realised is that we can transcend our sorrow and suffering through our understanding of Holy Scripture, and our own human reason and moral conscience. We can save ourselves. And even at that tender age the thought comforted me immensely. Because we didn't need to burn dollies or scatter white powder outside our doors. Through our own courage and conviction we can be redeemed. That is what I understood, talking to him as he drank the mint tea my mother always made. After all, what greater commitment can there be to the flourishing of humanity than to bring this message to all those willing to hear?'

He stopped. Sat on a nearby bench. I stood. Looking down at him.

'But it is a challenging task. An arduous path. One that it seems I may not be strong enough to continue.' He gazed up. 'I'm afraid I may be in the process of crossing a bridge from which there will be no return.'

A young couple ambled past us hand in hand, glancing briefly at Michael sitting on the bench. He stood and started to walk again with his hands clasped behind him.

'How do we know what is in our hearts? What is the true heart as opposed to the imagined or wished-for heart, because right now what is in my heart is a fear of letting go of something that has, for so long, given meaning to my life. And yet there is something else. Something urging me on into the unknown.'

I didn't know what to say to him. So I just let out the voice that was inside my head. And it said: 'I too am tormented.'

★　　★　　★

It was after that, I saw Isaac. In town. Strolling towards me in King Street with a young black woman on his arm. He just walked straight past. Didn't even look at me, never mind say hello. I stopped and checked to see if he would turn but he didn't. He just kept on going with his head held high like he had somewhere important to get to. Standing there staring at his back I knew I had it coming. The ice-cold reception. And that really I had nothing to complain about. Isaac could spite me worse than that if one day he took a mind to do it.

CHAPTER 24

MAMA RESTED HER elbows on the dining table, either side of her plate. Fingers woven together. That is how I remembered it. Then she cleared her throat.

'I am going to say this one time and one time only. And afterwards I don't want to hear another word about it. Not one mention. You understand me? All you need to do is listen and mend your ways. That is all. And the good Lord will take care of the rest.'

Then she looked at Kenneth. 'Kenneth Wong, I pray for you. Morning and evening. Day in day out on my knees in that room inside there. Begging the Almighty to help me to understand where it is you are getting all of this money to buy so much fancy clothes and gramophone and music that playing all hours of night when you come back in this house stinking of liquor. Where is that coming from because you not getting it from your father? I know that for certain. And sure as hell is hot, you don't have a job. Who would hire you anyway? There is not one damn thing you know how to do. And then last week you come with a car that I think maybe you borrow but six days later it is still out there with you coming and going in it. So remind me, when was it you got your driving licence?'

She didn't wait for an answer. 'This is all bad business, Kenneth. I can smell it. Just like I smell the ganja you busy smoking in your bedroom. You think I don't know? Not live long enough to recognise the smell of that evil weed and see the red bloodshot in your eyes? Well I know. So what you have to do is remove the padlock you put on your bedroom door so the maids can get in there and do their work. And stop doing whatever it is you are doing and go to school. It is as simple as that. And if you cannot bring yourself to do it then I will have to think to myself what else is to be done, because just like your father said to me, my praying isn't doing the damnedest bit of good.'

'It not nuh school.'

'No? So what is it?'

'College. All a yu keep talking 'bout school. It not school. It college.'

'College. Yes. Where one minute you are learning about sugar cane and banana agriculture and then bauxite mining and drilling for oil and fishing and tourism and something else and something more. Every month a different thing.'

'I never did nothing to do with no fishing.'

'It doesn't matter, Kenneth. The point is you cannot settle to anything. Year in year out your father is paying school fees but there is never anything to show for it.'

She sat tight-lipped as she turned over in her mind the sermon she wanted to deliver to me. And sure enough, five minutes later she put together her knife and fork, took a sip of ice-water and prepared herself.

'Fay, you are a married woman. A mother of two. Whatever go on between you and Yang Pao is your business. Husband and wife argue. That is life. But you can't keep running back here every time the two of you disagree. To and fro. Up and down like a yo-yo. And this time, coming here while you leave your children with him downtown, and staying out all hours of night doing God knows what. It is unseemly.'

'You are the one who wanted me to marry him.'

Well, if looks could kill, I would have dropped down dead on the spot. But it wasn't just look that she wanted to do because her hand was twitching and easing back just a little. Then she wriggled her fingers instead and rubbed her fingertips against her palms like she was drying them off.

'I am saying nothing about Yang Pao. A more respectful son-in-law I couldn't wish for. Whatever your troubles, I am sure it has nothing to do with him. Remember, madam, I have lived with you under this roof for many, many years. I know you.'

And then, holding her head in her hands: 'Father Kealey I am saying nothing about. But just like I smell the ganja I can smell the badness of that too. The two of you chasing each other from one end of Kingston to the next. No good can come of it. And him a man of the cloth.'

She looked directly at me as she stood up, sliding her greasy plantain fingers along the cloth and resting her hand on the table to steady herself as she bent down to pick up her napkin from the floor.

'The devil makes work for idle hands. Maybe you should think to get yourself a job instead of coming back here to live off your father, like he hasn't already provided enough for you.' And then, tossing the napkin on to her half-empty plate, she turned and walked away.

Daphne sat there. A prim pucker on her lips. So I just said: 'What?'

'Nothing.'

I looked at Kenneth shovelling the rice and stewed peas into his mouth.

'Yu nuh think I know what yu doing?'

Daphne piped up. 'Don't talk like that. What if Mama hears you? She hates it when you talk like that.'

'What she going do? Come back and cuss me some more? Anyway, Daphne, is not you I am talking to, is him.' I jut out my chin at Kenneth, sitting across the table, harpooning the red peas like fish swimming in the gravy.

'Yu not got nothing to say?'

'Yu don't know what yu talking 'bout, Fay, so just hush yu mouth and mind yu own business.'

'This is the way yu talk to yu big sista? Anyway, I know more than you think.'

He looked over at me with a sneer. And then he pushed back the chair, scraping it noisily along the polished mahogany floor, and got up from the table. I followed him to his bedroom, stopping at the threshold and leaning against the doorpost because I knew I wasn't welcome.

'Yu understand that what yu doing most likely going get yu killed? It not no game that going on out there.'

'What you know 'bout it?' He put a record on the turntable and turned up the volume so loud everything in the room started to vibrate to the sound of Toots Hibbert. When I walked over to lift up the needle he grabbed my hand so that it dragged across the vinyl and scratched a deep ugly groove all the way from the edge to the Studio One label.

'Now see what yu do! Why yu nuh stop yu meddling? This not no business for no woman. This is man's work. Yu get me?' And he tossed my hand away.

'Kenneth, I know Yang Pao started yu running errands for him. But Samuels wasn't no random shooting. He was killed execution-style. Yu understand? And the person who did it is the same man yu busy running with now.'

'Louis is my friend.'

'Louis DeFreitas is not your friend. He is a low-life pretender who fancy himself as some big-shot gangster, which he is not. Mouthing off all sorta political slogans he hear on the street or see written on a fence at the side of the road. Louis is a punk, not the people's saviour he reckons himself to be, no matter how many schools he builds or health clinics he supports. All his handouts only serve one purpose. To make the people beholden to him. Louis DeFreitas is a drug dealer and a warlord.'

Kenneth walked over to the door and held it open. 'Get out of my room. Yu so busy running down Louis when it was your own husband that introduce me to him.'

'That I very much doubt.'

'Yu know so much about it? Anyway, since when you start sticking up for Yang Pao? I thought yu hated him as much as …'

'As much as what?'

'As much as yu hate Mama.' He spat out the words. But with his voice lowered. Then he said, 'Just get out.' So I stepped outside and he slammed the door in my face. Hard. So hard it bounced back and had to be shut a second time. A few moments later I heard Prince Buster ringing out, full pelt: 'Al Capone's guns don't argue.'

I walked back into the dining room. Daphne was still sitting there.

'Mama will hear you.'

'And I should care?'

I took a whisky with me out to the veranda to catch some peace. Daphne followed.

'Karl been here today looking for you.'

'He came here?'

'After school.'

I looked up at her in surprise. What I felt? Gratitude. And perhaps some reassurance that maybe I hadn't been as dreadful a mother as I thought.

'What did he say?'

'Nothing. Just chatted, you know. He came to see you, that's all.' She sat down next to me.

'How was he?'

'Good. He looked fine.'

When I asked her if she knew when he might be coming back she shrugged her shoulders.

'Did you leave them both with Pao for a reason?'

I considered telling her about Samuels. DeFreitas. Everything. But decided against it. 'I can't cope with having them with me right now.'

She raised her brows. 'Have it your own way.' And then she got up and started to walk back inside.

'Daphne,' I called after her. She turned. 'How come you and me are always so up and down? Hot and cold all the time?'

She gazed out into the garden. 'I think you are a good person, Fay. But I get tired of listening to you argue with everybody.' Then, as an afterthought before stepping into the house, she said, 'And I feel hurt that you always lock me out.'

What was it about for me? The feeling of being judged by her. According to Mama's standards and codes of decency. Being judged by Daphne as though through Mama's eyes.

The next afternoon I went down to St George's to wait outside the school for Karl to come out. When he saw me he walked straight up and put his arms around me, which stopped my heart, because Karl, like me, wasn't a person given to displays of affection.

I offered to take him to Times Store for an ice cream but he said no, he'd rather go uptown, so we drove to Half Way Tree. To the soda fountain at the pharmacy.

Sitting in the traffic I said to him, 'You OK?'

'Yes.' But he was gloomy.

'How is school?'

'OK.'

'Matthews Lane?' He fiddled with the window. Up and down a couple of times. 'Things not so good down there at the moment?'

He gave the window another slide. 'It's OK.'

I waited for more but nothing came my way. 'It's good to see you. I was very happy when Aunt Daphne said you came to find me.'

He ordered a Coca-Cola float and I took a coffee. And then we walked out to find a table on the upstairs covered veranda. Karl ate some of the vanilla ice cream perched on top before using the spoon to mash the remainder into the soda. Squashing it against the side of the long glass and stirring it in.

'I don't like him carting us around town with him.'

'Your father?'

'Going to all the places he busy collecting money from. I don't like it. Even if the people greet him nice. Getting introduced to shopkeepers and market traders and them messing up my hair and saying how I look like him. And taking their free gifts.' He shook his head. Then smiled a little cheekily. 'Actually, that part is alright.'

'So that is why you so down in the dumps?'

'No.'

'No?'

'It was meeting her. Outside Times Store. And him making us go in and sit down with her and order ice cream. Pretending it was an accident but I knew it wasn't.'

I narrowed my eyes. 'Who are we talking about?'

'Gloria.'

'Gloria?'

He looked at me, wide-eyed. 'You know. Gloria Campbell.'

I couldn't believe it. That Pao would have the nerve to introduce the children to his whore.

'Are you sure it was her?'

He looked at me like maybe I'd called him stupid. 'I know who she is. I heard you talking about her. She said she was his friend and that Daddy helped her when she and her sister had some trouble. She even called me Xiuquan like she think she know me.'

'You heard me talking about her?'

'With Aunt Beverley. At Grandma's. On the phone sometimes.'

'Really?' I had no idea.

'And Daddy saying I was rude because I wouldn't talk to her. While Mui was shooting off her mouth about Father Michael and asking all sorta questions 'bout her daughter. As if I care. It made me mad.' He drained his glass. And then he stood the long-handled spoon in it, rattling it a little against the sides.

'Did you know she has a daughter?' he asked.

'Yes.'

'And he calls me rude.' He rattled the spoon in the glass some more.

'Your father didn't mean to insult you. He wasn't thinking, that was all.'

He raised his brows. Flared his nostrils. 'Anyway,' I said. Anyway what? Where was I going with this? What could I possibly say about his father and Gloria? So I changed the subject. 'Are you still seeing Father Michael? Going to Mass on Sunday? Catechism classes?'

'Yes.'

'And Mui?'

'You want us to stop?'

'No, Karl. I want you to go. Father Michael is a good man.'

Driving back downtown he said, 'Is Daddy really a thief and a criminal?'

'Yes.'

'Is that why the two of you had the fight? And you left?'

'In a way. But really, it was more about my worry. My anxiety that if the two of you stay there with him you'll end up ...'

'I know. I heard you.'

He sat silent for a while and then he said, 'I wanted to run after you. That day. After the fight.'

'You did?'

'Yes. I was just too scared to do it.'

I took my left hand from the steering wheel and patted him lightly on the arm. 'It's OK. It was probably for the best anyway.'

I pulled the car over at the kerb outside the school and he opened the door. 'Thursdays are good. I'm supposed to have cricket practice but I never go.'

'So see you next Thursday,' I smiled.

And then he leant across and kissed me on the cheek. For the first time in living memory. And said: 'It will all be OK, Mommy.'

CHAPTER 25

SISSY TOOK A Checker Cab to meet me at the Carib in Cross Roads. She loved going to the pictures so once a month that is what we did together. Anything with Doris Day, or Ginger Rogers and Fred Astaire.

That afternoon it was Doris Day. *The Glass Bottom Boat*. That was what she wanted to see.

'How yu gwaan?' is how she greeted me. I smiled. Four years since independence so she figured she could talk that way to me now. Like a kindred spirit. Her tease at the etiquette of how things used to be. Except we both knew that things hadn't changed. Not that much. Not really.

I linked her arm as we walked into the theatre together. Gently, because Sissy was frailer and slower than she used to be.

Afterwards we had dinner. Nothing elaborate. That wouldn't have been to her liking. Just a quiet, homely place, with wholesome Jamaican food.

'Yu likkle bredda done get himself a gun. Yu know that?' She was stirring the water with her finger, swirling the ice in a vicious circle. Then she reached into her wide-open mouth to search for a stringy piece of callaloo that was wedged between her back teeth.

'How yu know?'

'Like how I know everything.'

'On the breeze?'

She looked at me sternly. 'Dis not no laughing matter. Things getting real serious over deh. All sorta shooting and rape and murder. Person cyan even set foot outside deh door no more without vengeance raining down on deh head. It get so bad only last week a child go to di corner to di shop and somebody catch him and cut him wid a cutlass. That is how perilous ordinary everyday life is in West Kingston. And as fah every woman dat walking down di street or laying in her bed, well dat not even worth talking about. Dem kicking down people's door at night and doing whatever deh want.'

'What about the police?'

'Di police?' She laughed. 'Deh cyan do nothing. All deh do is beg and plead wid di people dem but what good yu think dat doing?' She shrugged her shoulders. 'Any minute now it will be all guns blazing. Not Calamity Jane singing "Whip Crack Away" and dancing on di table waving her gun in di air, but real honest-to-goodness gunshot wid bullets dat not fretting 'bout where deh landing.' She paused. 'So yu better get yu bredda outta deh. Dat is what I am saying to yu.'

'I talked to him the other night. About Louis.'

'DeFreitas? Dat bwoy been nothing but trouble since di day he born. Not even his own mother can stand di sight a him. Even though she living in di house deh doing like a mother supposed to.'

She reached for a toothpick. 'He busy lording it over Tivoli Gardens right now, shouting 'bout how he fighting fah di poor and dejected. Di sufferers. Don't get me wrong, dat struggle sure is righteous. But Louis? He mean and nasty. Only in it fah what he can get fah himself. No sensible person would trust him further than deh could spit.' And then she spat the stringy callaloo that was bothering her into the little square of white paper napkin, which she crumpled and placed on the table next to her plate.

'Di whore, Gloria Campbell, her mother tek sick. So she and di sista go back fi country in Westmoreland where deh come from and di old woman last just long enough fi say hello and wave dem goodbye. But no sooner than deh come back fi Kingston she close her eyes and never open dem again. So deh have fi go back fi face di funeral.' She sipped her ginger beer. 'And now yu going say how I know that?'

'On the breeze?'

'Same so. On di breeze.' And then she scraped the last piece of fish on to her fork and put it in her mouth.

I asked her: 'Yu think I would be that interested in what happening with Gloria Campbell?'

'Mock me if yu want, but who else would a tell yu all di things I do all these years?'

She was right. If it wasn't for Sissy I would never have known about Pao and Gloria. And Papa. And Kenneth and Louis. Actually, I wouldn't even have known about where babies come from, or the diseases that pass between men and women. If it wasn't for her.

'And if it wasn't fah all di palaver over di jade necklace all dem years back, what would yu know, eh? Where would yu

305

be without di news I bring?' She looked contented as she nodded her head and sucked up the last drop of her ginger beer. Through the red-and-white-striped straw.

It was the news of the gun that did it. Made me realise just how deep Kenneth was getting. And that I needed to talk to Papa. So next morning I went to find him. Downtown. Because ever since the Samuels incident and me going back to Lady Musgrave Road, he'd made himself completely absent. Gone to Chinatown for his breakfast, sitting in the shop in North Street all day, back to Barry Street for his dinner and mah-jongg until all hours, hoping that by the time his feet passed over the threshold at home Mama would be asleep in her bed with no chance of him getting caught in the crossfire between me and her.

But when I got to Hong Zi Wine & Spirits the place was empty except for his assistant, Alvin, who was busy loading liquor on to the old truck out back.

'He know I got to drive these things to Ocho Rios and somebody got to be in di shop when I go.'

'Have you seen him at all this morning?'

'No, Miss Fay, not yet. Most likely he still having his breakfast. But he soon come, fah sure.' And he carried on loading his crates.

I left Alvin and drove down to Barry Street. Too far for me to be walking in this heat and certainly not in this part of town. Not with some urchin holding out his hand and pleading with me every step of the way. 'Miss Chin, yu 'ave someting fah me?' To them every Chinese is a Chin and every Chin spells money. Serious money. So I drove with the windows closed for the air-conditioning and the tinted glass to ward off inquisitive eyes.

I squeezed the Mercedes into a space just down from the post office and made my way to Mr Lowe's cookhouse. And even though that walk from the car was such a short distance, still I could feel all eyes upon me. Every passing woman and man. Every higgler and juicy with their beer and sodas, shaved ice and syrup, coconuts, sugar cane, and strings of oranges. Heavily scrutinised I was. Not for being Chinese in Chinatown. But for being so elegantly dressed because looking like I did I should have been in King Street shopping for accessories and fineries not trudging around like a domestic searching for the week's best buys or dropping off the dry-cleaning.

Papa was sitting in front of rice and sausage. Bamboo steamers with *char siu bao* and shrimp dumpling at his elbow.

'Fay, what you do here? Yu want rice? Dim sum?' He waved his arm at the young waiter dressed in a traditional Chinese jacket. Mandarin collar, toggle buttons, patch pockets, black edged in gold.

'Soup?' Swinging his head towards the boy so his grey hair brushed his collar. Not like the crew cut so many of the other Chinese men preferred. Like Pao.

'Maybe some tea.'

'Yes,' he said and then shouted to the waiter, '*Cha.*'

The boy poured the jasmine tea and rested the pot on the table. After he walked away I watched Papa's hands manoeuvring the chopsticks between mouth and bowl. Scooping the rice, picking up the sausage in his pincer grip, even cutting through the bread of the *bao*. And I thought of Mama with her afternoon Earl Grey, and knife and fork that she considered so civilised, even if most of the time she preferred to use her fingers.

'Yu have something on mind?'

'Kenneth, and all dis money he got in his pocket.'

'You talk Jamaican, Fay. Wait till your mama hear you.' And he laughed. A warm-hearted, bright-eyed laugh, which made me smile.

'She hear me already.'

'Yes?' He laughed again, throwing his head back in delight.

'She cuss Kenneth over it the other night. Saying yu tell her praying not doing no good.'

'No good, Fay. Not one drop. Not with Kenneth or anything else. Though I not mention that part to her. I just stick to Kenneth. That way she and me worry 'bout same thing.'

'So yu worried then?'

'I worry enough, talk to her weeks back. But just yesterday, Yang Pao ask me same thing.' He finished eating and rested down his chopsticks. 'Say if maybe I can have talk with Kenneth because the boy bad outta hand and heading for trouble. So I tell him, I have no idea what Kenneth do. He have money. That is for sure. And he back-chatting everybody. And not go school. I know that. But what to do with him?' He wiped his hands on the napkin.

'He got himself a gun. You know that?'

Papa's eyes widened. 'Gun? Yu sure? How yu know?'

'Sissy.'

'Oh this not job for me, Fay. Yang Pao he know what to do. But he holding back. Want somebody else put leash on boy. But yu know, when it come to children, that is your mother's business. Me, I stick to wine and groceries.' He piled his dirty crockery together. Shamefaced.

I sat there thinking about her and her business and then I said to him, 'How come yu never lift a finger or even raise yu voice to stop her treating me so bad?'

'Fay.' He paused, clasping his hands together. 'Yu still not forgive me for that even though yu big woman now and all that misery behind yu?'

'I forgave you, even as a child. But I never understood it. Yu a big man, Papa. Successful. Determined. But not with her. Never with her. No matter what she say or do. No matter how bad she gwaan. There is always something that has you kowtowing to her.'

His jaw took on a guilty, hangdog look. So I said, 'I know yu love me. I've always known that. It just hard to remember sometimes when you never ever had the breath to say "Cicely, leave the child alone."'

He reached across the table and took my hand. 'Fay, yu know I love you. That is good. But remember, it is through your own strength that you survive and even if everybody see you as spoilt little girl, it not true. Yu strong. Yu full of courage. And to tell yu truth is only recent times I come to understand that yu can never judge a woman from what yu see on outside.'

'How come?' I poured some more tea just so I could lower my eyes and not have to look at him as he answered. In case it was to do with Gloria Campbell.

'It nuh matter. I see yu now.' And then he said, 'Life turn on a sixpence, Fay. Everything always changing. Yu can never tell what is in the future. How something unexpected can change everything. Change the way yu see yourself. Change the way yu see other people. Change the way yu see the world.' So it was about Gloria after all.

We sat in silence, him drinking some ice-water and me sipping the tea thinking about how much he liked that phrase about life and the sixpence.

Then I remembered what I'd come there for. 'What about Kenneth?'

'You talk Yang Pao?'

'Me? No.'

'Well, it already catch his attention so I know situation bad. I will think. Find something say to Kenneth.'

'Good, because he certainly isn't listening to me.'

Papa looked at his watch. 'Ah. Truck. Ocho Rios!' He stood. Grabbed his jacket from the back of the chair and started out of the door.

'It's OK, you go. I'll pay.'

'No need, Fay. All on account.' And he was gone.

I slowly finished the pot of tea and walked to the post office to check my rented box. As soon as I opened the slim grey metal door I saw it. The flimsy blue aerogramme from London. I slipped it into my purse and stepped outside back to the car. And drove to Constant Spring.

Tyrone was standing just inside the door. 'Fay.' He came over and hugged me. 'Looking good, gal.' Then he stood back. 'I still cyan get over how much yu look like Beverley. Honest to God, if I see yu in a dim light I would swear yu was my own sista. No wonder those boys down the wharf got no idea what going on.'

'Yu say that every time yu see me.'

'And every time I see yu, and every time I say it, it is true.'

We laughed. 'She upstairs?'

'Where else? Go on up. She expecting yu.'

I walked the full length of the store and climbed the pine staircase. Beverley was on the telephone discussing a shipment. I went over to the coffee-maker still gurgling with a fresh brew. Poured myself a cup. No milk. One spoon of raw cane.

I gazed out of the expansive plate-glass window and surveyed the neat counters in row after row of perfect order now busily browsed by the afternoon shoppers. And Tyrone, strutting the strut he developed right after Grandmother Chung told him that his mother had named him after Tyrone Power. That same swagger he had paraded in every nightclub we ever visited together.

She hung up the phone. 'So yu get a letter then? From Stanley.'

I pulled it from my purse and waved it in the air.

'Open it, gal.'

I tore into it and read.

Your situation sounds impossible. Trapped between Donaldson and Pao. You'll never get away from them as long as you live.

'So?'

'He says I must come to England.'

Her excitement turned to disappointment. 'I thought he might say that.'

'You disagree?'

'No.' She lightened. 'It makes sense. Jamaica not big enough for you to disappear out of reach of those two. Especially without a divorce.' Then she came over and hugged me.

'Not that I want yu to go. Yu know that.' She eased back and studied me. 'But I understand yu cyan go on like this. England got a future for yu, where yu don't have to be looking over your shoulder for Pao or Donaldson. Or Louis or Isaac, for that matter. Or bump into Gloria Campbell in the street.'

'It still a big decision. Not just for me, for the children as well.'

She stepped back and set herself while I marvelled at how she got away with wearing a tight red *cheongsam* like that. Edged in gold with some black embroidered birds on it. In the middle of the day. Never worrying that someone might mistake her for a different kind of businesswoman. But then Beverley never worried about anything.

'True. Big decision.' And then she added: 'And Father Kealey?'

'He doesn't come into it. I just want to make the right decision, that is all.'

'Well if England don't work out yu can always come back.' She grinned. 'I will still be here and, as long as I am, there will be a welcome for yu. Even mek yu a bona fide partner in the Emporium if yu want.'

We drove over to the Sheraton for lunch. Lobster salad and a cool Red Stripe beer. Sitting on the terrace overlooking the swimming pool with its almond trees and plumbago hedge.

'What yu tell Stanley anyway 'bout why he having to write to yu at a post-office box number?'

'I tell him the truth. That I think the maid steaming open the letters that going between us and that I rent the box in your name because it safer. Nobody can trace anything back to me.'

She took a forkful of salad and wiped away a little dressing from the corner of her mouth. With her lips open so as not to smudge her lipstick. 'Yu know if yu decide to stay that is alright as well. I don't want yu thinking that I'm pushing yu to go. If you stay I will be pleased to see you. We been laughing and scheming together for too long to have a little thing like this set us back.'

She was right. But then I started to think about the children and what it would mean for them to leave. Or stay. And I said to her, 'Yu ever think about what happen to Junior?'

'What yu asking me that for?'

'Is just that we never ever mention him. Almost like he never existed.'

'And?'

'I was thinking about Karl and Mui, that's all. And Junior came into my mind.'

'Well yu can get him outta yu mind. He is outta mine.' She looked across at the swimming pool with the tourists bathing themselves in the sun. And then she turned back to me and smiled as she raised the beer glass.

'You have to choose, Fay. Your decision. Absolutely. But yu have time. So let's just tek it easy and not feel like we got to rush into anything.'

CHAPTER 26

DAPHNE WAS SITTING on the veranda when I got back to Lady Musgrave Road. So I pulled up a chair next to her and eased off my shoes.

'Would you like Ethyl to bring you something cool to drink?'

'No, I'm fine. I'll just take some of the water you have there.' I poured a glass from the jug still jingling with the ice cubes. 'Something happen?'

'No.'

'So why yu sitting out here waiting for me?'

'Who said I'm waiting for you?'

'Don't fool with me, Daphne. I can see yu got something on yu mind.'

'Fay, you ever think that maybe Yang Pao is just doing the best he can? That maybe he's not as dreadful as you think?'

'What brings this on?'

She hesitated for a moment and then said, 'He was here earlier. Well all afternoon, actually.'

I raised my brows but didn't say anything. I knew he still had his regular visits with Mama.

'He's been good to us. That is all. Got me and Mama invitations to the reception at King's House when Queen Elizabeth came. And that was wonderful for her. Feeling so important.'

'And you too.'

She ignored me. 'And there was the shopping trip to Miami that he organised for Hampton to take us on. Plus all his visiting with chocolate and ice cream for Mama. He is not a bad man, Fay. Quite the contrary, actually. And he's good company as well. Pleasant manners, charming, funny.' She paused. 'Papa wouldn't be in business with him if he didn't like him too.' She shifted in her seat. 'In fact, nobody in this house has a bad word to say about him. Except you. Even the children always say how much they like being with him. That he is fun and they feel safe and have a good time.'

I thought she would never shut up as I sat there drinking the ice-water and not listening to a word.

'And all you do is run him down.'

I thought to myself: Does she really not know what Uncle Yang Pao gets up to downtown? When he's not sitting here drinking tea with Mama and charming and amusing her.

'All I am saying is that you argue with everyone about everything. Deliberately finding things to disagree with Mama about when all she is asking from you is that you act decent and pay some respect. Even Kenneth you following around the house to criticise.'

'You don't know anything about what is going on with Kenneth.'

And just so, he pulled into the driveway in the black Buick Skylark that Mama had referred to at dinner. A 1950s, two-door convertible Roadmaster. Getting out of it and walking to the veranda dressed in new shirt and shoes.

I looked at Daphne. 'Yu not even curious 'bout where he getting all this money from?'

'He told me he's been working for Yang Pao.'

I laughed. 'And that don't worry yu?'

'Pao isn't as wicked as you think.' And after giving herself some time to choose her words carefully, she said, 'All he wants is the wife he thought he'd married.'

'Well, if you know what he wants and you love him so much, you marry him.' And I got up and walked inside.

The truth about Kenneth? He was running with Louis DeFreitas and his gang of gunmen. Involved in all sorts of armed street violence, including clashes with security forces. All in the name of Louis's contrived political hostilities in which Kenneth was just a pawn. No matter how much he tried to convince himself otherwise.

Papa collapsed just two days after I had spoken to him about Kenneth. By the time I heard about it, Pao had already arranged for an ambulance to move him from the public hospital downtown to the private medical centre in Old Hope Road. Into the care of Dr Morrison.

Daphne had driven Mama to see him. That is what Ethyl told me. So I took a cab there. Papa's room was clean and fresh, overlooking the internal quadrangle garden crammed with colour and a single frangipani with a wooden seat surrounding it. A safety balcony rail across the open French windows and a gentle breeze wafting the chiffon drapes against the shiny mahogany floor. He looked comfortable in his crisp, white sheets.

'A stroke.' That is what Mama said. 'Paralysed down one side.' But really she seemed more inconvenienced than distressed.

'What does Dr Morrison say?' But instead of an answer all I got was the shrug of her shoulders and the sight of her back as she walked out of the room into the corridor.

I turned to Daphne. 'Where is she going?'

'She says she's been here too long. She needs some coffee.'

I drew up a chair next to the bed and took Papa's hand in mine while Daphne stood on the other side with a Kleenex wiping away a dribble of saliva from his chin.

'What a thing to be doing, eh?'

He smiled. 'Life turn on a sixpence, Fay. I couldn't think a nothing better to do.'

I laughed. 'Yu just say that like a real Jamaican.'

'Yu nuh think that is what I am?' And then he looked sideways at Daphne with a glint of mischief in his eyes as if to say: 'Don't you be reporting me to your mother now.'

Over the next few days he improved. That's what I wanted to believe anyway. He could sit up in the bed, drink from a straw and feed himself, with one hand. He could also hold a conversation of sorts, as long as it wasn't too long or too complicated. Never mind the little slur in his speech. But Dr Morrison wasn't convinced. According to him, Papa wasn't out of the woods yet. He suggested that the Chinese Sanatorium might be more comfortable. So we moved him, but all Papa did was complain about how he missed his Jamaican food and pleaded with people to bring him rice and peas and chicken, and saltfish fritters and bammy. When I asked him about the care he was receiving he said, 'It fine, Fay. Nurses kind and attentive. Everything good apart from all the time they serve Chinese food. They forget I am Jamaican as well.'

He had a lot of visitors. Men following under Pao's instruction to deliver yam and dumplings, fried plantain and boiled green bananas; and to entertain my father all hours permitted and some more besides.

'To tell you truth, Fay, it sort of tiring, even though the food is welcome.'

'Why don't you tell them to stop?'

'Yang Pao mean well. It good of him.'

Mama? I don't think she visited him more than twice. She just carried on. Complaining about the maids and hounding the long-suffering yard-boy, Edmond, over a garden that was never quite perfect enough for her. Even when I tried to talk to her about him there was nothing she had to say apart from: 'The good Lord cuts us down when he is ready.' And in the meantime she ordered the house and gossiped with Miss Allen. And played the piano. Singing to high heaven about the wages of sin and how we should 'Let the word of the Lord be a lamp on to our feet and a light unto our path', which made me wonder if she actually suspected something about Papa and Gloria or if her righteousness was all for me and Michael. Especially the Bible quoting: 'He that soweth to his flesh shall of flesh reap corruption, but he that soweth to the Spirit shall of the Spirit reap life everlasting.'

In the meantime, Kenneth enjoyed free rein. Coming and going from the house as he pleased. Driving his Buick, playing his music, smoking his ganja and finding cram space in his room for all his new belongings.

Daphne? She remained cheerful. Forever the optimist, or perhaps because she refused to see what was happening around her as she arranged more flowers in more vases; fiddled with the cutlery and napkins after the maids had set the table; fetched and carried one glass, a jug of lemonade, a bucket of ice, all in separate trips from the kitchen to the veranda. Brushing down her skirt at every turn as if disposing of a grasshopper that might have tumbled into her lap. All to the constant hum of some random tune that occupied her vocal cords and kept her from engaging in the simplest of exchanges.

'Your mama not such a bad person. Not like what you think.' This is what Papa said to me sitting up in the bed sucking on one of the tamarind balls I had given him.

'She doesn't give a damn about what is going on with you. You know that?'

'Ah, Fay. Yu still vex with her for what she do to yu? That not all there is to her, yu know.'

I patted his hand lightly. 'This really what yu want to be talking about right now?' And then I took his hand, raised it to my lips and softly kissed the back of it.

He smiled. 'Maybe it the only thing I should have on my mind. How to help yu understand the suffering your mother had that turn her the way she is. And how to beg your forgiveness for being such a good-for-nothing father.'

I rested a finger against his lips. 'Hush. Yu need to tek it easy like Dr Morrison say.'

'Tek it easy, Fay? That is all I ever did when it come to you and her. I would even lay in my bed at night and practise to myself what to say to her next day. How I would say: "Cicely, you leave that child alone. She didn't do nothing to you except get born, and that was none of her doing." I would mek up long-long speeches 'bout how I understand the miserable time she had with her own father, and the mother who run away to Panama and leave her. And how the old man treat her bad and make her fall pregnant with Stanley. All of that I was going to say before telling her how wrong she was for beating yu and chastising yu the way she do. All of that, but I never said any of it.'

'Papa, I know yu love me.'

'So yu say, but I know that not truth. Not whole truth anyway.'

The nurse was at the door in her white uniform and starched cap, telling me it was time to leave. Visiting hours over. 'We don't want to exhaust the patient.' That is what she said while standing guard in the room to make sure I left.

After that, for his own reasons, Papa decided to spend every visit repeating over and again the sad, sad tale of Mama's loveless life. A mother who abandoned her; a drunken, womanising father who forced himself on his own sweet, innocent child; a wretched, dreary existence in the packed-solid-hard-dirt-floor hut she and her father shared. The same hut they kept the slaves in all those years before, on that same banana plantation on which her father, Mr Johnson, was the foreman. And when Mr Johnson finally got them rooms in town, how Mama cooked and cleaned and washed and ironed while the old man lorded it around Ocho Rios with a different woman every night of the week making so much noise when he came home it would wake up Mama and keep her wide-eyed listening to the rhythmic thumping of the springs on his bed. And how, come morning, she would have to fix breakfast for whoever his latest woman was, and maybe even fill her a bath carrying the water in pails from the standpipe in the yard and heating it over the coal stove. And her nothing more than a child.

Such was the tragedy of my mother's life until Papa agreed to marry her, pregnant as she was with Stanley.

'Why did you do it?'

'Marry Cicely? I didn't know anybody else, Fay. Old man Johnson brought me from wharf very same day I land in Kingston. Took me to banana plantation to help out. Earn money cook for workers, do laundry for great house, run errands for him. That is how it was. I was just boy. Only Chinaman on plantation. When I finally leave it I set up shop with gold mother give me when I set sail from China.' He paused and swallowed. 'I needed wife. That was the thing. Good African woman so people not think I prejudice against them.' He stopped. I wiped the spittle from his lips. 'Funny thing, they still prejudice. Chiney, they say, robbing the black man with high prices in shop. Have no right to make living when negro out of work or getting starvation wages on plantation. That is what they say, never mind I selling goods as reasonable as I can and giving them credit. Even lend them money when times hard. Some of them so aggravated I have African wife, shout nastiness in street. But it nuh matter.

Cicely have husband and father for child and Mr Johnson have daughter off his hands. That is how life turn on a sixpence. And in truth how they talk and what they do completely different. They spiteful but they still come shop, chat Cicely. They happy. Feel at home. Come back. It good for business.'

Another time he said: 'I good businessman. But inside I feel like lost boy with nowhere to go.' He paused for breath. 'I make money. Grocery shop in Ocho Rios. Liquor store in Kingston. Montego Bay. Wholesale warehouse. That is how the years go by. Only thing I have to remind me of who I am is name of shop. Hong Zi Grocery Store. Hong Zi Wine & Spirits. That is me. Hong Zilong, Hakka from China. Not Henry Wong that British immigration officer name. But who know that except Cicely? Who but her ever see this lost little boy and take pity on him? Give him chance for family. Wife and children. The things that give life meaning. Long before she know what future ahead of me. Who else know the mistakes I made?'

He turned his stare away from the washbasin in the corner of the room and looked directly at me.

'But I am sorry. Truly sorry for what my weakness mean to you. All the years of hurt you suffer.'

'Me and Mama, that is between us. You, Papa, I love. I always have.' And then I leant over and kissed him on the forehead, as I remembered my child's hand in his. Chinese New Year, when every street in Chinatown would be strung with continuous firecrackers that banged and fizzed for three hours from start to finish. And afterwards you would be ankle-deep in the red paper left behind.

★   ★   ★

The Friday before I bumped into Gloria Campbell, right there in the sanatorium, in the corridor outside his room, he pulled the sheet up tight around his neck and then flattened it down over his chest like he was ironing it smooth before saying, 'Sissy tell me you hire private detective and know all about Gloria.' I didn't say anything. 'You two not so different as you think.' He reached out his good hand for the glass resting on the side. I stood. Picked it up and supported his back as he leant over to sip the water.

'You rich young woman, big house uptown, fancy clothes, Mercedes-Benz drive Kingston. Gloria poor, mek living doing things we don't talk about. Sure-sure. But inside, you the same. Deep wounds of sorrow. And if it wasn't for seeing it in Gloria, I would never have seen it in you.'

CHAPTER 27

DAPHNE WANTED ME to go with her. To buy a dress. A dress for a date. I grabbed both her hands and danced her around. Swinging her arms in joy and excitement.

'Who it is?'

'Someone I met on a shoot.'

'Really?'

'Assistant hotel manager.'

'Called?'

'Lincoln.'

'Daytime or evening?'

'Daytime.'

I suggested we visit GC's dressmaker instead, but she said no, there wasn't time. Chung's Emporium? She said not something Chinese. So the next morning we went to town, into the hustle and bustle, battling the traffic, the crowd and the noise. What we found eventually, after searching every downtown store, was a high-necked shirtwaist dress, sleeve-less with a full pleated shirt in polka-dot navy and white cotton.

Afterwards, we took a late-afternoon lunch in an upstairs balcony restaurant overlooking King Street. That was when I saw them. Across the street. Pao on bended knees, tying Mui's shoelaces. Karl standing next to her while twisting and turning his head to survey the people brushing past. Then Pao straightened up and said something to him, after which he took Mui's hand and they set off up the street towards me.

I watched them for two blocks. From Harbour Street to Tower Street. Hand in hand. Pao holding Mui. Mui holding Karl. Only letting go whenever they encountered a person or obstacle that refused them linked passage. Resuming their connection at the earliest opportunity, their hands seeking and finding each other like magnets. Without even the need to look down. They were together. For the whole world to see. A father strolling blissfully up the street with his two children on a sunny Saturday afternoon. No one could mistake that.

The most astonishing part? They were talking. Chatting all the way along. Mui looking up side to side. Karl directing comments to her, or to Pao. Over her head. Pao answering and waving his free hand about. Acting out his conversation the way he liked to. All three of them smiling and laughing. With a casual, easy familiarity I could not believe.

'What you so busy staring at?'

I jut out my chin towards them. Daphne turned around to look, but didn't say anything as they reached the corner by the post office and headed off down Barry Street.

On Monday morning I went to visit Papa. Sitting with him until just before Hampton was due to arrive with his lunch. Ackee and saltfish, which would still be piping hot in the shut-pan from Ma. I excused myself. A meeting with Dr Morrison. It was later, while on my way back to say a final goodbye to him, that I came face to face with her in the corridor. Almost like she had been spirited there in some bizarre twist of fate to give me the opportunity to look this woman in the eye and come to terms with who she was and what she meant to both my husband and my father.

So I invited her to join me for coffee. Just like that. Like it was an ordinary everyday occurrence. The words spilling from my mouth before I had even considered the implications or consequences. And she said yes, which sort of surprised me. Why would she do that when I had been so high and mighty at our previous chance meetings? But now here we were strolling next to the banana trees and yellow hibiscus edging the corridor, breathing in the fresh, damp air after the rain.

We walked in silence to the restaurant, collected the tray cafeteria-style and waited for the woman to fill the cups. Which she did, pouring in milk before I had a chance to decline. So with that already done, I decided to leave the sugar. And even as we approached the table with its damask tablecloth and small vase of anthurium, the same question echoed over and over in my head. 'What are you going to say to her?' I had no idea.

So I just said: 'Do you love him?' Like we were already in the middle of a conversation.

'Pao?'

I nodded even though I wondered if perhaps she'd thought I meant my father.

'Do you?'

She was shrewd, this Gloria Campbell, trading one question for another.

'Never even liked him. Not in the slightest.' That is what I said even though I knew the truth is always more complicated.

'So what you marry him for?'

I took a sip of coffee and dabbed the corner of my mouth with a paper napkin. Then I placed the cup back in the saucer, resting it on the napkin I had positioned there to soak up the slight spill from the woman behind the counter. Playing for time. Just the same way I had straightened my skirt and pulled the chair up to the table with careful deliberateness.

And then I told her about being the fair-skinned, blonde-haired child of a black African mother. And Mama's nightly ritual of instructing the maids to plait rags into my hair so that come morning it would flow out into a magnificent display of cascading curls. And how everyone called me Shirley Temple and talked about 'On the Good Ship Lollipop' as if this was the highest accolade that could be bestowed upon me.

She looked at me in disbelief. Gloria. Toying with the handle of the cup but scarcely raising it to her lips.

'This will probably be the only time that you and I talk like this, so I think we should just be open and honest. There is no reason not to be.' Why did I say that? Why did I even think it? What was it that was driving me to disclose all of this to Gloria Campbell? Of all people. And then, sitting there gazing across the table at her smooth black skin and troubled but patient eyes, I realised what it was. I wanted to be included.

With her. Because she was something to Papa, Pao and Michael that I was not.

'Everybody thought that Mama resented it, my hair and the attention, but that is not true. She was the one, after all, instructing the maids to make the curls. She was the one who had me twisting and turning in front of company to show off what a beautiful blonde daughter she had produced. Mama only turned sour after my hair changed to brown when I was five years old.' And then I thought about the other things. With Stanley. But I didn't mention that to her.

Instead, I told her about pleading with my father to let me board at Immaculate so I wouldn't have to return from school to Mama each day, and about her accusation that I was playing at being white with my new friends.

When the server came to the table to collect the dirty crockery I asked her to bring me a top-up. She seemed startled, sour even, at my request. But she did it anyway, noticing when she lifted up the cup that I had taken milk and enquiring if I wanted sugar. It felt like too much effort to explain. And really it didn't matter. So I just smiled and said, 'No, thank you. That's very kind.'

It was after she brought the second coffee that I told Gloria about Isaac. Meeting him outside the Carib as big and as black as a man could be. Putting him in a taxi and taking him to Lady Musgrave Road so that Mama could silently seethe. A black man on her veranda. Not serving her afternoon tea but sitting there, sipping her beer and acting like a welcomed guest.

The surprise on Gloria's face was to be expected. Especially at my mention of Isaac. But there was also a look of recognition. So I guessed she'd heard some of it before. Maybe from Papa.

'The steam was practically coming out of her ears. It was the most gratifying sight I had ever seen.' I laughed, still relishing the memory of Mama's indignation.

'The funny thing was, Isaac was actually good company. Not too bright but very humorous and I thought caring. And after a while I really grew to like him and I thought he liked me. So when Mama told me to marry Pao I thought Isaac would have something to say about it. But all he did was sit there with the cigarette in his hand as if it had nothing to do with him. And eventually, when I pressed him, all he said was, "Do whatever yu want."' Which I said in real Jamaican just to show Gloria I could do it.

So it was done. It was out. The sordid tale of Isaac Dunkley and the stinking little room above the butcher's shop in Cross Roads. The whole story served as sufficient explanation of why I took up with Isaac to spite Mama. And then married Pao to spite Isaac, which was the question she had asked me. It made some sort of sense. Even if it wasn't the truth. Not the whole truth.

But why belittle Isaac to her? Calling him 'not too bright' when actually I'd learnt so much from him. Maybe I didn't want her to think he meant more to me than he did. Maybe I was protecting him. Him being a communist and all. Maybe it was bitterness over the last time I saw him. Or maybe it was just my light-skinned snobbishness. That old habit. Anyway, the truth was, it was a relief to say his name. Out loud. After all this time.

'All of my life I thought that everything could be solved inside my own head. All I had to do was to be smart enough.

And I would disappear into this head for hours and days, thinking and thinking and thinking some more. But you know the problem with that? You can only think what you can think. You can only see things the way you see them. You can only understand them the way you understand them. So in the end you just go around and around in circles getting even more confused and exhausted. And when I tired I would just stop and decide that everything would be fine. Just to get a rest. Then I would rally myself and carry on with nothing having been resolved. That is what I did running between school and Mama, and then Matthews Lane and Lady Musgrave Road. It was all I could do because escaping from that internal madness takes courage. You have to step outside of your own head. You have to be prepared to let someone else in and believe that it is possible to expose your vulnerabilities and inner torment to them without feeling invaded.'

And then I told her about Michael because I wanted her to understand that I had learnt something. That I'd learnt to give up fear and embrace hope. I'd become brave enough to trust someone.

But what I saw in her face wasn't comprehension, it was astonishment. So I simply said, 'I know you know.' And she smiled. 'I know about your daughter as well, at St Andrew.'

She waited awhile and then she said, 'Fay, what is all of this about?'

'I want you to know that I don't hold any malice towards you. I also want to apologise for my mention of the necklace the last time we met. It was spiteful and I am sorry. The past is the past, Gloria. What happened happened. So be it, but the future is a different matter. I suppose I just wanted you to understand something about me. Know me, not only what is said about me. We have shared such a lot it seems there should be more between us.'

I stopped. And then I said, 'How old are you, Gloria?'

'Forty-three.'

'I have just turned forty and I have spent almost all of that time trying to spite someone: first Mama, then Isaac, then Pao. And I have never ever stopped to think, I mean really think, about who I am or what I want. I have never had any sense of direction about my life. I have just stumbled from one disaster to the next trying to make the best of a bad job.' I thought of Stephenson and Hutton. Meacham and Donaldson. 'Trying to salvage something from my misery. And now, finally, I want to change my life.'

But as soon as I said it, I knew I'd made a mistake. Given too much away. Because what was on my mind was the UK Ministry of Labour work voucher I had applied for and my letter to Stanley asking him to enquire about a clerical position at the builders' merchants where he was working.

And, realising my error, I got up from the table abruptly and said, 'Walk with me to the car park and I'll give you a ride back to Barbican.'

The drive was straightforward. I already knew the way, which, if it surprised her, she didn't mention. She just sat there quietly in the car while I negotiated the uptown traffic feeling grateful for her lack of curiosity over what I meant about changing my life. Strangely, the silence was comforting. Like two old friends resting easy in each other's company.

When I pulled up outside her house she opened the door and stepped out. Then she bent down and stuck her head into the car and said, 'Thank you.' And I got the feeling she wasn't just talking about the ride. There was a look of appreciation in her eyes like she had seen something new yet familiar. And in that single moment I understood what my father had fallen in love with, and Pao too. The irresistible combination of intelligence and compassion that made Gloria Campbell so completely beautiful. She took you in. Without questions. Without conditions. Without judgement. Because what she had, and offered, was an absolute acceptance of you. Gloria Campbell had faith in humanity. It took my breath away. So much so that I didn't even manage to say goodbye before she closed the door and walked to her veranda.

I waited at the kerbside and watched her as she climbed the steps and disappeared into the house. Regretting that I had not known her sooner. Not known her differently.

CHAPTER 28

PAPA'S FUNERAL WAS soured by Pao being there with the children. He was standing in the garden with Karl and Mui either side of him, holding their hands so tight it seemed the blood would drain from their arms. They were timid when I approached. With a glazed look in their eyes.

I leant over to speak to them but no amount of 'How you doing?' or 'How is school?' could coax a word from either.

'The children quiet right now but it don't mean they don't miss you. Anytime you want to come home is alright with us.' He had a self-satisfied air about him.

I straightened up and walked away with an ache in my heart and a coldness in my stomach.

The sadness I felt for the passing of Papa I didn't know what to do with. So I buried it. Deep inside because what I wanted Pao to see was a vision of me as fresh and as alive as I could be. Not bruised and battered from the constant bickering with Mama and the loss of the father I had only recently come to know. That was the face I showed to him. With my back turned, I dropped the mantilla and let myself breathe away the tears that did not come.

Michael was standing at the cathedral door dressed in purple, white and gold, talking with Daphne. I took his hand and shook it.

'Thank you. The Mass was beautiful.' He smiled and rested his other hand on top of mine so I was clasped and held firm.

And then Daphne said, 'Especially at the end when you said: "Remember also, O Lord, Thy servant Henry who has gone before us with the sign of faith, and rests in the sleep of peace." That was nice. Papa would have liked that.'

I didn't know that he would. Not any of it. Not even the soprano singing 'Ave Maria' in Latin would he have appreciated. It was all too religious for him. All too Catholic for his taste. But then the funeral wasn't really for him. It was for us. And I would have had no other voice but Michael's ringing out in that cathedral '*In Nomine Patris, et Filii, et Spiritus Sancti*' regardless of Mama's protestations. What won her over in the end? Michael was now Roman Catholic Bishop of Kingston, consecrated just weeks earlier. And for Mama, status always counted.

When we got back to the house the place was full of well-wishers, eating and drinking and expressing to Mama their deepest sympathies. And so overwhelmed was she with her grief and crocodile tears that she had to sit throughout, with Miss Allen at her side, so that everyone had to go down on bended knees in order to grasp her hand and peer up at her with their condolences.

Who all of these people were I had no idea. None of them had anything to do with my father. Apart from a handful of fellow Chinese businessmen who kept to themselves, standing on the lawn with ice-water in hand, talking to each other in Hakka.

For whatever reason, Pao stayed away. Thankfully. I'd already seen enough of him, standing in the cathedral crossing himself and confessing to Almighty God that he'd sinned in thought, word and deed, and then following that with some long-drawn-out conversation with Mama in the garden. About what? Who knows. I only watched it from afar.

'This is Lincoln,' Daphne said to me.

I looked up at this very tall, very slim, very handsome man, with a clean-shaven, chiselled face. Dressed in a well-tailored dark-grey suit.

'My sister, Fay.'

He put out his hand. I shook it. His grip was firm but gentle. Soft. Like he'd been making reservations and checking guest accounts his entire life.

'Not the best circumstances for us to meet,' I said with as much of a polite smile as I could muster.

'I guess not.' He tightened his lips across his teeth.

'Lincoln is down from Runaway Bay. Just for a few days. Business.'

I nodded. I had no idea what to say to him. Then I saw Mr Lowe making his way across the lawn towards me. Threading a path deliberately through the crowd.

I excused myself. 'It's lovely to meet you, Lincoln. Let's catch up later or tomorrow perhaps.'

I walked over to Lowe. 'I have something for you. Your papa leave with me. For safekeeping.' That is what he said. Quietly. Standing at my side. At close quarters.

I rested my hand gently on his arm. 'Thank you.'

He smiled, revealing the small gap between his two front teeth. And then he stroked his stringy beard. 'You come get when you want. I always have ready for you.'

I knew about the money. Papa told me just two days before the second stroke took him.

'US dollars, Fay. Lowe keep for you.'

'Where you get so much cash from?'

He laughed. Mischievously. Then he lifted his good hand and with his index finger beckoned me towards him. So I leant over while he whispered in my ear.

'Me and Gloria money-lending business.' And then he eased himself back against the upright pillows with an enormous grin on his face. 'Always cash transaction that.'

'US dollars?'

'You have to keep reliable currency, Fay. Jamaican money devalue. And every time they change government all you have is worry 'bout what going happen next. US dollars, that is as solid as the gold in your mother's teeth.' He chuckled. 'Cicely, she get house and life insurance and every penny in bank. That is plenty. But you I want to have something for self. Something your mama not have anything to do with.'

'What about Daphne and Kenneth?'

'Their mama will look after them. But God help us what she decide to give to that boy. Yu see what bad business he already mek for self with money he have? What calamity he mek if he have more?'

'Papa, all this talk when you sitting here as strong as an ox.'

'A man got to mek arrangements. I not last for ever. Maybe this week, next week, next month I gone. And then what? You want me die and leave you all in a mess?'

★   ★   ★

Well, it wasn't a mess exactly. Mama did get everything just as Papa said. The part he omitted to tell me was that he hadn't made a will. So she inherited all his worldly goods by right of being his widow, including the supermarkets, wine store and wholesalers, which he'd promised to Pao. Told him so practically on his deathbed, a few days after telling Mama the very same thing.

She was incensed. 'Everything he want to give to Yang Pao?'

'They were in business together.'

'So you say.'

'I don't just say it. It was a fact. Week after week delivering supplies to the hotels on the north coast. Partners. For years. So Pao's sweat and tears is in those shops as well.'

'So now you remember he your husband? Now he got himself some serious money.'

I slammed the coffee pot down on the table. 'That has nothing to do with it. Papa made a promise to Pao.'

'But to give everything to him? Lock, stock and barrel? Just like dat? Even when he tell me I say to him, "Yu sure dat is what yu want to do? Yu certain yu not delirious meking a decision like dat?"'

I laughed at her yu and dat.

'What the hell you find so funny?'

'Nothing.'

'So what yu laughing at?'

'Nothing. Nothing at all.'

'Nothing at all? Yu should be thinking 'bout what going happen to yu brother. Yu think about that?' And muttering to herself: 'Sit there talking 'bout nothing at all.' And then to me:

'Yu father die and giving away di boy's future. Yu think dat is a laughing matter?'

'Kenneth? Yu joking? Kenneth not interested in nuh shopkeeping.'

'How many times have I told you not to be talking like that in this house? Yu think yu such a big woman yu can come here and do anything yu like? Talk to me after any fashion that tek your fancy? I will tell you now that as long as the good Lord is in his heaven so too am I mistress of this house where you will show the respect I expect from you.' So that is how it ended because Mama cannot hear the Jamaican in her own voice.

A week later she told Pao to come up to the house for afternoon tea. She wanted to talk to him. This I had to hear. So I positioned myself, out of sight, at the far-end living-room window. What I could see was Pao balancing the cup and saucer in one hand, while reaching with his other for the plate of sandwiches Mama was passing to him; and her with her Earl Grey tea and sugar tongs, like she believed she was the actual, real-life Lady Musgrave herself.

'As you know, Henry had it in mind that you should have his businesses. I understand that. After all, you are his only son-in-law, and mine, and the two of you were partners in supplying groceries and suchlike to the hotels. And I know you have been doing that together for some good time. But this is my problem. Kenneth. What will Kenneth inherit if I grant this wish of Henry's?'

Then she told him, 'Kenneth is not an easy boy. I am sure you have noticed. And even though I have prayed for many long hours, it seems that my prayers are in vain. This is the thing. If you could see your way to helping Kenneth learn about the supermarket business then perhaps in a few years' time, when he has mastered his trade so to speak, we could divide the business so that you could have, for instance, the wine merchants and wholesalers, and Kenneth could have the supermarkets. How does that sound to you?'

'Well, Miss Cicely, I think it is very fine of you to be thinking about Kenneth's future. It is what a good mother would do. But I am not sure if Kenneth is that interested in the supermarket business.'

'Let's just give it a try, shall we? And in the meantime let us say that you have control of Henry's business concerns. You are the general manager, if you like. Carte blanche. And Kenneth is your apprentice. And as for income, let us just split that fifty-fifty between the two of us, and you can pay Kenneth a salary out of your share. How is that?'

And then she offered him more tea. In truth? I actually felt sorry for him. The manoeuvrer had been manoeuvred. Mama didn't even seem to care that her plan was doomed to failure. Kenneth wasn't going to enter the supermarket trade. Not now, not ever. Not with Louis's fast-and-easy money calling him, and the fun he was having flaunting his power and gun around town. It wasn't going to happen. No more than Pao was going to drink the tea or eat the cake with both his hands full of crockery.

So he just stood up and walked over to the side table next to where Mama was sitting and rested down the plate and saucer. And then he said, almost with a bowed head, 'Thank you, Miss Cicely.' And left.

★   ★   ★

When she told Kenneth about her plan he said no. He wasn't nuh shopkeeper and he wasn't going to do it. So she threatened to throw him out of the house.

'Where will yu park yu fancy car then? And play yu music and smoke yu ganja? Because the money yu making not going stretch to maids and tennis court and swimming pool. Coming and going like a lord. Eating and sleeping and leaving your dirty laundry behind. Yu think yu can pay for all that on what you mek? Yu would have to sell your soul to the devil, whoever he may be, because God knows whatever yu doing got evil written all over it.'

So Kenneth decided to stay at home and start working at the supermarket. But it couldn't last and within weeks Sissy was telling me that Kenneth was still running with DeFreitas, leaving groceries in vans parked at the kerbside while he hurried off to do whatever Louis wanted.

I said to him, 'Kenneth, Papa talk to yu 'bout all this before he die?'

'All what?'

'Louis.'

He stiffened, ready to walk away. 'Yu going start with that again?'

'Do you understand why?'

He shrugged his shoulders and pouted his lips. And then he started down the veranda steps towards his car. I followed him.

'It is because I care about you. You are my brother. I love you. Louis DeFreitas is bad. He's no good for you.'

'What the hell you know 'bout Louis or anything for that matter? This is Jamaica. Things happening. A man got to mek his mark. Not be loading cans a bully beef on no supermarket shelf. He got to know where he belong. Know what he stand for and who he stand with.'

He opened the car door. I rested my hand firmly on the frame.

'You are not a man. You are a boy.'

'A man, Fay. Twenty years old. Old enough to do whatever I want.'

I looked at him standing there with the keys in his hand. 'Louis is a warlord.'

'Look who is talking, Mrs Yang Pao. Anyway what you know 'bout what the poor got to put up with? Living hand to mouth in some dirt yard with a zinc sheet over their head for shelter; sharing three standpipes and two public bathrooms between five thousand people. No work. No money. No food on the table. Fretting every time yu set foot outta yu yard that somebody going beat yu or murder yu. Having to stick a gun in yu pocket just to walk to di corner fah a loaf a bread. Survival. That is what it is.'

'Survival? What do you know about survival? Yu call this survival?' And I turned and waved my free arm at the house.

'Get out my way,' he said as he tried to loosen my grip of the car door.

'Kenneth, the gun in your belt not putting food on anybody's table or a roof over anybody's head. It is lining Louis's pocket. There not nothing noble 'bout stealing goods off the wharf, or selling ganja, or shaking down people for the money they owe to Louis.'

I removed my hand. But instead of getting into the car he just stood there. And then he said, 'I would rather be dead

341

than spend the rest of my life being a Chiney shopkeeper.' After which he did get into the car and drove away.

I would have talked to Papa, but he was gone. So there was nothing else to do. Except the last thing in the world I wanted to. Go and see Louis.

Sissy tried to talk me out of it. 'If yu go stick yu head in di lion's jaw not nobody going to be surprised if he just close his mouth on yu.'

Beverley was worried. 'After all this time? How yu going explain to him who Kenneth is to yu?'

Tyrone even offered to come with me but I said no. Why involve an innocent person?

CHAPTER 29

1966

TIVOLI GARDENS, TO a person like me, was a completely different country. Not just because of the absence of well-tended flower beds or the hiss of sprinklers on manicured lawns, but because of the modesty of the housing and the dry, dusty earth that swirled up around you, and the sea of black faces examining your every move. People, just sitting there in the heat of the afternoon; resting on the corner doing nothing at all; maybe mending a broken bicycle; whittling a piece of wood; a child banging a stick, rhythmically, on the solid dirt ground. All in a deadly silence that you know is reserved for you. The outsider.

Not that I'd forgotten that day in Back-O-Wall, as it was back then. Back in the 1950s when it was the most notorious slum in West Kingston. Home to the largest dump at Bumper Hall; the largest sewage-treatment plant; the two largest maternity and public hospitals; the blood bank; the morgue; the abattoir; the largest public cemetery in the English-speaking

Caribbean; and all the funeral parlours of downtown Kingston. Back-O-Wall before it was demolished and redeveloped into Tivoli Gardens where, Kenneth was right, the sufferers suffered. I just wasn't convinced that Louis DeFreitas was their saviour.

One of his men at the wharf had given me a phone number. When I called it, he told me to come. 'Louis, we can meet for lunch anywhere.'

'No. It time I stop running after you.'

Louis's house was a two-storey affair with a narrow wooden balcony upstairs. Painted pale blue and white apart from the spots of yellow on some of the windowsills where maybe he was in the process of rethinking the colour scheme. I parked Tyrone's Toyota and was locking the door when I heard a voice shouting out to me, 'Nobody going do nothing to dat parked there. Everybody know dis is my house.' I didn't have to look up to know it was Louis.

I opened the gate and walked past the breadfruit tree up the steps towards him. He was wearing black trousers and a long-sleeved grey shirt, with a pattern of small white diamonds in it. Standing there with the stick balancing his wiry frame.

'Yu change yu car?'

'It belongs to a friend.'

'Too fraid to bring yu Mercedes down here?' He laughed mockingly at me. At my ridiculous snobbishness.

'So come. Sit yuself down and let me get yu a drink.' Then he went inside and when he came back he was being followed by a woman carrying a tray with glasses, ice cubes and a jug of lemonade.

'This is my mother, Clorinda.' She rested the tray on the table and turned to me, wiping her wet hands on her apron.

I shook her hand. 'How do you do.'

'And, Mama, dis here is Fay Wong even though she play me for a fool and convince me dat she was Beverley Chung. Can yu believe a thing like dat? A woman who would be so deceitful.'

I felt the cold clam of fear.

'Onoo got yu tings fi settle.' And she walked back inside.

Louis sat down, positioning his walking stick against the side of the chair, and smiled to himself as he poured the lemonade into the glasses. Then he picked up one and offered it to me.

'Nuh worry yuself. There not no poison in it.'

I took the drink from him as he reached for the other glass and put it to his lips. He sipped. And afterwards raised his arm to make a toast.

'To friendship. True friendship, Fay Wong.'

I swallowed some lemonade. It was cold and refreshing with the perfect balance of bite and sweetness.

'How did you find out?'

'How I find out? Your brother. Give di whole game away complaining to me 'bout how his sista vexing him interfering in his business. How he cyan tek di constant antagonising and questioning 'bout what he doing and castigating – you like dat word – castigating his friend and confederate, yours truly.' He raised his bad leg and rested it on the stool in front of him.

'So now yu come here for what? And before yu answer me know dat I am intrigued. I cyan wait to hear what yu got to say. So mek yuself comfortable and tek yu time. Whatever it is will be worth listening to. Of dat I am certain.'

He eased himself back in the chair with a smug grin. Then he reached under the table and pulled out a small Chinese paper fan and started to waft the air around him, with the birds and flowers dancing to and fro at the side of his face.

'You make a mistake, Louis. And I thought it was simpler to leave it alone.'

'Simpler?'

I waited while he sipped his drink and readied himself to speak.

'Yu know how I finally put two and two together? It was when yu brother tell me dat his sista had di naked nerve – dat is what he say, naked nerve – to call me a crook when she married to dat swindling Chinaman Yang Pao. And how she drive 'round town in dat maroon Mercedes like she think she di First Lady a Kingston Town. So I say to him: "Maroon Mercedes?" Because dat is unusual, Fay. Yu have to admit it. Why yu no choose black like everybody else?' He didn't wait for an answer. 'So I tek a drive up to Constant Spring and step into Chung's Emporium to tek a look at Beverley Chung. Not in di dim light a di wharf at night or some corner of a dark restaurant, but in broad daylight. Bright Jamaican sunshine. And yu know what I discover?' He smirked. And then he held up the fan. 'Dat is where I get dis from.'

I crossed my legs. 'I want you to let Kenneth go.'

'Let him go?'

'You know what I mean, Louis. Stop him running errands for you. The boy should be in college. You know that.'

'College?'

My foot started to wiggle with impatience. 'I'm asking this of you as a friend.'

346

'A friend?' He paused. 'Yu know, Fay, di bit dat vex me. Really disappoint me. Was finding out dat all di time we busy meking friends yu was reporting everything to di police. Di police, Fay. Yu know how dat hurt me?'

'Louis,' I placed both feet on the ground and leant forward in the chair, 'they had me over a barrel.'

'A barrel?'

'Nothing bad happened to you. Yu still in business doing what yu do. Two years later, Louis, and yu still the king a Tivoli Gardens. Nothing I ever said was going to bring you down.'

'Did yu know dat fah sure all di time yu busy spouting to Donaldson 'bout me?'

I fiddled idly with my purse as it rested in my lap. Took another sip from the glass.

'Yu brother is a grown man. He will mek up his own mind. He big enough for dat. Not like dat son a yours who is truly still a bwoy. As for you, I am going to let yu drive outta here in yu borrowed car. But don't mek no mistake. I not forget about this. I just cyan mek up my mind as yet what to do wid yu. Maybe something, maybe nothing.' He wafted the fan some more. 'I say dis for yu, though. Yu got some guts coming over here.'

As I reached the car I shouted back to him, 'What do you want from me, Louis?'

'That remains to be seen.'

I had no idea how Louis found out about Donaldson. But as it turned out, I didn't hear anything from him. Not before events overtook us. Because after so many years of suffering and grievance, and public unrest, and political accusation and condemnation, and drug trafficking and turf wars, West Kingston erupted with open gun battles between rival gangs and armed confrontations with the police. So much so that on 2nd October the government had to declare a State of Emergency.

But before West Kingston could be settled, Kenneth was dead. Shot in some gunfight and bleeding to death in the middle of the street. Because, despite all my warnings, Kenneth could not bring himself to stay away from Louis DeFreitas.

It was hours later when the security forces came to the house to tell Mama what had happened and asked her to come to the hospital to identify his body. But she wouldn't go. Said she couldn't face it. So Daphne and I went. When they pulled back the cloth covering him I felt my knees buckle under me. It seemed impossible that all that blood could be his. Soaked into the blue shirt he'd bought only the previous week.

Then, taking my eyes off him, I saw the other trolleys, five or six of them. Bodies wrapped in shrouds. And, for the first time, heard the wailing that was coming from the other side of the door. From the corridor we had only moments before passed through, deaf to this world.

A policewoman took me by the elbow as we stepped outside into the crowd of mothers and sisters hanging on to each other in their anguish and grief. And the nurse led two other women into the viewing room we'd just come from.

That is when Daphne started to sob, screaming and flinging her arms in the air and hurling herself hard against the wall. She slid on to the cold, tile floor and lay there, clawing at her chest like she was trying to rip the blouse and skin from her breast. With tears streaming down her face and a wailing that was coming from deep inside. I dragged her to her feet and supported her as we walked to the waiting police car. But I didn't know what to say, so we just sat there quietly next to each other in the back seat, with me stroking her arm.

When we got home I discovered that Mama had locked herself in her bedroom and wouldn't let anyone in. Even my attempts to talk to her through the closed door were met only with silence. Daphne also took to her room, although I could hear her crying from the other side of the house. So I went in there and, sitting on the edge of the bed, rested my hand on her back. It was moist with sweat as she lay there on her stomach with her face buried in the pillow.

'Daphne.' But that was it. All I could think to say.

She turned over to look at me. 'This is your fault.'

'My fault?'

'For arguing with him and driving him out of the house.'

'I didn't drive him out of the house. He's been running around West Kingston with Louis DeFreitas for months.'

What came next I didn't expect. Her clenched fists beating into me with fury. I put both my arms around her and drew her to me. To comfort her and protect myself. When she wriggled and tried to tug away, I held her closer.

'Daphne, it isn't my fault.' She tossed her head aside. Snot from her nose landed on my cheek. I wiped it off and rubbed my damp hand on the sheet.

'This will kill Mama. That is what you want, isn't it?' And then she shouted: 'Get away from me. I hate you.'

I stood up and walked to the door. Then I turned and asked, 'Do you want me to call Lincoln?'

'Lincoln? No, that is all done.'

'Really?'

'He didn't want to know me after he found out about Pao.'

I closed the door behind me and went to the telephone. But I couldn't keep my hand steady enough to dial the number, so I had to call Ethyl to do it. The screaming that erupted from me was a surprise. The blubbering too. But there I was yelling at Pao about how Kenneth's death was his fault. Turning an innocent boy into a hoodlum. Crying so much I could barely get out the words.

'Exactly what you had to do with it, I don't know. But I know this. If Kenneth hadn't been working for you he would never have met Louis DeFreitas. Never have gotten involved. And I tell you this, I'm not going to let you do the same thing to Karl.' And I hung up the phone.

But really, I knew it wasn't true. In my heart, I knew Daphne was right. It was my fault. My fault for getting involved with Louis and betraying him. And afterwards, for not being able to protect my own brother. The flood of tears? More guilt than grief.

I telephoned Louis.

'I didn't have nothing to do wid it, Fay. Di bwoy went out deh when I tell him not to. I wasn't anywhere near Spanish Town Road when it happen. A stupid, trivial argument over nothing. That is all it was. And dem start shooting and nothing could stop it. I sorry fi yu. But Kenneth was a law unto himself. A hot-headed bwoy if ever deh was one. And yu know dat yuself.'

He was right. I did know. Then I said, 'Louis, last time we talked you mentioned something about Kenneth being a grown man but Karl still being a boy. What did you mean?'

'Mean?'

'Why did you bring Karl into it?'

'I don't know. I cyan even remember.'

Minutes later Pao's car was screeching into the driveway. When I went to the door I realised that Mama was sitting on the veranda. I hadn't even heard her leave her room. Pao came up the steps and went straight over to her, kneeling with both knees on the hard tile floor.

'Miss Cicely, I am so sorry to hear about what happen to Kenneth.'

I didn't know he had that kind of sympathy in him.

She took his two hands in hers and told him it wasn't his fault.

'I know you did your best. Kenneth was not a good boy. We tried. What more can we do? This is just the Lord's way of punishing me for all the things that I should have done and didn't do, and all the things I did that I should have thought better of. This is for me to ponder on, not for you to blame yourself.'

I didn't know she had that kind of remorse in her.

They stayed there holding hands. And after a while he got to his feet. And Mama went back into her bedroom.

I stepped out on to the veranda.

'I was hoping I would see yu,' he said. 'So I could give yu this.' Then he reached into his right trouser pocket and fetched out something in his clenched fist.

When I raised my hand on his instruction he placed it into my open palm. Michael's missing rosary. The Seven Sorrows of Mary.

'Where was it?'

'I had it.'

'All this time?'

'I took it while yu sleeping in the hospital. I thought maybe it would mek yu pay more attention to Mui.'

He was covered in regret. I could see that from the way his body was hanging. Loose and slumped. Not firm and upright like he usually was. Regret. Not just about the rosary but about that night. About our marriage. Maybe about his whole life.

He stuck his right hand back into his pocket. Stroked his chin with his left. And then, looking away from me, towards the garden, he said, 'All I wanted was a wife and family. So I could be decent and respectable. Have a reason for doing things. Children to pass things on to. Otherwise, what is the point of anybody living?' He thought for a while and then said, 'And you.'

'Me?' I was angry. 'So what are you passing on to your children?'

He looked confused. 'Everything is for them, Fay.'

'No, Pao, it isn't. It's all for you. What would they do with the gift of Chinatown?'

We stood in silence. Long enough to know that neither of us had anything else to say.

'Thanks for the rosary,' I said.

'I reckon it right yu should have it back.'

Kenneth's funeral was small. That is how Mama wanted it. Just family and the household help. Pao was there, of course, at her beck and call; supporting her as she lumbered her way along; easing her down when she wanted to sit; taking her weight when she wanted to stand. It was Pao she leaned on. With Miss Allen at her other side. And Daphne trailing behind, looking every bit the dutiful daughter. But surplus to requirements.

Why Pao decided to bring Karl with him I had no idea. Perhaps he wanted to show him what comes from a life on the streets. As a deterrent. Maybe. Not that Pao was setting much of an example. But to be fair to him he wasn't selling drugs or carrying a gun in his hip pocket and getting involved in shootouts.

What troubled me was seeing Louis a little distance off in the cemetery. And then Karl wandering over to him and the two of them engaging in conversation. Like they knew each other.

I went to check what was happening. 'You know this man?'

Karl looked first at me and then at Louis. Nervously. 'He's a friend of Uncle Kenneth's.'

'And you are talking to him because?'

'He call me over.'

Louis's eyes had that same inquisitive stare. The one I saw on the wharf the first time we met.

'I didn't mean di bwoy no harm. We passing di time a day, dat is all.' He smiled and slapped Karl on the shoulder. 'Dat not so?'

I took Karl by the arm and we walked back to join the others. 'I want you to stay away from that man.'

'He scares me, Mommy.'

'He scares me too.'

That was the moment I knew for sure I had to leave.

CHAPTER 30

'HOW COME YOU never say anything about God?'

'God?' Michael looked at me across the dining table of empty plates and dishes. 'What would you like me to say about God?'

'You are a priest. Aren't priests supposed to talk about God?'

Where we were? In Negril. On the West End cliffs. Far away from the seven miles of white sandy beach for which the town is famous. In a little cottage overlooking the sea with no telephone, electricity or hot water, but with the most magnificent sunsets, beyond compare according to Beverley, as the orange globe dipped over the horizon. Where the locals dive into the clear, blue water of a Caribbean cove from high above in the trees. For tourist dollars.

How we got there? In Papa's maroon Mercedes because we couldn't trust Michael's Chevy to make the journey from Kingston, through Spanish Town, over the mountains to Mandeville, down through Black River and along the coast to Savanna-la-Mar. Four, maybe five long hours' drive. Over hills and down valleys. Not a journey for an old jalopy. Not even one as pretty and gleaming as Michael's.

What I had told them at home? I was going away for a few days. The least said the better.

Michael was already dressed in casuals when I picked him up at Half Way Tree. A mauve open-neck shirt and dark grey trousers. So there we were, having finished our one-pot dinner of gungo-peas soup cooked by a maid at Hagley Park Road, where Beverley and Tyrone had been living since GC's death, transported and warmed by us over the one-ring Calor Gas stove. Sitting on a wooden-railed balcony. Enjoying Beverley's unrivalled sunset, sipping our Appleton Special.

And since I told him I expected a priest to talk about God he said, 'God is simple, without composition of parts. God is perfect, lacking nothing. God is infinite, not being physical, intellectual or emotionally limited. God is immutable, incapable of change in spirit or character. God is one, in essence and existence.'

'Reciting St Thomas isn't what I meant.'

'No?' He brought his thin lips into a smile. 'So what did you mean?'

What we were doing there? Having some time together because I was going. To England.

So I asked him to come to Negril with me. To give us some private space to think and talk. To figure out what future might be possible for us. If at all.

We lit the kerosene lamp and rinsed the dishes under the cold-water pipe, but I could still feel the tackiness under my fingers. So we boiled water and finished off the plates and bowls. Made coffee. Sat on the balcony. Looked out across the darkened cliffs. Listened to the lap of the Caribbean against the rocks.

'Will you come with me?'

He acted as though startled. 'To England?'

He was stalling. He knew exactly what I meant. 'Choices come to us from God.'

'So it's God now?'

'It always was, Fay.' He paused. 'But it seemed we had other things to discuss. Like your divorce.' He smiled, deepening the dimples in his cheeks.

'We barely talked about that and you know it.'

He ignored me. Sipped his coffee.

'So even when we think we have free will, we do not. Our choices are compelled by Him.'

'That isn't what you said about what happened in Back-O-Wall.'

'It isn't? What did I say?'

'You said we are responsible for our actions.'

He threw his head back and laughed. 'That is also true.'

'You can't have it both ways, Michael.'

Except he could, because according to Michael, God created us with different desires but it was up to us to choose. Up to us to deliberate over them and decide whether to act in this way or that.

'Yet, the very process of deliberation is also compelled by Him since our reasoning power is a potential given by God.'

It sounded like a lecture he'd received at the seminary, straight from the pen of Aquinas.

'Otherwise we act from habit and that is making no choice at all.' He pulled his lips together weakly. 'There is a saving grace, though. St Thomas tells us. Because however ingrained our reactions are, given time and the inclination to reflect, we can still resist our impulses. We can still go against a habit.'

'What impulse are you trying to resist now?'

He didn't answer. But actually he didn't need to. Because in order to be there in Negril, at that moment, he must have offered some explanation at Bishop's Lodge. Had packed a bag. Had allowed himself to be driven there. To be alone with me. Through his own free will.

We hadn't discussed sleeping arrangements. But after the moth got into the glass globe and spluttered the lamp, we decided it was time for bed, and went into the only bedroom together. Instinctively. Without a single word being spoken by either of us. And in the dark, we undressed, slipping into the cool, cotton sheets at precisely the same moment. Each of us from the opposite side of the bed. And lying there in the stillness of night, Michael reached out and put his arm around me. And I rested my head on his shoulder. Aware of my nakedness. Not with the lost and lonely feeling of rejection I had the time Mama stripped me. Nor the bitterness and resentment I had with Pao. Not the anxiety of approaching loss as with Freddie. Or the superiority I hid behind with Isaac. No. It was something completely different. A feeling of reassurance and familiarity with the smell of the Pears soap wafting off his skin and the firmness of his body against mine. Like an invisible cloak had masked any awkwardness between us, leaving no questions or doubts to be answered or untangled. No dread to overcome. No uncontrollable feelings to be gratified. Just the simplicity of the moment. So it was with a sense of ease that I raised my leg and laid it across his. And that was enough.

Over the next two days we ate and swam in the fresh river-water pool and dozed in the shade of an almond tree, with the hair on Michael's shapely and muscular legs reminding me about his mother being Indian. And we talked endlessly about everything, including what he was doing that day in Back-O-Wall.

'Visiting my mother.'

'Your mother? In Back-O-Wall? That was where the yard was? The one from your childhood.' He nodded. 'And they didn't know you? Those men.'

'I was a child who left a very long time ago. Anyway, Back-O-Wall was a big place. And a cassock means what? Persecution by the foreign Catholic invaders? Not like the obeah woman with her spells and potions, or the self-ordained preacher calling on God in his heaven while he molested young girls under the pretext of exorcising the devil.'

'Bitterness, Michael?'

He turned to me with furrowed brows. 'A cassock is not sacrosanct.'

'And your mother never wanted to get out?'

'She said my father took her there and abandoned her. So that was where she belonged. With the rest of the discarded and dejected.'

'Where is she now?'

'She died just before they bulldozed the place to make way for Tivoli Gardens.'

I looked at him like I knew there was more.

He blushed. 'I will not lie to you. But there is nothing I can say.'

I waited. Then I said, 'The person you were running the errand for that day, was it Bishop Langley?'

'Fay, please.'

So I stopped.

When, in the car, we finally talked about England again, he said, 'The truth is I feel at home with you. At home, where I can breathe and rest and be myself. That is such a long way from Back-O-Wall where I always felt like an outsider, even as a child. Or at Bishop's Lodge where all of the time I am so conscious of trying to be good and working to be better. But that truth, like all truths, is in the mind. Where we create them. And that is not the same as having faith. In God and the Scriptures.'

'You once told me that faith is not static. That it causes us to learn more about God so we can create our own happiness.'

He smiled. 'But are we to settle for imperfect happiness on earth rather than the bliss of union and fellowship with Him?'

I had no answer for that so we sat silently for the rest of the journey back to Kingston. When we reached Half Way Tree he said, 'Faith is revealed in an active life aligned with the ideals and example set by Jesus Christ. It is the exercise of reason and the practice of virtue.'

'That applies to everyone,' I said. 'Not only priests.' But he didn't reply. He just got out of the car. And then standing on the sidewalk he leant his head in and said, 'I will come.' But the handle was already out of his hand and before I could say anything the door had shut and there was only glass between us. So through the window I mouthed, 'I love you.' And he mouthed, 'I love you too,' before turning and walking away.

Mama was sitting on the veranda when I pulled into the driveway.

'Daphne tell me you leaving.' She looked up from her embroidery. I sat down on the armchair next to her. With the side table between us. And the sprinkler whirling around as it watered the afternoon lawn.

'You want to say something to me about that?'

She thought for a while. Her fingers moving nimbly with the cloth and thread. 'I can understand it. Your life been nothing but one misery after another. Me included. Better one soul be saved than every single one of us going down with the ship. Drowning in our sorrows.'

'Is that what you are doing, Mama? Drowning in your own sorrows.'

She picked up her scissors and cut off the green silk. And started to rethread. With yellow. A bright canary-yellow. Putting the loose end of the thread into her mouth to moisten it before focusing her attention on the eye of the needle.

'When yu born and grow up the way I did yu come to understand a lot of things. The first thing yu understand is that a woman like me with no education to speak of, except for reading the Bible like the missionaries teach me, such a woman has no chance of making anything of herself. Not in this world. Not the one I was living in anyway. And then with a father like mine.' She sighed. 'Well that not even worth going into. So yu soon come to see that the best yu can hope for is a considerate husband who can be tolerant and forgiving. And who can provide.' She continued with her cross-stitching. 'But where do yu find a man like that when yu already with child? And only a child yourself. Where indeed. Especially since the African had nothing himself. And didn't know how to do anything apart from sweat from labour and toil. Just like he did on the plantation for three hundred years. And then spend every penny he earned in ways that decency would prohibit me from mentioning.' She looked over at me. 'I wanted more than that for my daughters.' Then she stared down at her hands again, carefully manoeuvring the needle through the cotton of the altar-cloth. 'And there was your father. Whom I had known since we were children on the plantation. And who was willing to marry me. Me, of all people. A man with ambition. The kindest man yu could ever hope to meet. The man who brought us to all this.' She levelled her eyes across the veranda and garden. 'God rest his soul. All from one little shop in Ocho Rios.'

'And that is why you chose Pao for me?'

'A Chinese man, Fay. With a shop and money in his pocket.' Her brows furrowed. 'Of course I didn't know then what I know now. About how he put that money in his pocket. Didn't know then what I have learned since Kenneth died. Not that I am here passing judgement. Yang Pao does as he do. Everybody start somewhere. Just like your own father.'

'What do you mean?'

That is when she told me about the crocus bag stuffed full of US dollars that Papa found under his shop in Ocho Rios. So much money they were afraid to count it. So they just hid it. And how the American man it belonged to threatened to kill them if they didn't give it back to him. So Papa made him a deal and he settled on buying Papa the liquor store in Kingston in exchange, because the shop cost far less than what was in the bag.

'Where did it come from? The money.'

'It was 1920s prohibition, Fay. They were running rum and molasses from Cuba and Jamaica.'

'My father was a rum-runner?'

'He was no such thing.' She was indignant, looking over at me for the first time. 'There was no prohibition in Jamaica.' She turned her attention back to her sewing. 'But that is how things start. And later, when he wanted to clear out of Jamaica and go back to Chicago, he sold your father this house at a good price. Because I don't think he paid anything too much for it himself.' She lifted up the cloth to admire her needle-work. Holding it at arm's length against the bright sunlight.

'Every penny your father made after that was through his own hard work, diligence and prudence. Week in, week out. For forty long years. I want you to remember that.' There was pride in her voice. A rare tone for my mother.

'Is that why you didn't like me spending time with him?'

'Because of the liquor? No. It wasn't that. No shame in that.' She bit on her lower lip slightly. 'The truth? Because he gone and you going? It was because he favoured you so much. When you little. With the blonde hair that made you look so innocent. Which I know was me encouraged it. With the curls and such. But him and you, it reminded me of how my father used to favour me.' She paused. 'When he was in a good mood.'

'Nothing like that ever happened with Papa, you know.'

362

'So you say. But it didn't stop me thinking about it. When you young. Or worrying that you had some wickedness in you. The same wickedness that was in me. To make my father do what he did.'

Tears started to form in her eyes. So I stood up, walked over to her and removed the material from her lap. And then I took her hands in mine.

'It wasn't your fault, Mama.'

She snatched herself away and reached for her embroidery on the side table where I had rested it. 'Still. There got to be something.'

I parked myself back in my chair and watched while she concentrated on her stitching. Forcing back her tears. I thought about Stanley. 'That morning in the bedroom with Stanley. What was that?'

She shot a defensive glance at me. 'What Stanley tell you?'

'Nothing. He said it was nothing.'

She looked down into her lap, concentrating on thread and scissors. 'That is right. Nothing. Nothing except a message from the devil to remind me that evil is just under the skin. Waiting there. In the blood. To send me to hell if I let it.'

And then she fell silent. And I knew she was done talking about it. So I said, 'I'll write.'

'Write to Daphne. She will be the one to miss you. She talking to Karl and reading books with him about England like she almost wish she was going with you.' And then she said, 'And as far as Stanley is concerned, you can just say hello to him from me.'

CHAPTER 31

DAPHNE NEVER EXPLAINED to me about what happened with Lincoln. Even though I asked her. More than once. Frankly, she didn't seem that disappointed. More like she was relieved. As if a burden of unwanted responsibility had been lifted from her shoulders. Like maybe a life with Lincoln wasn't what she had in mind. All hotel and tourists.

And then remembering the comments she'd made about Pao being good company and not as bad as I thought. And him sitting on the veranda with her being 'charming and amusing'. I wondered. Perhaps 'Lincoln finding out about Pao' wasn't what I'd taken it to mean.

When I told her about leaving she wasn't surprised. Only startled at the suddenness of the decision. After all, she'd watched my growing unease over Karl's relationship with Kenneth. And sensed my worry about his future, especially with Pao as a father.

She had softened, too, in the weeks after Kenneth's death. Had come to terms with the fact that I had also lost a brother, and that despite our differences we were still sisters. That blood was thicker than tears.

'You don't think maybe it's a little dramatic?'

'I refuse to lose my son to this reckless violence.'

She didn't say anything. She knew what I meant. So I just handed her what was left of the money I'd collected from Mr Lowe.

'Here, I want you to have this.' She lifted the lid of the shoebox and looked inside.

'Where you get all this from?'

'Keep your voice down,' I said to her, 'Mama will hear you.' And then: 'It's legal tender, that's all you need to know. Yours now so keep it safe. Get yourself some independence from her.' I motioned my head towards the veranda where Mama was sitting.

I didn't tell Daphne any more, despite the confusion on her face and questions on her lips. No need to explain why I couldn't pay the money into the bank. Too much inquisition over its source. And I certainly couldn't take it off the island with me. Too many restrictions on foreign currency. Too high a risk of having it confiscated at the airport. Never mind arrest. Besides, finance in England was secure. Stanley had arranged a job for me in the office at the builders' merchants. So my army clerking experience was going to come into its own after all.

'What am I going to tell Mama?'

'Why tell her anything? Just spend the money and keep it to yourself.' Then I looked her earnestly in the eye.

'But, Daphne, you have to promise me one thing.' She was nervous. 'Don't give Mama or anyone else Stanley's address. He left here thirty years ago and has never been in touch with her. And he doesn't mean to start now. You understand me?'

'But how can I keep a thing like that from her?'

'If I can't trust you then I'm not going to give you this.' I waved in front of her the postcard on which I had written Stanley's address in London. 'And then you'll never be able to contact me. Is that how you want it to be?'

She thought on it. 'Give me the address.'

'I am serious, Daphne.' I pulled back my hand. 'Never been more serious about anything. Trusting you completely now not to be giving this to Mama or Pao so he can send his musclemen to bring us back.'

'I don't think he would do a thing like that.'

'No?'

'I know what he is, Fay. Kenneth told me about the errands he ran for him so I know it wasn't just delivering groceries. But there is another side to him.' She paused, thinking carefully about what she was going to say. 'Well, I just don't think he would do that.'

I didn't see any point in arguing with her over what we thought Pao might or might not do, so I just said, 'Do you promise?'

And she said, 'Yes.' While holding out her hand into which I placed the postcard.

The plan, I'd been working on for months. Ever since Karl told me that the police had arrested him for stealing a bow and arrow from a King Street store. And how angry the constables were that their sergeant made them drop the charges and apologise to Pao.

'You just took them? The bow and arrow.'

'We never pay for anything, Mommy.'

366

I understood. That was how life was with Pao. 'What were these constables called?'

'Mutt and Jeff.'

'Mutt and Jeff?'

'That is what Daddy called them because they look like the comic strip. It was a big joke. Even the sergeant was laughing.'

The day I went to North Street police station, the duty officer smirked as he picked up the telephone and said, 'Tell Mutt and Jeff to come out front. Somebody want to see them.'

When they came through the door they were just as to be expected. One of them tall and thin, the other short and squat, both looking as dim-witted as their namesakes.

'We can help yu?' They were grouchy. Still stinging from the embarrassment.

'I think maybe you can.'

We stepped together into the afternoon sunshine and while we strolled I explained to them what I had in mind. Later, sitting under the shade of a tamarind tree in East Queen's Street, the deal was done. Because, in the end, it was all a matter of money. The only question was whether they actually had the wherewithal to do it. What we agreed. But since I had few options, I decided to take a chance.

'Yu really think yu can trust them?'

'What options have I got, Beverley? Honestly. Can you think of something else?'

She stirred her coffee. 'I'm not questioning your plan, Fay. But Mutt and Jeff?'

I rested my elbow on the table. 'Who else would even think about crossing Pao?'

She sighed. 'I know.'

I changed the subject. 'Daphne took some old snapshots of Karl and Mui to work with her and turned them into passport-sized photographs.'

'And Marjorie Williams got all the travel arrangements in hand, promising me that she will not breathe a word of this to anybody. She still grateful for yu saving her from drowning at the Guide picnic.' She paused. 'And talking of old school-friends, you know Hazel Brown sent the manuscript of her book to Freddie?'

'Really? Hazel? She actually finished her book?'

'Wonders never cease, eh? So I suggested she send it to him and it seems like his Bamboo Tree House Press is going publish it.' She sliced her fork into the sweet-potato pudding. 'And in this letter that Freddie sent her back, according to Marjorie, Freddie said that his wife died. Ovarian cancer.'

'He told her that?'

'Maybe hoping she would tell you.' She looked purpose-fully down as she slipped the pudding into her mouth. Chewed and swallowed. And then she said, 'Yu think maybe yu should write to him?'

'Freddie?'

'Why not? Yu going to England. His wife dead. What harm would it do?'

'Yu nuh think it sort of contrived?'

'Contrived? How can true love be contrived?'

I laughed. 'True love?' And then I wondered if maybe I should say something to her about Michael, but decided against it. 'I am happy for Hazel about her book. But Freddie? I wouldn't know what to say to him.'

When Mutt and Jeff told me that their sergeant had booked leave to go to Miami, I knew this was the moment. So I went to Bishop's Lodge to ask Michael a favour. It was the first time I'd seen him since Negril. He was different. Softer, more relaxed, gentler, with a bright, shining sparkle in his eyes. Actually, his whole body was different. More fluid somehow as he moved around the desk to open the French windows on to the garden.

We stepped outside. Him flowing with an ease I'd never seen before. Not even in Negril.

'I have a favour to ask of you.'

He didn't say anything, just took me by the elbow as he headed between the gap in the poinsettia to the secluded lily pond beyond. I wanted to slide my arm down and take hold of his hand but didn't dare. And right then I think he read my mind or maybe he had the same thought because suddenly he let go of me and clasped both of his hands firmly behind his back.

He walked slowly and deliberately towards the arbour. In silence. And then he seated himself in the shade of the rambling purple and white wild orchids. He crossed his legs, in the only way his cassock would allow. Not in that ankle-on-knee way that Isaac would, but like a woman or true gentleman. And then he rested his hands on his knee. And looked up at me. And smiled while pointing to the adjacent bench for me to sit.

What I wanted to do? Throw my arms around him. Feel the weight of his body against mine. Its bulk. Its warmth. I wanted to stroke his skin and bury my nose in his neck to smell the Pears soap. I wanted to run my fingers through his wavy black hair. I wanted to press my lips against his. I wanted to touch his nakedness.

'That is not for now,' he said, reading my mind again. 'Another time, another place.' And then, jutting out his chin towards the lodge: 'My next appointment will be here soon.' He smiled. 'Anyway, so much more time you and I will have.' That was how certain he was. Like the world was at his command.

I sat down on the bench across from him. 'There is a chance to leave in the next two weeks. So I need to speak to Karl urgently. Will you let me see him on Sunday?'

His mood hardened. 'The children are with Pao now. If you want to see them you will have to make arrangements with him.'

'I can't do that and you know it.' My voice was higher, my tone sharper than I meant it to be. Why? Because something had come between us. A separation. A distance that I couldn't bear to be there. The worst part? That it seemed OK with him. Michael was comfortable keeping me at arm's length. I breathed in and out slowly. To calm myself.

'Let me speak to him on the phone then. It's the only opportunity I will have. Here at Bishop's Lodge. After Mass.'

'Fay, I can't ...'

But I didn't let him finish. 'This is my window, Michael. I might not get another one. Not soon anyway. Maybe not at all. Please don't stand in the way of that.' I paused and then I said, 'It's your future too.'

He stood. 'After Mass then. I'll find an excuse to bring Karl back here.'

His two o'clock appointment was walking up the path towards us as we approached the lodge door.

'Father, thank God in his heaven that yu here. When I walk past the office just now and see it empty I fret that maybe yu forget about me.' She mopped the sweat from her brow as she hurried to catch up with us, switching her shopping bag from one plump arm to the other. 'There not nobody else on this wretched earth that understand me and the troubles I face other than you.'

He took her puffy hand in his. Clasping it between his own. 'Good afternoon, Miss Clarice. How well you are looking today.'

And she did. Look well. Actually, she was glowing. Despite the fullness of her in the scorching afternoon heat.

She looked at me. 'Yu nuh think this man sent to us straight from the good Lord himself?' But she didn't wait for my answer. 'Yessir. That is the truth. Everybody I know say the very same thing. Woman and man. Even the chillen he have the patience to listen to. Whatever ailing or afflicting yu, a good half hour with Father Kealey will set yu right.'

He let go of her hand and bowed his head slightly. 'Would you like to wait for me in the office?'

She walked into the cool lodge entrance while I hung back at the door, and Michael watched her disappear from view. Then he said, 'All of this is happening so quickly. So close to Christmas. I will have to follow you.'

So I spoke to Karl on the phone that Sunday. Sitting in the living room at Lady Musgrave Road. Trying to be as discreet as I could, despite being interrupted by Ethyl carrying a vase of flowers. I waved my hand at her to tell her to get out while

I confirmed the arrangements with him. Because he too was ready to go. He too had seen the truth of his father's life. He too had met Gloria Campbell. He too had been frightened by Kenneth's death.

The hardest part was saying goodbye to Sissy. Without saying it. But she knew.

'Might not be seeing yu for a while then.' That is what she said to me while giving me a sideways glance. In the car, after seeing *The Great Caruso*. A movie as old as the hills but a favourite of hers. And mine too. For the music. Like the Celebrity Seasons at the Carib we so much enjoyed. World-famous opera singers and ballet dancers performing for us. Right there in Kingston.

'I guess.'

'Yu got to do what yu got to do.' She stared out of the car window. 'I reckon it best anyway.' Pause. 'In the circumstances.'

I gazed out at the stationary traffic, remembering the lolli-pop doll she'd given me when she left Lady Musgrave Road.

'Yu know, Sissy, yu been more mother to me than Mama ever was. Caring for me day after day. Tending to all my cuts and bruises and ups and downs. Never having a cross word for me no matter what happened, torn clothes, wet bed sheets, all my antics mimicking Nancy's mother next door. All the things I lost or broke or discarded like a child does. All the misery with Mama. Shielding me as best yu could, comforting me when I needed it. Listening to all my woes. Even saving food for me from your own plate.'

'Oh don't start wid all a dat.'

'No, Sissy, I'm serious.' I eased the car forward as the traffic started to flow. 'And yu know the thing I will always love you for? That you thought I was perfect. Like you whispered to me on the veranda steps. "You are perfect. Don't let anybody mek yu forget it." Who else in this world would think a thing like that about me?'

'What yu trying to do? Get the whole audience bawling in the aisles?'

I turned towards her as she wiped a single tear from her cheek. 'The truth, Sissy? You are the one who taught me what motherly love is. If I have any such thing to give to my children it is because of you.'

'Yu have it, gal. All yu have to do is let it out.'

After I pulled the car over to the kerb to drop her off, I reached into the back seat for the gift I'd brought for her.

'What dis?'

'Unwrap it and see.'

It was a record. Doris Day.

'Something to stick on that gramophone Papa bought you.'

And then, as we stood on the sidewalk together, she hugged me. A close, warm-hearted, long-drawn-out embrace. More confident, more committed than the last time we said good-bye. On the veranda steps the day she left Lady Musgrave Road.

'And nuh bother thinking 'bout no letter writing. I never took to that. Yu can send me a postcard once in a while when the fancy tek yu.'

On the way home I called in at the post office and sent a telegram to Stanley. 'All set. We are coming to England.' And I gave him the flight details.

★   ★   ★

Pao had the children practically under house arrest. Ever since Kenneth's death. Constantly guarded by his men every minute they were away from Matthews Lane, escorting them to school, to church, to see Michael. Always there, waiting with a car to transport them to their next destination.

But when the day came, with their sergeant away in Miami, Mutt and Jeff were as good as their word. Grabbing Pao's man, Milton, outside Karl's school and while Mutt was arresting him, Jeff dragged Mui from his car and put her into the taxi in which I was waiting. Waiting and wondering. Wondering if I was doing the right thing. Wondering if we would hate England. If England would hate us. If I would ever get over my regrets about abandoning Jamaica. Or if I didn't leave, my regrets about staying. Wondering if Karl really believed what I'd told him about why we had to go. Or really believed what he'd told me about why he wanted to. If Mui would ever forgive me for snatching her away from Pao and her life at Matthews Lane. Away from Zhang and Hampton and Ma. And the country she loved so much. And, of course, there was Pao who, despite his bad ways, was still more father to them than I was mother. Wondering if maybe it was not too late to change my mind.

But it was. The children were in the taxi and Milton was on his way to the police station to be detained until after our flight left.

Daphne was at the airport. With Beverley and Tyrone standing next to each other like they were ready to take to the dance floor. Beverley looking as fresh as she did that first day we met when she shouted out, 'Hey, gal' and asked me if I had anything to say for myself. Tyrone still with his boyish

374

good looks, which gave me a sudden flash of him bent over the piano keys at Grandmother Chung's. Seeing them there filled my head with music. The Bournemouth Club, Silver Slipper, Club Havana. Freddie. The days and nights with GC, eating and drinking, dancing and laughing like we hadn't a care in the world. We were vibrant then, like they were now. Full of their hopes for me.

Daphne? She had a hangdog look. Just like the one she wore at Papa's funeral and Kenneth's too. Her death-face because either me or her or both of us was dying. That was how it seemed to her. As she stood there amidst the airport's festive decorations.

So much I wanted to say to all of them. But with Mui creating such a commotion our parting was rushed and chaotic. We were through the gate before I could blink an eye, their waving arms out of sight.

Then we sat in the departure lounge, with Mui kicking and screaming to be returned to her father. And me watching the turning heads of other passengers and trying to reassure them that all was in order.

A stewardess came over wanting to examine our tickets and passports for a second time. 'This is definitely your child?'

'Yes, she is.' I turned to Mui. 'Tell the lady I am your mother.'

She was silent but nodded her head.

'Then yu need to get her to calm down.'

It was Karl who managed it in the end. Kneeling on the ground in front of her and holding her hands in his.

'Yu see how Uncle Kenneth get killed? And all the shooting and everything that going on? It dangerous. And me? I was heading the same way as him. Wandering off down that same road if I wasn't careful. Because Uncle Kenneth was working for Daddy and Daddy not no angel. Yu old enough to understand that. And what would you be doing anyway in the middle of all that trouble? That is what Mommy is trying to save us from. Growing up in bedlam. You get that? England is safe.'

I looked at Karl kneeling there and remembered the day in King Street that I watched them walking up the road with Pao. Swinging their linked arms and talking to each other. Chatting in that casual way I had never managed. This fourteen-year-old boy and eleven-year-old daughter of mine. My children, who were growing and grown. Karl tall and wiry, running his hand through his hair and tugging up his trousers in the same way Pao would from time to time. Mui, sturdy and strong-minded, bonded to Matthews Lane and the life I had now snatched her away from. Why? Because I wanted them to have a better future. Not just for their safety, but for their flourishing. I wanted them to bloom like I never did. I wanted them to have opportunities I never had. I wanted the possibility for them to have and make their own choices. Not act out of habit or within the confines that somebody else laid down. Me? I wanted the freedom and space to find out how to love them. Like Sissy loved me. Like a mother ought to love her children.

Mui's crying eased. 'He is still my papa.'

'Yes he is and always will be. But you know, Mui, you know that what I say is true. You and Zhang talk about the plight of the people. And it is good to care about that. But what happening in Jamaica is not a Chinese revolution. It is drug dealing and gang war.'

'My papa doesn't do any of that.'

'No he doesn't. But it is there waiting for us if we don't leave. And Daddy, he will know this is the right thing as well. Because he loves you too and would want to see you grow up safe and happy.'

He gave her a Kleenex to dry her tears. And then she leant against me and allowed me to put my arm around her shoulder.

She looked up at me. 'I didn't say goodbye to him.'

'No. But one day you will say hello to him again.'

The plane raised its nose above the Blue Mountains and headed north. Karl was in the window seat. Mui sitting in the middle, next to me. Sleeping. Clutching Athena, Sissy's lollipop doll I had brought for the journey.

I opened my purse and fetched out the airmail paper. The letter I wanted to finish before I landed.

You are a priest, Michael, all you ever wanted to be. A wonderful, loving priest whose calling is Jamaica. How could I take you away from that and rob Jamaica and the Jamaican people of all the good you will do in the years to come? I couldn't do it. And if I did, I would never be able to forgive myself.

And then I wrote: *Just remember this. I love you.* Because I wanted him to know it. Not just watch me mouth it through a closed car window. So it was done. Signed and sealed. The end of one life, the beginning of another. With a good deal of sadness for so much of my life that had been wasted and misguided.

I thought of Pao with all of his contradictions. Dishonest and honourable, ruthless and tender, selfish and considerate. All at the same time. With the most graceful and poetic hands I'd ever seen on anyone. Woman or man. And his voice. That smooth tenor singing 'Roses of Picardy'. Even in the middle of a crowded street. Human and flawed, just like me. And in that moment what I hoped? That he would forgive me. That he would come to understand this was for the better. For them. Karl and Mui. Because really, what did Pao ever do to me? Apart from want something I could never give him. And what was so bad about the way he was a father? Nothing. Except the example he set by being himself.

I reached down to the floor and picked up Athena, who had slipped from Mui's sleeping grasp. And then, placing the doll back in her lap, and resting my hand on her arm, I looked out of the window. And wondered what kind of England was waiting for us.

ACKNOWLEDGEMENTS

It took me seven years to write *Pao*. The second novel in these three interlinked books, *Gloria*, took two and a half years. As did this current work. So this is the end of a very long journey. Three books, three lives, three quests for redemption. But one story, one island, one love.

Thank you to Helen Garnons-Williams for reading and scrutinising draft after draft. Fresh and enthusiastic like each time was the first. Thank you for being so smart, unremitting, patient and kind. I know how lucky I am to have had you as my editor these past years.

Thanks also to Sarah-Jane Forder, the most lovely of copyeditors. And to all at Bloomsbury, especially Alexa von Hirschberg. My agent, Sophie Lambert at Conville & Walsh. Thank you for being there for me, by my side and on my side.

Thank you Amanda Harrington for your friendship, support and encouragement every page of the last fourteen years. May Whyte for your love and affection. And my family – Donna, Shelly, Sebastian, Pru, Wain and Sally – who continue to put up with me in all my weird and wonderful ways.

Most of all, thank you to my mom for loving and believing in me.

I have drawn on many different sources during the writing of this book, most notably the following: *Aquinas: Selected Philosophical Writings* by Thomas Aquinas, selected and translated by Timothy McDermott (Oxford University Press, Oxford, 2008); *The Shopkeepers: Commemorating 150 Years of the Chinese in Jamaica 1854–2004* by Ray Chen (Periwinkle Publishers Ltd, Jamaica, 2005); *Rise and Organise: The Birth of the Workers and National Movements in Jamaica 1936–39* by Richard Hart (Karia Press, London, 1989); and *Time for a Change: Constitutional, Political and Labour Developments in Jamaica and Other Colonies in the Caribbean Region 1944–55* by Richard Hart (Arawak Publications, Kingston, 2004). I have also referred to other classic texts, including Dante's *The Divine Comedy* and Milton's *Paradise Lost*. The epigraph is from St Thomas Aquinas, *Summa Theologiae*, 1a, question 96, article 4.

ALSO AVAILABLE BY KERRY YOUNG

PAO

Shortlisted for the Costa First Novel Award

Fourteen-year-old Yang Pao arrives in Jamaica from China with his mother and brother. They are to live with Zhang, the 'godfather' of Chinatown, who mesmerises Pao with stories of glorious Chinese socialism.

When Pao takes over the family's affairs he becomes a powerful man. He sets his sights on marrying well, but when Gloria Campbell, a black prostitute, comes to him for help, they begin a relationship that continues even after Pao marries Fay Wong, the headstrong daughter of a wealthy merchant.

As political violence escalates in the 1960s the lines between Pao's socialist ideals and private ambitions become blurred. Jamaica is transforming, the tides of change are rising, and the one-time boss of Chinatown finds himself cast adrift.

'With grace, authenticity and humour, Young lets Jamaica's political history shine through the life story of her charming yet fallible hero. Brilliant'
DAILY MAIL

'A punchy tale of pungent characters and impassioned entanglements'
INDEPENDENT ON SUNDAY

'*Pao* confirms Young as a gifted new writer. Her novel is a blindingly good read in parts, both for its mesmeric story-telling and the quality of its prose'
OBSERVER

GLORIA

'A highly evocative portrait of a country in transition, and of one woman's search for self-awareness and self-respect'
MAIL ON SUNDAY

Gloria Campbell is sixteen years old when a single violent act forces her to flee her hometown to forge a new life in Kingston. But while Forties Jamaica is awash with change, a black woman is still treated as a second-class citizen. When Gloria finds her way to a house of ill repute on the edge of the city, she is enthralled by the glamorous, financially independent women within. It is here that dreams of social change are instilled in her, and she must choose between the life she has made for herself and the one that might be.

Alive with the energy of a country at a crossroads, this is a story of love in many forms, and of one girl's evolution from a frightened teenager on the run to a woman fully in possession of her own power.

'A vivid portrayal ... Heartfelt, sparky and affecting ... A chronicle of multicultural Jamaica, both in its cultural richness and in its strife and tensions'
GUARDIAN

'A brilliant, observant read'
YORKSHIRE POST

'Gritty and also funny and very real'
MONIQUE ROFFEY, AUTHOR OF THE WOMAN ON THE GREEN BICYCLE

ORDER YOUR COPY:

BY PHONE: +44 (0) 1256 302 699; BY EMAIL: DIRECT@MACMILLAN.CO.UK

DELIVERY IS USUALLY 3–5 WORKING DAYS. FREE POSTAGE AND PACKAGING FOR ORDERS OVER £20.

ONLINE: WWW.BLOOMSBURY.COM/BOOKSHOP

PRICES AND AVAILABILITY SUBJECT TO CHANGE WITHOUT NOTICE.

WWW.BLOOMSBURY.COM/KERRYYOUNG

BLOOMSBURY